My Mother Told Me Stories

By I. M. Ramsey

The contents of this work, including, but not limited to, the accuracy of events, people, and places depicted; opinions expressed; permission to use previously published materials included; and any advice given or actions advocated are solely the responsibility of the author, who assumes all liability for said work and indemnifies the publisher against any claims stemming from publication of the work.

All Rights Reserved
Copyright © 2023 by I. M. Ramsey

No part of this book may be reproduced or transmitted, downloaded, distributed, reverse engineered, or stored in or introduced into any information storage and retrieval system, in any form or by any means, including photocopying and recording, whether electronic or mechanical, now known or hereinafter invented without permission in writing from the publisher.

Dorrance Publishing Co
585 Alpha Drive
Pittsburgh, PA 15238
Visit our website at *www.dorrancebookstore.com*

ISBN: 979-8-88812-211-2
eISBN: 979-8-88812-711-7

The characters and story events in this book are fictitious. Any similarity to real persons, living or dead, is coincidental and not intended by the author.

DEDICATION OF BOOK

It is with a grateful heart that I would like to dedicate this book to **Joan Seko**. I met Joan after contacting the Seattle Japanese Cultural Center as I was seeking a diversity reader willing to read my manuscript to ensure cultural and historical accuracy. As a very young girl Joan, along with her family was incarcerated at Minidoka Internment Camp, near Jerome, Idaho during the years 1942-1945. Joan's writing and editing skills, as well as her knowledge of Minidoka and that time period were of immeasurable assistance to me. She is a remarkable woman!

ACKNOWLEDGEMENT

I would like to acknowledge and thank **Dr. Cami Eastep** for her copy-editing expertise and assistance in reviewing this book. She was the very first person to read my manuscript from beginning to end. Her encouragement and assistance in finding and correcting those pesky mechanical inconsistencies in spelling, grammar, and punctuation was amazing and incredibly helpful.

Finally, I would like to acknowledge the support of my husband, **Jon**, for his enduring and endearing belief in me.

Table of Contents

Part I – Walla Walla, WA, 1963
    Chapter One - The Rumpus Room's Secret 1
    Chapter Two – Mushrooming in the Blues 13
    Chapter Three – Story of Miss Wren 29
    Chapter Four – Death of a President...................41
    Chapter Five - An Experiment 49
    Chapter Six – The Spelling Bee 67
    Chapter Seven – The Accident 77

Part II - Seattle and Bainbridge Island, 1942 - 1948
    Chapter Eight – Executive Order 9066 89
    Chapter Nine – The Letter............................99
    Chapter Ten – Goodbye My Father 113
    Chapter Eleven – Leaving Seattle 121
    Chapter Twelve – Puyallup Assembly Center, 1942 133
    Chapter Thirteen – Minidoka Interment Camp, Idaho ..145
    Chapter Fourteen – Minidoka, 1943 159
    Chapter Fifteen – Minidoka, 1944 171
    Chapter Sixteen – Tragedy at Minidoka 185
    Chapter Seventeen – Going Home 195
    Chapter Eighteen – Fate Calls 203
    Chapter Nineteen – The Visitor 209
    Chapter Twenty – Walter Gibson 217

Part III - Walla Walla, WA, 1964
    Chapter Twenty-One – Forgiveness 237

Terms

Nikkei – people or persons of Japanese heritage.
Issei – first generation of Japanese immigrants.
Nisei – second generation of Japanese heritage born in the United States.
Gaman - Japanese term of Zen Buddhist origin which means "enduring the seemingly unbearable with patience and dignity."

Fictional Characters Highlighted in the Novel
Tatsuno Family
Hiroki Tatsuno – Hitomi's Father
Junko Tatsuno – Hitomi's Mother
Hideo Tatsuno – Hitomi's eldest brother
Mio Tatsuno – Hideo's wife
Enji Tatsuno – Hitomi's second brother
Kazuko Tatsuno – Enji's wife

Murato Family
Akio Murato – Hitomi's first husband
Masako Murato – Hitomi's young daughter
Hiroki Murato – Hitomi's son

Inaba Family
Mr. Inaba – Tulip farmer from Mt. Vernon
Mrs. Inaba – Wife of Mr. Inaba
Grandma Inaba – Mother of Mr. Inaba
Kame Inaba – the Inaba's oldest daughter
Mikio Inaba – the Inaba's son
Tome Inaba – the Inaba's youngest daughter

Seattle Gibson Family
Mrs. Elizabeth Gibson – Walter Gibson's aunt (Aunt Liz)
Emily Gibson – Mrs. Gibson's fourth and youngest daughter
Clara Gibson – Mrs. Gibson's third daughter

Walla Walla Gibson Family
Walter Gibson – Hitomi's second husband
Hitomi Gibson – Walter's wife
Mabel Gibson – Walter's mother
Megan Gibson – Walter and Hitomi's daughter

Introduction

In the fall of 2002, my daughter and I were in Cape Town, South Africa doing research for my doctoral dissertation. We were investigating the lived experience of political perpetrators who had committed human rights abuses during the Apartheid era and who'd received political amnesty through the Truth and Reconciliation Commission as well as forgiveness from family members of their victims. Our research involved interviews with victims, family members, and political perpetrators. After nearly three months of working in Cape Town, we found ourselves at the Office of Home Affairs to get our visas extended.

While standing in one of the lines to meet with a visa clerk I noticed a young man looking back at my daughter and me on several occasions, listening to what we were saying. It was obvious from our accents that we were Americans. Cami and I had been following the news of pending war with Iraq after the 9-11 terrorist attack on American soil. We found ourselves right behind him as he brought out his passport and responded to the clerk's inquiry by saying, "I am from Iraq." He turned around and smiled at us in an apologetic manner. I felt the need to say something to this young man as my daughter and I had been expressing our dismay at the possibility of war with Iraq. I said to him, "Sir, excuse me, but I want to apologize to you for the aggression that our country is showing against your country. I am very sorry your people are having to face the threat of possible war with my country."

The young man smiled at me and said, "I don't blame the people of America for this threat. You have families just like I do. The leaders and politicians of countries make war, but it's the people that suffer." I was stunned by the incredible insight this young man showed and his graciousness to my daughter and me. The chance encounter planted the seeds for writing this book.

The story starts with the adventures of a ten-year-old biracial girl named Megan growing up in a small town in the southeastern corner of Washington

State in the early 1960s. Megan has the usual struggles of growing up that most children have, but her concerns are complicated with the reality that she is half-Japanese and half-White. She also struggles with one concern that is unique to her and that is to understand why her mother is overly protective and hovering, so different from the mothers of her friends. The mystery grows when she discovers pictures of her mother standing with a little Asian girl that she had never seen before in front of a drab and desolate looking building somewhere in an empty and arid landscape. On the back of the picture is written, *Minidoka, 1943*.

The first section of the book is seen through Megan's eyes as she tries to make sense of the many questions that arise about life, racism, discrimination, and her mother's earlier years before her birth. The second section of the book tells the story of what her mother, Hitomi, experiences after the attack on Pearl Harbor and the heart-breaking disruptions that turn her life upside down. Hitomi's pre-war life is destroyed, and she must re-build her future from the ashes of the past.

I wrote this novel to honor and remember an American people whose story is not often told. It is the story of how Japanese Americans were treated as enemies of America in the aftermath of the attack on Pearl Harbor. It is a story of how they endured this humiliation with dignity and resilience. Executive Order 9066 signed by President Franklin Roosevelt in February 1942 opened the door for the federal government to relocate over 120,000 Japanese Americans living along the West Coast to ten internment camps that were quickly established in California, Nevada, Utah, Arizona, Wyoming, Arkansas, Colorado and Idaho. The majority of these people were born on American soil and were U.S. citizens. Due to their Japanese ancestry, Japanese Americans were required to give up their homes, businesses, and lives without complaint and were incarcerated for the duration of the war. Very little has been written about this tragic period in American history, in large part because traditional Japanese culture teaches that one must bear the unbearable and endure hardship with dignity and patience. Most of the survivors rarely spoke of their incarceration and often their friends, children, and grandchildren had no idea of what they had gone through.

This novel is a story of ordinary people going through extreme discrimination and disruption of their lives. But it is also a story of surprising kindness, generosity and friendship, of forgiveness and reconciliation, and the enduring love of family.

Part I
Walla Walla, Washington

1963-64

Chapter One
The Rumpus Room's Secret

My mother told me stories. Even now, after all these years, if I am in a quiet place and close my eyes, I can hear her voice rise and fall in a lilting singsong rhythm. As a young girl I thought my mother was beautiful and wise. She often let me brush her hair for what seemed like hours while she told me stories. Her voice smiled in contentment as I teased waves on the side of her head; or wrapped curls in a silhouette on her forehead. My hands were small, but agile and I took great care to make sure the brush did not tug her head. I hated it when Mother suddenly stopped mid-sentence to say sharply, "Megan, careful, you're pulling my hair." The fascinating world of words and stories would suddenly pop like a bubble at her reprimand.

My mother told me stories of carefree girlhood days, of magical little animals bravely defending their fellow creatures, of people living in faraway exotic lands, and stories that helped me cope with my childhood sorrows. But she never told me stories of her difficult years in Minidoka, a Japanese internment camp during World War II. Nor did she tell me stories about my sister. The sister I never knew existed until I discovered her one spring day while playing in the rumpus room that was attached to the back of our house. In the early 1960s, nearly every house in our neighborhood had a large multi-purpose space, the antecedent of today's family rooms.

Our back room was not set up for play nor was it particularly pleasant. The large area held things you might find in a basement, laundry or game room. I always had the feeling that *other beings* lived there. I may have gotten this idea from my father who once told me to stay out because he had set several mousetraps. He was annoyed with the family cat, Karl, who had given up an active hunting life for long days napping on the overstuffed living room sofa. My father came from the rumpus room one morning with a mouse dangling from each of two traps he held in his hands.

"Walter!" exclaimed my horrified mother. "You're frightening Megan with those dead creatures!"

Up until that moment it hadn't crossed my mind to be frightened. But upon hearing the horror in my mother's voice, I clutched her arm.

"See what I mean, Walter. She's terrified. You'll give her nightmares!"

I did not let this last remark go unnoticed. Sure enough, I had difficulties going to sleep that night and many more, insisting upon crawling into bed with my parents. But that was long before I found my sister in the rumpus room.

I was ten that spring day in 1963 and quite bored with myself. School was out for spring break, keeping me at home with no friends to play with and nothing interesting to do. I wanted to play Barbie dolls with Sarah and some other friends from school. But my mother, true to form, insisted that I was too young to ride my clunky old bicycle to Sarah's house. Secretly, I fretted about my mother's hovering ways, but I just nodded my head and began counting the days until spring break ended and I could see my friends again at school. It was a sunny spring day, and I was feeling put out with my mother. She always spoiled my plans for a good time.

It was hard being the youngest child of an anxious, overly protective mother. It was even more difficult being a child from a biracial family, a situation not common in the sixties and almost nonexistent in the rural Southeastern Washington community where I spent my childhood. I never heard my parents talk about the difference between them, but even as a small child I saw people stare at my Japanese mother whenever she and Father were together. In my childish mind I thought they made a striking pair. Father was tall, over six feet and my mother, a slender wispy woman with delicate Asian features. As an adult now and looking back I realize that my parents lived in multiple social worlds. They had a private life at home, a life with friends and neighbors who knew them as the Gibsons, and then a life they encountered whenever they went outside of their close, warm, and supportive circle. I often thought that was why my mother was so protective of me.

Mother worried about everything. Even on the warmest days, Mother sent me off to school bundled up like a little old lady. I was always the first girl in the fall to wear tights to school, as Mother feared that I would get pneumonia. The tights felt good on crisp September mornings riding the old yellow bus to school. But by the time lunch was over and the afternoon recess had come, I managed to rid myself of those ridiculous garments of torture. The first time I took them off and ran around the baseball diamond in my sturdy oxfords, I got blisters on both heels so badly that I hobbled for several days.

I overheard my Aunt Mary telling the ladies at a church potluck that Japanese mothers were very devoted to their children. The other ladies nodded their heads in agreement. At times her devotion could be humiliating. I loved my mother's special way of making sushi, and she made it for me whenever I wanted it. But she had no idea the shame I experienced at lunch one day when Bobby Barker wanted to trade his peanut butter and strawberry jam sandwich for something in my lunch. All I had to bargain with was my mother's sushi rolls. Of course, Bobby had never seen a sushi roll, let alone tasted one.

When he saw it, he exclaimed, "What's that Megan? It stinks!"

His comment drew the attention of several of our friends who soon began chanting, "Stinky stuff, stinky stuff! Megan eats stinky stuff."

I sank into my chair with shame. Why couldn't my mother be like other mothers and pack peanut butter and jam sandwiches, or Twinkies, or something from the grocery market? The burden of being her daughter weighed heavily in my life.

My brother Hiro was ten years older than me and although we were not close enough in age to be playmates, he was a good brother, and it gave me comfort to know that I was not alone in the world. Our mother worried and fussed over him as well, but he was always patient with her – much more patient than most boys might be at his age. I guess that's how I came to tolerate my mother's eccentric ways with good grace.

Hiro would look me in the face and say, "Megan, our mother is special, and we must take good care of her."

It would be years before I understood the significance of his words, but I did love my mother dearly. No matter how much I chafed at her hovering, I knew there were reasons beyond my understanding that explained her overly protective ways.

I. M. Ramsey

That spring day in 1963, I'd been playing dress-up all morning with my cat, Karl. He'd been patient as I dressed him in doll clothing and strolled him around the house in my old baby buggy. But when I tried to put a yellow and white gingham bonnet on him, the one Aunt Mary made to match my yellow Easter dress when I was four, he let me know he'd had enough. He shot me a haughty look, hissed and then jumped out of the stroller, hiding somewhere under the bed. I was at loose ends and feeling sorry for myself. If Karl wasn't going to let me dress him up, then I would dig through some of my mother's old dresses and try them on myself. I knew she kept several old leather suitcases in the back room where she stored clothing that she wasn't ready to give away to Goodwill.

I usually ventured with trepidation into the back rumpus room. My imagination ran wild with vivid images of tiny furry rodents zipping across the old tile floor. But today my boredom gave me courage and I boldly ventured in. The room seemed cool with a musty smell like my father's garden dirt. The shelves along one wall held a combination of canned fruit, jams, pickles, and empty jars awaiting the summer's bounty from Father's garden. Mother learned to can from my father's mother, an austere, wrinkled woman scarred by the depression years. Grandma Mabel Gibson had lived with us for as long as I could remember. In fact, I couldn't remember a time that her no-nonsense presence had not been a part of the Gibson family household.

Grandma Gibson preserved everything she got her hands on. "Waste not, want not," was her favorite mantra as she looked with an accusing eye at my barely touched oatmeal bowl.

"Don't be wasteful, Missy. During the Depression, a grown man worked a full day for a bowl of hot oatmeal."

I didn't know whether to believe Grandma Gibson or not. I suspected she stretched the truth, just to prove her point, but being an obedient child by nature I would tentatively dip my spoon into the disgusting bowl of gray goo.

Often, my mother would intervene. "Now Megan, just try a bite or two of that oatmeal."

That was easier said than done; the spoonful of morning mush had an uncanny way of increasing in volume in my mouth.

The filled fruit jars made a colorful mosaic along the wall in the rumpus room. Yellow peaches that were the salvation of my morning cereal bowl, slender green beans snapped in perfect bite size pieces, creamy white pears, and bright red stewed tomatoes that Mother used to make her famous Sunday evening stew. Every Sunday afternoon throughout the winter, Mother gathered vegetables and the week's leftovers from the refrigerator, then added a jar of her summer stewed tomatoes. The kitchen would fill with a tantalizing aroma of vegetables, chicken stock, and herbs that left my mouth watering and my stomach growling long before the family sat down at the kitchen table and Father bowed his head for grace.

The top shelves were lined with jams, jellies, and preserves made from the raspberries, boysenberries, and strawberries my father grew in our backyard. Every year, Father threatened to pull out all the berry vines against my mother's protests. Gardening was the only topic I ever heard my parents argue about.

"Walter, you know how much we need those berries."

"But Hitomi, the raspberry and boysenberry vines take up too much of the back yard. If I take them out, we could have more potatoes."

Father took great pride in his yearly potato crop. He grew a variety called Red Pontiacs and these spuds were large by any standard, some the size of a small grapefruit. Father always checked the farmer's almanac to determine which day was best for digging his potatoes. He'd let me know at supper that tomorrow was spud-digging day. As a small girl, it was great fun.

I still remember how the crisp October air made my nose tingle and my breath float heavenward in long wispy streams. We must have made quite a picture in those days. Me in my overalls and my father, tall and lean, wearing his old red plaid flannel shirt, the one he constantly tossed into my mother's mending basket. He insisted the shirt still had years of good wear. Mother would shake her head in bewilderment as she threaded her needle to patch yet another hole in Father's shirt. Father was frugal, the child of Depression parents and German stoicism.

In the corner of the back room, I found two old satchels with the monogram WG etched on the clasp. Mother had told me they belonged to Father and the WG stood for Walter Gibson. He had given them to her back in the war years. At any rate, the old leather satchels had been around as long as I could remember.

My eyes adjusted to the dim light in the rumpus room as I focused on the old leather bags. What a good place to search for fancy dress up clothes. With some tugging and pulling, I dragged them out from the corner. Cautiously, I unlocked the clasp of the first satchel, half expecting a little mouse to jump out and scurry up my arm, but there was no such surprise. Instead, I found neatly folded dresses, which I'd never seen my mother wear. I pulled out a lovely lavender silky dress with a little jacket and tried it on. It felt smooth and slinky on my bare legs. I knew I would look even more elegant if I could find a pair of Mother's open toed heels to sashay around in. With mother's heels on I would be just tall enough to see myself in the mirror hanging on the wall above the counter where she kept the old, chipped enamel laundry tub.

Eager to find one of my mother's old purses or hats to top off my outfit, I searched carefully, lifting each folded garment without success. But below several layers of dresses, a tissue-wrapped package appeared, and my heart quickened with the anticipation of a matching scarf. But when I unwrapped the tissue, I was surprised to see that it was not a scarf, but a small pink dress. The bodice was made with delicate tucks and the large white collar was trimmed with lace. Three red embroidered roses adorned each side of the collar. The roses were connected with a vine of tiny green embroidered leaves. Even with my girlish eyes I could see that the beautiful stitching was carefully done. This was a special dress. But to whom did it belong? As I lifted it out of the tissue, I saw that it must have belonged to a small girl.

Inside the second satchel I found a plain brown paper sack. Someone had folded the top of the sack over very neatly and closed it with yellowing cellophane tape. This only made me more curious, but I didn't know if I dared look inside. That would mean breaking the seal. Grandma Gibson always said I was the most curious child she had ever known – always asking questions and getting into mischief. She was never very patient with me, not like Mother who took my inquiries with great patience and seriousness.

"Now Hitomi, you spoil that child. The Bible says that children should be seen and not heard. When I was a girl, a child would get a smart rappin' on the knuckles if she got into something that she shouldn't." I looked at Grandma Gibson's gnarled knuckles and wondered how many rappings she had gotten. From the looks of her hands, plenty. But Mother's quick look in my direction silenced my tongue. It was awfully hard to keep the words in my mouth, but I knew there would be a huge fuss if I didn't.

Later, when Grandma was out of the kitchen, Mother drew me to her side and kissed the top of my head and said, "Megan, you are such a good girl!" Her words took the sting out of Grandma's disapproval.

The battle to know what was in the paper sack went on for several minutes in my mind. Surely, mother wouldn't care if I took one little look, and if I was careful, I could retape the sack and no one would ever know. Hadn't I done that with Aunt Mary's Christmas package when I was eight?

While Christmas shopping with my Aunt Mary I saw something in Knickerbocker's Five and Ten store window that made me stop and stare. It was the Real Tears doll that I'd seen in the Christmas edition of the Sears and Roebuck catalog at home. I had carefully circled the picture of the doll with my father's black ink pen and written Megan next to it. I showed the picture to my brother, mother, father, and Grandma Gibson with big hints that the Real Tears doll was the only thing I wanted for Christmas. I had no luck with my brother who said it was too expensive for him to buy. My Grandma Gibson said I had enough dolls and when she was a child, she was perfectly content with her corncob doll wrapped in scraps of calico. That didn't bring me much comfort, but very little of what my Grandma Gibson said ever soothed my worries.

Father said it was too late to order the doll and Mother just looked at me and said, "Megan, Christmas is about giving to others, not worrying about what you are going to get. I don't want you to grow up selfish. Selfishness leads to heartache."

The only heartache I felt at the moment was despair at the thought of waking up Christmas morning without my dream doll under the tree. But standing outside Knickerbockers, there she was, looking at me from inside her pink cardboard box, wrapped in a soft yellow blanket.

"Aunt Mary, come see Real Tears! This is the doll I want for Christmas! Mother says I should think about giving to other people at Christmas, but I only think about how sad I'll be when I open presents on Christmas morning and Real Tears won't be there."

"Well Megan, sometimes nice surprises come to little girls who think about other people. Who knows, maybe Real Tears will find her way under your Christmas tree after all," smiled Aunt Mary.

Her words stirred hope in my heart. But the next week as Father and I came home from running an errand to the grocery store I looked in the window of Knickerbockers and saw that Real Tears was gone from the window display. My heart sank and my hopes for a joyous Christmas vanished.

I was in a mopey mood and very quiet during supper that night. Father looked at me quizzically and Mother asked if I felt ill. I just shook my head and went to find Karl. Sometimes he comforted me by curling up in my lap and purring. But not tonight. He jumped off my lap and went bounding upstairs into my parent's room to his favorite hiding place under their bed. I knew he was there because his big fluffy black tail with the little white tip swished back and forth from under the bedspread. I lifted the cover to retrieve him and came face-to-face with a large pink box. I was sure it was the Real Tears box, but I didn't have time to pull it out and investigate because just then Mother called me to help her with the supper dishes.

Sleep came with difficulty that night as I schemed and schemed on how to get a better look at that box. Maybe I could take a quick peek tomorrow while Mother and Grandma Gibson baked cookies. Morning brought fresh thoughts of the mysterious box. I wandered out to the kitchen where Mother and Grandma Gibson had prepared breakfast.

"It's about time you got up. Your mother and I have been up since half past five lighting the fire, getting breakfast ready and gathering the makings for cookies. Never did I know a child so lazy in the morning as you, Megan!"

Mother gave me a sympathetic look, but the look also told me to keep my mouth shut. I didn't think that 6:30 was sleeping in, especially on cold winter mornings. I really wanted to snuggle down deeper in my flannel sheets, spooning with my cat Karl. I couldn't tell Grandma Gibson that the only reason I'd gotten up this early was because I wanted to solve the mystery of the pink box. The chance came sooner than I anticipated. Right after breakfast mother called me into her bedroom.

"Megan, would you please fold these towels on the bed while Grandma and I start getting the dough ready for sugar cookies? asked Mother. "Then come downstairs to the kitchen and help us cut out cookies. I know you love doing that."

"Yes, Mother," I responded. "I'll be down to help you and Grandma as soon as I'm done with the laundry."

I quickly finished folding the towels just the way Mother liked them. She always folded them in half, and then in half again, and finally in thirds, making neat little stacks of towels to put away in the cupboard outside the bathroom. This was my chance to see if Real Tears was under the bed. Quickly I knelt down and peeked under the bedspread only to discover that – nothing was there! I couldn't believe my eyes. I blinked and then blinked again. But no amount of blinking revealed the missing pink box.

Just then I heard a crash and the sound of glass breaking on the hardwood floor downstairs. Mother, Grandma Gibson, and I all ran for the living room just in time to see Karl batting another Christmas ornament off the tree.

"Megan, get that creature out of the house before he brings the entire tree down!" sputtered Grandma Gibson. "I don't know why you let that cat have the run of the house. Houses were made for people."

Poor Karl, I would have to sneak him up to my bedroom later. But for now, he was banished to the cold winter air. I felt sorry for him huddled up on the welcome mat on the front porch. But I had other things to think about. While sweeping up the broken glass I noticed many new packages under the tree. One looked the size of the box I had seen under my parents' bed the night before.

All day the mystery of the box whirled through my brain. But Mother and Grandma Gibson kept me so busy I didn't have a single moment to slip away and investigate further. We expected my brother Hiro home from college that afternoon. The entire family would drive to the Greyhound station to meet the evening bus from Seattle. Hiro studied engineering at the University of Washington and hadn't been home since Thanksgiving break.

Mother was beside herself with anticipation at the thought of his arrival. She reminded me of the many last-minute preparations and my legs were much younger and sturdier than hers. I climbed the stairs to the upper story many times that morning; one hundred and sixty steps in all. There were seven steps to the landing and nine to the top and I made five trips, up and down, carrying towels, linen, bedding, and laundry items. By noon I was exhausted and very petulant. After lunch Mother asked me if I would like to help her and Grandma deliver cookie plates to several of our neighbors.

"Megan, your grandma and I are going to deliver cookie plates to the Sheldons, the Bakers, and the Barnetts. Do you want to come with us, or do you want to stay at home?"

Finally! This was my chance to search the house. I put on an exhausted expression and yawned expansively. "Goodness, but I'm tired. I think I'll just sit by the stove and read my Nancy Drew mystery."

"Okay, but don't go out of the house and keep the doors locked. If the phone rings don't answer it. If it's important they'll call back and I don't want anyone knowing that you are home alone. Do you understand me, Megan?"

"Mother! I can manage just fine by myself." This last statement came out with a twinge of guilt, because I planned to solve a mystery, which had nothing to do with Nancy Drew.

I tried to act relaxed, but inside I felt as if I would split open with anticipation. It seemed that Grandma Gibson took forever to get her hat, boots, winter coat, and gloves on, but finally I locked the door behind them with my mother's final instructions echoing in my ear. "Megan, don't answer the door for anyone."

I watched Mother and Grandma cross the yard and open the gate to Bill and Bitsy Sheldon's front walk. I held my breath as I peeked through the kitchen window, waiting to make sure that Bitsy was home. A huge sigh of relief whistled through my lips when Bitsy finally opened the door and Mother and Grandma disappeared inside. Whew! I knew it would be a full half hour before they would appear again, and they still had cookies for the Bakers and Barnetts across the street.

Quickly, I found myself on hands and knees carefully inspecting one of the boxes under the tree. The card read, *Merry Christmas to a special girl who thinks about others, love Aunt Mary.* I knew Aunt Mary wouldn't think I was so special if she knew I'd opened my present before Christmas day. But I figured this was my present and opening it a little early wasn't really so bad – it wasn't like I was stealing anything.

Carefully I examined the package and realized it had been wrapped rather quickly. No doubt, the work of my Grandma Gibson who didn't think that gifts needed any fancy wrapping. True to her parsimonious ways, three tiny pieces of cellophane tape held the package together – a piece of tape on each end of the package and a small piece of tape on the bottom.

Slowly I peeled the tape back, being extra careful not to rip the paper. As the wrapping fell away, I gasped to see the box with my dream doll inside. She lay there wrapped in her fuzzy yellow blanket, with her eyes half shut and real dark hair sprouting out of her head. I was in heaven! Even now as an adult and after all the passing years, I remember the absolute joy that pulsated through my heart as I took Real Tears out of her box and cuddled her in my arms. I managed to unwrap and re-wrap Real Tears three more times before Christmas and no one was the wiser. I felt a twinge of guilt, but when I opened my gift from Aunt Mary for the fourth and final time on Christmas morning, the squeal of sheer happiness in my voice was genuine.

I looked at the brown paper sack in my hands as the memories of Christmas two years earlier vaporized in my mind. There was no colorful Christmas tag with my name on it and I knew that the contents of the sack were not for me, but I had to know what was inside. Using my Christmas package opening technique I carefully pulled back the cellophane tape. The contents within would change my life forever. I found secrets in the sack, secrets of a past that I didn't know existed.

I found pictures of long wooden buildings sitting in a landscape of dust with no trees or flowers. The buildings looked desolate, barren and lonely. Barbed wire fencing surrounded the buildings and made it look even more inhospitable. I didn't understand what I was looking at, but I knew this wasn't my family's neighborhood.

Even more puzzling, I saw a picture of my mother standing with her brother, Uncle Hideo. She held a baby in her arms and standing between my Uncle Hideo and Mother, was a small girl wearing the pink dress I'd found wrapped in the tissue paper. I looked for my father but didn't see him. *Who was the little girl?* I turned the picture over and saw the words, *Minidoka, 1943*, written on the back. I found another picture of my mother holding the baby with one arm and her other hand resting on the shoulder of the little girl in the pink dress. On the back of this picture I read, *Hiroki, one year, Masako, three years.*

My first thought was to skip into the house to show Mother the pictures and to ask her to explain all that they meant. But I hesitated. I wasn't afraid Mother would scold me for being too curious, or for prying into packages that weren't addressed to me. But I knew there would be a moment when her eyes would widen with surprise as she saw what I held in my hand. The surprise would quickly deepen into some long-forgotten sadness as she recognized the snapshots.

I saw that look in my mother's eyes one day when she asked the butcher at the local grocery store for a fresh salmon fillet. The butcher said he'd already sold all the fresh salmon for the day, but he could sell Mother some frozen fish he'd stored in his backfreezer. As we passed the counter a few minutes later, Mother pretended not to notice the butcher cutting a large fresh salmon steak for another customer, smiling broadly and saying, "Yup, this fish came in fresh just this morning. Yesterday it was swimming in the Pacific."

But I noticed and saw the dark sadness of shame in her eyes as Mother quickly turned her head. Somehow, I knew that my questions would bring her sadness.

She would be tender, but her voice would resonate with finality as she would say, "Megan, I cannot tell you this story today."

I knew all this in my heart, so I carefully placed the pictures back into the paper sack, all the pictures but one. The snapshot of the little girl in the pink dress with the big white collar embroidered with three little roses intrigued me. Her face looked so familiar, but I had never seen her before. I said her name quietly, *Masako*. I liked how it sounded.

The afternoon shadows climbed the walls of the rumpus room as I carefully folded each garment and returned it to the old satchel. I placed the paper sack where it had originally laid inside the second satchel on top of one of Mother's old wool dresses. With effort I shoved both satchels back into the corner and tidied up my afternoon play. Usually, I was not so neat, but today I had discovered a secret and the burden of such a secret made me feel older, wiser. I knew now that there was a life that my mother had never shared with me, and that knowledge quieted my usual spirited self. The snapshot that I slipped into the back pocket of my pedal pushers would be a reminder to me of that life. Now my mother and I both had a secret and for some reason, that comforted me.

Chapter Two

Mushrooming in the Blues

It was a spring ritual to look for tasty morel mushrooms that grew amongst the fir and Tamarack that forested the Blue Mountain Range of Oregon and Washington. Our family had hunted mushrooms for as long as I could remember. Even now, so many years later, I remember the joy and anticipation of this annual adventure. In my mind, I see the family sitting around the kitchen table with Father and Grandma Gibson discussing whether they thought this season would be a good mushrooming year. They would carry on forever debating the best locations to find the elusive morel mushroom.

My father had his favorite places to look. I remember the excitement when he got the mushroom baskets down from the attic and dusted them off. Grandma Gibson would prepare a delicious picnic lunch and pack it in cardboard boxes that Father brought home from the hardware store in the old Drumheller's Building where he worked as an accountant. The lunch included cold chicken breasts that Grandma Gibson fried in her homemade seasoned breadcrumbs, beans baked for hours in brown sugar and tomato sauce, and of course Grandma Gibson's special apple pie. Mother told me the secret to Grandma Gibson's apple pie was the three different types of apples she used in the filling: Golden Delicious, MacIntosh, and Gravenstein. Grandma always kept enough of these apples down in the cellar to make pies for our first mushrooming hunt of the season. By spring, the apples from the previous fall were wrinkled and shrunken, but regardless of their appearance, Grandma worked her magic, and the pies were always the hit of the day. I can't really say what I loved best about our family's mushroom hunting ventures – finding the curious morel mushroom or sitting on the back end of our 1956 Ford station wagon eating Grandma's apple pie.

Mother helped prepare food for the big event, but I knew her heart was never truly a part of the activities. Father and Grandma Gibson loved tramping through the forest looking for fungi, but Mother was hesitant, even timid in the woods, preferring to hunt mushrooms close to the car. She had a terrible fear of losing her way in the forest. She thought every tree looked just the same and was easily intimidated by the tall grasses, ferns, and undergrowth that proliferated in the Blue Mountains. Her concern and worry about getting lost extended to me as well. Whenever we went mushroom hunting, I had strict orders to stay near my father or another member of my family.

Mother grew up on Bainbridge Island located in the Puget Sound area, a thirty-five-minute ferry ride from downtown Seattle. She was the youngest daughter of a successful strawberry farmer. Her father sold his large juicy strawberries to select wholesale grocers in Seattle, as well as vendors at Pike's Place Market, a public market center that looked over the waterfront of Elliot Bay. She grew up enjoying the life her parents had worked extremely hard to achieve. Her father was *Issei*, first generation Japanese American. Grandfather arrived with his bride of two months in 1908 with nothing but $60 and a basketful of clothes when they arrived. Grandfather and Grandmother Tatsuno settled on Bainbridge Island where they worked in agriculture for a large tomato farmer. After a few years, Grandfather Tatsuno saved enough money to lease an acre, which he cultivated with tomatoes.

He and Grandmother rose at 4:30 in the morning, leaving their two young sons sleeping as they picked until 7:00 when Grandmother returned to the house to awaken the boys and prepare breakfast. While Grandmother prepared the morning meal, Grandfather sorted tomatoes by size, color, and shape, packing them carefully into flat, slat-sided boxes for the market. He would eat breakfast, and then head down to the ferry on his bicycle pulling a cart filled with tomatoes for delivery at Pike's Place Market. Grandmother would spend the day watering and tending tomato plants while taking care of her two young sons. By the time the boys were old enough for school, they'd already learned to help Grandmother with many of her daily tasks in and around the greenhouse. Grandfather returned from the market late, sometimes not until 7:00 in the evening. After dinner he went to his storage shed and built more wooden crates to transport the tomatoes. Grandmother put the boys to bed, then joined Grandfather in the shop, sorting and packing tomatoes for the next day's market. Those were difficult years and although I never knew my grandparents, Mother told me stories of how her father and mother spent their early years in America working, working, always working.

By the time my mother was born in 1918, Grandfather Tatsuno had leased additional acreage next to Bob Sabers, a farmer on Bainbridge Island. The Alien Land Law prohibited Grandfather from purchasing land. However, Bob was a good neighbor, and a lease was agreed upon by the two men. Grandfather went from raising tomatoes to growing strawberries, a special variety called Marshall Strawberries known for their deep red color and sweetness. Marshall Strawberries were coveted at regional markets during the late spring and early summer months.

My mother was the only girl, the youngest child, and pampered by every member of the Tatsuno family – Grandfather, Grandmother, and her two brothers, Enji and Hideo who were six and eight when she was born. She told me wonderful stories of her girlhood growing up in a warm, loving family. In a hatbox, high on a shelf in the closet of her and Father's bedroom were the dolls that her parents had given her for *Hina Matsuri* when she was seven years old. *Hina Matsuri*, Girl's Day, happens on March 3rd, and on this day, it is tradition for parents to give their daughter a doll shrine. Sometimes Mother got the hatbox down and would carefully pull out a small palace shrine and figurines dressed in traditional Japanese clothing. Two dolls were warriors who guarded the court people, but I was most impressed with the Emperor and Empress dolls. The Empress was clothed in a twelve-layered ceremonial robe called *juhnihitoe,* a garment made of vivid red cloth. My mother became a Christian when she married Father, but I knew the traditions of her Japanese ancestry stayed close to her heart.

Sometimes Mother got a dreamy, faraway look in her eyes as she told me stories of pleasant Sunday afternoons spent in tea ceremonies sharing sesame cookies with her girlfriends. I would run up to her bedroom and get her tortoise brush and comb set. She'd make herself comfortable in one of the kitchen chairs next to the oil furnace, prop her feet up on the footstool, and I would brush and comb her hair.

"*Hina matsuri* is a girl's festival, Megan. It is a very exciting time for girls, awaited with much anticipation. Girl's Day is an occasion where parents pray for their daughter's happiness and development. I remember one special *Hina matsuri* your grandmother gave me a kimono made of beautiful silk cloth. The kimono was a traditional gown your grandmother made especially for me to celebrate this occasion. She made the tiniest, most even stitches by hand. I think her hand stitching rivaled the stitches made on any modern sewing machine. Your grandmother's embroidery work was also exquisite. Her embroidered roses were famous for their beauty and perfection."

I thought about the little pink dress with the big white collar and three tiny, embroidered roses I had discovered in the old leather satchel and wondered if my grandmother Tatsuno had sewn the garment and was almost tempted to ask. But somehow, I knew this was not the right moment to reveal my secret knowledge.

"I wish your grandmother Tatsuno were here to teach you how to make beautiful stitches, but she's gone now, Megan. Everyone is gone. Only your Uncle Hideo and me are here."

"When did my grandmother die?"

"Long ago, Megan. Long before you were born, during another life and another world."

I never knew my maternal grandparents. They both died before I was born and whenever I asked about their passing, Mother always told me I must wait until I was older before she'd tell me that story. I only knew something terrible had happened, causing my grandfather to lose possession of the family farm and he had died from grief. At least that's what Aunt Mary told me, but Mother never talked about what happened to Grandmother and Grandfather Tatsuno. She'd just pull me close to her and say, "you and Hiro are all that I have left of my family now. Except for your Uncle Hideo, there is no one that has blood of my blood. I love your father and his family, and they are your family, but they are not of my lineage, only Hiro and you are, which makes you both so precious."

I knew Mother worried about me and Hiro. She fretted that something might happen to us. But knowing all this didn't dampen my spirits for exploring the woods. The discovery of finding mushrooms always held adventure and fun times. But Mother didn't enjoy the great outdoors or mushroom hunting. Father accepted this, Grandma Gibson was tolerant, but it would be many years before I truly understood her worry.

That spring Father invited our neighbors, Bitsy and Bob Sheldon, Aunt Mary and Uncle Henry, Sarah Williams and her parents, and the O'Loughlins from church to go with us. I knew the picnic would be fine because even though Grandma Gibson made the best apple pie ever, my Aunt Mary's specialty was double fudge cake.

She made it on special occasions and would bring it out with a laugh saying, "Henry says the only reason he married me was for my double fudge cake."

"Now Mary, you know that's not the only reason I married you! I like your lemon meringue pie too," Uncle Henry would say with a wink.

I loved my Uncle Henry and Aunt Mary. Uncle Henry was Father's younger brother, but they looked so much alike, people thought they were twins. Uncle Henry was an engineer and worked at the U.S. Corp of Army Engineers in Walla Walla. Uncle Henry and Aunt Mary never had any children and they treated me like their own child. Aunt Mary always sewed my Easter dresses and knitted me warm wooly scarves every Christmas. I couldn't remember one of my birthdays where they hadn't been a part of the celebration.

It was hard to believe it was nearly June because the weather was unseasonably cool. May had an abundance of rainy days. Grandma Gibson said the rains were a blessing because the moisture brought up the spring mushrooms throughout the forest floor in the mountains. The old logging road my father took to get to his favorite mushrooming grounds was full of ruts and I thought we'd never get there. Finally, Father drove the old station wagon into a large turnout. At one time this turnout had been a loading area for logging trucks. Tree stumps, rotting limbs, and bark were scattered throughout the area, so Father was careful where he parked.

Sarah's parents drove behind us in their blue Chevy Truck and pulled up beside our station wagon. Sarah and I squealed in delight to see each other. Sarah was an only child. She and I were best friends, and we were like sisters except we didn't live in the same house. We were inseparable at school and went to the same church, Pioneer Methodist on East Birch Street. Sometimes I wished I could be more like Sarah. Grandma Gibson said she had a *sunny disposition*. Nothing bothered Sarah and even though she had a naughty streak, she never felt guilty about the mischief she got us into. Sarah thought up the craziest plans and then stood innocently by when the chaos inevitably broke out.

One day in the third grade, Sarah unhooked the cage latch holding Jimmy Silvers' six mice he had brought to school for show and tell. No one noticed her doing this as we all went out to play for recess. But recess was cut short when we suddenly heard Miss Martin scream in terror. We rushed back to the room in time to see Miss Martin hop on a chair by her desk. Boy, did Jimmy get it that day! He could not convince Miss Martin he had securely latched the cage hook after showing the class his pet mice. Miss Martin told Jimmy he was never to bring anything alive to show and tell again. In fact, show and tell time was suspended for the next few weeks.

We missed math that day because it took nearly a full class period to find all of the escapees. The last mouse was found in Janet Field's desk, chewing on her peanut butter sandwich left over from lunch. Miss Martin made Janet cry when she scolded her for being a messy child and said she couldn't go home until she had cleaned out her desk.

All and all, it was a bad day at school, but Sarah was as chirpy as a sparrow. No one ever found out that she was the one to set the mice free. She made me take a vow of silence on a bird feather we found on the playground the next day. I kept my word but felt guilty every time I saw Jimmy Silvers.

No one ever suspected Sarah of being a devil child because she was sweet and charming. She never talked back to her parents or teachers, did her homework and chores at home, and could converse with any adult in the politest way. But behind those innocent eyes and rosy lips was a mischievous spirit. I found Sarah exciting, and I was giddy with joy at the anticipation of our mushrooming day together.

Mother gave me a tin whistle to wear around my neck with strict instructions to listen for her occasional call. Sarah and I were to follow the buddy system and hunt together, staying within hearing distance of Mother's whistle. Mother gave one long whistle, and I returned her call with two short shrills. When it was time for lunch, Mother was to give three long whistles to alert everyone that it was time to eat. I usually hunted with Father or Aunt Mary, holding their hand as we searched through the coniferous forest. But this year I had Sarah to hunt with, and Mother, always the anxious angel, had dreamed up the whistle method to keep tabs on us.

The day was warm and splendid. Sarah and I soon stripped off our sweatshirts and tied them around our waists as we tramped through the forest looking for mushrooms around the roots of the many Tamarack and firs. I found the first morel mushroom and let out a squeal to mark the occasion. It was just like finding Easter eggs. Sometimes I imagined little forest elves scampering through the forest dropping morels for us to find. Mushrooms just popped up in places I had looked only moments earlier. It was the ultimate hide and seek game.

Now and then, Sarah and I heard Uncle Henry, Father, or Mr. O'Laughlin calling to say that they had found a cluster of morels, or calf brains, or cauliflower mushrooms. Sarah and I would run to the spot and begin picking them as quickly as we could. Occasionally, Mother blew her whistle, and I returned her call with my two sharp shrills.

We had been hunting morels for an hour or so when Sarah said, "Look Megan, let's follow this deer path. It's going toward that cluster of Tamarack trees in the distance. I bet we'll find lots of morels there."

"Perhaps, but that's a long way off from where our families are looking. Don't you think we'd better tell our parents first?"

"Naw, just blow your whistle a couple of times so your mother knows where we are."

"Okay, but I still think we should tell somebody before we take off."

"You worry too much, Megan. Why do you think your mother gave you that ole' whistle anyway? Use it."

"Okay, okay," I said as I gave two short blasts on my tin whistle.

Mother returned my call with one long blast. Off we went along the deer path. Sure enough, Sarah was right. We walked only a short distance when we came upon a huge bunch of morels, growing in a beautiful cluster around some decaying stumps. It was the mother lode, and we excitedly began cutting the mushrooms.

Everywhere we looked there were mushrooms. It was as if a magic fairy waved her wand in every direction and mushrooms had sprouted up. Hiro always let me use his favorite pocketknife, which he kept in the old Quaker Oats can on the bookshelf in his bedroom. The knife was a gift he'd gotten on his twelfth birthday. It was a beauty. The pocketknife handle was made out of deer antlers and was polished as smooth as marble. I unfolded Hiro's pocketknife and cut the mushrooms along the stems. Sarah and I had nearly filled our baskets when we sat down to take a rest. We assessed our bounty and concluded that these were the most mushrooms we had ever found.

"Sarah, should we go back and get another basket?"

"No, it would be a waste of time. If we tie the sleeves of our sweatshirts together, we can carry the mushrooms that way. Our parents will be amazed at how many we have found if we fill our baskets and our sweatshirts. Let's go find more."

Off we went looking here and there, yelling with delight when a new patch of mushrooms was found. We were so intent on finding mushrooms that we didn't notice the passing of time. But, after a while, the air got cooler, and the sun stopped smiling through the trees. Our baskets and sweatshirts were filled to the brim with no room for another mushroom. I regretted using my sweatshirt as a sack because a sharp wind was blowing, and my fingers were feeling numb from the cold.

Suddenly, I realized I hadn't heard my mother's whistle call since we had taken off on the deer trail some time back. The original deer track we followed had diverged into many other tracks and now Sarah and I had no idea which way to go.

"You'd better blow your whistle and let your mother know where we are," said Sarah. "Besides, I'm starving, and I can't wait to have some of your Aunt Mary's double fudge cake."

"I'm hungry too, and awfully cold," I complained as I pulled the whistle out of the neck of my shirt. I blew two short shrills and waited to hear the usual long shrill from Mother's whistle. I strained my ears, but only the wind in the pine trees could be heard.

"Try it again and blow harder this time," demanded Sarah.

I drew in a deep breath and gave two blasts on my tin whistle, but only the whispering of alder leaves responded to my call. Now I was really getting worried. *Where was Mother? What would Father do if he were in this situation?* The trees all looked alike, and they seemed to stretch forever in every direction.

"We're really lost, aren't we Megan? Your mother will be cross with us," said Sarah through chattering teeth.

That thought crossed my mind as well and only increased my anxiety. I was tired, hungry, cold, and feeling as if the forest was a puzzling maze. I knew it was way past noon from the growling sounds of my stomach. Sarah and I sat down under a gigantic Tamarack tree and huddled close together to keep warm. I could see the stems of mushrooms that we had excitedly cut only a few moments earlier. As I stared at the stems, I suddenly had a thought. The mushroom stems were a clue to where we had been. If Sarah and I followed the stems of the mushrooms we had cut, perhaps we could backtrack to the deer trail we had originally taken.

"Sarah, I have an idea! Look over at that tree. See the white stems of morels we cut a few minutes ago. Let's walk over there and while you stand marking that spot, I'm going to explore a bit and see if I can find another place where we cut mushrooms. Perhaps we can make our way back to the deer trail if we locate enough of the mushroom stems we've already cut."

Sarah and I walked quickly over to the mushroom stem patch. Sarah marked the spot while I walked in a semi-circle pattern to see if I could find any other stem patches. I was thrilled to catch sight of another place where mushrooms had been cut. Sarah came running towards me. This time, I marked the spot, and she did the searching. Patch by patch we slowly worked our way back along the forest floor. Sometimes it was difficult to find any stem patches and we would look at each other in despair. But just when we thought that we had come to the end of the trail, one of us would give a whoop of joy after spotting yet another mushroom cutting spot. We had been tracking the stem patches for a half hour when Sarah gave a holler that made my heart lurch with hope.

"Megan! I found the deer trail! We can't be too far away from where we left our parents. Blow your whistle and see if your mother answers," yelled Sarah.

By now my lips were blue with cold and it took all my pucker power to get enough air to make a sound. I gave two puny shrills and listened with anticipation. There it was! Far away we caught the faint shrill of Mother's whistle. I gave two more blasts on my tin whistle and this time there was no doubt as Mother's whistle returned my call with clarity. Our legs were not so weary as we moved quickly down the deer path.

I caught a glimpse of my father's familiar red plaid shirt in a clearing, and then suddenly he was there wrapping his long arms around me and Sarah. Mr. Williams was close behind. Sarah and I forgot all about being lost in our excitement to show our fathers the many mushrooms we had found. But my father hadn't.

"Megan, do you have any idea how worried your mother has been? She's been so upset, and we have spent the past hour looking for the two of you."

The elation of successfully finding our way back to where we had first begun seemed to pale in the realization that our parents had been worried for our safety. I was no longer hungry. I just felt ill. Father noticed the expression on my face and the drag in my walk because he wrapped his old wool sweater around my shoulders and took my sweatshirt stuffed with mushrooms. We walked slowly back to the car together.

Sarah chatted excitedly with her father, giving him an account of our adventure. In animated detail she told him how we lost the trail and discovered the way back by following the patches of cut mushrooms. No chatter escaped from my lips. I weighed the complexities of life as I walked silently by my father. Mother, my Aunt Mary and Uncle Henry, and Grandma Gibson were standing in the clearing by our station wagon. When Mother saw me, she burst into tears and hid her face in Uncle Henry's chest. Her slim shoulders shook as she sobbed. I couldn't help but notice the difference between my mother and Sarah's mother, who held out her arms as Sarah flew towards her.

"Sarah, I could just bonk you on the head for giving me the scare of my life," exclaimed Mrs. Williams. "Don't pull another stunt like that as long as you live! Do you hear me, young lady?"

"Yes, Mother! But look at all these wonderful morels that Megan and I found. We used our sweatshirts as gunny sacks after we filled our baskets. Don't you think we are clever girls?" said Sarah with pride bursting from her voice.

"Indeed, you are! These mushrooms will be tasty as a side dish with the pot roast, I've saved in the freezer," purred Mrs. Williams. "Look Lawrence, I think Sarah found more mushrooms than you and I put together."

I stood next to my father as he talked with Mr. O'Laughlin about the weather and the great mushrooming season. I felt invisible, yet oddly the focus of everyone's attention. Awkwardness and uncertainty settled upon my body like a shroud of despair. I was surrounded by waves of chatter and all I wanted was for Mother to kiss the top of my head and tell me everything was fine. But Mother wasn't well, and I heard her tell Aunt Mary she had a headache. Aunt

Mary gave her a blanket from their car and Mother slipped into the back seat of our station wagon and laid down. Grandma Gibson and Uncle Henry unloaded picnic treats from the boxes in the back of the station wagon. Grandma Gibson gave me a sympathetic look as she and Uncle Henry carried them to the back of Mr. Williams' pickup.

"Come on everyone, let's have lunch now," called Grandma. "No sense wasting any of this good food."

But I wasn't hungry now. Our adventure did not seem to slow Sarah down. Her plate had a large piece of cold chicken breast fried to a crisp in Grandma Gibson's cast iron skillet and then chilled in the cooler. Grandma Gibson had spent most of yesterday preparing the picnic lunch for today. I could see the pleasure on Grandma Gibson's face as people ooooohed and aaaaahed over her garden potato salad made from Father's Red Pontiac potatoes and the baked beans that had simmered for hours in the oven. Sarah's plate was piled high with these goodies along with a large slice of her mother's freshly baked bread slathered with sweet butter and blackberry jam. I was usually the first one in line to fill up my plate, but today I was not hungry. My stomach felt empty and shrunken, but I didn't feel like eating.

"Come on Megan," cajoled Sarah. "Your mother will be alright. My mother said she has wounds from the war. You gotta eat some of your grandma's good food or she'll feel bad."

The ride home was quiet. I sat in the front seat between Father and Grandma Gibson. Mother lay in the back seat, covered by Aunt Mary's *Around the World* patchwork quilt. She was not at the breakfast table the next morning, only father sat at the table reading the Union Bulletin and drinking his cup of black coffee. Grandma Gibson made the usual morning mush but there were no canned peaches to brighten up the insipid gray goop. It was a dismal day.

Sarah was her normal chatty self at school and told our teacher about our adventures. Mrs. Kramer said we were amazing and resourceful. She had our class play a game of *what to do if you were lost in the woods*. I forgot my worries and felt like the heroine as Sarah and I shared the story of getting ourselves unlost in the woods. The good feeling disappeared when I got off the bus and waved goodbye to Mr. Harvey, our school bus driver.

Grandma Gibson was in the kitchen peeling potatoes, carrots, and onions to add to her pot roast she was preparing for supper.

"Megan, your mother is in the living room darning socks. Go spend some time with her."

I was surprised at the gentleness in Grandma Gibson's voice. I looked at her with questions in my eyes, but her face never changed. Only her voice told me that she understood my worry.

"Come here, Megan," called mother. "I'm in the living room darning your father's socks one more time. I never knew a man to wear out the toes of socks like your father."

My mother looked very pale and tiny sitting in the large, overstuffed chair, but I knew it was her favorite chair to darn in because that corner had the best lighting.

She kissed the top of my head and all my worries spilled out as I cried, "Mother, I'm so sorry I scared you by getting lost yesterday. Sarah and I found mushrooms everywhere we looked. I wanted to find the most mushrooms so you and father would be happy with me."

"I understand, Megan. But you did give me a start when you were gone so long, and I couldn't hear your whistle. I imagined all kinds of terrible things happening to you and I'm afraid I worried myself into quite a headache."

"Are you still angry with me?"

"Megan, I was never angry with you. Just worried that something terrible had happened."

"Sarah's mother was upset but she didn't get sick like you did."

"I know. It's hard to explain, but when you lose someone or something very dear to you and the Fates return what was lost, then the gift that the Fates return becomes even more priceless. Do you understand what I am saying, Megan?"

"Not really, Mother. I was with Sarah and together we were able to figure out our way back to our starting point. Don't you think that was good?"

"Yes, yes, Megan! Of course. I'm really proud you stayed calm and thought your problem through to a solution. My worries overwhelmed me because you are all that I have. Hiro is nearly grown and away at college, but you are my pearl of joy. Come sit here and let me tell you a story."

Mother moved over in the big armchair, and I slipped in beside her.

"Goodness Megan, you are growing so big! We barely fit together in your father's chair."

I was growing, which made me secretly glad. If I steadied myself at the bathroom sink and stood on my tiptoes, I could see myself in the medicine cabinet mirror. I had used a little step stool for years to brush my teeth or comb my hair, but now on tippy toes I could see myself in the bathroom mirror. Yes, I was definitely growing.

Mother began her story.

Many years ago, in a remote fishing village on Okinawa, there lived a poor fisherman, Ikuro, who toiled from dawn to dusk on his ancient fishing vessel. He was so poor that he owned only one pair of zori. Zori are wooden sandals worn by fisherman as they work in the water or on boats hauling in their fishing nets. Ikuro was a simple man and grateful for the fish he caught each day. His catches were often small, but once sold at the market, he received enough yen to make payments to keep his boat. The small catches gave him a little extra for rice and sake to go with the fish he dined on each evening. He was happy and content.

Each day he would wake before dawn, launch his boat, and head for the open waters. He loved the familiar smells and rituals of his daily work on the boat. Some days the sky was so blue he found it difficult to distinguish where the ocean ended, and the sky began. One particular day there was a light easterly breeze that carried his vessel to his favorite fishing waters. He was fairly successful, finding several schools of tuna, which weighed his small boat down considerably. He began pulling in his net to empty the last haul of the day when a sudden freak wave smacked his boat on the port side. The sudden thrust of the wave, along with the weight of the fish in the boat and the fish in the net, rolled the small vessel dangerously on its starboard side flipping Ikuro into the cool depths of the Pacific Ocean.

This was a dangerous situation! Being separated from the boat meant facing certain death. But as Ikuro emerged from the sudden plunge, he grabbed the fishing net that floated behind the boat and pulled himself back to the boat. It took great effort, but he managed to pull himself into the vessel. Ikuro lay on the bottom exhausted, drenched, and shaking at his close encounter with death. Ikuro was grateful to all the ancestral gods for his good fortune. Even the loss of the large catch in his net did not dampen his joy at cheating a certain disaster and he still had the day's catch in the hull of his boat. But as the thrill of his res-

cue diminished, Ikuro suddenly realized that he had lost his zori, the only footwear he owned.

Now this was a grave situation and darkened the thrill of cheating death. The loss of his zori meant he'd have to work on the boat and walk along the shore with bare feet. His ability to work quickly and effectively would be limited without sandals to protect his feet. Ikuro was despondent at the loss of his zori, but work he must, with or without sandals.

No matter how carefully Ikuro worked, he often cut his feet on the sharp coral reef or broken shells that lay hidden in the sand. Each evening he hobbled home where he sat on the floor and smeared animal tallow on his bruised and bleeding feet. He'd carefully wrap his feet in clean rags and for a short time he felt relief from the biting pain. Each morning he prayed to his ancestral gods, asking them to have mercy and send a great school of tuna. But each day he caught just enough fish to pay for his ancient vessel and a little sake to accompany his evening rice and fish. At the market he gazed longingly at the zori wishing for a pair to protect his tormented feet.

There was no more joy at dawn as he painfully made his way to the boat. Every step brought agony and often the rags that he used to wrap his feet would be stained with blood. He couldn't move as swiftly when his small vessel encountered a school of tuna and it was impossible for him to obtain the most prized catch, the bluefin tuna. Their extraordinary size made it difficult for him to get the leverage he needed to pull them in. His rag covered feet slipped on the wet surface of the boat and he'd lose his grip on the nets allowing the bluefin to escape.

One morning as Ikuro hobbled to his boat, he was surprised to see a pair of beautiful zori, sitting on the bow. They were placed in such a way that all he needed to do was simply slip them on. Amazed, he looked around to see who might have left them there, but there was no one. He picked up the zori and examined them carefully, noting the exceptional handiwork and sturdy toe thongs. Surely, some itinerant sandal maker had delivered them to the wrong vessel. Excitedly he walked up and down the shoreline asking his fellow fishermen if the sandals were meant for them. Although the zori were much admired by all, no one knew where they had come from or who had ordered them. For seven days, Ikuro left the sandals on the bow of the boat when he left in the evening, and for seven mornings the sandals were waiting exactly where he had placed them the night before.

On the eighth morning when he found the sandals again on the bow, he sank to his knees with a brimming heart and thanked the gods of the sea and all his ancestors for this wondrous gift. For at last, he knew that these marvelous zori were his. But Ikuro was greatly worried the ocean would again claim his sandals so he took great caution to tie rope around the sandals and attach the strands to the boat so they wouldn't be lost if he should fall into the waters. The ropes bound to the boat made walking awkward and catching fish difficult. Whenever Ikuro saw a great school of tuna the ropes impeded his ability to get to the nets quickly. By the time he was able to throw the nets overboard the school of fish was gone, and the catch became smaller and smaller.

Ikuro became so obsessed with protecting his sandals he spent more and more time focusing on them rather than the work of fishing. Eventually he could not even bring himself to work in the water or on the boat for fear he might lose them. Instead, he began sitting at home, in his humble abode, looking at his sandals, while his friends went out to sea. The day came when the man took the boat away because Ikuro had not paid him in many days. Ikuro lost the means to make his livelihood, and he had nothing but his precious zori. All he could do was to sit on the shore, look out to sea, bereft of all things, except for the zori he cradled in his arms.

My mother let out a long sigh when she finished telling me the story.

"That is a very sad story, Mother. Did Ikuro ever get his boat back and was he able to fish again?"

"Well, that story is for another day, but do you understand better now why I was heartsick with worry when you did not answer my whistle calls?"

"Yes, I think I do," I said. "But the story also tells me that precious things should not be overly sheltered, because that ruins everything."

"Indeed, you are wise. That's the lesson your mother must remember, and will, in the future."

Mother looked at me and for the first time in two days I saw the worry lines on her brow disappear. Crinkles around her eyes appeared as she smiled at me. I knew I was forgiven.

Chapter Three
The Story of Miss Wren

The summer of '63 was filled with endless days of brilliant sun, the kind of hot days for which Walla Walla was famous. The mild spring days of May and June evaporated as the summer days of late July and August brought blistering temperatures of 100 plus degrees. My room was on the second story of our house and air conditioning was a luxury unheard of in the sixties. At night, I laid on top of my bed clothed only in my underwear. Mother placed wet washcloths on my chest and forehead to provide relief from the sweltering heat. Both windows in my corner bedroom were open in hopes of creating a cross breeze. Occasionally I felt a cool easterly wind gently sweep me. But then the heavy warm night wrapped itself around my roasting body. Finally, I'd fall asleep only to wake up the next morning sprawled on the covers with the washcloths dry and stiff on my pillow and bed covers. August seemed to last forever, but slowly the summer mellowed into autumn and the evening temperatures became noticeably cooler. Yet the days were still intense. I overheard Father and Grandma Gibson talking about the unusually hot fall.

"Walter, the weather this year reminds me of the autumn of 1937. We had eighty-degree weather up until October that year, said Grandma. "I don't think we had a killing frost until after Thanksgiving."

"I remember the summer of 1937. We didn't get any rain the entire month of August and the blueberries just dried up on the bushes. Farmers really suffered that year," said Father.

I reluctantly put my swimming suit away in the bottom drawer of the old oak dresser in my room where Mother stored my summer clothes. I hated to give up my carefree summer days of freedom for school days sitting at a desk practicing cursive or doing math problems. This year was no exception, although I secretly looked forward to being in the fifth grade. Mrs. Kramer was the fifth-grade teacher, and everyone knew she was the best teacher in Walla Walla. I was officially an "older student" and assigned to the big kids' room.

The first morning of school I popped out of bed with no cajoling from Mother or scolding from Grandma Gibson. I was excited about my new school supplies, especially my box of sixty-four crayons. I had coveted such a box since my friend Sarah proudly displayed hers on the first day of school the year before. It took a great deal of talking to convince Mother that getting the larger box was a financial advantage. I sold her on the idea that I wouldn't need a new box of crayons all year since the box of sixty-four had a built-in crayon sharpener in the back. I would be able to keep my crayons razor sharp and ready for any art project Mrs. Kramer assigned.

I was tempted to waste a few minutes cuddling with Karl who looked especially cute curled up on my pillow with his white face tucked under his bushy black tail. But I knew mother would have breakfast ready by the time I put on my school clothes. Mother spent extra time at the sewing machine working during the hot weeks in August to sew my new school dresses. I loved how crisp and cool my white blouse felt under the velvety smoothness of my new plaid jumper. My red socks from the five and dime store matched the plaid in my jumper perfectly and there wasn't one scuffmark on my new brown oxfords.

I was excited about the day and all the adventures that the school year would bring! I dawdled over my morning oatmeal eating only the banana that Mother carefully sliced on top. I spent the rest of breakfast stirring the gooey gray mass around and around, hoping no one would notice. It worked that morning because Grandma was busy talking with Father about a letter that she had gotten from a family friend in Oregon. Mother was packing my lunch box when she spied the yellow school bus coming up the street.

"Megan, here comes Mr. Harvey! He won't be happy if he has to wait for you on the first day of school. Go brush your teeth and grab your book bag." I ran upstairs and gave my teeth a quick swish, swung the book bag on my back and ran back downstairs in time to give Mother a quick peck on the cheek.

I was greeted by Mr. Harvey's toothy smile as I climbed up the steps. Mr. Harvey had driven the school bus for generations of children. He was kind, dependable, and tolerated no mischief making. One year he kicked some of the older boys off the bus and made them walk home when he discovered they'd been lighting matches and smoking in the back of the bus.

"Good morning, Miss Megan! Are you ready for the fourth grade this year?"

"No, Mr. Harvey! I'm in the fifth grade this year!"

"Nah, really?" he smiled.

"Yes, I'm in Mrs. Kramer's class."

"Well, Megan, you just shine this year for Mrs. Kramer!" Mr. Harvey gave me a quick wink as he pulled the door closed behind me. I spied Sarah sitting in the middle of the bus waving me back.

"Hi Megan, I saved you a seat! Come sit with me. Hey, I like your new jumper. Did your mother make it? My mother said that she wasn't going to do any more sewing for months because she was tuckered out from making all my new school dresses."

I plopped down in the seat next to Sarah and said, "Thanks for saving me a seat. I like your new gingham dress and that Scotty dog your mother sewed on your pocket is really cute."

"That Scotty dog your mother sewed on your pocket is really soooooo cute."

I looked up, shocked to hear my words being mimicked in a sarcastic way. My eyes stared into a pair of bright blue ones. A tall skinny boy draped his body over the seat in front of me and stared back with mockery in his face.

"What's a matter? Can't you talk, Jap eyes?"

I had never seen this wild and outrageous boy before, and I really didn't know what to say to him.

Sarah tugged on my arm and advised, "Just ignore him, Megan. He's one of the Henderson kids that just moved into the ole Henry house. The Hendersons have a bunch of kids and Billie is the meanest one of all."

That was my introduction to Billie Henderson and the beginning of our miserable relationship. He became the bane of my existence. Unfortunately, Billie not only lived on the same street I lived on, but he was also in Mrs. Kramer's room. I wasn't sure exactly why I was the brunt of his bullying, but he never missed a chance to throw a verbal punch whether I was on the playground, on the bus, or walking home.

Throughout that fall I tried to sit behind Mr. Harvey in the old yellow school bus. Sitting there, I felt relatively safe from Billie's verbal jabs because no one dared to say mean things in Mr. Harvey's earshot. Sitting in the front seat also allowed me a quick get-away home. Our house was where Mr. Harvey stopped the school bus for pick up and drop off on Catherine Street. If I made a quick dash, I could be halfway in my yard and almost to the front porch before Billie, his many siblings, and the other children exited the bus. Sometimes I wasn't so lucky, and Billie would shout nasty, hurtful remarks at me.

"What ya 'fraid of, Jap eyes? Why don't you just go back to where you came from?"

One particularly difficult day, I came rushing into the kitchen and Grandma Gibson exclaimed, "Whoa! Slow down, Megan. Why are you so fired up and in such a hurry?"

"It's that nasty mean Billie Henderson. He's a wild, hateful boy and says the meanest things to me. I hate him!"

"Megan! You know better than to say you hate someone. The Bible says if you hate someone, it is the same as wanting to kill them."

"I'd kill him if I could."

"Gracious sakes, Hitomi! Did you hear that child?"

Mother was in the rumpus room sorting laundry, so her voice was muffled as she called for me.

"Megan, what's this I hear?"

I wandered into the rumpus room to talk with my mother. I hadn't been in there since summer, and I couldn't help but look in the corner at the old leather satchels. I was tempted to ask mother about the dress and pictures but kept the idea to myself.

"It's Billie. I hate him!" I wailed.

"Why Megan. What's he done?"

"Billie calls me Jap eyes. I don't have Jap eyes. I have American eyes, just like Father."

Suddenly, I felt confused. Here was my gentle Mother looking at me with her beautiful Japanese eyes and I was telling her how much I didn't like them.

"Mother, I love your eyes, but when Billie calls me Jap eyes, I feel bad inside. Billie is just a bully."

"Yes, I understand Megan. Help me sort the rest of this laundry and then come to the kitchen and I'll tell you a story."

It didn't take long for Mother and me to sort the rest of the laundry. She was very thorough and methodical about her sorting. Whites in one pile, towels in another, sheets in a third pile, and finally dark clothing. She started the whites and then we both went into the kitchen where she poured some milk into a small saucepan for hot chocolate. I anticipated an extra special story because Mother put a big white marshmallow in the steaming cup and smiled as she set it on the table in front of me.

"Now be careful Megan, it's really hot." She sat across from me and smoothed the tablecloth with her hands. "Let me tell you a story about little Miss Wren."

Little Miss Wren lived in a beautiful valley where the sun shone every day. There were many splendid trees throughout the valley that gave shade to the birds and beasts during the heat of the day. Some of the trees were tall firs that stood straight as an arrow with their graceful boughs swaying gently under the heavens. There were oak trees with plentiful acorns for all the squirrels in the valley and giant maple trees with leaves as large as the moon. These leaves gave shelter to little Miss Wren when the evening rains fell. The raindrops made singing sounds as they plopped into the crystal-clear stream that meandered through the middle of the valley. Tiny minnows lived in the stream where they darted here and there amongst the colorful pebbles that lay at the bottom of the streambed. Miss Wren shared these surroundings with many friends. Each day brought lilting songs from the meadowlarks, chirrups from the squirrels, and peeps from her mice friends who made burrows under the tall grasses.

One sunny morning, Miss Wren was taking her morning bath when Charlie the squirrel came rushing toward the stream.

"Miss Wren, Miss Wren, there is danger here! An invader has come to our valley!"

"What is an invader? I don't know what an invader is. Should I be worried?" asked Miss Wren.

"Oh yes, indeed! An invader comes with a shadow, and he preys upon all those who are small."

"What does this invader look like?"

"Look! There is his shadow now!" Far down in the valley Miss Wren saw a dark shape on the ground moving slowly and silently up the valley towards her.

"Quick! Find cover before he sees you." yelled Charlie as he jumped into a hollow hole in the maple tree with graceful boughs that draped over the stream.

I. M. Ramsey

Miss Wren flitted silently up into the maple tree and hid underneath a large leaf. She watched the shadow grow larger and larger and her feathers quivered as she heard the screech of a large red hawk. It landed in the fir tree on the other side of the stream, just above the burrows where her mice friends lived. She watched with great horror as the invader suddenly dove to the ground and caught one of the mice that had been slow to scurry into her nest underground. The hawk flew off with the mouse in its talons. Miss Wren couldn't believe that such tragedy had happened in front of her eyes on such a lovely sunny day.

Fear descended upon the little valley, and fear held every bird and small beast in its awful grip after that day. No longer did the meadowlarks sing their lilting songs, nor did the squirrels chirrup, or the mice peep as they made their nests. The little minnows didn't play tag among the pebbles in the stream because the invader even dove into the water and took them away. The valley became a silent place with only the occasional triumphant scream of the hawk when he made a kill.

Miss Wren's heart quivered with anxiety and worry as the invader plucked his helpless victims from their homes. What could she do to help her friends when she herself lived in fear for her life? Terror paralyzed her and kept her quaking, hidden behind the large maple leaves.

Each day brought tragedy and sorrow. Poor Millie lost nearly all her mice children to the talons of the hawk. Only Alfie, her youngest son, survived the attacks because he was swift as a bullet and could reach the tunnel in the blink of an eye. But he was also reckless, spending more time in the open, and this tormented Millie with endless worry.

Alfie was Miss Wren's favorite mouse child of Millie's many offspring. He was funny and amused her in the good days of the peaceful valley with his backward flips and his ability to stand on his front paws. Yes, Alfie was athletic and a very special mouse. Miss Wren worried about his safety as she watched him from her hidden defense in the old maple tree by the stream.

One day, several weeks after the invader came to the valley, Miss Wren sat in her usual hiding spot behind a big leaf on one of the lower boughs of the graceful old maple tree. She rarely budged from this spot because of her fear of the invader and his talons. From her hiding place she could see up and down the valley and it gave her a sense of security as she kept a vigilant eye for the shadow. From her secretive perch she saw Alfie gathering weeds and twigs to line his nest. He darted here and there, going further and further from the safety of his home. He was unaware that the shadow was moving up the valley, but Miss Wren saw, and her heart nearly jumped out of her breast. Alfie was in imminent danger. If he didn't make a quick get-away he would soon be in the claws of the giant shadow! Miss Wren didn't know what to do. Alfie was too far away for her to warn him, and Miss Wren was frozen in fright and couldn't utter a peep, let alone a warning.

The shadow stealthily gained on Alfie as Miss Wren peeked from around the leaf. Suddenly, the invader plummeted earthward directly towards Alfie. Without a thought for herself, Miss Wren shot out from her hiding place like a tiny rocket and hurled herself towards the invader, giving his head a stinging peck as they passed each other in the air, just inches from the poor startled Alfie! Alfie raced back to his underground nest in a split second. Miss Wren felt great rage at the invader as she cut a quick corner in midflight and struck the hawk again on the head. The hawk screeched in surprise because he couldn't see what was hitting him. Again, and again Miss Wren flew over the hawk and pecked him on the head. Little feathers flew and the hawk screeched in pain as he tried to elude his attacker. Miss Wren lost all sense of fear. Instead, she felt strong and powerful. She realized the invader was now the one who was fearful. That emboldened her to continue pecking at his head. The invader flew this way and that way trying to rid himself of the pesky wren, but he couldn't shake her off. Across the valley they sparred, until with one last screech the hawk flew up and over the forest trees and disappeared beyond the horizon. Miss Wren lit on a tall fir tree and looked as far as she could over the horizon, but there was no sign of the invader. She looked to the earth below and saw no dark shadow.

From that day forward, the shadow was never seen again. Peace and tranquility returned to the beautiful little valley. Alfie grew up and had a big family that he amused with his somersaults and paw stands. Charlie the squirrel gathered acorns again and hid them in his favorite holes for his friends. Misty and Miss Wren lunched together on bright red berries that grew in the valley and the minnows could be seen playing tag in the crystal-clear stream. Serenity and kindness prevailed, and harmony could be felt throughout the valley.

"So, you see, Megan, even little creatures have great power when they stick up for what is right. Just stand up to Billie and tell him to stop calling you those ugly names. Think about little Miss Wren the next time Billie calls you

Jap eyes. Think about how she stood up to the invader and chased him out of the valley. I think you can do that."

I wasn't so sure I could stand up to Billie. He seemed big and very powerful. Mother didn't understand how intimidating and hateful Billie acted. But I liked her story, and I thought about the peaceful valley all through dinner while my parents and Grandma Gibson talked about the day's news. I thought about Alfie and how close he had come to being snatched up in the shadow's talons while I practiced my spelling words with Father, and I thought about Miss Wren as I lay in my bed and saw the pumpkin moon peering in through my bedroom window. I was still thinking about Mother's story as I boarded the bus the next morning. Thank goodness the seat behind Mr. Harvey was still available. This was not the moment to flex my muscles with Billie Henderson. I avoided him most of the day and this must have frustrated him because I barely escaped the bus, running for home, when I heard Billie close on my heels.

"Hey! Jap eyes. Why don't you just run back to slant-eyed land! Nobody wants Japs living around here."

I thought about Miss Wren and swung quickly around, nearly tripping Billie with my sudden move. "Says who?" I demanded.

"Says me. Do you want to make somethin' of it?" snapped Billie.

"Yes, I do!" I clenched my fingers into a fist and popped Billie in the nose.

Blood began dripping out of Billie's nose and he burst into tears, crying, "I'm gonna tell my mom on you!"

I don't know who was more shocked, Billie Henderson, or me. I couldn't believe I had hit another person, but what surprised me even more was that Billie the monster became Billie the crying boy. The sight of him crying stopped me cold in my tracks. I was confused and ashamed of myself. Billie grabbed his nose and started running up the street. I heard him crying as I walked slowly up our driveway. I wasn't in a hurry to get in the house, there was too much to think about.

"What's the matter child, cat got your tongue?" inquired Grandma Gibson as she sat peeling carrots at the table.

Normally I would have been excited at the sight of Grandma's gnarled fingers peeling carrots because for all her sharp words, Grandma Gibson made the best carrot soup in all the world. But the thought of a warm bowl of Grandma's creamy carrot soup did not lift my mood.

"No, Grandma, I'm tired from thinking so much at school."

"Well, take your things up to your room and don't leave them scattered around the house. Your mother and I are forever picking up after you."

I put my book bag in my room and started downstairs when the telephone rang on the kitchen wall. I had a sinking feeling that this telephone call had something to do with Billie Henderson and me. I sat down on the top step of the stairs where I could hear the conversation below.

"Hello, Gibson residence," my mother said sweetly.

A very long silence ensued, and I found myself holding my breath.

"I see, Mrs. Henderson. I'm sorry Billie's nose is bleeding. I hope it's not broken, but Billie has been bullying my Megan since school started and that must stop. Yes, I will talk to Megan, but if there are further incidents of him intimidating Megan, I will have my husband Walter talk to the principal about Billie. You can be sure of that."

"Gracious sakes alive, Hitomi!" cried Grandma. "What mischief has that child been up to now?"

"Now Mother, I'll talk to Walter about this situation, but I'm going to talk with Megan first."

My heart sunk further as I flew back to my room and flung myself on top of the bed. Karl jumped up on the bed and snuggled in my arms. But nothing could comfort me now. I felt terrible. The world was ending. I was the worst person on earth. I heard my mother come into my room and pull a chair up close to my bed.

"Megan, Billie's mother called. She says you hit Billy in the nose and made it bleed. She's afraid that his nose might be broken."

I burst into tears at the thought and buried my face in my mother's lap. I didn't want Mother looking at me with her sad, disappointed eyes. I just couldn't bear to see that look.

"I stood up for myself just like Miss Wren," I cried. "I'm sick of Billie calling me hateful names."

"I understand, Megan. I would never encourage you to strike another child, but I admire you for standing up to Billie's bullying."

"You do?"

"Yes, I admire you for telling Billie to stop calling you names. I don't think he'll be bothering you again. It's unfortunate this incident took place, and I don't want you hitting other children, but I'm proud that you stood up to injustice. Now, go wash your face and dry your eyes. I need your help setting the table and making the salad for dinner."

I was quiet at supper that night. Grandma Gibson kept giving me pointed looks but didn't leak a word about the afternoon drama. I knew Mother had told Father the details of the telephone call from Mrs. Henderson, but he didn't reprimand me. Sometimes I found grown-ups confusing. I thought I was in big trouble, but no scolding came. Billie's crying face loomed in my mind. I was bewildered by how a toughie like him could suddenly melt into a crying baby.

As I lay in my bed that night with Karl purring in my ear, I knew I had learned something very important that day. It was good to stand up for myself, but maybe not in the way I had. The most remarkable thing I learned was that bullies were just people hurting inside and they acted tough so that no one would see their pain. Billie's broken face had revealed that secret truth. His face haunted my dreams that night and I woke up several times thinking about what I should do to make peace with him.

It was dark and very cold when I tiptoed down the stairs and headed toward the rumpus room. I didn't like visiting the back room at this hour of the night, but I couldn't sleep until I had accomplished my mission. Slowly I opened the door and turned on the light. The light reassured me as I shuffled across the cold linoleum with my bare feet to where Mother folded the family's laundry. In one neat pile lay several of my Father's handkerchiefs. I chose a dark blue paisley one and tiptoed back up the stairs to my room. Digging in my book bag, I found some notebook paper and pencil and wrote a note.

It said, "Billie, I'm sorry I hit you. Here's a handkerchief to dab your nose if it starts to bleed. I promise not to hit you again. I hope you never call me Jap eyes. Your friend Megan."

I felt better after I wrote the note and tucked it into my book bag. Karl was still curled up on my pillow when I hopped into bed, but he slid under the covers and snuggled up in my arms. I was soon warm and sleepy again.

At school the next day, I picked my timing carefully. When the class was in the art room carving pumpkins for Halloween decorations, I raised my hand and asked Mrs. Kramer if I could go to the bathroom. Quickly I slipped into my classroom, retrieved the handkerchief and note, and placed them inside Billie's desk.

I wasn't sure if this was the right thing to do, but I knew I felt so much better, as if a gigantic load had been lifted from my back. Billie didn't say anything to me all day, but I caught him looking at me when we lined up for the afternoon recess. It was only a glance, but his face was a study of curiosity, not revenge.

I took my usual seat behind Mr. Harvey on the way home and was out of the bus in a streak. I was almost to the house when I realized there was no name calling from Billie. I stopped and turned and saw his tall skinny frame walking along with some of his siblings and other kids who lived further up the street. He didn't even look at me.

Mother stood at the sink scrubbing red Pontiacs from Father's potato bed. Father and I had dug them up the previous Sunday afternoon and I knew that they would taste wonderful with the pot roast Grandma Gibson was preparing.

"How was your day at school, Megan?" asked Mother.

"Fine. We carved pumpkins for Halloween, and I get to bring it home on Friday."

"How big is your pumpkin? Do you want Father to get off work early on Friday and pick you up from school?"

"No, I can manage, Mother."

"Hmmm, yes, I think you can manage, Megan."

Mother and I exchanged knowing glances. I felt happy inside again. I realized I hadn't felt this happy since the first day of school. I ran up the stairs and tossed my book bag on the bedroom floor. Karl was curled up in the center of my bed just like a doughnut, head laying on the bed, eyes closed, and his little triangle chin pointing to the ceiling. I scratched his throat and gave him a kiss on his velvety soft paw. He purred deep in his throat. Life was good and I felt as if I had solved one of its most puzzling mysteries.

The next day at recess, Mrs. Kramer chose Billie Henderson and Jimmy Silvers as captains for the baseball teams at morning recess. Of course, they both chose the boys first. When just the girls were left everyone gasped in surprise when Billie chose me first instead of Angela Harrison, who was a better baseball player than most of the boys in our room.

I overheard Bradley Baker ask Billie, "Why dyuh' pick Megan? She's the scrawniest girl in our room."

"Yeah, but she runs fast!"

I. M. Ramsey

I felt joy in my heart as I joined the team. I don't remember which girls were chosen after that, or if we won the baseball game. I just knew I had forgiven Billie and that he had forgiven me. We could live together in the same universe, even for all our differences.

Chapter Four
The Death of a President

Our entire fifth grade class was bustling with excitement because today, Friday, November 22, 1963, was the long-awaited spelling bee day. Six weeks earlier, Mrs. Kramer had given the class a list of 500 words to learn in addition to our weekly spelling words. This list comprised the words for the spelling bee. The winner would have his or her picture taken and printed in the Union Bulletin and receive a brand new, ten-speed bike from the hardware store in the old Drumheller's Building.

I wanted to win the spelling bee because my father was the accountant for the hardware business at the Drumheller Building. Father would be proud of me if I won the spelling bee. The gold, ten-speed bike had sat in Drumheller's front window for a month with a big sign announcing it was the grand prize for Sharpstein School's fifth-grade spelling bee.

For weeks I had been practicing the words on the list. At first, it seemed impossible to learn all the words. Learning to correctly spell 500 words was no small feat. But everyone in my family got involved. Each night after reading the evening newspaper, Father would pull out his large pocket watch. He'd wind it carefully and look at me saying, "Megan, my watch says half past seven and that gives us thirty minutes to learn ten new words – three minutes per word."

I would plop myself down on the footstool in front of father's overstuffed chair, lean my back against the side and wait for father to give me the first word.

This had been going on for weeks. Saturday mornings, Grandma would quiz me on words that I had learned through the week as she cleaned the breakfast dishes. Sunday evenings, Mother would sit by the kitchen table while I brushed her hair and gave me fifteen new words from the list. Karl listened by the hour to my repetitive spelling. He would lay on my bed with two front paws tucked under his chest, his tail elegantly wrapped around his side, and listen to me go over and over my spelling words.

Occasionally he blinked his eyes when I would exclaim, "Drat! I missed that one!" and then yawned in boredom as I tried the word again.

The spelling contest was well underway and getting very exciting when the telephone began ringing with an insistent voice in the hallway of Sharpstein Elementary. In the sixties, when I was a student going to school there, a telephone was mounted on the wall in every hallway and shared by the teachers in that area. The teacher who was least occupied at the time usually stepped into the hall to answer the telephone and take the message. That morning, the telephone just rang and rang.

I was worried because Mrs. Kramer had just given Nellie McCall the word *exiguous* to spell. There were only three of us who had not misspelled a word. If Nellie missed this word, it would go to Bradley Barker, and if he misspelled it, I would have a chance to win the spelling bee and the grand prize. I could hardly stand it because I knew how to spell *exiguous*! With only three of us left standing the tension was intense. Nellie began spelling slowly, e - x - u - g - u - o - u - s.

"I'm sorry Nellie, but that is not the correct spelling," said Mrs. Kramer.

Disappointment registered on Nellie's face.

"Whew," I thought. "Nellie missed the 'i' in exiguous. I wonder if Bradley will get it right?"

The telephone kept ringing and Mrs. Kramer glanced at the window of the door that led into the hallway, then gave the word to Bradley. Without hesitation, Bradley jumped in and spelled, e- x- i – j –u –o – u –s. He had a triumphant look on his face that crumbled in disbelief when Mrs. Kramer said, "Sorry Bradley, but that is incorrect." It was my turn, and I knew I would get it right because I had spelled *exiguous* to Karl five times last night.

The telephone continued ringing and Mrs. Kramer said, "I'm sorry, Megan, but wait a moment because I need to answer the telephone. Everyone else is either out to recess or preoccupied. Now children, I don't want any talking or discussing of the spelling word while I am out of the room. If I find out that this word was discussed while I'm gone, the spelling bee will be cancelled immediately, and no one will win the prize. If Megan misses this word, then Nellie, Bradley, and Megan will have the chance to try another word."

Mrs. Kramer looked sternly at everyone and went out to answer the telephone. Silence reigned as we all looked at each other. Mrs. Kramer was gone a very long time and some of the boys began to fidget in their seats. Whispering soon broke out. Nellie and I exchanged worried looks, but finally Mrs. Kramer came back. Her face was ashen white as she stepped back into the room.

"Children, something terrible has happened! The president of the United States of America, John F. Kennedy was shot in Dallas, Texas and may yet die. Bow your heads and pray fervently that he is spared."

All the children looked stunned, but I was mad! How could this happen when I was just about to win the spelling bee and the beautiful ten-speed bike? I didn't want to pray for the president because Father would be so proud of me if I won the spelling bee. But I obediently bowed my head while Mrs. Kramer fervently prayed for the well-being of our president, John F. Kennedy. The telephone began ringing again and she stepped out to answer it. I noticed that there were several other teachers in the hallway looking worried. But my only thoughts were of the spelling bee and the preoccupation with having a chance to spelling *exiguous*.

When Mrs. Kramer finally returned to the classroom, she announced that school was being dismissed early and the school bus would be in the loading area in fifteen minutes. The children who did not ride the school bus were to line up in the hallway while teachers called their parents for transport. I just couldn't believe that the spelling bee was over. I wasn't the only one worried because Bradley waved his hand madly in the air.

"Mrs. Kramer, what about the spelling bee? Doesn't Megan have to spell *exiguous* to see if we continue on?"

"I'm sorry about the spelling bee, Bradley," answered Mrs. Kramer. "This is a national tragedy, and the school officials feel it is important students are home as soon as possible. The spelling bee is cancelled for now and I will have to see when we can reschedule it. In the meantime, I want each of you to pray for President Kennedy. The combined efforts of all our prayers may be the only hope he has."

My heart sank. It wasn't fair. I was on the pinnacle of fame and fortune and then this had to happen. No way was I going to talk to God about saving President Kennedy. I didn't even know him.

That evening, my parents and Grandma Gibson sat huddled in front of our black and white television as Chet Huntley and David Brinkley brought forward the tragic events of the day. Their faces were drawn and sober as they listened to the broadcasters announcing that the thirty-fifth president of the United States, John F. Kennedy, had been shot in Dallas, Texas around 12:30 p.m. that day, rushed to the hospital, and pronounced dead thirty minutes after being shot.

I sat with my parents and Grandma listening to Chet Huntley.

I heard him say in his broadcast, *"There is in this country and there has been for too long an ominous and sickening popularity of hatred. The body of a president lying at this moment in Washington is a thundering testimonial of what hatred comes to and the revolting excesses it perpetuates. Hatred is self-generating, contagious, it feeds upon itself, and explodes into violence."*

I felt sad about my selfish desire to win the spelling bee and my refusal to pray for the president. If only I had prayed for him, maybe he would have lived.

Mother said, "Megan, it's time you started getting ready for bed. I'll come up and get your bed turned down while you put on your pajamas and brush your teeth. Give your father and grandmother a kiss goodnight."

I dutifully did as Mother asked, but the events of the day weighed heavy on my heart. I had failed President Kennedy because I had not prayed for his well-being. My austere grandmother's unusually warm embrace, and my father's "sleep well tonight, Megan" brought me no comfort. As we climbed the stairs together my mother's gentle arm lightly resting on my shoulders soothed my troubled heart.

"It's been a very sad and shocking day today, Megan, and you seem quiet tonight. I know you are sad about President Kennedy's assassination. Is there anything on your mind that you would like to talk about?"

"I think I may have caused President Kennedy to die today."

"What!" exclaimed my mother. "How could you have possibly caused President Kennedy's death?"

"Today at school we had our spelling bee contest. Nellie, Bradley, and I were the last three up. Mrs. Kramer gave Sarah the word *exiguous*, and she missed it. Then Bradley tried spelling *exiguous,* and he missed it. The telephone in the hall kept ringing and ringing. Just when it was my turn to spell Mrs. Kramer went to answer. The call was about President Kennedy being shot and I never got a turn to spell *exiguous* and I knew how to spell it! I really did, Mother. But Mrs. Kramer said that we all needed to pray for President Kennedy. She said his life depended upon us asking God to save him. I didn't pray for him, and I think that is why he died."

Mother gently wiped the tears from my cheek. "Go brush your teeth Megan, and I'll tell you a story once you are done and have your pajamas on."

Soon I was tucked in my covers. Mother didn't even shoo Karl from my bed when he poked his furry little face out from under the blanket. He always curled by my side at night.

Mother smiled at me and began.

This happened a long time ago when I was a young girl like you. My best friend was Polly Summers, and her parents owned a small bakery on Bainbridge Island. The smell of freshly baked bread and cookies was intoxicating when you walked into their bakery. Polly's mother's cinnamon rolls were famous, and it was always a treat when our family got them for special occasions.

The year Polly and I were in the fifth grade, a gymnasium was built on the school grounds so that students had a place to play and exercise during the cold winter months and when the weather was bad. A number of local men worked on the project as many of them had children attending the school. They volunteered their time and expertise to support the effort in getting the project completed. Some of the men helped with the framing, laying the concrete floor, wiring, plumbing, or whatever their construction expertise might be.

One day that fall, Polly's Mother arrived about noon and brought a huge pan of iced cinnamon rolls to our classroom. The smell of warm cinnamon filled the class room with an aroma that caused all our stomachs to growl even though we had just finished lunch. Our teacher, Mr. Jenkins greeted Mrs. Summers with a smile, and they chatted briefly for a few moments. Then Mrs. Summers set the large bakery sized pan of rolls on a table at the back of the room.

Our teacher dismissed us for the noon recess, and we all went out to the playground.

Polly said to the girls hanging around together, "I think my mother brought those cinnamon rolls for our class."

"Really!" said one of our friends in the group. "I love your mother's cinnamon rolls and I always beg my mother to get them for Saturday morning breakfast."

Polly smiled with pleasure when she heard this compliment. Soon we all chimed in with admiration for Mrs. Summer's cinnamon rolls. Some of the boys in our class drifted over and joined in with the compliments. Soon the entire class surrounded Polly enquiring when we would get to eat the rolls. Polly had never experienced so much attention in her life, and anyone could see she reveled in the praise.

Finally, the bell rang for afternoon classes, and we all went back into the school. Our teacher was at the end of the hall talking with the principal as we entered the classroom. Polly announced that everyone in the class could help themselves to a cinnamon roll. We all rushed to grabbed one before they were gone. Only one girl, Dorothy Anderson, stood back while the rest of us munched away on the warm gooey rolls. I had never eaten anything so delicious.

Polly encouraged Dorothy to have a roll, but she shook her head and said, "Are you sure those rolls were meant for us?" Polly assured Dorothy that her mother wouldn't have left the rolls in the classroom if she hadn't intended for the class to enjoy the treat. Dorothy just shook her head in doubt.

Most of the cinnamon rolls were consumed by the time our teacher, Mr. Jenkins came back into the classroom. He was appalled by what he saw. I had a sinking feeling in my stomach that what we had done was wrong. The delicious cinnamon roll I had just eaten didn't set well on my stomach when I saw Mr. Jenkin's shocked face. He told all of us who had eaten a cinnamon roll to line up along the back wall of the school room. That included every student in class except for Dorothy. I felt like I was standing against the wall of shame and Mr. Jenkins, usually so patient and kind, gave us the lecture of our lives. He told us that the cinnamon rolls had been specifically prepared for the men volunteering on the gymnasium project to thank them for their time and services. Mrs. Summers had made the cinnamon rolls just for the workers.

I hung my head in shame along with all the other students in my class. We all felt bad, except for Dorothy, who sat at her desk coloring while we got scolded. I wished with all my heart that I was sitting next to her coloring, rather than standing along the wall of shame.

Mr. Jenkins asked us what we should do to make the situation right. We shuffled our feet and looked at each other not knowing what to say. Finally, one of the students suggested that we all bring money to class the next day and give it to Mr. Jenkins to buy a couple of dozen cinnamon rolls from Mrs. Summer's bakery to give to the workers.

Mr. Jenkins thought it over and agreed this was a good idea. He told us to bring whatever allowance we could to school the next day and the money would be pooled together to purchase cinnamon rolls for the workers. We were a quiet group of students that afternoon. The next day Mr. Jenkins collected all the money and when Mrs. Summers brought another batch of rolls around noon, he gave the money to her. After Mrs. Summers left, Mr. Jenkins told us that he was proud of our class. I'll always remember his very last words. "Remember students, when you do something wrong, make it right, and then forgive yourself."

"Now, Megan," my dear little mother concluded, "forgive yourself for not praying for President Kennedy? You did not kill him. The person who pulled the trigger took his life, not you. Some things cannot be changed just because we pray that they will. It is only normal for you to want to win the spelling bee and win the big prize. The lesson to learn, Megan is to think about others, do right by them, and everything else will sort itself out the way it should."

By the time mother had finished her story, kissed me on the forehead, and tucked the covers around my shoulders, the heavy cape of sadness that burdened me was gone. Mother understood. Knowing that she did made me feel better. The world might be falling apart, but here in my cozy little bed, with Karl curled up next to me, purring like a tractor, I felt safe and at peace.

Chapter Five

An Experiment

It was a very quiet Thanksgiving that year. People were mourning the death of President Kennedy. Aunt Mary and Uncle Henry came over the evening of November 25th to watch President Kennedy's funeral with Mother, Father, and Grandma Gibson. I saw a tear slip down Aunt Mary's cheek when she saw Kennedy's little son, John Jr. salute his father's casket. It was a heart tugging sight, and it seemed the whole world was in mourning.

I felt especially mopey because I had been looking forward to seeing my brother Hiro for Thanksgiving. But he called Mother and Father and said he would be staying in Seattle over the holiday. This was Hiro's third year at the University of Washington's School of Engineering. Fall quarter would be ending shortly after the Thanksgiving break and a project in one of his engineering classes would be due. He needed more time to work on it, but he said he'd be home for Christmas.

I think Mother was sad that Hiro wasn't coming home, but she didn't say anything as she helped Grandma Gibson prepare corn casserole and pumpkin pie to take to Uncle Henry and Aunt Mary's house for Thanksgiving dinner. It'd be just the six of us, but I was used to being the only kid at the dinner table.

The weeks between Thanksgiving and Christmas flew by quickly. About two weeks before Christmas, Father and I drove up to Tollgate in the Blue Mountains and cut down a Christmas tree for the house. When we got back, Father trimmed the trunk, set it in the Christmas tree stand, and brought it into the house. The fragrance of freshly cut fir permeated our home with the smell of the great outdoors. I was eager to get the tree decorated, but we always waited until Hiro came home. He loved wrapping the string of bubble lights around the tree while I hung the many glass ornaments that Grandma Gibson had collected over the years. Everyone's eyes would light up with pleasure when Hiro plugged in the lights and the bubbling colors brought Christmas magic to our home.

I was happy to have my brother home for the holidays. Hiro was twenty and officially an adult. He usually spent hours talking with Uncle Henry about boring engineering stuff as Uncle Henry was an engineer at the U.S. Corp of Army Engineers in Walla Walla. But he always treated me like a peer, and it was nice not being the only kid among all the adults. He'd make me cinnamon toast or pop a big bowl of buttery popcorn while we played Monopoly or Chinese Checkers during some of the long winter evenings. Christmas was the season of endless joy in my world, and I hated to see the holidays end. But the days of family closeness and holiday happiness came to a close as we all crawled into the car to take Hiro to the Greyhound station. It was time for him to head back to Seattle, his college classes, and life at the university.

As for me, I would be returning to the ordinariness of Mrs. Kramer's fifth grade class and reunion with my best friend Sarah. She lived on the other side of town, and it had been two weeks since we last chatted. I couldn't wait to hear what she had gotten for Christmas and to show her the charm bracelet that Hiro had gotten me in Seattle. It was my favorite gift. I loved it even more than the pretty pink cardigan sweater that Mother and Father had given me, or the newest Nancy Drew Mystery from Aunt Mary and Uncle Henry. Grandma Gibson knitted me a pair of mittens for Christmas. I knew I was a lucky girl.

Sarah smiled with joy when she saw me. "Megan, guess what? We have a new girl in our class! Her family just moved to Walla Walla during the Christmas holidays. Her father is an emergency doctor at St. Mary's Hospital," Sarah said excitedly. "Wait 'til you meet her. I think you'll like her as much as I do."

"How do you know all of this Sarah? Classes are just starting. How do you know so much about the new girl?" I questioned.

"Because I've already met her," she answered excitedly. "She moved into a house down the street from us. This huge moving van arrived in our neighborhood the week before Christmas. Mother took a casserole to their house a few days later to welcome the family to the neighborhood and I got to go along. That's when I met Christine. She has the longest hair you have ever seen. She wears it in two long braids that reach to her waist. She's always flipping them over her shoulder. There she is now! Come meet her. It's really hard being the new kid halfway through the school year so let's be really nice to Christine."

I nodded my head in knowing agreement. Just then the bell rang so Sarah wasn't able to introduce me to Christine. We managed to slip into our seats just as Mrs. Kramer walked into the room.

"Welcome back class. I hope you all had a good Christmas vacation," said Mrs. Kramer as she smiled at all of us. "We have a new student in our class, and I would like to introduce you to her. This is Christine Parsons and she just moved here with her family from Seattle. I expect you will all make her feel welcome and right at home in our class. Now let's stand and say the pledge of allegiance to the flag to start our day."

Christine was the loveliest creature I had ever seen. Her hair was a golden yellow just like Sarah said. It was so long that her two braids hung nearly to her waist in the back. She had the biggest blue eyes and the creamiest skin of any girl in our class. When she looked my way, I smiled at her, and she smiled back at me. I really hoped that we would be friends.

Mrs. Kramer began class with exciting news. "We weren't able to complete our spelling bee contest before Thanksgiving break because of the tragic assassination of President Kenndy," she began. "But I've given it some thought, and I think it would be good if we started again with a fresh list of 500 words. However, there were three students who were very close to winning the spelling bee. I'm going to give you all a chance to decide if you think we should start anew, or if we should give Nellie, Bradley, and Megan the chance to finish up their competition?"

Boy oh boy, I really wanted to win the spelling bee and the thought of going through the exercise of studying new words and preparing for the spelling bee all over again, made me tired. But I remembered Mother's story of the cinnamon rolls and doing the right thing. Her words echoed in my ears, "*Megan, think about others, do right by them, and everything will sort itself out the way it should.*"

"Ok class, all those who think we should start the spelling bee over again with a new list of words, please raise your hand," said Mrs. Kramer.

Everyone's hand shot up in the air, everyone except for Nellie, Bradley, and me. For a second, I hesitated, and then I slowly raised my hand.

"My oh my, that does seem like a strong majority," said Mrs. Kramer. "Well then, here is the new list of 500 words that I want you to study for the next six weeks. Come Valentine's Day, we'll have our spelling bee! I want to encourage all of you to take some time each day and study a few words. That's the best way to ensure that you learn all of them."

That night around the dinner table I filled the family in with all the happenings of the day. I excitedly told them about the spelling bee and the new list of spelling words to learn.

Father looked at me over his bifocals and said, "Well Megan, we've got our work cut out. We'll start working on those spelling words right after the supper dishes are done." He smiled and gave me a wink.

"We've got a new girl in our class. Her father is an emergency doctor at St. Mary's Hospital, and they just moved here from Seattle the week before Christmas. I think we will be friends," I said.

"Yes, it has been the news of the town," said Father. "St. Mary's hasn't had an official emergency doctor since old Doc Powers retired last fall."

"It's about time," chimed in Grandma Gibson. "With the influenza so bad this year, the hospital has been shorthanded."

Father and Grandma Gibson's conversation began to fade out of my mind as they droned on about the news of the day. My mind wandered to the golden ten-speed bicycle sitting in the window of the Drumheller's Building. I kept dreaming of seeing it parked in our garage, ready for me to fly free on sunny spring days. My heart was set on winning that bike!

The next day at school I ate lunch with Christine and Sarah. Mrs. Kramer let kids push their desks close together during lunch, with the rule that everything was returned to orderly rows before we went to recess. Christine smiled and giggled at every story Sarah told and she was not shy about sharing stories of her own adventures at her previous school. I was soon to find out that although Christine looked like an angel, she loved to play practical jokes as much as Sarah did, especially on the boys in the room. Things began popping the very next day. Christine and Sarah dawdled as they came in from noon recess and were the last ones to hang up their coats in the cloak room next to the classroom. They giggled and whispered as they sat down at their desks.

Sarah leaned over and whispered to me just before Mrs. Kramer called the class to order. "Just wait until recess time. The boys in class will not be the first ones out on the playground! Christine and I made sure of that."

I looked at her quizzically and asked, "What have you done?"

"Just wait and see," said Sarah. "The boys are always the first ones out to the playground and won't let us swing during the entire recess time. But we've fixed them."

The afternoon dragged on and I had a hard time concentrating on getting my math assignment done. Of course, the lesson was on fractions, and I found them tedious to do. But finally, I finished my last problem just as the afternoon recess bell rang. I put my assignment in the basket on Mrs. Kramer's desk labeled "Mathematics" and then headed to the cloakroom to get my winter jacket. I was met with a very funny sight. Someone, and I suspected I knew who, had taken each boy's coat, turned the sleeves inside out, and then put them back on the coat hooks in a mixed order. There was much confusion as the boys hurried to find their coats and fix them to wear properly. Bradley's mittens were found in Frank's coat pocket and Frank's mittens were lost. Frank finally found his mittens tucked in the toes of his rubber galoshes. Billy's stocking hat was hanging on the edge of the ceiling light. Billy was trying unsuccessfully to toss up one of his gloves to dislodge it. What a chaotic sight and even funnier to hear the boys grumble and complain about who had done this. The girls were laughing, but no one was laughing harder than Christine and Sarah.

Just then Mrs. Kramer came around the corner and said, "What's all this commotion about? You are losing precious recess time!"

All the girls quickly skipped out to the playground, found their favorite swings and teeter totters, while the boys tried to get their winter coats straightened out. I felt a pang of remorse as the boys got less than ten minutes of recess time that afternoon. There was much grumbling and finger pointing from the boys that day with complaints that the girls were being unfair, and the girls saying the boys were jerks. It was the beginning of the practical jokes that became the bane of Mrs. Kramer, our long-suffering teacher. It was also the beginning of rivalry between the boys and girls with each group demonizing the other. I had never experienced these kinds of feelings before, but in some ways, I felt empowered by being a part of the "girls" group.

I. M. Ramsey

A few days later Nellie found a dead mouse in her desk. Whoever put the mouse in Nellie's desk didn't know what a tough girl Nellie could be and was probably disappointed at her lack of annoyance at the discovery. When Nellie found the poor rodent in her desk, she calmly picked it up by the tail and dropped it on Jimmy Silver's desk, who then plunked it on poor Jenny McDougal's desk. Jenny stood frozen in fright, but Mrs. Kramer came over and picked up the mouse and put it in the waste basket for the school custodian to discard after school. She reprimanded everyone for the commotion and insisted that we get back to work.

Secretly, I was relieved that the poor mouse hadn't landed on my desk as I was creeped out about rodents of any kind – dead or alive. I just shivered inside because I wasn't keen on finding a mouse in my desk.

Several days after the dead mouse incident, Katie Donaldson and Betty Ann Jenkins came back from lunch recess and found rubber snakes curled up on their school books inside their desks. The rubber snakes looked so real that both girls screamed in terror, which really upset Mrs. Kramer. She had just started working with a reading group while the rest of us practiced our cursive writing. The classroom serenity was interrupted by Katie's blood-curdling scream, followed a few seconds later by Betty Ann's horrified screech. Chaos ensued as both girls slammed their desk lids down and rushed to Mrs. Kramer's side.

It took a few minutes for Mrs. Kramer to get to the root of the problem and she was clearly annoyed when she discovered the lifelike rubber snakes in each of their desks.

She lectured the class saying, "As much as I like a practical joke, pranks can cause so much disruption that it is hard to get any learning done, and I won't have it. This nonsense has got to stop. It's been going on too long now and if I find out the culprits of this mischief there will be a price to pay."

Everyone loved Mrs. Kramer and knew she was strict, but fair. Her words seemed to sober the pranksters for a while, but only for a while. Over the next week or so peace and calm returned to the class, that is until Lenny Powell got a note on his desk, supposedly from Mrs. Kramer. Now Lenny had the worst handwriting in the class. It was hardly decipherable. Mrs. Kramer was always speaking to Lenny about "slowing down" and taking more care with his writing.

The note Lenny received read, "You will need to stay after school today for thirty minutes in order to practice your writing skills. Before you go home you will write the following sentence one hundred times in your best handwriting, *I will carefully practice writing cursive every day.*"

When the dismissal bell rang that afternoon, the usual noise erupted as children bustled around putting away their books, and getting their lunch boxes, coats, and boots from the cloakroom and headed out the classroom door. That is, most of the class except Lenny who remained dutifully at his desk. He pulled out his notebook and began carefully writing the required sentence, line after line. Mrs. Kramer had stepped out of the room to take some papers down to the front office, but when she returned a few minutes later, she was surprised to see him still sitting in the classroom.

Our class had a library period that day and Sarah and I were chatting about what book we were going to report on as we stuffed our library books into our school bags. We overheard Mrs. Kramer talking to Lenny as we finished and went to get our coats and boots.

"Lenny, what are you still doing here after school? Shouldn't you be getting your things together to go home for the day?" Mrs. Kramer enquired.

Lenny looked up from what he had been doing with a very confused look on his face. "But you told me I had to stay after school and practice my cursive writing before I went home today. And that's just what I'm doing!" Lenny said empathically.

"Now what led you to believe that is what I wanted you to do today, because I don't recall asking you?" countered Mrs. Kramer.

Lenny reached for a wadded-up piece of paper on his desk and handed it to Mrs. Kramer. She opened it up and read: "you will need to stay after school today for thirty minutes in order to practice your writing skills. Before you go home you will write the following sentence one hundred times in your best handwriting, *I will practice writing cursive every day.*"

Mrs. Kramer frowned as she said, "Lenny, you've been snookered. I didn't write this note as I don't require students to stay after school unless I talk to them myself. That isn't to say you wouldn't benefit from extra practice writing cursive, but it isn't fair to require one student to stay after school for something I wouldn't ask other students to do as well. You just gather your things together and hop on home."

"Thanks Mrs. Kramer," said Lenny gratefully. "I was afraid I would get in trouble for being late for my newspaper route. I've got to get home and fold papers."

"Run along Lenny. I'll see you tomorrow." Mrs. Kramer said.

The next morning, our class faced a very serious and sober-faced Mrs. Kramer. We started the morning as we did every morning with the Pledge of Allegiance to the Flag, but then things took a change.

"Students," began Mrs. Kramer. "I've seen our close knit, hardworking community of students turn into competing rivals. As I've said in the past, I don't mind a practical joke once in a while, but too many of them disrupt the class and causes chaos in our learning schedule. A practical joke can be annoying and can make someone feel foolish, but when a joke turns mean and harms someone in a serious way, then we have to stop and look at the damage it does."

I felt terrible inside and I think many others felt the same way because I saw their heads hanging down in shame.

Mrs. Kramer continued, "Someone left a note for Lenny yesterday, saying he needed to stay after school and do some extra homework. That person impersonated me and caused Lenny to feel embarrassed and punished when he really hadn't done anything wrong. It caused him worry because he had an after school commitment of delivering the newspaper. People in his neighborhood depend upon him to get their daily paper but staying after school made him late to get his delivery from the Union Bulletin, made him late to get the papers folded and delivered on time. That was not a practical joke, but a mean joke, and we are just not going to have that in our classroom."

Mrs. Kramer paused for a minute and looked around the classroom and then continued. "None of us like to have a joke played on us, nor feel ashamed when others see our frustration, our fears, or our vulnerabilities. Competition and rivalries are common experiences, but if we can't feel how others feel this can lead to treating people who are different than we are in demeaning and inferior ways. These intense rivalries create a situation where some people are always privileged and on top, while other people are not seen as equal and find themselves at the bottom. We need to see everyone in this classroom, whether you are a girl or boy, whether you are short or tall, whether you have blonde, brunette, or red hair as important human beings with potential to make the world a better place. We need to have empathy for those who are different than we are. Empathy is the best way to develop friendship, cooperation, and community.

Starting tomorrow we are going to have an experiment in empathy for two days. Do you all know what empathy means? It means that you are willing to walk in someone else's shoes and try to experience and feel what they are experiencing and feeling. I want each of you to reach in this basket as I come around the room and pull out one envelope. Inside that envelope you will find a slip of paper that says gold team or gray team. I will tell you what the rules for the next two days will be."

I was excited about this game and wondered what team color I would get. I also felt that something very important was going to happen in the next few days and I was both worried and excited to see what would happen.

After everyone had gotten their envelope, Mrs. Kramer went up to the black board where there were two teams identified: Gold team and Gray team. She began at the back of the room and worked her way up to the front row asking students to open the envelope and show the team they had gotten. Then she wrote that student's name under the gold or gray team, depending upon which team they chose. I picked an envelope with gray team written on it. Sarah picked an envelope with gold team, and Christine was placed on the gray team. I knew that Sarah was disappointed that she hadn't picked the same team as Christine and me. But she smiled at us when Mrs. Kramer said the gold team would have all the privileges the next day, and the gray team would be the privileged team on Thursday. Then she wrote the rules on the blackboard. We children were very quiet when she had finished writing. I began to think that this game wasn't much fun after all.

Mrs. Kramer said, "listen up students. I want you to pay careful attention as I read these rules, because that is how we will conduct class for the next two days. The team designated as the gold team of the day, will have these advantages and privileges.

The gold team will have five extra minutes for each recess of the day. That includes the morning recess, lunch recess, and afternoon recess."

"That's not fair Mrs. Kramer," blurted Wesley Foster. "What about the gray team? Don't we get to play longer too?"

"Not tomorrow," said Mrs. Kramer. "You are not a gold team member tomorrow, so you will not get the same advantages or privileges."

Groans could be heard around the room as students who had gotten envelopes containing gray team realized that they would not have as much play time as their gold team counterparts.

"Additionally," Mrs. Kramer said, "the gold team will get their lunches first. They will only have ten math problems to solve tomorrow, instead of twenty, (more groans emerged around the room), and they will get to spend five extra minutes reading time in the library."

Sarah had a big grin on her face, but Christine just scowled at her. Sarah had been my best friend since first grade, but I wasn't very happy about the way she was acting, and it made me angry at her.

"Finally," Mrs. Kramer said, "every student who is on the gold team will wear a bright gold button pinned on their shirt for the day. The gray team will wear a gray button on their shirts to ensure that everyone has their status identified for the day. Now, are there any questions?"

We sat in our seats looking annoyed, confused, or smiling. I knew that the smiling students were the gold team members and that they would be on top the next day.

The day passed quickly, but I didn't like the way Sarah suddenly began to act superior to me. When I tripped and almost fell coming in from recess, she said to me in a haughty voice, "Megan, if you weren't so clumsy, you'd walk on your two feet rather than stumbling over them!"

I was so confused. This wasn't like Sarah at all. We had been friends forever, since I first met her at Sunday School and then in the first grade. What had happened to make her change from a friend to a stranger?

At supper that night I told my father and mother and Grandma Gibson about the empathy game we were going to play the next two days at school.

"What has brought this all on?" asked Grandma Gibson. "I don't see how you can learn about empathy by letting one group of students have more privileges than the other. Doesn't make sense to me at all. What's become of education these days?"

This was certainly an area that I could agree with Grandma Gibson. Usually, we didn't see eye to eye on very many things, but I couldn't see how I was going to learn one thing about empathy if Sarah was going to act superior to me.

"It sounds like everyone in your class will get a chance to have special privileges," my father said. "On the day you are on top, it might be good for you to remember what it feels like when you weren't."

I thought about that for a bit. "Mrs. Kramer said that empathy was about learning to think and feel what it is like to walk in someone else's shoes," I told my father. "Is that what you mean when you say that when I'm a gold team member and have more privileges I should remember how I felt on the day when I had to do everything last?" I queried.

"Yes, that's exactly what I mean," said my father. "If you are always on the winning side and you never experience disappointment, you develop a sense of entitlement. You never really understand how others think and feel. I think this is a good experiment. Come on now. Let's help your mother clean up the table and get these dishes washed and put away. That will give us just enough time to practice your spelling words before you head for bed."

The next morning at school Mrs. Kramer pinned a bright gold paper button on each student who belonged on the gold team, and a dull gray paper button on the chests of the gray team members. She spent a few minutes going over the rules of privilege that were written on the blackboard before our day began.

Things moved along quite normally until the first recess call when Mrs. Kramer said, "Gold team, put away your reading books and you may be dismissed for morning recess. Gray team, since you are not of the privileged group, you must stay in your seats and study reading comprehension for an additional five minutes."

Sarah and the other gold team members cheerfully, and may I say, with superior looks on their faces, put away their books and went to the cloak room to get their coats, boots, and mittens and were gone in a flash. I looked around the room at the remaining students and there were no smiles, just glum glances. It sure didn't feel fair, but it was even worse when we finally got to go outside for recess. The gold team students had all the swings and gym equipment, and Sarah and Nellie were playing Double Dutch rope skipping with some of the other gold team girls. When Christine and I tried to join, Sarah said arrogantly, "You girls are on the gray team and that means you aren't allowed to play Double Dutch with us. You are not good enough to play with the gold team."

Christine's mouth formed a big "what" and I retorted, "You know I'm a better rope skipper than you are Sarah!"

But no amount of cajoling or reasoning would change their minds. Christine sat down on the steps looking very dejected and I joined her, feeling very put out with Sarah and the other gold team girls. Recess was not fun that morning.

Lunch was even worse. The gold team was dismissed for lunch a full five minutes before the gray team. Mrs. Kramer had brought cookies that day and by the time the gray team was dismissed to get lunches, there were no cookies left, just tantalizing crumbs. Lunch recess was a repeat of the morning recess and by the afternoon I was in a dark mood. Starting tomorrow I was going to get back at Sarah and Nellie when I was a gold team member. But it wasn't just Sarah and Nellie, all the gold team members were treating the gray team as inferior and second rate. Even Mrs. Kramer acted like we were not the brightest students in the class.

That afternoon in our "pop up" spelling test to practice for the upcoming spelling bee, Mrs. Kramer, always chose a gold team student to spell the word first. Even if they missed the word, she would praise them as if they were the best spellers in school! I knew every word because father and I had been practicing each night since Mrs. Kramer gave us the new 500 word spelling list. But I never got a chance to spell one word that day. It seemed that Mrs. Kramer just looked past me as if I was invisible.

By the time we got to the afternoon recess, the gray team members were very unhappy. Tempers flew when Martin Corn called Lucas Powell a "jerk" because he tripped him while playing Capture the Flag.

Lucas retorted hatefully back, "You are the clumsy one. If you weren't on the gray team, you wouldn't be so clumsy!"

That didn't settle well with Martin and before you know it, they were pushing and shoving each other all over the field. Martin ripped Lucas's shirt pocket before the playground supervisor pulled them apart. She had each one of them by the arm and marched them into the principal's office when Mrs. Kramer came out to blow the whistle, signaling the end of recess time.

I fully expected Mrs. Kramer to say something about the playground altercation between Martin and Lucas, but she just marched us into the classroom, and we began our final hour of school working on our history lesson.

By the end of the day, I was in a very bad mood. I didn't walk Sarah to the cloakroom to get our coats and lunchboxes, in fact, I wouldn't even look at her. It was hard to have any warm feelings toward her, and I didn't see how this could be a lesson in empathy. Sarah was being so uppity I felt left out and upset. The only solace I felt as I walked out of the classroom was the thought that the next day, I'd be a gold team member. I couldn't wait to make Sarah feel just as badly as I was feeling right then.

There was a storm in my heart and a darkness that I had never felt before. I didn't like any of the gold team members and I didn't like Mrs. Kramer. It seemed she favored them and didn't even care about the gray team members; we were her students too! I couldn't figure out what I was supposed to learn from this experiment. My father and I had just finished reviewing my spelling words when he asked me how my day at school had gone?

"Just terrible!" I cried out. "Mrs. Kramer plays favorites with all the gold team members and Sarah acts so superior. I don't like the way Sarah looks down on me. She acts like I don't do anything as well as she does. It's just not fair Father! Mrs. Kramer didn't call on me to spell one word, even though I was the first one up out of my desk. She looked right past me like I wasn't even there!" The dark words just spilled out of me, and I could feel my hands clinch into fists.

"Hold on Megan," my father said kindly. "It's my understanding that tomorrow the teams will be switched, and you'll be a gold team member. Am I right?"

"Yes!" I retorted. "And I'm going to make Sarah feel as badly as she has made me feel today."

"Well, you might remember how badly you felt today when Sarah was so unkind with you. Perhaps you could treat her like you wished she had treated you today," said Father.

"She didn't treat Christine and me nicely," I said. "I don't think we should be nice to her."

"Well, let's see how you feel about that tomorrow night," Father said wisely. "It's time for you to get your bath and get your pajamas on for bed. Here, let me give you a goodnight kiss."

Father's words soothed me, and it felt good to feel his kiss on my forehead, but I still had a storm brewing in my heart.

The next morning my heart was full of hope and eagerness as I sat at my desk. I had a bright gold button pinned on my blouse, and I felt happy and strong. Today was the day when I was the superior student, and I wouldn't be ignored by my best friend or anyone. I felt big and I felt bold. I looked across the aisle at Sarah and she didn't look happy, not like yesterday. She had a downcast expression on her face as she looked straight ahead. There was a gray button on her dress and the drabness of the gray matched her face. Suddenly I felt sorry for her, but I didn't know what to say.

Instead, I looked behind Sarah at Christine, who was also sporting a bright gold button and she flashed me a brilliant smile.

Just then Mrs. Kramer spoke to the class. "Good morning students. Today we have switched up the teams and the students with gold buttons will have the longer recesses, fewer math problems, and more time in the library. Are there any questions?"

"If not, then we will begin today with our weekly reading comprehension test. I will pass out the Weekly Reader and you will be given thirty minutes to read this week's edition. Then I will give you the reading comprehension test. Let's see if we can beat last week's score. I'm sure that the gold team members will do well, but I would encourage all of the gray team members to read very carefully as I know you have more difficulty remembering the content," she said.

Out of the corner of my eye I saw Sarah's head droop further. Sarah was one of the best readers in class and I just didn't understand how Mrs. Kramer could say Sarah did not comprehend the tests. Of course, everyone knew that Katie Donaldson and Martin Corn usually got the lower reading scores, and they were on the gray team today, but Sarah was a star reader.

Once the reading was done and the test was given, Mrs. Kramer instructed us to trade tests with a classmate, but she added that gold team members were to double check gray team members tests because everyone knew they had a tendency to mess things up. Groans and protests erupted among the gray team students, but Sarah sullenly handed me her test and I gave her mine.

I was surprised because Sarah never missed any reading comprehension questions, but this day she had four wrong answers. This was unthinkable and I hated to write 6/10 on her paper, but I did. I looked at her sympathetically when I returned her test, but she didn't look at me. I had 10/10 on my test, which made me very happy. But I felt sorry for Sarah. Even more so when Mrs. Kramer told us at noon that we hadn't beaten last week's reading comprehension score and it was because of the gray team members as they had missed more questions than usual.

Recess that day was no fun. I missed Sarah's happy chatter and familiar companionship. She leaned against the concrete school building, looking forlorn, but when I asked her to come play hopscotch with me and Christine, she just turned away.

Lunch wasn't any fun either. Usually Sarah, Christine, and I would cluster our desks together while we munched on the lunches our mothers had prepared, comparing our food and making trades now and then. But not this day. Sarah sat by herself, eating lunch very quietly. I wanted her to join us, but Christine said that we couldn't mix with the gray team people because they weren't as good as us. That didn't seem fair, and I saw Sarah's face scowl when she overheard Christine's words. Nothing seemed right that day.

I went home feeling sad, not angry like I had the day before, but very sad.

"What's the matter with you," Grandma Gibson asked me when I got home? "Did you get into trouble today?"

"No, no I didn't. I was looking forward to being a gold team student today, but it didn't turn out quite as good as I thought it would," I said.

"Well, a person never feels very good when they don't treat other people kindly," Grandma responded bluntly.

I nodded my head in agreement and went to find Karl. He was curled up in his favorite place, right smack dab in the middle of father's easy chair in the living room. I picked him up and snuggled for a while as I tried to sort out all the confusing things in my mind.

How could I be so angry at Sarah one day when she acted uppity and self-important? Then feel sad the next day when I was the privileged one? I had looked forward to being on the gold team, but it hadn't been any fun at all. I felt sad for Sarah and the other kids who were being constantly put down. It didn't make me happy to have all the advantages as I thought it would. Why not, I wondered?

Karl was no help in figuring this out. I went to find mother, but Grandma Gibson said that Bitsy Sheldon was feeling poorly, and mother was at her house helping Bitsy get dinner prepared for her family.

After the dinner dishes were washed and dried, Father sat down with me to work on the spelling list. "Ahh, here is a good word to start with," said Father. "Can you spell *perspective,* and do you know what it means?"

"Yes, I can spell perspective," I said. "*P-e-r-s-p-e-c-t-i-v-e,* but I don't know what it means."

"Well, get the Webster's Dictionary from the bookcase and let's look it up," said Father.

As I got up from the footstool by Father's chair I tripped over Karl. He gave an annoying yowl as I stepped on the tip of his tail.

"Put that creature outside," Grandma Gibson said sternly. "That cat is always underfoot and thinks he owns the house. He could do with a stretch outside."

I bent down and scooped him up in my arms and cuddled him as I walked out the door. I whispered in his ear, "Don't worry Karl, I'll sneak you in before I go to bed tonight."

I got the big red Webster's Dictionary from the bookcase and plopped back down on the footstool. It took me a few minutes, but I finally found that pesky word "*perspective"* and began reading the definition out loud to father. There were several definitions, six in all.

When I was done, Father said, "Why don't you read definition four again."

It read, *a specific point of view in understanding or judging things or events, especially one that shows them in their true relations to one another; the ability to see things in a true relationship.*

"Do you understand what that definition means?" Father asked.

"Does it mean that in order to understand things in a true relationship you have to see it from another angle and not just your own?" my forehead wrinkled in furrows as I answered.

"Yes, I think so," said Father. "Perspective taking means that you look at events from different positions other than your own. For example, Mrs. Kramer is trying to help all of the students in your class understand what others feel when mean spirited things are done. We call that empathy, or perspective taking."

"Do you mean I was being empathetic when I couldn't be mean to Sarah today, because I remembered how it felt when she was mean to me yesterday?" I asked.

"Yes, precisely that," said Father. "You were angry with Sarah last night. You thought she was being superior and uppity, and it hurt your feelings. So much that you looked forward to being on the gold team today and making her feel as bad as you did yesterday. Is that how you felt?"

"I was angry when I came home from school yesterday, and I really wanted to make Sarah feel bad. Those feelings all went away today when I saw how sad she felt. I remembered how sad I felt, and I didn't want Sarah to feel that way. Being on top didn't feel right when I saw her so sad," I said to Father.

"I'm glad you are trying to understand perspective taking," said father. "If you can learn to see another person's point of view, even if you disagree with them, it will save you much sorrow and misunderstanding as you go through life."

The next morning at school Mrs. Kramer had a large blanket in the reading area on the classroom floor and after our Pledge of Allegiance, she asked us all to come over and sit on the blanket. We were a sober-faced and serious group of students that morning as Mrs. Kramer began the morning discussion of the last two days of school.

"How did you students like the last two days of school?" she asked.

"I hated it!" began Martin. "I hated being on the gray team and feeling like everyone on the gold team was better than me."

"I hated it too!" cried Sarah. "When I was a gold team member, I felt I was the best, on top, and nothing could stop me. But when I was a gray team member it seemed like everything went wrong. I couldn't do anything right. And it felt like my friends didn't care about me." Sarah looked at me with sad, soulful eyes.

"I wanted Lucas to feel like he was a loser too," said Martin. "Especially after he kicked me, just because he thought I wasn't as good as him."

Soon everyone was saying how unhappy they had been, and they didn't feel as if they had any friends at school. Even though I didn't say anything I felt exactly the same way.

"Well students, do you think we should continue this experiment?" asked Mrs. Kramer.

"No!" we all shouted.

"Go back to your seats and get those awful gold and gray buttons and let's throw them away!" said Mrs. Kramer.

We scrambled and retrieved those dreadful symbols and threw them in the wastebasket. I saw Sarah ripping her gray paper button into tiny pieces before tossing them away. I did the same and so did Christine. We all smiled at each other as we tore those ugly symbols into tiny little scraps. It felt like a huge black cloud lifted from the classroom and that sunshine was streaming in.

"Doesn't that feel better?" Mrs. Kramer enquired with a big smile

"Yes!" We all yelled together.

"Does it feel like we are one team again?" she asked.

"Yes, it does!" we cried back.

"Does it feel good being friends again, rather than trying to outdo and play mean tricks on each other?" she asked.

I felt joy in my heart as Sarah put her arms around Christine and my shoulders. I wrapped my arm around Sarah's waist and smiled at Christine as she did the same. Life seemed good and I knew that I had come back home.

Oh yes! Things seemed right again.

Chapter Six

The Spelling Bee

It was the day we had all been waiting for, the day of our fifth-grade class spelling bee! The excitement had been building for a couple of weeks, especially on the days of our weekly pop-up spelling rehearsals. In the past few weeks, since the empathy experiment, our class had grown closer together and were working even harder on our scholarly achievements. Not just individual achievements but celebrating our group achievements as a class. Mrs. Kramer praised us every day for improving as a class on our Weekly Reader comprehension quizzes, our math tests, but even more on our great spelling skills. Everyone in our class was succeeding.

I could hardly go to sleep the night before the spelling bee. Father and I had worked hard every night after Mrs. Kramer gave us the list. However, the final week before the big spell-off the anticipation and effort grew to an incredible urgency. Even Grandma Gibson told me she would help Mother with washing and drying the evening dishes in order to give Father and me extra time to review the spelling bee word list.

That night, before the big day, my dreams were filled with spelling bee drama. In my dreams I couldn't find my classroom and ran up and down the halls of Sharpstein School anxiously looking for Mrs. Kramer's room. But in my dream, I couldn't find it. Morning came, but my final dream kept haunting me. There I was, the last student who hadn't misspelled a word. In my dream, Mrs. Kramer asked me to spell a word, but it was as if I'd gone deaf. I could see her lips move, but I couldn't hear her voice at all. I leaned forward, straining to hear the word when suddenly the classroom began shaking as if we were in an earthquake.

"Megan! Megan! It's time to get up. Today's the big day," mother said as she shook my shoulder. I woke up with a start and looked at my mother with startled eyes. I wondered if the earthquake in the dream had been her shaking and trying to awaken me.

I rubbed my eyes and said, "I had the most terrible dream Mother. I dreamed I was the last student in our class that hadn't misspelled a word and I was on the verge of spelling the winning word. But in my dream, I suddenly became deaf and couldn't hear the word Mrs. Kramer gave me. It was just awful."

"Well, this isn't a dream, Megan. Today is the day and you had better get up and get dressed and down to breakfast. Your father is already at the kitchen table drinking his coffee." I popped out of bed with no more insistence from Mother.

At the breakfast table, Father said, "Megan, you have time for that extra piece of toast with your mother's raspberry jam to give you good luck and energy today." He smiled at me as he pulled on his overcoat and headed out to warm up the car and scrape the frost off the window.

I wasn't hungry and I could barely eat the bowl of oatmeal sitting in front of me, let alone another piece of toast with jam. No sirree, I was ready to get on with the day. Mother reminded me to brush my teeth, so I went to the bathroom and gave them a quick swish, then grabbed my coat and rushed out the door to the waiting car.

Mother stood in the doorway waving to me and saying, "Good luck today!"

I furtively waved to her as I stepped into the car. During the snowy days of winter, Father often dropped me off at school in the mornings on his way to work. Today was one of those days. As I got out of the car, he patted my arm and gave it a little squeeze for good luck. I gave him a grateful smile and ran to catch Sarah and Nellie walking towards the front door. They were chattering about the spelling bee and how worried they were about the bonus words that Mrs. Kramer had given us only a couple of weeks earlier.

"I wish we had gotten that fifty-word bonus list earlier," said Nellie. "I know I should have studied them more, but I just ran out of time."

"Me too," agreed Sarah. "Those words are so hard. I don't know where Mrs. Kramer got them, and I don't know what most of them mean."

I hadn't known the definition of the fifty words on the bonus list either, but Father had insisted that I look up each word and write the definition before I worked on spelling them. It had taken me ten days. I had just finished looking up the last of the bonus words on Sunday, which gave me only this week to review them. But I felt confident.

The classroom was a bustle of activity when we entered. Everyone was chattering about the exciting day ahead. Classes would convene as usual during the morning, but after lunch recess, the spelling bee would take place. I was excited and could hardly concentrate on anything that morning. Time seemed to drag along. Finally, the lunch bell rang and Sarah, Christine, and I put our desks together to chat about the upcoming event.

"Who do you think will win the golden ten-speed?" asked Christine. "It's such a beautiful bike. My older brother has a black ten-speed bike, but it's not half as shiny as the grand prize. I have a one-speed, but I would love to have a ten-speed so I could beat my brother. Whenever we ride bikes, he leaves me in the dust."

"I bet Nellie wins the grand prize," piped up Sarah. "Or maybe you Megan. You are a good speller."

My heart gave a little flutter of joy to hear Sarah say I was a good speller, but then I remembered mother's words that it wasn't good to act proud.

I smiled at Sarah and said, "Thank you Sarah. That's really nice of you to say, but there are lots of good spellers in our class. Both you and Christine have done well in our pop-up spelling practices."

Both of my friends smiled at me, and I realized that everyone likes it when someone compliments them.

After lunch we got our winter coats and gloves and headed out. The previous weekend the county had received a skiff of snow, followed by another four to five inches during the week, bringing plenty of snow to make snowmen and snow angels around the playground. The boys engaged in snowball fights during the week with a few stray snowballs hitting unexpected players on the playground.

The air was filled with squeals of surprise, but it was all in good fun. My friends reveled in the rituals of winter and so did I. Today was no exception as we put the finishing touches on our snow "woman." It had taken all week to create her. Instead of a round base Nellie, Sarah, Christine, and I spent two days shaping the base of the snowwoman in a triangle shape to look like a skirt. We were proud of our effort. The next level was a perfectly shaped round snowball for her middle and a smaller snowball for her head. We had shaped her head and carved it in such a way that it looked like she had braids wrapped around the crown of her head. Today we put the final touches on her face. She was a beautiful snowwoman, and we were enthralled.

We stepped back to admire our handiwork just as the whistle blew to end lunch recess. Without hesitation we all raced into the school building. The spelling bee was about to begin! Mrs. Kramer had brought several large thermoses of hot chocolate and lots of delicious cookies for us to enjoy. It was a party atmosphere, and everyone was excitedly awaiting the rules of the spelling bee.

There were twenty students in our class and Mrs. Kramer had drawn our names out of a box and created two groups of ten. One group of ten students would line up at the front of the room and Mrs. Kramer would begin by asking the first student to spell a word. If spelled correctly she would go to the next student and give that student a different word. This process would continue until a word was misspelled. When that happened, that same word would be given to the next student in line to spell. If spelled correctly, then she would give a new word to the next student in line.

When we were given a word, we were required to say the word out loud, then spell it, then say the word again. Each group of ten students would have fifteen minutes and then the second group of ten students would stand in front and spell for fifteen minutes. This rotation would continue until there were two students left on each team. The four students would come up to the front and a final spell off would begin.

I wasn't in the first group of ten students who were chosen to begin the spelling bee. That was fine as it gave me time to settle my nerves and see how the process would unfold. And so, it began. My close friends Sarah, Christine, Betty Ann, and Janet were all in the first group of students. Only Nellie and I weren't in the first group, so we sat close together eagerly watching our friends.

Mrs. Kramer gave Bradley Baker the first word of the contest, *unconscious*.

"Unconscious," said Bradley. "u-n-c-o-n-s-c-i-o-u-s, unconscious."

"Correct!" Responded Mrs. Kramer. "Bobby, the next word is for you. *Example.*"

"*Example*" said Bobby. "*e-x-a-m-p-l-e, example.*"

"Correct!" Mrs. Kramer said. And thus, it continued. No one misspelled a word in the first round of the spelling bee and my classmates all took their seats with smiles on their faces. Whew! They had made it through the first round.

The second group of ten students went to the front of the classroom. I was so nervous I could hardly stand still, but I could feel Nellie next to me shuffling her feet, which made me feel better knowing that I wasn't the only nervous one. My first word was a short word, but quite tricky if you hadn't studied it carefully.

"Megan, your word is *knack,*" said Mrs. Kramer.

"*Knack, k-n-a-c-k, knack,*" I said.

"Correct!" said Mrs. Kramer.

Whew! I thought with relief.

Everyone in the second group made it through the first session without anyone being disqualified. Nellie and I sat together and waited to see how the next round would go. No one was disqualified until the third session when Katie Donaldson was given the word, *hemorrhage* and forgot the "h" in the middle of the word. She sat down with disappointment written all over her face. *Hemorrhage* then went to Martin Corn, and he used a "j" instead of a "g" and he had to sit down. The word went to Betty Ann, and she missed it too! Betty Ann added an extra "m" and now the first spelling group was down to seven members. *Hemorrhage* went to Sarah and luckily, she spelled it correctly.

At the end of that round there were only five spellers still qualified to continue. Round three had been brutally hard and half the group had been disqualified. I wondered how our group would fair.

Round three didn't go very well for our group either. When our third session ended there were only seven students who hadn't misspelled a word. The spelling bee continued and by the time we were starting our sixth round of competition each team was down to the final four spellers, two on each team. I couldn't believe my good fortune. I was one of the final four. Father and I had worked hard every evening for the past two months to prepare for this competition and the hard work was paying off.

Mrs. Kramer explained that in the competition of the final four she would also draw words from the bonus list she had handed out a week ago. The bonus list had words that were tricky, and I could feel a little knot of worry building in the pit of my stomach.

We went back and forth for quite a while correctly spelling words such as *chauffeur, camaraderie, questionnaire, and reservoir*. Christine and Bradley represented the final two of group one and Nellie and I represented the final two of the second group. Bradley stumbled on the word *zucchini*, putting a second "n" in the word, so the word passed on to Nellie. She spelled it correctly, so Bradley had to sit down. Now it was only Christine and me standing undefeated on our team. She was given the word *camouflage* and she spelled it without blinking. The next word was *entrepreneur*. I held my breath as Nellie spelled it.

She began, "*entrepreneur, e-n-t-r-e-p-r-e-n-e-r, entrepreneur.*"

"Incorrect!" said Mrs. Kramer. "Megan, please spell *entrepreneur*."

"*Entrepreneur, e-n-t-r-e-p-r-e-n-e-u-r, entrepreneur.*" I said.

"That is correct!" said Mrs. Kramer. "Nellie, please take your seat. Well class, we are now down to the final two spellers, Christine and Megan. Let's begin this final spell off." The next word went to Christine, then to me, and back and forth for several rounds. Then came the word *perspective*, which was given to Christine.

"*Perspective, p-r-e-s-p-e-c-t-i-v-e, perspective,*" said Christine.

"Incorrect." Said Mrs. Kramer. "Megan, please spell perspective."

Christine looked distressed and puzzled. I could tell that she thought she had spelled it correctly, but I knew she had indeed spelled it wrong.

I took a deep breath, remembering my conversation with father, many weeks ago. I had looked *perspective* up in the Webster dictionary and we had talked about its definition, "*a specific point of view in understanding or judging things or events, especially one that shows them in their true relations to one another; the ability to see things in a true relationship.*"

I knew I could do it and I began spelling it, "*perspective, p-e-r-s-p-e-c-t-i-v-e. perspective.*"

"Correct!" Said Mrs. Kramer. "Congratulations Megan! You have earned the honor of winning this year's Sharpstein School's Fifth Grade Spelling Contest! I'm so proud of every one of you today as I have never had a group of students go so many rounds before a word was misspelled. You are all winners and each of you will receive a free book at the Public Library when you take them this card. And Megan, you will be the winner of the ten-speed bike that has been sitting in the window at the old Drumheller's Building! Saturday morning, which is tomorrow, at 10:00, the *Union Bulletin* newspaper photographer and a reporter will interview you and take your picture with the bicycle. There will be a very big story in the Sunday *Union Bulletin* about our exceptional fifth grade class, the spelling bee, and Megan's picture will be on the front page!"

Everyone came up to congratulate me, even Christine who was so disappointed when she missed spelling the word *perspective*. But she didn't show envy or disappointment, just sweet words of "well done" and a smile of congratulations.

Sarah came up and grabbed my arm saying, "Megan, I'm so happy that you won the spelling bee! You are a hard worker and I know you deserve this win! I'm going to talk my mother into taking me down to Drumheller's tomorrow so I can see you get your picture taken for the newspaper. It will be so exciting!"

"Thanks Sarah!" I said. "I'm so happy you are coming! My parents will be proud of me, especially my father. He spent every night for weeks drilling me on those spelling words. He should be the one to win the prize."

"I'm glad you won the bike," said Sarah. "Maybe we can go for a ride around Pioneer Park on Sunday. Try to talk your mother into it."

"I'll try," I said. "But you know how overly protective she is."

"I know," said Sarah. "But we'll be eleven soon and I think we can handle ourselves just fine. I know my mother will let me."

"Yes, I'll do my best and I'll let you know what Mother says."

Bright and early and fifteen minutes before 10:00 a.m. my father, mother, and Grandma Gibson climbed into the Ford station wagon and drove to the old Drumheller's Building. Sure enough, Mrs. Kramer was there talking with the Union Bulletin reporter. The UB photographer was also there, the Principal of Sharpstein School, and a number of my classmates. Even Aunt Mary and Uncle Henry were standing in the crowd outside Drumhellers.

My heart was bursting with happiness, and I could see that father was also proud of me. I hadn't realized how much this "five minutes of fame" really meant to me. In that moment I realized that everyone loves recognition, and we all crave the adoration of others. I was no exception!

Mrs. Kramer introduced me and my family to the Union Bulletin reporter and he asked all kinds of questions. The reporter's first question is the one I remember most clearly, even though I'm a grown woman now, with children of my own. He asked, "How is it that a young slip of a girl like you managed to out spell everyone in your fifth-grade class?"

I didn't quite know what to say. But I took my father's hand, and then looked shyly at the reporter and said, "Well, I couldn't have done it without my father's help. He drilled me on my spelling words every night after the dinner dishes were cleaned and put away. He had me look up words in the Webster's dictionary and then I'd practice spelling the word. We did that every night. It took forever." I felt my father give my hand a gentle squeeze and I knew that I had said the right thing.

Just then, Mrs. Kramer spoke up saying to the reporter, "Well Ned, I have the brightest group of fifth graders in this entire valley! Every student in my class did exceptionally well in this spelling bee. The competition was fierce, but Megan is a dutiful student and her conscientious and consistent effort to learn that list of 500 spelling words really paid off when it came to the spelling contest."

I glowed in all the glory and wanted the day to last forever. I remember putting my hands on the handles of the golden ten-speed bicycle and the flash of the camera as the photographer took my picture. It was amazing to see the photo the next morning on the front page of the Sunday UB. Father brought the paper in from the front porch and the article was admired by the entire family. Mother got a pair of scissors from the kitchen drawer and cut the picture and story out of the newspaper. Later that day our neighbor, Bitsy Sheldon, brought another copy over to mother.

"Thank you, Bitsy," said Mother. "Now I can send Hiro the picture and story. I wanted to put a copy in our family scrapbook, but I also wanted Hiro to read the story of Megan's spelling bee win! He'll be proud of his sister."

The only thing that marred that perfect day was Grandma Gibson. She caught me smiling at the UB photograph and reading the article and she said, "Now look here Missy. Don't get too high and mighty with yourself. Just when you think you are at the top of the mountain is about the time you fall off the edge!"

Grrrrr. I didn't need to hear this from Grandma Gibson. She always had a way of bringing me back to earth. I thought about her words again that night as I lay in bed with Karl cuddled by my side. I fell asleep wondering just what she meant. There was nothing that could spoil winning the ten-speed bicycle.

Chapter Seven
The Accident

I had been walking around on cloud nine ever since I won the fifth-grade spelling bee. Mother took me down to the City Library and I turned in my free book slip and chose, *The Lion, the Witch, and the Wardrobe*, by C.S. Lewis. I loved the magical world I escaped into when I read. I had never actually won anything in my life and getting the book and the ten-speed bike was a memorable experience. When I think back on my childhood, the wonder of that time still stays with me.

After school each day I popped out to the garage and admired the golden shininess of my new bicycle. Mother had relaxed the rules of someone always being with me when I took the bike out for a ride. She knew I was responsible and realized I was growing up. Anyway, I could ride the bike around our block as much as I wanted as long as I didn't cross any of the streets where I might encounter a car. It was a small win, but one I cherished because it felt like freedom to me. The breeze tossed my hair as I rode up and down, around and around, the block. It was especially fun on sunny spring days when I didn't have to wear a coat and I'd feel the wind through my blouse, making me feel I had wings and was flying.

I waved to various neighbors that I encountered on these rides, and I always stopped and chatted with Bitsy Sheldon. She would ask me how I was doing, or ask about Hiro at the university, or about my mother. I felt a sense of freedom, belonging, and being grown up on these excursions. I had been working up my courage to ask Mother to let me go riding with Sarah and Christine at Pioneer Park. I couldn't rely on her saying yes. It wasn't because we lived far away, but there was the big problem of crossing Division Street. I kept putting the request off.

On several occasions, Sarah and Christine rode their bicycles to visit me, but then they'd take off to ride through the park as they headed home. They both lived near Whitman College and had to cross Alder Avenue. But neither of their mothers seemed overly concerned about them crossing this busy thoroughfare. They would ride down to the traffic lights on the corner of Alder and Clinton and then walk their bikes across the road when the light turned green. It irked me some to know they were both allowed to ride to the City Library and the YMCA, but I was taken by my mother or my father wherever I went.

I spent some time filling Karl in on my woes and frustrations. This usually occurred in the privacy of my room, or on the front porch swing. He'd lay on my bed with his tail curled smartly around him, and his two front paws folded in and tucked under his white creamy chest. He watched me sleepily while I went on and on.

"I just don't get it Karl. Why do Mother or Father have to drive me everywhere I want to go, on their schedule, and all my friends get to ride their bicycles wherever they want to go in town? It just isn't fair," I moaned. Karl would blink his sleepy eyes, yawn, and then lick himself with his pink raspy tongue. He never gave me any tips for settling the problem, but he sure was a good listener.

Grandma Gibson was no help at all. She would look at me over her glasses, and then say, "Why are you so mopey Missy?"

"Mother and Father won't let me ride my bike to the library or the YMCA for my swimming lessons without one of them coming along. I don't think it's fair because all my friends get to go by themselves," I complained to her.

"Listen here, young lady," Grandma Gibson would say sternly. "When I was your age, I didn't know how to ride a bicycle, nor did I own one. With seven kids in the family, we were all lucky to have food on the table and a bed to sleep in. There were three of us girls and four boys, and we girls all slept in one bed until we were in high school. In those days you didn't go anywhere unless you walked there on your own two feet."

Boy, did I hate those "listen here young lady" lectures. But I knew Grandma Gibson was right. I was pretty lucky to own a ten-speed bike. None of my friends had such a nice bicycle. I just didn't have freedom to ride it wherever I wanted to go.

The spring days got warmer and sunnier. We were just getting into May with the end of the school year only a few weeks away. Sarah and Christine told me a number of baby ducks had recently hatched near the big duck pond at Pioneer Park. I really wanted to see them and decided to do my science observation project on baby ducks. Mrs. Kramer announced that our class was doing a special science project. We were to observe an animal, or bird and then write an essay of five characteristics that were unique to the animal or bird we were observing. At first, I planned to observe my cat Karl, but lots of kids were focusing on their pets, so I decided to do something different. I also thought that doing my project on baby ducks might be the way to convince my mother to let me ride my bike to Pioneer Park with Sarah and Christine. It was worth a try.

At school that day Sarah and Christine begged me to ask my parents if I could go bike riding with them on Saturday morning. After school I found Mother and Grandma Gibson in the back yard planting garden seeds. Father had rototilled the garden a few weeks back and put in Walla Walla sweet onions starts as well as chard and lettuce seeds. There was a faint line of green emerging in the seed rows. It was always exciting to see the garden beginning to sprout. Father had bought some tomato and pepper plants from one of the local nurseries in town, which Mother and Grandma Gibson were now planting.

I wasn't very fond of getting my fingers in the dirt during planting, but I really enjoyed going out into the garden during the summer and early fall and helping mother harvest a variety of vegetables as they ripened and matured. I especially loved picking tomatoes with Mother, but I didn't like picking the bush beans or getting cucumbers off the prickly vines.

Mother and Grandma looked busy and preoccupied. I wasn't sure if this was a good time to pose the question, but I took a deep breath and resolved to try.

"Megan," my mother said. "How was your day at school?"

"Pretty good," I responded. "Mrs. Kramer assigned a new science project. She said it will involve a naturalistic observation with a written report describing what we observed."

"Why don't you grab that shovel on the back patio and help your mother finish planting the last three tomato plants?" said Grandma Gibson. "I'll just sit on the patio chair and give my ole back a rest."

Mother glanced up from where she had been kneeling and nodded toward the shovel on the porch.

"Sure Grandma," I said. Normally I would have been more reluctant, but I thought that having Mother all to myself would make it much easier to lay out my bike riding plans.

I walked over to the porch, grabbed the small shovel, and walked back over to where mother was waiting for me. She had a measuring stick that Father had cut for her to space the tomato plants exactly eighteen inches apart. Father was a precise farmer, and there wasn't a garden in Walla Walla with as straight of rows or evenly distributed plants as Father's garden. The precision of the rows was a vision to see and a source of great pride to the Gibsons.

Mother once told me she was a child of the soil. I wasn't exactly sure what that meant, but no doubt it had to do with her growing up on a berry farm on Bainbridge Island. Mother also grew beautiful flowers in the front of our house. Every year as far back as I could remember, she planted nasturtiums, zinnias, and marigolds around our house. I knew I wasn't a child of the soil because I didn't like getting my hands in the dirt, certainly not like my mother, father, or Grandma Gibson. I preferred curling up in a chair with Karl on my lap and reading the day away. But today, I dutifully put the shovel in the garden dirt and stepped on the spade with both of my feet as the blade sank a good six to seven inches into the soil.

"That's good," Mother said. "Now do it again until we have a hole about ten inches in diameter and about seven inches deep. That will be the perfect size to plant these tomato starts."

I worked the ground until I had a hole that met Mother's approval. While she carefully pulled the tomato plant out of the nursery pot, I broached the subject of riding my bicycle to Pioneer Park and used the science project as a reason to do so.

Mother thought the project sounded interesting and asked what animal I planned to study. "I thought about observing Karl, because I think he is an interesting creature," I said. "But I've changed my mind to do something a bit more novel." I looked at Mother out of the corner of my eye to see if she was listening and then I continued. "Lots of the kids in my class are observing their family pets and I think I should observe something in the wild. Don't you?"

"Yes, I think that's a good idea," Mother agreed." Do you have any ideas of what kind of bird or animal you'd like to observe? It's harder to observe an animal in the wild, and you won't have as many opportunities to do that. Maybe your father has an idea or two."

"That's just it, Mother. Sarah and Christine told me a number of baby ducks have hatched at Pioneer Park. They're going to ride their bicycles to Pioneer Park on Saturday and asked me to ride over there with them. Sarah is going to write her naturalistic observation on squirrels, and Christine is going to write about the pheasants housed there. I thought I'd observe and write about baby ducks. Don't you think that would make an interesting science project?"

"Hmmmm," said Mother. "Yes, I think studying baby ducks would be a very interesting science project. This is certainly the time of year when the ducklings are most plentiful. Baby ducks are cute, so they would be an excellent subject to learn more about." Mother continued, "There's the concern of riding your bicycle to the park. I know you've been stretching your wings riding your new bike around the neighborhood block and gaining more confidence."

I held my breath as it seemed Mother was seriously contemplating allowing me to go.

"Let's talk this through with your father tonight and see what he thinks," Mother said. "I know you're growing up, and if you're with your friends, I think it should be fine."

I couldn't believe my ears. Had I really heard my mother say it would be fine to ride with my friends to Pioneer Park? I kept a calm face and started digging the hole for the final tomato plant, but inside I was jumping for joy. This might really happen. I couldn't wait until Father got home that night and see what he thought. I knew if Mother was fine with the plan, Father would be too.

Sure enough, Father gave his approval saying he thought I could go Saturday morning. However, there would be some rules to consider. The most important being that I would have to get off my bike and walk across every street we had to cross – no riding the bike across busy streets. I soberly nodded my head and promised to take the utmost care in crossing streets. This was my red-letter day, and I was more than willing to agree to anything as long as I got to go with Sarah and Christine.

The next day I shared the good news with my two best friends. They were as excited as me and the three of us had a wonderful time planning everything we would do Saturday morning. Sarah and Christine would meet me at my house mid-morning and then we would caravan to Pioneer Park to do our naturalistic observations. Mother had said I just needed to be home in time for lunch on Saturday. It was all set, and I could hardly maintain my excitement.

Saturday morning finally came. No one had to nag me into getting up that morning. It was a beautiful spring day with blue skies and sunshine, a perfect match for what I felt inside.

After breakfast I helped Mother with chores around the house. This involved dusting the furniture in the living room, watering the house plants, stripping my bed sheets and taking them down to the rumpus room where the washer and dryer were already humming away with the towels. But the time flew by quickly and before I knew it Sarah and Christine were knocking on our front door. I grabbed a small rucksack that used to belong to Hiro and headed out the door to get my bike from the garage.

Mother called me back saying, "Megan, don't forget your sweatshirt. It's still cool outside and you need something to keep you warm."

I went back into the house for my sweatshirt then headed out to the garage. I saw Father in the garden preparing the rows to finish planting the rest of the vegetable seeds. I waved to him as I got my bike. He waved back and returned to his gardening.

Mother stood on the back porch and said, "Megan, remember be home in time for lunch. We'll see you then and be careful."

"Yes Mother, I'll be very very careful," I promised with a big smile. Then off we went down the street towards Pioneer Park.

The breeze tossed my hair about and it felt good. I was free and independent. Once we were at Pioneer Park, we rode our bikes to the big duck pond at the south entrance. The pond encompassed a large portion of the park and had a small island at one end. We saw several duck families, but I decided to observe one family in particular. There was a mother duck with five tiny ducklings paddling behind her and one duckling riding on her back. The ducklings must have only been a few days old because they looked smaller than some of the other groups of duckling we had seen. They looked like fluffy ping pong balls bobbing on the pond.

The mother duck and her squad of babies swam along the edge of the water towards the island at the far end. The ducklings were fun to watch as they darted here and there, chasing a bug or flying insect. But they always returned quickly to their mother's side crowding up close to paddle along with her. Sarah, Christine, and I followed the mother duck and her babies on the path that paralleled the edge of the pond. The duck family meandered here and there as they swam to the island. The little family finally settled down in a small inlet where a large rock jutting from the island created a shallow cove. The mother duck stood on the large rock preening her feathers in the sunshine while her babies splashed about in the cove.

Sarah sat close by watching several squirrels chasing each other up and down and around some of the trees in the park. She kept complaining to me that she didn't know how she could be expected to describe the squirrels when they would not hold still long enough for her to make note of their size and color. I sympathized with her and was grateful I had caught the duck family sheltering in the cove by the island. In the distance I could see Christine sitting on the ground at the pheasant cage busily writing in her notepad.

I got my notebook and pencil out from Hiro's backpack and started writing down the description and activities of the sweet little duck family. The ducklings had fluffy yellow bellies, the top of their heads was black and all of them had a dark line that ran across each side of their tiny heads at about eye level. I also noticed that even though they were quite small, each duckling had perfectly shaped webbed feet that helped them paddle efficiently through the water. They looked like they had tiny brown rubber stockings on. The ducklings cheeped constantly to each other and their mother. By the time the mother duck completed her grooming ritual, the ducklings were ready to move on. Mother duck slid into the pond again with one of the ducklings attempting to climb on her back. With much struggle and effort, the tiny duckling finally succeeded. I saw them turn the bend by the island with one of the baby ducklings snuggled atop the mother duck's back taking a wee nap.

Christine finished her pheasant observations, and we went looking for Sarah. The scampering squirrels had taken her on quite a chase, and we found her on the other side of the park, close to the big gazebo. The sun was getting high in the sky, so I knew I needed to head home for lunch.

The day had warmed up considerably and I took my sweatshirt off and tied it around my waist We hopped back on our bikes and decided to ride through the park towards the tall berm on the west side where neighborhood kids loved to sled when the winter snows came.

"Let's race down the hill and see who can get to Catherine Street first," challenged Sarah. And off she went.

"No fair, wait up," hollered Christine as she took off after her.

I was completely taken off guard but wasn't going to let Sarah's challenge go unmatched. Quickly I stood up on the bike pedals pushing down hard to get my momentum going. Before I knew it, I was going down the berm at great speed. Suddenly I felt the bicycle's wheels lock up as the sweatshirt around my waist came loose and got caught in the spokes. I found myself flying over the handlebars and landing on the concrete sidewalk headfirst. I felt a sharp pain on my left arm and even more pain on my forehead where I felt a huge bump beginning to form.

"Sarah! Christine! Help me!" I screamed.

Christine and Sarah both came back quickly to where I lay, immobile on the sidewalk.

"Oh no!" Sarah cried. "Your forehead is all bloody."

I felt faint as I touched my face, aware now of the warm stickiness of blood.

Christine quickly took charge and told Sarah to ride as fast as possible to my house and get my father. She stayed with me as Sarah took off. Several people gathered around wanting to help, but Christine kept them back saying that my parents were on their way. Everything hurt and I only wanted my father and mother. It seemed forever, but Father finally arrived in the family station wagon. He raced out of the car with Mother right behind him. It was such a relief to see them. I showed Father the large lump on my left arm, and he just nodded. I heard him say to Mother that he'd have to take me to the emergency room because it looked like my left arm was broken. He also told her that the doctor would need to check if I had a concussion as I had a nasty bump on my forehead.

Father extracted me from the pile-up on the sidewalk and carried me over to the car and gently laid me on the back seat.

"My bike, my bike," I cried.

"Don't worry Megan," my mother said. "Your father got your bike and put it in the back."

I felt woozy and wondered if I was going to die, but I lay quietly as Father sped to the hospital. He parked the car and then gathered me in his arms and carried me to the emergency entrance. Mother was by his side holding my hand. As a young girl I thought my father was hopelessly old. He wore glasses and his dark hair had lots of gray areas, especially around his forehead. He was a tall man, over six feet in height, but built on the slender side. People would probably have described him in those days as bookish looking with his glasses and quiet demeanor. But that day, Father was my hero and being in his arms lessened the dull pain in my arm and forehead. Mother followed us and I could see fear and concern in the wide openness of her eyes.

Still holding me in his arms Father told the emergency room receptionist that his daughter had been in a bicycle accident and needed a doctor. The lady called the nurse to the front. The nurse took us all back to a large room divided by several white curtains. She pointed to one of the examining tables and Father laid me down as the nurse drew the curtain around the table. The nurse said that Dr. Parsons was seeing another emergency case, but he'd come shortly. She asked my parents to wait in the emergency room while she went to brief the doctor.

"What happened, Megan?" my mother implored.

I felt tears in my eyes and felt ashamed to think I had caused my dear mother so much worry. "I didn't mean to have a wreck, Mother," I cried. "It happened so fast. Sarah said she was going to race us down the hill to Catherine Street and she was off before I could even think. I raced after her and my sweatshirt slipped off from around my waist and got caught in the front bicycle wheel as I started down the berm. The next thing I knew I was flying in the air. I'm so sorry to scare you like this and I didn't mean to crash my bike. I hope it isn't wrecked for good."

The tears flowed down my cheeks, but mother grabbed my hand and squeezed it.

"Hush now Megan, it's not about the crash, or wrecking the bike. I was just shocked at the thought of losing you. You've given us such a scare. Walter, as soon as the doctor comes, we need to give your mother a call. I know that she's sitting at home wringing her hands," Mother said.

The door opened and in walked the nurse and Dr. Parsons. I recognized Dr. Parsons as he had picked Christine up from school several times when the weather had been snowy and icy. But it was Mother who caught my attention. At the sight of Dr. Parsons, she began squeezing my right arm so hard that it hurt worse than my injured one. I heard her gasp and saw the oddest expression of fear, shock, and sadness come over her face. She was staring at Dr. Parsons.

Part II
Seattle and Bainbridge Island
Washington State

1942 - 1948

Chapter Eight
Executive Order 9066

Hitomi woke with a start, her heart racing under a dark blanket of smothering dread. She took a deep breath and felt a slight fluttering of the unborn child she sheltered in her womb. The movement was delicate, like the wings of a butterfly. But each day the fluttering became stronger, letting her know that the life within her was growing. It was dark outside; the morning light still hours away. She looked at the clock and saw it was only 4:30 in the morning, but she knew that her sleep was done for the night. She slipped out of bed, pulled a sweater over her nightgown, then checked her sleeping daughter in the next room.

Masako had just turned two years old in January. Hitomi thought she was the most magical being she had ever known. She remembered how her heart swelled with joyful emotion after Masako was born and she had lovingly seen the perfection of her tiny fingers, toes, and rose petal mouth. Each time she looked at her, Hitomi thought, "This is the most beautiful child I have ever seen, and she is mine!" Masako was asleep in her crib, her small round arms thrown up over her head as she lay on her back. Hitomi could see her chest rise gently as she slumbered in the early morning hours.

Hitomi went into the kitchen to prepare a cup of tea and to wait for the coming dawn. It seemed the world was going crazy, falling apart, changing in ways that she never dreamt possible. Her husband, Akio, was in Maui with his parents. He had left her and Masako at their small apartment on Capitol Hill in Seattle and flown out ten days earlier, but it seemed he had been gone an eternity. Akio was a second-year law student at the University of Washington. He had withdrawn from his studies for the winter quarter and returned home when he learned of his parents' difficulties at their pineapple farm on Maui after the attack on Pearl Harbor. Although he had two younger sisters who lived on the Big Island, much closer to their parents, Akio was the eldest son and he felt it was his place to return and help them during this difficult time.

Hitomi remembered the tenderness of Akio's kiss and warmth of his arms as they said farewell at the door of their apartment. It was only a fleeting goodbye as he had to rush to catch the bus that would take him to the airport. She remembered his parting promise to telegram her once he arrived on Maui. The telegram had been brief. He had arrived safely but wasn't sure how long he would be there. She longed for his comforting presence and wished him by her side. Akio knew how to subdue her fears and she felt safer and more secure with his arm around her. But now he was in Hawaii, trying to help his struggling parents save their small farm.

Ever since the attack on Pearl Harbor there had been whisperings of Japanese-Americans disloyalty. Some Japanese-Americans had been arrested, others detained, their loyalty to country and home questioned. Her father and two brothers were worried, and she could see the collected strain on their faces when she and Akio visited them at Christmas.

But yesterday, February 19, 1942, her worst fears were realized. It had come across the radio and in the Seattle Times that President Franklin D. Roosevelt had signed Executive Order 9066, giving the federal government the power to relocate 120,000 Japanese Americans in the Pacific Northwest to internment camps, away from coastal areas. Areas along the Pacific coastal regions were considered high-risk target areas for hostile attacks. Bainbridge Island, just a short ferry ride from Seattle, Washington, was identified as one of the areas where Japanese Americans would be removed. Her parents, Hiroki and Junko Tatsuno, along with her two older brothers, Hideo and Enji, operated the family berry farm on Bainbridge Island.

Hitomi had been shocked to hear the executive order and wondered when her family would be forced to relocate. She and her brothers Hideo and Enji had all been born in the United States and were American citizens (Nisei). But her parents were first generation Japanese immigrants (Issei) and not allowed to become naturalized citizens. If it hadn't been for the generosity of the Sabers to lease some of their acreage to her parents, they wouldn't have been able to develop the berry farm.

Hitomi never heard her parents bring this subject up, but she had heard her brothers and Akio talk about it on several occasions. After many years of leasing the property, the Sabers sold the acreage to her parents, but the legal documents were filed in Hideo and Enji's name. Although her brothers were legal citizens as they had both been born in the United States, they worried about not inheriting the farm when their parents passed away. The brothers had worked alongside their parents since they were schoolboys and the family's combined sweat, sacrifice, and work ethic had helped the farm flourish. Tatsuno strawberries were famous at Pike's Market as well as at other market areas throughout Washington State and the entire family took quiet pride in the lusciousness and quality of their berries.

Hideo had called Hitomi the previous night to check on her and Masako. They talked late into the evening regarding the Executive Order and what that might mean for all of them. Hitomi asked about her parents and Hideo shared deepening concern regarding their father.

"Father is deeply upset and very agitated," Hideo told Hitomi. "He doesn't know what is going to happen to the farm if we are forced to relocate. Enji thinks we should try to sell the farm, but that kind of talk gets Father angry and upset. I told Enji to back off. But today's news may mean we have to act sooner than later."

Hitomi loved the quiet wisdom of Hideo. Even though he was eight years older, he had always been a caring brother and when she was younger, he had listened to her childish woes without teasing. Over the years, a close bond of understanding had developed between the siblings that had seen them through more than one crisis. Not that Enji wasn't a good brother, he was. But Enji was outgoing and quicker to laugh. He was popular at school, witty, smart, and other children were drawn to his warm and funny ways.

Hideo was quiet, more traditional and adhered to the old ways. He had never married and still lived with their parents on the family farm on Bainbridge Island. Hideo had been a fine student, excelling in his studies. He secretly wanted to attend the University of Washington in Seattle but gave this opportunity to his younger brother. At the time, there was only enough money for one brother to attend college. Hideo felt an internal pressure as the oldest son to help his parents work the strawberry farm.

Enji studied at the University of Washington and received his bachelor's degree in business. This achievement was the pride of the Tatsuno family as he was the first one to earn a college degree. Hideo was very proud of his brother and never a word of resentment was heard from him. After graduating Enji returned to Bainbridge Island with his young bride and helped his parents expand their market capability. The family business had flourished and grown as Enji found new market connections. Kazuko, Enji's wife and Junko, started a small produce stand on the farm. They worked hard to make it successful and soon developed a loyal customer base. Enji talked his brother into expanding an undeveloped acreage to add raspberry and boysenberry vines to extend the berry season into the early fall. These enterprising measures had proved profitable.

"How's our mother doing?" asked Hitomi.

"Well, Mother has grown very silent in her worry. I'm concerned about both our parents, but Enji and I are trying to make arrangements for this year's berry harvest and that is our most pressing concern. If you can slip over here this weekend, I think it would soothe our mother's heart to see you and little Masako," responded Hideo.

"Yes, I'll come over Saturday morning. I can take the 10:20 ferry. Can you meet us? I'll bring some sesame cookies as I know Mother loves them," Hitomi said.

"I'll be there. Be careful, my little sister," Hideo said.

Their conversation had occurred only last night, but she worked for Mrs. Gibson as a caretaker, and she had much to do before the visit to Bainbridge Island. The thought of the many things she needed to do wearied her before she even started. The growing life she carried brought her joy, but also fatigue as she faced the day's tasks.

Hitomi awakened the next day to a rainy Saturday morning. The dreariness of the weather matched her own mood. It seemed to her the whole world was weeping. Emily, Mrs. Gibson's daughter, had offered to give her a lift to the ferry terminal, an offer for which Hitomi was deeply grateful. She had carefully packed one small suitcase for both her and Masako. But it was a monumental endeavor to manage Masako, the suitcase, check in, and then get on the ferry. It was a rough crossing with white capped waves and several times during the thirty-five-minute trip Hitomi was nauseous. By the time they arrived at the terminal, she felt quite ill and very relieved to see the farm truck with the Tatsuno Berry Farm emblem painted on the door waiting in the parking lot. Hideo came running out to help her. He swooped Masako up in his arms, making her giggle. He gave his sister a quick hug and grabbed the suitcase.

"I'm glad you came, sister," said Hideo. "You'll be a comfort for Mother and Masako will bring a smile to Father's face."

The brother and sister sat in companionable silence as Hideo drove to the family farm. Hitomi loved Bainbridge Island. She loved the familiar roads, the homes, the trees, and rustic surroundings where she had spent her growing up years. Seattle had an exciting hustle and rhythm. But Bainbridge was home, and her heart felt at peace as she viewed the approaching family farm. Her parents and brothers had developed this acreage from rambling brush and brambles to a neat, well-ordered and comely haven. She knew it would destroy her parents, especially her father to lose all of this. And for what purpose?

That evening, after the supper dishes had been cleaned and put away, the family gathered around the dining table. Enji and Kazuko had come over and the conversation grew serious.

"Have you heard anything new with regards to the executive order and what that might mean for us?" Hideo asked Enji.

"Not much at this point," said Enji. "But it's quite clear that people of Japanese ancestry along the West Coast are seen as a national security threat. That includes us, brother."

Hideo slowly nodded his head.

"But aren't we quite isolated here on the Island?" asked Kazuko. "We're surrounded by water. What harm could we do?"

"We know we would do no harm, but the attack on Pearl Harbor has heightened the military's fears that the Naval Station on Sand Point in Seattle could be another target," responded Enji. There is growing suspicion that there may be spies or individuals who have sympathies for the nation of Japan."

"We are Americans!" Father Tatsuno's voice exploded in anger. "You do not harm the hand that has sheltered and fed you!"

Hitomi looked at her father and then with concern at Masako who had fallen asleep on her grandmother's lap. She quietly slipped over, picked up the sleeping child and carried her to the bedroom. Earlier in the evening Hitomi had given Masako a bath and readied her for bed. The little one had crawled up on her grandmother's lap, patted Junko's wrinkled cheeks with her baby hands, and then fallen asleep in her grandmother's loving arms. Hitomi gently laid Masako in bed. The tiny child instinctively curled up on her side and placed both hands under her check. She reminded Hitomi of a small baby duckling nestled in the soft yellow blanket that Junko had made for her. As Hitomi looked with loving eyes upon her sleeping daughter, she felt a grip of fierceness awaken in her heart, it burned like a fiery ember. Whatever happened, she would protect this beautiful child and the babe yet unborn.

From the bedroom, Hitomi heard the anger and frustration in her father's voice. She knew it was intensified because of his desperate fear of losing everything he had struggled for his entire life. It had been difficult for her parents when they first arrived. Not everyone on the Island or surrounding area had accepted them. Hiroki and Junko had worked hard during those early years to carve out a life for themselves and their children. It hadn't been easy. But as the years passed, warm and supportive friendships developed amongst the small community of Japanese-American farmers on Bainbridge Island. Friendships were also forged with people in the broader community and certainly with the Sabers, their closest neighbors. The community had come to trust Hiroki, his farming expertise, his business dealings, and his integrity. The community looked forward each year to the luscious berries that the Tatsunos grew on their farm and sold in the markets around the region. Year by year, kind interaction upon kind interaction, and through good business dealings, the Tatsunos had gained the trust and confidence of everyone they met. Hitomi knew that the worry of losing this trust, built over a lifetime of relationships, was causing her father as much anguish as the worry of losing their property and home.

Hitomi quietly slipped back to the living room and sat down on the sofa beside Hideo. Her father paced restlessly back and forth by the dining room table, running his hands through his hair.

"I'm not leaving the farm!" he said empathically. "I'm not leaving everything that we've worked so hard to build over these many years. The land, the business, our home, it's all we have."

"But Father, we have no choice if the order is to evacuate," implored Hideo. "If we don't comply, we'll be detained, or imprisoned for violating a federal law. We have each other and we will endure this together. With Akio in Hawaii and the instability there, we will need to step up and help Hitomi. She is going to have your grandchild and we can't abandon her during this time of uncertainty."

Hideo's voice of reason sunk into Hiroki's mind, and he slumped into one of the dining room chairs and put his hands in his face. It broke Hitomi's heart to see her strong and capable father in such despair. The family sat quietly for a few moments, each in deep thought, knowing that they faced an uncertain future, but finding strength in Hideo's words.

Enji broke the silence, "I bumped into Bob Sabers today when I was in town mailing some letters. He asked about you, Father, and said he was shocked and angry about the executive order. He told me to let you and Mother know you've been great neighbors and that he'd help you in any way possible."

For the first time Junko spoke. "Barbara Sabers and I have been friends for years. I remember the spring I was sick with pneumonia and was in the hospital for nearly a week. It was the spring of your senior year at the university, Enji. Your father and Hideo were working day and night getting ready for the strawberry harvest. I was so sick, but Barbara came over twice a day for three weeks, fed the chickens, and helped me with the laundry and evening meals until I was back on my feet again."

Her eyes teared up as she recalled the memory.

"I remember, Mother," Hideo said. "I also remember the time you helped Barbara for nearly two months after she fell off the ladder and broke her arm. You did double duty all those weeks."

"Yes, those were hard times, but we got through them," she said with a quivering voice.

Hideo spoke again, "We need to keep our wits and not panic. In the meantime, we continue preparing for the spring strawberry harvest, which includes trimming the raspberry canes, and building more berry picking carriers. We were in short supply last year and some of the carriers are getting really old. Let's move forward and take one day at a time and deal with whatever comes, when it comes."

The weekend passed quickly, but a calmness had come over the family after the Saturday evening conversation. Life was still uncertain. There was a war in Europe and things were heating up in the Pacific. But Hideo's words had brought a focus that steadied the course and gave them a plan for what they needed to do now. And that was to live life doing the things they would have normally been doing at any other time and to deal with the future as it came.

Sunday was a beautiful spring day on the Island. Life seemed almost normal as the family gathered for the mid-day feast that Junko, Hitomi, and Kazako prepared while the brothers worked around the farm and prioritized the tasks for the upcoming strawberry season.

After the lunch dishes had been cleaned and put away, Hitomi and Kazuko went out on the front porch and sat together in the swinging chair. They swung quietly watching Masako run and scamper in the lovely spring sunshine. Hitomi felt a joy in her heart as she watched Masako kicking up her heels like a playful lamb. She was so much freer here on the farm. The tiny apartment on Capitol Hill was affordable but living in the city had its drawbacks. Especially now that she had a child to raise and another one on the way. There was no place for Masako to play outside, just concrete sidewalks, streets, and endless traffic. There was a park several blocks away and Hitomi made it a point to take Masako there, whenever weather and work allowed so that she could run, play, and swing to her heart's delight. But here at the farm, green grass and freedom to explore were just a step away.

Kazuko and Enji had not yet been blessed with a little one of their own. Hitomi could see the wistfulness in Kazuko's eyes as she watched Masako. But Kazuko never talked about the fact that she hadn't conceived, and Hitomi never broached the subject with her. Kazuko had grown up in the San Joaquin Valley, near Stockton, California. Her parents were tomato farmers, so she felt comfortable working alongside Enji on the berry farm and this had added great support to the Tatsuno family. Unlike many young women of her day, she had gone to college and majored in Business. She had met Enji at the University of Washington and then graduated the same year in the same program. Hitomi had always admired Kazuko's confident ways and had looked up to her as an older sister.

"What do you hear from your parents in Stockton?" asked Hitomi as they sat out on the porch watching Masako play with some barn kittens.

"My father is worried about the threat of relocation just like the rest of us and he believes it will happen very soon. However, my mother is in denial about it. I worry about them being so far away, but both my brothers live there, and I know they'll stand by my parents whatever happens."

The two women were interrupted by Junko who joined them out on the porch.

"Your father is not feeling well this afternoon," said Junko. "He won't tell you this himself, but he's been experiencing chest pains the last couple of months. Ever since the attack on Pearl Harbor. I've told him to get checked out by Dr. Parks in town, but he says it's nothing serious. I still wish he would get his heart evaluated before the spring harvest begins in earnest. He gets tired so much sooner than he used to, but he just keeps pushing himself."

"Have you told Hideo and Enji?" asked Hitomi. "Maybe they could persuade him to make a doctor's appointment."

"Yes, the boys know, but they've had no more success in getting your father to visit the doctor than I have," Junko said mournfully.

The afternoon passed in peaceful conversation as the sun sank into the sea. Hitomi thought about her mother's words but didn't say anything as her father seemed rested and in good spirits at breakfast the next morning. It was Monday and Hitomi planned to take the afternoon ferry back to Seattle. For the most part, it had been a very pleasant weekend. She hated to leave the serenity of the island and she was grateful for the time with her family. She disliked the thought of returning to the empty apartment and wished Akio was there waiting for her.

She hugged her father longer than usual as they said their goodbyes on the front porch. He patted her arm and asked when she would be able to come again.

"Soon, Father. I'll try to come again very soon. It's so good for Masako to play here at the farm. The city's no place for a little one to frolic and play."

"Come again, as soon as you can, and bring some of your sesame cookies when you do," smiled her father. "And bring your little lamb to frolic here at the farm. Your mother and I miss the sound of Masako's sweet voice and your gentle face when you are gone, my daughter."

Hitomi was touched by her father's tenderness. He had always been a kind father, but not sentimental or openly affectionate. She knew he loved her profoundly, so these unusual words warmed her heart intensely.

"Good-bye, Father, I'll see you soon," said Hitomi. And then she left her father standing on the porch and walked down the steps to the truck where Hideo waited to take her to the ferry terminal.

She promised Hideo that she would come again to visit, but it would be a couple of weeks before she would have the chance. He said that he would call her the next weekend to see how she was doing and to check on whether there was news from Akio. Hideo slipped a five-dollar bill in her hand and said, "Take this and get a taxi to your apartment. I don't want you riding the bus burdened with a suitcase in your condition. You must take care of yourself, Masako, and the baby yet to come."

Hitomi looked at her brother with grateful eyes. He had always been there for her. Hideo picked up Masako and she hugged his neck with her baby arms. He waved goodbye as he climbed back into the truck. They watched him drive away until the farm truck disappeared around the corner.

Hitomi hoped there would be a letter from Akio, but when she arrived back at the apartment and checked the mailbox, there was no letter. She walked sorrowfully to the elevator and the empty apartment.

Chapter Nine

The Letter

Hitomi worked four days a week as a home service provider for Mrs. Elizabeth Gibson. Mrs. Gibson lived on Capitol Hill just a few blocks from Hitomi's apartment, so it was an easy walk to her place of employment. Hitomi was grateful for the work as it helped pay for the expense of their little apartment and whatever groceries were needed. She helped Mrs. Gibson with light housekeeping, shopping for the weekly groceries, preparing meals, and assisting her with physical therapy exercises. Mrs. Gibson was a kindly woman in her sixties. She had lost her husband a few years earlier and enjoyed Hitomi's quiet and competent ways. She took pleasure in being a surrogate grandmother to little Masako and would read stories and rock her to sleep at naptime.

"Good morning, Hitomi," Mrs. Gibson cheerfully greeted them at the door. "I missed the frolicking lamb!" She gave Masako a hug and kissed her baby cheek.

Hitomi smiled and asked, "How are you feeling today Mrs. Gibson? Did you have a pleasant weekend?"

"Oh yes, this was Emily's weekend with me, and she doesn't make me do my exercises like the other girls do," she said with a twinkle in her eye.

Mrs. Gibson had four daughters and each one took a long weekend every month to stay with their mother. Hitomi cared for her the other four days of the week. Mrs. Gibson had suffered a stroke two years earlier and although she had made a remarkable recovery, regaining both her ability to speak as well as her physical well-being, she was less steady on her feet than she had been before her stroke. Emily was her youngest daughter and close to the same age as Hitomi. She had an affable personality like her mother and unlike her three older sisters, she never pushed her mother to do her physical therapy exercises. All of Mrs. Gibson's daughters were nice to Hitomi, but Emily and Clara, the two younger daughters, were the most fun loving, leaving little treats for Masako.

"What about you, Hitomi?" asked Mrs. Gibson. "How was your weekend at Bainbridge? Saturday was such a miserable day with all that rain and wind. I worried about you crossing the Sound in that storm."

"It was a pleasant weekend on the farm with my family, and you are right, the ferry ride over Saturday was rough," said Hitomi. "Now, what would you like to do first after I get your bed made and floors swept? Your meal planning for the week or your physical therapy exercises?"

"Well, I might as well do my exercises with you as I've had three days off. Emily and I took little walks around the neighborhood instead of doing those ridiculous exercises. I get so tired of doing them," she said with a complaining voice.

"I know you don't like to do them, but I think they've really helped with your balance and made you stronger," said Hitomi.

"Yes, I reluctantly agree with you, but that doesn't mean I like doing them," Mrs. Gibson said with a toss of her head.

"I know you don't like to do them," Hitomi said with a smile. "But let's just get them over with and then I'll fix you and Masako a lovely lunch."

Later that afternoon, they sat around the dining table and discussed the menu for the week. Mrs. Gibson's needs were simple, but ever since her stroke she had been placed on a very careful diet, which she followed faithfully. One of Hitomi's responsibilities was to prepare the weekly menu in collaboration with Mrs. Gibson. Each week she shopped for groceries at one of the neighborhood markets, typically the closest one on Broadway Avenue. Hitomi usually went right after breakfast on Wednesdays. Early in the day there weren't as many shoppers and unless the skies were full of rain it was always a pleasant walk to the market. Masako stayed with Mrs. Gibson and played while her mother did the weekly grocery shopping.

Hitomi and Masako always slept over on the days she worked for Mrs. Gibson. Although Mrs. Gibson insisted that she was fine staying alone at night, her daughters hired Hitomi with the stipulation that she spend nights with their mother during the week. It had worked well in the past year with Akio up late studying every night. Now that he was in Hawaii, the weekly companionship was a comfort for both Mrs. Gibson and Hitomi.

The next morning, Hitomi bustled around preparing breakfast and getting the morning chores done. She was delayed getting out the door to do the grocery shopping, but her annoyance disappeared when she stepped out and saw the sun and cloudless blue sky. There was no place in the world where one could experience such glorious blue skies as in Seattle. She took a deep breath and quickened her step as she walked up to Broadway Avenue and the market.

She put her two grocery bags in the cart and started walking down the produce aisle when a man approached her. She had seen him before and knew that he was an employee of the market, so she didn't think his approach was unusual. But she was startled when he grabbed the cart and stuck his big boot in front of one of the wheels, causing it to jerk to a stop. He was a large man, rotund in circumference, with thinning hair, and an angry expression on his face. He wore one of the market's red aprons and the name tag pinned to his chest read: Frank, Meat Department.

"What are you doing in here?" he angrily asked her.

Hitomi was taken back. No one had ever spoken to her like this before and certainly not in this store. She shopped here every week and had often seen this man working in the butcher section. Although he wasn't as friendly as some of the other store employees, he had never made her feel uncomfortable when he waited on her.

"Uhhhh, I'm doing the weekly grocery shopping for my employer, Mrs. Gibson," she stammered.

"Not anymore!" He said roughly. "We don't let slant-eyed traitors patronize this store. Not after you people bombed our ships in Honolulu and killed good men."

Hitomi was stunned and frightened. She silently picked up her two bags and started back out of the store, when another younger man blocked her path. He wasn't wearing a store apron but wore a white shirt and tie with a name tag that read: Walter Gibson, Accountant/Manager. Hitomi thought he looked too young for a store manager, but that was what his tag said.

Frank spoke up loudly.

"Walter, I'm getting rid of the riff-raff from the store before she steals something," he said.

'I'm leaving now." Hitomi said quietly.

"Listen, Frank," spoke Walter authoritatively. "I've seen this woman shopping here many times in the past year and there has never been any indication that she would do anything illegal. It's not your place to decide who shops here and who doesn't. If a situation comes up you bring it to me, but you don't make that decision. Now get back to work!"

Frank huffed off to the meat department muttering under his breath.

"It's okay, really," Hitomi said shyly. I don't want to cause any trouble. I can shop somewhere else."

"You will shop here, just like you do every week," said Walter. "And I'm going to walk down the aisles with you and help you get your groceries."

"Oh, no, you don't need to do that," said Hitomi with a worried look on her face.

"I would do this for anyone, and today that person is you," he said with a broad smile. "Besides, I think you know my aunt."

Suddenly it clicked in Hitomi's mind. This man had the same last name as her boss, Mrs. Gibson.

"Are you related to Mrs. Gibson?" Hitomi asked with curiosity.

"Yes," said Walter. "My dad and her husband were brothers. She's my Aunt Liz. You must be the young woman with the 'frolicking little lamb' my Aunt Liz fondly talks about. She was so sad after losing my Uncle Henry, and then having that stroke. But she says that you and your daughter have brought a spark of sunshine back into her life."

"Thank you for telling me this," Hitomi said. "My parents live on Bainbridge Island, and I don't get to see them very often, so Mrs. Gibson has been a wonderful substitute grandmother for my daughter. She's very kind to both of us."

"I'm sorry about the ugly encounter just now," said Walter. "I don't know what got into Frank. He's usually a very steady guy, but I think everybody's nerves are on edge with the war going on and the uncertainty after the attack in Hawaii."

They chatted together as she gathered the grocery items on her list. While she shopped a comfortable sense of friendship developed, but when she was done shopping, an awkwardness fell upon her. Hitomi looked up shyly at Walter Gibson. He was tall and much younger than she had first thought, but he had the same broad smile she'd seen on his cousin Emily's face, which lightened her heart.

"What is your name?" he asked

"My name is Hitomi Murata," she said.

"Now listen, Hitomi," he said. "I know how kind and helpful you've been to my Aunt Liz. Both my cousins Emily and Clara as well as Aunt Liz have told me of your care. I work here every week day and I'll keep my eye out for you on Wednesdays. Don't be afraid to come and get your groceries here. What happened at Pearl Harbor is a tragedy of unbelievable proportions. But that act of war was not caused by you. I want you to feel safe shopping here. Call on me if you need anything. Promise?"

Hitomi felt tears begin to well up in her eyes, but she fought them back. Mr. Walter Gibson's concern completely overwhelmed her, but she was grateful for people like him and people like Mrs. Gibson.

"Thank you, Mr. Gibson," she said. "You've been so helpful to me today and I appreciate knowing that you are here if I should need assistance. Thank you again."

"Just be careful," said Walter. "Good people sometimes take their frustrations out on others when they feel pressed upon. And by the way, you can call me Walter."

Hitomi thought about his parting words as she quickly walked back to Mrs. Gibson's house. The world had changed, and she didn't feel as secure and safe as she had when she woke up this morning. But Walter Gibson's kindness buoyed her spirit.

Back at the house she found Masako dressing and undressing her favorite baby doll. Mrs. Gibson was sitting close by working a crossword puzzle while keeping an eye on Masako.

"You are back," she said cheerfully. "Were you able to get everything on the grocery list?"

"Yes, I was able to get everything," said Hitomi.

She wasn't sure whether she should say anything to her employer about the incident at the market. She didn't want to worry her, but she also felt she should be forthright about what happened. Hitomi hated to admit it to herself, but the entire event had shaken her, and she wasn't sure she felt safe returning to the market to do the weekly shopping. Even after Walter's reassurance that there would be no further incidents, she felt uneasy.

"I met your nephew, Walter Gibson, at the market this morning," said Hitomi.

"You did?" Said Mrs. Gibson with a smile. "Walter is the son of my husband's brother Wesley. Henry and I had four girls; his brother Wesley and wife Mabel had two boys. Walter and his younger brother were close to Clara and Emily as they were growing up and I remember some rousing good times with those mischievous cousins.

She prattled on. "Walter graduated from Seattle University in Business a couple of years ago and then got his accounting degree. He's been working at the Market on Broadway for at least a year and done well for himself. As young as he is, he's now the store manager and accountant. You can imagine how proud his parents are of him."

"He seemed really nice and helped me out of a terrible situation at the market today," Hitomi said with a shaky voice.

"Really? What happened," asked Mrs. Gibson as she looked at Hitomi with concern.

"I had just started shopping when one of the employees grabbed my cart and stopped me," she explained. "He told me to get out of the store because traitors were not allowed to shop there."

Hitomi felt her throat constrict at the memory of the dreadful encounter with Frank.

"Why, I never," exclaimed Mrs. Gibson with great indignation and concern. "That is a terrible thing to happen. I'm going to report him to the owner of the market."

"Oh no, please don't," said Hitomi. "Walter intervened and took care of the situation. He even walked the aisles with me getting the groceries. He told me he'd keep an eye out for me on Wednesdays as he didn't want me to feel unsafe. But the truth is, I feel embarrassed and awkward about the situation. And frankly, scared to go back. I might go to the larger Safeway store down the block, even though it is further."

"These are worrisome times," Mrs. Gibson said with empathy. "I know the president's order to relocate certain groups of people along the West Coast has everyone in turmoil. President Roosevelt is completely wrong, and this order will cause more harm than it will prevent. Just look at what happened to you today. This is not right. I've been thinking about you and Masako ever since the order came out last week. With your husband in Hawaii and you all by yourself with the little one, I think you should move in here with me, until your husband gets back. Have you heard from him yet?"

"Akio telegrammed me when he landed in Maui, but I haven't heard from him since. He told me it was much worse than what he expected, and he didn't know how long he would be there," said Hitomi. "Our rent is paid up through the end of February, this month, and we are not on a lease, just month to month rental. Are you sure your daughters would want you opening your house to strangers?"

"Oh, yes, they would," Mrs. Gibson retorted. "And you are no stranger to me. You've been like another daughter caring for and helping me this past year. Besides, I love having you and Masako here. And look at your condition! Your baby will be due in another four or five months. You are the one that will need care!"

The week passed quickly. Friday evening came and Emily came to spend the weekend with her mother. Mrs. Gibson's two older daughters were in their mid-thirties, both married and with children. Her two youngest daughters, Emily and Clara, had been born eight and ten years later, so it was almost as if she had raised two separate families. Although quite different from each other, all four daughters got along well and were devoted to their mother's well-being.

"See you next Tuesday," Mrs. Gibson said to Hitomi. "And remember to talk with your landlord about moving out of your apartment the first of March."

Emily looked quizzically at her mother and then at Hitomi compelling her to explain Mrs. Gibson's invitation.

"I think this is a good idea," said Emily. "I'll talk to Clara and the sisters about the plan, and I think you should move in with Mother. It would be good for her, and I know Catherine and Evelyn will be supportive. Let us know what you decide."

Hitomi was anxious to reach home and check her mailbox to see if there was a letter from Akio. She felt anxiety and expectation grow stronger with every step she took. It had been three weeks since Akio's telegram and she yearned to hear from him, to feel that connection of love that bound them so closely together.

Hitomi pulled the small collection of mail from the mailbox in the lobby and felt her heart leap with joy when she saw a slim white envelope with *Air Mail* posted from Maui, Hawaii. She recognized Akio's bold hand script on the envelope. Her first instinct was to rip the envelope open and read the letter in the lobby, but she quietly slipped the letter into her bag and took the elevator up to their third story apartment. Hitomi waited until she had unpacked her few things and taken care of Masako. Once these things were attended to, she sat down in the chair by the window that overlooked the street below. She began reading:

February 12, 1942

Island of Maui, Hawaii

My dearest Hitomi,

The situation here in the aftermath of the attack on Pearl Harbor is much graver than what I expected. Martial law was enacted within hours after the attack and each day more restrictions are put into place. Although my father was not initially arrested, nor has he been to this point, my uncle on the Big Island was arrested, interrogated, and detained for over a week as a "person of suspicion." Mother lives in dread that Father will be arrested, although I don't see that as likely since they are not in Honolulu or the Big Island. It seems that currently there is a system of "selective detention" and I'm hoping that my parents will not have to endure that injustice.

When I flew in to Honolulu, I was detained for nearly six hours and questioned as to the nature of my visit. I was fingerprinted and issued identification papers and told that I must have them on my person at all times as I would need to produce them upon demand. I'm glad that I didn't bring my camera with me as it would have been confiscated. We are not allowed to carry cameras or to take photos anywhere outside.

The military has imposed a strict curfew and habeas corpus has been suspended. I don't know for how long. Father has been prohibited from hiring the seasonal workers he has depended upon for so many years to help with the harvesting of his pineapple crop. Packing and shipping is also restricted, and it looks as if this year's crop will not be picked and may rot in the field.

My darling, I think of you every minute that we are separated. I knew you were the one for me when I first saw you in Professor Stratton's Introduction to Philosophy class at the University. You were so serious and yet so lovely. I wanted to make you smile, but there isn't much to laugh about when you are studying the likes of such great thinkers as Plato and Socrates. Those days seem so long ago, but the memories live in my heart. I think of our unborn child and beautiful Masako. I wish I could feel her baby hugs around my neck. I know I should be there with you, and I feel torn between my love for you, my duty to my parents, and my growing sense of duty to our country.

If we will be free again, I know I must help in the fight to have this freedom for all of us. There is a civilian group forming that is called the "Varsity Victory Volunteers" which will help construct some of the military bases in the Pacific. Forgive me Hitomi, my dearest love, but I feel compelled to join them and to do my small part to help in the fight for freedom. And to show my loyalty to the country where I was born.

My love for you is as endless as the ocean that separates us now. The winds that sweep the Island and head towards the mainland carry my love to you. When you feel the whisper of the breeze caress your face, know that this is my kiss upon your cheeks.

I am forever yours,

Akio

Tears rolled down Hitomi's cheeks as she finished reading Akio's letter. "What will become of us?" she whispered to no one and yet everyone.

She picked up the rest of the mail, which was made up of local grocery flyers, an electricity bill, and a letter from the apartment managers notifying Akio that the apartment complex would no longer be available for rent since he was not enrolled as a student at the University of Washington. The letter went on to say that the apartment must be cleared out for cleaning and the keys turned in to the office by 5:00 p.m. on Saturday, February 28th. Hitomi had not been aware that being a student at the university was a criterion to rent an apartment at the complex. She wondered what had precipitated this eviction. The letter was dated February 20th, but she had not seen it in the mailbox when she had returned from Bainbridge Island on Monday. It must have arrived the next day. Today was Friday, February 27th, which gave her only one day to pack and get things cleared out of the apartment. Hitomi was filled with panic, shock, and disbelief. What could she do?

She picked up the telephone and called Mrs. Gibson's residence. Emily picked up the phone after several rings saying, "Hello, this is the Gibson's residence. Emily speaking."

"Hello, Emily," said Hitomi. "I just got home a short while ago and found a letter from the apartment manager saying I must be packed and cleared out of the apartment by 5:00 p.m. on Saturday evening. That is tomorrow! I wanted to speak with your mother to see if her invitation might still be open for Masako and me to move in with her."

"Oh, I think you must come live here, but let me get her on the telephone," responded Emily. "Just a moment and I'll get her."

"What is this I hear?" enquired Mrs. Gibson, with a surprised tone in her voice. "Emily says you must move out of your apartment by tomorrow night!"

"Yes, that's what the letter from the apartment manager says," said Hitomi. "I'm upset about it, especially the short turnaround time to vacate the apartment. The apartment is mostly furnished, but I do have cooking pots, dishes, some bedding, and my mother's rocking chair besides clothing that I need to pack. Akio's textbooks and law books, clothes, and personal items are also here. It's so overwhelming."

"Don't you fuss about a thing," comforted Mrs. Gibson. "Walter has a car. I'll call him to see if he can help bring your things to my house. Emily says she'll come over tomorrow and help you." Relief flooded Hitomi's heart. The goodness of some people was incredible. She didn't feel alone now and knew she could manage with Emily and Walter's help.

"Thank you with all my heart Mrs. Gibson," cried Hitomi. "How can I ever repay you for all your goodness and generosity?"

"Don't you worry," said Mrs. Gibson. "That's what neighbors do for each other. You dear thing. Get some rest and Walter and Emily will be over in the morning to help."

Hitomi began organizing her kitchen items with a lighter heart. She wanted to sit and write Akio after reading his letter, but that would have to wait until she had some quiet time at Mrs. Gibson's house. On her way in she had noticed a number of empty boxes by the garbage bins outside the apartment building. It looked as if someone had recently moved and put the empty boxes out for collection day on Monday. She made several trips up and down the elevator with Masako until she had enough boxes.

Hitomi began packing immediately and didn't stop except to make a simple dinner of rice and vegetables for Masako and herself. By nine o'clock that evening she had most of the kitchen things packed and ready to go. She was exhausted but decided that she should call Hideo and update him on Akio's letter and her plan to move to Mrs. Gibson's house.

Hideo was angry when he heard about the letter from the apartment complex requiring her to vacate by Saturday night. Hitomi told him about Mrs. Gibson's invitation to move into her house. He was relieved to know that she had a safe place to go. Hitomi told him about Akio's letter with updates about the martial law restrictions in Hawaii. She finally told him about Akio's plan to join the Varsity Victory Volunteers to help build military bases in the South Pacific areas.

"Did Akio give you any idea when he might be able to return to the mainland?" asked Hideo. "It doesn't sound like he'll be able to return to his law studies this year."

"No brother, he didn't say when he will be coming home," said Hitomi. "He wrote that he wanted to serve and help with the fight for freedom. I'm really scared, but I know he's going to do what he believes is the right thing to do. I don't want to burden him with my fears and worries."

"It would make me feel much better if he was with you," Hideo went on. "Especially with the baby coming. Two young children are a big responsibility for a woman alone. Would you consider moving back to the farm?"

"I've thought about returning to the farm, but my employer Mrs. Gibson has been kind to Masako and me. If I leave Seattle, she would have to find a new companion to help through the week. Mrs. Gibson's daughters are with her on the weekends, but she still needs someone during the week as they have busy lives with their families and work. For now, it is probably best that I stay here in Seattle. How are Mother and Father doing?"

"Mother is her quiet self, but I'm worried about Father. He doesn't have the energy he used to have, and I don't know if it's because he is depressed and worried about what will happen to the farm if we are relocated, or if it has to do with the chest pains he's been experiencing. He refuses to see Dr.

Parks and get his heart evaluated. Do you want me to come over on the early morning ferry and help you move your things to Mrs. Gibson's house?"

"I would love to see you, brother," said Hitomi. "But I don't think it is necessary for you to take a day away from the farm to help me. Mrs. Gibson's daughter and nephew are coming over in the morning. They will move my things."

"Ok, I'll check in again with you next weekend, but let me know if you need anything," said Hideo. "How's the little one? Can you come back to the Island in a couple of weeks for a visit? We'd all like to see you and Masako, especially Mother."

Hideo's last sentence warmed Hitomi's heart. It made her happy to know that Masako was a gift to the family.

"Yes, brother, I'll plan to come to the farm again in a few weeks," said Hitomi. "Once I get myself settled at Mrs. Gibson's house, I'll let you know her address and telephone number."

Hitomi peeked in on Masako and saw she was sleeping soundly. She looked like a little angel; her Raggedy Ann doll clutched under one arm. Hitomi tucked the blanket around Masako and brushed the hair off her forehead. She never tired of looking at her sleeping daughter. After checking her daughter, Hitomi crawled into her own bed completely spent by the trauma and emotional upheaval of the past few days. Her sleep was filled with a troubling dream of seeing Akio running towards her and Masako. The wind was tossing his hair, his arms outstretched, his face filled with love and longing. Just as the little family was about to embrace, Akio tripped and began falling into a large black hole that suddenly opened up in front of him. He continued falling, falling, falling. She awakened calling his name. Sleep did not return easily, but when it did, she dreamed again that he was falling into an abyss of endless darkness.

She awoke in the morning feeling as if she had not slept all night, but after fixing a cup of hot tea she felt she could face the day. The dream was very disturbing, but she knew it was only a dream and there was much to do before Walter and Emily arrived to help her.

By mid-morning Hitomi had packed most of the contents of her little apartment. She had almost finished boxing up Akio's textbooks when Walter, Emily, and Clara knocked on her apartment door. Masako squealed with delight as she recognized Emily and Clara at the door. Visitors were rare at their little apartment and the sisters were a surprise to Masako and her joy at seeing them created a party-like feeling.

Their arrival made Hitomi feel better. With the four of them working together, the apartment was completely empty by early afternoon. They returned to Mrs. Gibson's house with her belongings. Clara left for an appointment downtown and Emily said she would keep an eye on Masako leaving Hitomi free to clean the apartment. Walter took her back and offered to help her clean.

"Are you sure you have time to help me this afternoon?" she enquired. You've been so generous to help this morning."

"My mother believed that men should know how to do housecleaning, so my brother Henry and I were raised with household chores," laughed Walter. "I'm very proficient with a broom and a mop."

His eyes smiled at her as they stepped into the apartment. Hitomi was shy around most people, so it surprised her how comfortable Walter made her feel, just like being around her brothers. They worked in congenial silence with Walter wielding the mop expertly throughout the house. By mid-afternoon the apartment was cleaned, and Hitomi dropped the key off at the office and signed the papers releasing her from the rental agreement.

"Aunt Liz says you grew up on Bainbridge Island," commented Walter as he drove her back to Mrs. Gibson's house. "Does your family still live there?"

"My parents own a strawberry farm on the Island," responded Hitomi. "That's where I grew up with my two older brothers. How about you, Walter? Where did you grow up?"

"In a small town in Eastern Washington called Walla Walla. My father is a pharmacist, and just recently retired. He and my mother own a home there. In fact, they still live in the house where my brother and I spent our childhood. Henry and his wife Mary also make their home in Walla Walla. He is an engineer and works for a private firm."

His eyes turned serious, and his voice lost its brightness.

"The war is ramping up in Europe and the Pacific. Both my brother and I may be called up to serve soon," he said with seriousness. "I think it is just a matter of time. This war is changing all our lives."

Hitomi looked at him and nodded in understanding. It seemed the war left no one untouched. They reached Mrs. Gibson's house and Hitomi thanked Walter for all his help. She waved goodbye and turned to walk up the stairs of Mrs. Gibson's house to face the task of unpacking and getting settled again.

Chapter Ten

Goodbye My Father

The days passed quickly as Hitomi and Masako settled in with Mrs. Gibson. A warm bond of friendship grew between the two women to the point that it was not an employer and employee situation, but a relationship more akin to mother and daughter. Masako delighted Mrs. Gibson with her childish chatter, questions, and wonder for all the new discoveries the big house held. Hitomi's move into Mrs. Gibson's house relieved her daughters of weekend care. They visited frequently to check in on their mother. But with Hitomi living there it freed them up, which was especially helpful to the two oldest daughters, Catherine and Evelyn, who had families of their own.

It had been three weeks since she had moved in with Mrs. Gibson. Hitomi was making plans to take the Saturday morning ferry to Bainbridge Island to visit her family. She talked with Hideo each week to let him know how she and Masako were doing. She had written Akio and sent the letter to his parent's address in Maui, but she hadn't received a reply. She shared with Hideo how worried she was about him.

She woke Friday morning to the telephone ringing and quickly got out of bed to answer it, wondering who would be calling so early in the morning. It was Hideo calling her from Bainbridge.

"Hitomi, are you sitting down?" Hideo asked.

Hitomi thought that this was an odd question to ask and so unlike her brother.

"I just woke up," said Hitomi. "What time is it? Is everything alright?"

"I'm calling to let you know that Father is gone," said Hideo.

"What do you mean, gone?" said Hitomi in a troubled voice. "Where has he gone?"

"I mean he has passed away. Father woke up in the night experiencing chest pains and he collapsed on the floor," reported Hideo. "I took him to the emergency room, but he lost consciousness and never recovered. His heart just quit. Mother is beside herself. Is it possible that you could come today and be with her?"

"Hideo, this is terrible news!" cried Hitomi. "Yes, I will come. I'll need to make arrangements for Mrs. Gibson, but I can be on the 1:10 afternoon ferry. I'll see you then. I just can't believe this is real."

Hitomi's hands were shaking as she hung up the telephone. Her heart felt as if it was exploding in her chest and the anguish of her father's death swept over her in waves of grief. "Father, father," she cried. "I will never hear your voice again." She didn't know how she could bear his loss, but the tasks at hand demanded her attention. She knew she must carry on.

Her voice choked up as she told Mrs. Gibson of her father's death. Mrs. Gibson reached out and drew Hitomi into her arms.

"There, there," she said in a consoling voice. "Go ahead and grieve in my arms. I know the pain of losing people you love so dearly you don't know if you can face life without them. Clara was going to spend the weekend with me anyway and maybe Emily can stay for whatever days you will be gone next week. It'll just depend upon her schedule at the hospital. But don't you worry."

"It seems I'm constantly in your debt, Mrs. Gibson," Hitomi said sadly. "I'll call you when I get to the farm and let you know when I can return to Seattle."

"Let me call Walter and see if he can take you to the Ferry Terminal," offered Mrs. Gibson. "I hate to see you taking the bus with your suitcase and the little one. Makes it so hard."

"I don't really want to bother Walter," worried Hitomi. "I'm causing everyone enough trouble as it is."

But Walter was agreeable and said that he could take her during his lunch break. They rode to the ferry terminal in thoughtful quietness. Walter carried Masako and the suitcase to the office and waited while Hitomi bought the ferry ticket at the counter. He walked over to the viewing area and waited with her for the arrival of the ferry.

"I'm very sorry about your father's death," said Walter. "I've never lost a close family member, except for my Uncle Henry. It was hard to see my father suffer. He and Uncle Henry were close. It knocked the life out of him for a year or so, but time helped him recover from the loss. He said losing his brother left a big hole in his heart but seeing my brother Henry and me together helped to fill that hole. I hope Masako and the child that is coming can help fill that emptiness in your heart. They each have a little of your father in them."

Hitomi looked at him and saw that his eyes were filled with kindness and understanding. She had never met a person that could capture the essence of what she was feeling quite in the way Walter Gibson could. She recognized in that moment that in his own way he was a good-looking man. There were no stirrings of romantic interest for Walter, because she was deeply in love with Akio. But she felt a strong bond of friendship and care for him, much like the bond she felt for her brothers, particularly Hideo. She felt a calmness and trust with Walter knowing instinctively she could always count on him.

She looked up into his clear blue eyes and said, "Walter, you're one of the kindest men I know. I feel safe with you. I hope and pray that one day I can repay you for all the kindness you've shown in my time of great sadness." She touched his arm and then she walked down to the gate towards the ferry.

Hideo was waiting for her at the ferry terminal. He looked haggard and tired, and she knew he hadn't slept all night. He took her suitcase and put it in the back of the truck and then picked up Masako.

She patted his cheeks with her sweet baby hands and said, "I sorry, I sorry you sad, Unck."

Hideo gently smiled at Masako acknowledging her sweetness and then kissed her cheek.

"Where is Father now?" questioned Hitomi.

"His body is laying at the mortuary being prepared for cremation," responded Hideo. "Kazuko helped Mother get Father's clothing together for the wake, which will take place Sunday morning. Mother wants a traditional Japanese funeral and the people at the Mortuary are being very kind to accommodate her wishes."

"Will Father be clothed in a suit or a traditional kimono?" asked Hitomi.

"In a suit, but Mother is putting together the traditional items, which will be buried with him in his casket," continued Hideo. "But she seems befuddled and confused at times. I think she is still in shock."

"I'm sure she is in shock," responded Hitomi. "I can't believe that he is gone and that I won't be able to see him when I go home." Their eyes met briefly for a moment in the car and then Hideo looked forward, continued driving, and nothing more was said.

Friday afternoon was a blur. Hitomi felt as if she was in automatic mode, moving from one task to another, comforting her mother, caring for her child, preparing the evening meal, but feeling numb. Only the sense of duty and need to keep busy kept her going. That night she could not fall asleep because pictures of her father kept crowding her mind. She could see him clearly and he was always working; building wooden strawberry carriers, pulling weeds, mowing the grass between the strawberry rows, putting out straw, picking berries, loading the truck with crates of berries for market. Always working, always moving, and always with that determined look on his face.

"Father, I love you," she cried. "I never showed you enough how much I loved you, and now it's too late." She felt so sad inside. The realization that she would never come home to the farm again and see him working in the fields, never see him look up at the approaching truck and recognize that she was there, never again would she see his smile of welcome and happiness at the arrival of his only daughter. These realizations hit her hard. Her pillow was wet with tears. She heard Masako stirring in the crib next to the bed and she gently slipped her hand in to comfort and reassure her child. She felt Masako clutch her hand and then slowly relax as she fell back to sleep.

She remembered Walter's last words to her; "There is a little of your father in Masako and the child that is coming." These words were a healing balm to the pain she felt in her heart and finally she slept.

The next morning, Hitomi helped her mother prepare the home in the traditional way by covering the shrine in the living room with white paper to ensure that there were no impure spirits. Her mother carried a small table and placed it near the shrine. She covered it with a white cloth and placed incense, flowers, and a candle on top of the cloth. Hitomi went with her mother and Hideo to the mortuary to take her father's suit as well as items, which would be put into the casket. Her mother brought Hiroki's sandals, a white ceremonial kimono, a small knife, and six coins for the River of Three Crossings.

Hiroki looked serene in the casket, just as if he were sleeping. Hitomi found it comforting to see him looking so peaceful and rested. She had written a short letter telling him she would miss him and thanking him for giving her a good life in America. She told him she knew he had sacrificed so many of his own dreams to ensure her well-being and that of the entire family. She kissed the letter gently and put it in one of his hands that was folded atop his chest. He would never read it in this life, but it gave her solace to think he might read it in the next.

Sunday morning the family gathered at the Mortuary for the wake. Hitomi was surprised and deeply touched to see so many of their friends and neighbors there to give final respect to her father. Afterwards the coffin was removed and taken to the crematorium chamber. They would return at a later time to pick up his ashes in the urn that had been chosen to hold her father's final remains. Many people in the community including their neighbors, Bob and Barbara Sabers, were kind in their condolences. The sad day finally came to an end.

Hitomi called Mrs. Gibson to let her know that she would be returning to Seattle on Wednesday afternoon. Mrs. Gibson had assured her that Clara and Emily had set up a schedule where one or the other of them would stay with her until Hitomi returned. Mrs. Gibson reassured her that she would look forward to her return on Wednesday and she was not to worry about her care.

The next few days were very busy for Hitomi as she helped her mother pack up her father's clothes and personal items for distribution at a local church. Hitomi was surprised to see Enji and Kazuko with Hideo when he returned from town after delivering the items to the local church. All of their faces looked stricken when they came into the kitchen where Hitomi and Junko were preparing the evening meal.

"What is it?" cried Hitomi. "Has something happened?"

"Yes, I'm afraid so," said Enji. "There was news in town today that Lt. General DeWitt has signed Exclusion Order No. 1, which authorizes the federal government to remove all people of Japanese ancestry from Bainbridge Island. We are ordered to register at the evacuation center at the old Winslow dock."

"When do you have to register?" asked Hitomi, her heart racing. "How soon must you leave?"

"We are being relocated in six days, on March 30th," said Hideo. "We'll register in the morning when we take you to the ferry terminal for Seattle."

"No, I can't leave you," cried Hitomi. "I must stay here and take care of Mother. I'll go wherever she goes."

"I don't think that is for the best," cautioned Enji. "You do not live here now, and you can't lie about that when we register. There is the possibility that Mrs. Gibson can shelter you and Masako in Seattle. You've got the baby coming and you have to think about your children."

"Enji is right," said Hideo. "It is best for you to return to Seattle. The relocation there may be delayed, perhaps long enough for you to deliver the baby. We have no idea where we are going and the travel may be long, which would make it difficult for you."

Kazuko wrapped her arms around Hitomi and the two women held each other in a comforting embrace. "Little sister, listen to your brothers," said Kazuko. "We'll take care of Mother, and you must take care of your children. Akio may be able to return soon and it will be easier for him to find you if you are in Seattle."

Kazuko's final words made Hitomi realize that returning to Seattle was the best thing she could do for the time being. But her mind raced with so many questions and worries. Where was her family going? How would she be able to contact them? When would she see them again? How would she be able to do this on her own? Her anxieties mounted with each question.

Just then they heard a vehicle drive up to the farm house. Hideo looked out the window and announced that Bob and Barbara Sabers were outside. He went to the door and invited them to come in. Bob spoke first.

"Barbara and I were just in town to do some grocery shopping and we heard the news that people of Japanese ancestry on the Island must register for relocation," he said. "We wanted you to know that we find this very offensive, and we are against it. If you have to leave, don't worry about your farm. We'll take care of it for you, for as long as you are gone."

The Tatsuno brothers were stunned by Bob's generosity. The entire family sat in silence for a few minutes. Finally, Hideo spoke up.

"Bob, this is incredibly generous of you and Barbara. Our family has been in shock since the Executive Order came out in February. Now with Father's death, I didn't think it could get any worse. But when I saw the announcement this morning that we had to register for relocation, it felt as if our sorrows would never end."

Enji shook his head in agreement. "We only have six days to get everything ready to leave, and we have no idea where we are going or how long we will be gone. The uncertainty just intensifies the hardships. I can't speak for Hideo, but I feel that we shouldn't take advantage of your generous spirit. We know how much work it will take maintaining our farm and your farm at the same time. It will be costly to you not only in time and energy, but financially, too."

"Would you be willing to buy the farm for a small price?" asked Hideo. "With the understanding that you would keep the profits from the harvests you produce while we are gone. But if and when we return, we would have the option to buy the farm back at a reasonable price."

Bob thought a minute and then looked at Barbara. She took his hand and held it as an understanding passed between the two of them. He cleared his throat before he spoke.

"Barbara and I have talked this through, even before learning about today's order for mass removal. Your family have been good friends to our family for many years. You were there when Barbara broke her arm, and your father took my berries to Pike's Market on more than one occasion when the old truck broke down. We couldn't have asked for better neighbors. We'd be willing to buy your farm for $5.00 with the contract written that when you return, you could have it back for the same price."

For the second time that day the Tatsumo family were speechless. Tears began rolling down Junko's cheeks. Hitomi and Kazuko each put an arm around her shaking shoulders and held her tight.

"I'm so grateful and humbled by your generous offer," said Hideo. "I don't understand why we are a threat to this country, but if being removed from our homes keeps others safe, then I am willing to do just that. It would be our small part to help in the war effort."

Bob Sabers shook his head.

"It's just not right," said Bob. "You and your family, and the other Japanese families here on Bainbridge Island, for that matter anywhere along the West Coast, pose no threat to this country's safety. I don't care what the military or federal government says. They don't know you like I know you. And what I do know is that this is a serious violation of your civil rights!" His voice had grown louder as he spoke, and it was obvious to everyone in the room the intensity of his words came from a deep moral outrage.

"Thank you, Bob," said Enji. "Thank you, Barbara. Thank you for this generous gift to our family. Hideo and I will prepare a simple contract and bring it over tomorrow for you to sign. Then we can go down to the courthouse together and get the deed filed and recorded."

"Yes, that is a good idea," said Hideo. "We all plan to return after the war, but we don't know what the future holds. If something should happen to Enji or me, or both of us, then the farm would legitimately be yours and no one can question that. There isn't anyone else that I would want to have the farm, but you and Barbara."

The men shook each other's hands in agreement and Junko hugged Barbara. Once again, the thought of how wonderfully kind some people could be went through Hitomi's mind. Bob and Barbara took their leave and the family turned to the task of getting themselves and the farm ready for their departure.

The next morning, Hideo and Junko took Hitomi and Masako to the terminal to catch the ferry back to Seattle. It was a sad and tender goodbye. Hitomi had no idea when she might see her family again.

"When will I see you again?" she asked with pleading eyes.

"I don't know," said Hideo. "We are scheduled to leave the Island on March 30th, which is next Monday. I'll call you Sunday night and perhaps you can meet us when the ferry docks at the Port of Seattle. I'll have more information by then."

"Alright," said Hitomi. "Promise me you'll call?"

"Yes, I promise," said Hideo. "You can count on that."

Junko held Masako, gently kissing the top of her head. She handed the child to Hitomi and then hugged them both in a long embrace.

"Goodbye my dear little mother," whispered Hitomi. "Hideo will take good care of you. He is a good son."

Hideo gave Hitomi a quick hug, kissed Masako on her forehead and then Hitomi walked bravely into the terminal with her suitcase and child before turning around to wave farewell to her brother and mother. Hideo stood with his arm protectively around his mother, sadness on both their faces, as they waved goodbye.

Chapter Eleven
Leaving Seattle

Hideo called on Sunday night as he had promised. He sounded tired but resigned.

"We are ready to leave in the morning," said Hideo. "We will board the ferry *Kehloken* at the Eagledale dock, you know, on the southern side of Eagle Harbor. If you come down to the docks in Seattle around noon tomorrow, there is a good chance you'll be able to see us as we get off the ferry. Wear something bright and I'll look for you."

"I'll wear my red sweater that Akio gave me for Christmas," said Hitomi. "I'll look for you." They visited a bit longer as Hideo filled in the details of their activities on the Island during the past few days and then they said goodbye.

Hitomi had been worrying incessantly about how she would be able to contact her family. Hideo had told her they still had no idea of where they would be going. She shared her worry with Mrs. Gibson.

"I can't believe the cruelty of what is happening," said Mrs. Gibson in dismay. "They are literally tearing families away from their homes and their neighbors. I just don't understand it."

"I don't either," said Hitomi. "But my brother says that he is willing to do this if it keeps people along the West Coast safer. I just don't understand how this kind of removal makes it safer."

"Well, it doesn't," said Mrs. Gibson emphatically. "Anybody with a functioning brain and heart can see it is out and out discrimination against Japanese Americans. I don't see them rounding up German Americans by the droves."

The realization of what Mrs. Gibson was saying began to awaken Hitomi to the real root of the problem. She nodded her head in understanding.

"I have some stamps and envelopes in my desk," said Mrs. Gibson. "I want you to take some. Write my address and put postage stamps on each of the envelopes. Give them to your brother when you see him at the docks tomorrow. He can send a letter letting you know where they are when they finally reach their destination. Here, I'll show you where I keep them."

Mrs. Gibson handed Hitomi six envelopes, six sheets of stationery, and six postage stamps. Hitomi folded the stationary sheets in half and placed one in each of the envelopes. She addressed all the envelopes with Mrs. Gibson's Seattle address and then placed postage stamps on the envelopes. When Hitomi was done, she smiled at Mrs. Gibson saying, "This is a good idea. I feel better knowing that my family will have some way of communicating with me."

The next morning after the breakfast dishes were put away and Mrs. Gibson had done her physical therapy exercises, Hitomi put on her red sweater and gathered Masako to catch the bus to the docks. She had taken the six stamped envelopes and tied them with a small bit of string making a neat little packet of the letters and tucked them into her bag. She told Mrs. Gibson that she'd be back in a couple of hours and then she headed out.

When she arrived at the docks, she saw a crowd of people congregating on one of the piers. It looked as if there were newspaper people, reporters, photographers, and other people waiting for the *Kehloken* to arrive. As she looked out over the open waters, she could see a ferry in the distance approaching the docks. Her heart began to race, and anxiety grew at the worry she wouldn't be able to get close enough to see her family. The wait seemed to take forever, but finally the ferry docked and the crowd surged forward.

Hitomi held Masako in her arms and tried to move to the side of the crowd so she could get a better view of the passengers as they disembarked. She saw soldiers holding guns with bayonets standing on the dock. Her heart sank at the sight of these armed soldiers. She wondered if they'd allow her to say goodbye to her family.

After what seemed a very long wait, a few people began walking down the plank and then the numbers grew. Hitomi strained her eyes to catch a glimpse of her family, but she did not see them. She was overwhelmed at the sight of the many people she knew from the Island. She saw two soldiers, one on each side of elderly Mrs. Noritake supporting her as she walked unsteadily down the plank to the dock. She recognized the Hoshimoto family, the Haradas, and the Tanakas. Mrs. Tanaka was not Japanese, but Filipino. With loyalty she chose to go with her husband instead of being separated. Hitomi's heart was heavy to think that this elderly couple, married for so many years, were being incarcerated when they should be growing old together, peacefully on the island they loved.

Masako had grown very heavy in her arms and still Hitomi watched. She was about to give up in despair when she finally saw her brothers coming down the plank to the dock. Hideo and Enji carried two suitcases, one in each hand and walking a short distance behind them was Kazuko. She had her arm under Junko's arm, supporting her as they walked from the ferry to the dock. Hitomi was shocked at how frail her mother looked. She had aged so much in the past six days from grief, uncertainty, and the disruption caused by the forced removal. It had taken a terrible toll on her. But yet, there was a dignity in her posture that was undeniable. Hitomi swallowed the lump in her throat. It took all her courage, but she approached a soldier keeping the crowd back and asked him if she could possibly say goodbye to her family.

"Please sir, is there any way I could say goodbye to my elderly mother?" pleaded Hitomi. "She just disembarked from the ferry and is waiting in the crowd at the back of the line. My brothers are with her, and I may not see them for a very long time." The soldier was young and seemed uncertain of how he should respond to Hitomi's request.

He looked at her and Masako and a change came over his face as he said, "Can you point your family out to me? What are their names? You stay here and I'll bring them to you."

Hitomi pointed her brothers out to the young soldier and said that her family's surname was Tatsuno.

"There are four of them, my two brothers, my mother and my sister-in-law," she said. "They are standing towards the end of the line. Both of my brothers have gray overcoats on, and my mother has a brown tweed coat with a fur collar. Do you see them? Just over there."

The young soldier said something to his partner and then told Hitomi, "You stay here. I'll be back."

Hitomi clutched Masako closely to her heart, hope stirring in her veins as she watched the young soldier walk in the direction where her family was standing. She saw him speak to her brothers and point towards her. Hideo and Enji looked her way and nodded to the soldier. He beckoned the family to follow him, and they walked towards the place where she was waiting.

Hitomi could hardly believe this was happening and wanted to run towards them. But she stood quietly as they traversed the dock towards her and Masako. When her mother saw Hitomi and little Masako, tears began flowing down her cheeks. Hitomi reached out with one arm towards her mother, then looked pleadingly at the young soldier for permission to hug her mother. He nodded and she broke away from the crowd and embraced her mother. Hideo set the suitcases down and took Masako from Hitomi so that she could hold her mother longer. Both women wept.

The young soldier said quietly, "I'm sorry but I can only give you five or six minutes to say your farewells."

Hideo nodded in understanding. "Little sister, we only have a very short time. Let us visit a moment before we must leave."

Hitomi nodded, but her mother still clung to her. She put her arm around her mother, pulling her close and then looked at her brothers. Enji spoke first.

"We've been told that we will be transported to California by train, but we were not told the exact location. We prepared the contract to sell the farm and property to Bob and Barbara and were able to get the deed filed in the courthouse, so that is all done. Here is a copy of the deed, which I'm hoping you can keep safe for us. If you are forced to leave Seattle, please ask Mrs. Gibson to keep it filed at her house, just in case they take papers away from you."

He handed an envelope to her, which she placed in her bag.

"Yes brother, I will do as you ask," said Hitomi.

Hideo then spoke. "Bob and Barbara said to leave the house as is and that they would check it frequently. We packed photos, documents, and legal papers in labeled boxes and stored them in the hallway closet."

"Is there anything else I should know?" She asked.

Both brothers shook their heads. Hitomi reached into the bag that she had slung over her shoulder and pulled out the packet of stamped and pre-addressed envelopes, which she handed to Hideo. She reached in again and pulled out a lunch sack with four sandwiches, a thermos of tea, and sesame cookies, which she handed to Kazuko.

"Hideo," she began, "I've prepared these six envelopes with stamps and Mrs. Gibson's address. Promise me that that you'll send a letter to me wherever you end up. I need to know. It will torture me not to know where you are."

Hideo nodded and tucked the packet of letters in the inside pocket of his overcoat.

She looked at Kazuko and continued, "I made some sandwiches and cookies to sustain your strength as the journey may be very long. It's not much; I wish I could have done more."

"Thank you, little sister," said Kazuko. "We will think of you when we eat this lunch."

The young soldier motioned to them that it was time to go. Hitomi hugged her brothers, then Kazuko, and then finally her mother. She felt her mother's shoulder tremble as silent tears slipped down her cheeks.

"Bye bye, Unck," said Masako in her baby voice. "Bye bye, Ant. Bye bye, Gamma." And then the soldier escorted them back to the line where they would board a train to California. Hitomi stood quietly, watching them walk away. For a brief second Hideo stopped, placing one suitcase down, then put his hand on his heart, and extending it to her in a final gesture of affection.

Hitomi thought her heart would break, she felt so much pain. She held Masako tight in her arms, wishing that Akio could be there to support her through this terrible moment. But she knew it was up to her and only her, to be strong. She put her hand to her lips and waved back to Hideo. Then she watched and waited until they were out of sight. When she could no longer see them, she sadly turned to make her way back to Mrs. Gibson's house.

Three weeks later a letter arrived from Hideo. He wrote:

April 14, 1942
Owens Valley Reception Center
Manzanar, California
Dear Little Sister,
We were on the train for several days and arrived at a high desert area in Central California. We were weary from the constant clatter of the train, but at least we were able to move around on the train during the journey

south. Once we arrived here, we were put on buses and driven to a place called Owens Valley Reception Center. The camp is still under construction and a number of the facilities are not yet completed. The biggest inconvenience is that the sewer system is still being built. The lack of privacy is very difficult for Mother and Kazuko.

I'm worried about Mother; she cannot handle the food as it consists primarily of army rations. She has lost weight and Kazuko has been trying to get her fresh vegetables. Kazuko brought a bag of rice with her and has managed to get some cooked for mother, but it is quickly getting used up. Enji has been seeking an outside contact to acquire more rice and I'm working with a group of men in the camp to see if we can get some crops growing to supplement the canned meat that is given to us for every meal.

We miss the beauty of the Island and think of you often. I'll write you again to give you an address once things get settled here.

My love to you and Masako, Hideo

Hitomi was relieved to receive Hideo's letter but disheartened to see there was no return address. She'd have to wait for Hideo's next letter to write him. She still hadn't heard from Akio and wondered if he had actually joined the Varsity Victory Volunteers as he had indicated he might do in his first letter.

The next day she was surprised to see Walter pull into Mrs. Gibson's driveway. Both Walter and Emily got out and started walking up the sidewalk to the house.

"Hello Walter," said Mrs. Gibson. "What are you two doing here? Emily, did you leave something when you stayed with me this weekend?"

"No, Mother, Walter and I came to see you and Hitomi," said Emily. "There are posters all over Seattle with announcements about removal of Japanese Americans. Have you seen them?"

Hitomi's heart lurched. What would this mean for her and Masako?

"No, we haven't," said Mrs. Gibson. "Were you aware of these notices, Hitomi?"

"No, there weren't any posted when I got groceries last week at the Market," said Hitomi.

"They just started putting posters up today," said Walter. "Officials came into the market and asked if they could put notices up on the bulletin board at the entrance as well as on the doors."

"I saw workers nailing them to telephone poles and I asked for one," said Emily. "I brought it here for you to read. It doesn't give you much time to pack and get ready for departure."

The poster read, "*Pursuant to the provisions of Civilian Exclusion Order No. 17, this Headquarters, dated April 24, 1942, all persons of Japanese ancestry, both alien and non-alien, will be evacuated from the above area by 12 o'clock noon, P.W.T., Friday, May 1, 1942.*

Hitomi and Mrs. Gibson stood in stunned silence as they read the poster in its entirety. Hitomi felt as if she would faint. She sat down on a chair and put her face in her hands.

"What am I going to do?" she asked. "What can I do?"

"It says the responsible member of each family or each person living alone must report to the Civil Control Station this Saturday to receive further instructions," said Emily. "Walter and I can go with you to get this taken care of and help you get further instructions."

"I would be so grateful," said Hitomi. "I'm really scared to do this on my own."

"Well, you are not going to do this on your own," said Mrs. Gibson emphatically, 'I think this is a terrible thing and I have half a mind to hide you away in my house until this craziness is over!"

"Now, Mother," implored Emily. "We can't do something that is illegal, but we can help Hitomi get through the hoops."

"Thank you, Mrs. Gibson, for your kindness and loyalty to me," said Hitomi. "But Hideo says we shouldn't do anything that would cause detainment or imprisonment. I wouldn't want anything to happen to you. I'm just so glad that Emily will go with me."

"I know you are right," Mrs. Gibson went on with resignation. "But rounding up Japanese Americans and putting them in camps is just wrong. You were born in this country, just like my girls!"

Emily broke the awkward silence saying, "Mother, you can watch little Masako tomorrow while Walter and I go with Hitomi to register and get more information. Getting all the information that is available is the best thing for Hitomi right now so she can plan and have some knowledge of what she needs to do."

The next morning, well before the eight o'clock hour, Emily and Walter arrived to take Hitomi to the Civil Control Station in downtown Seattle. By the time they'd arrived there was already a large crowd of people waiting to get registered and get their instructions for evacuation. It bolstered Hitomi's spirits to have both Emily and Walter with her, but she hated the idea of them having to endure the long wait. But they did so cheerfully and the easy conversation between the three of them helped lift her spirits. It was nearly 11:00 o'clock in the morning, a wait of nearly three hours, before it became Hitomi's turn. She was asked to complete paperwork, which included questions regarding the number of people in her family, her address, and other relevant information. After Hitomi completed the paperwork, an instruction sheet was given to her stating she was to return on the afternoon of Friday, May 1. This was only six days away. She and Masako would be in the second group to depart for Puyallup Assembly Center, also referred to as Camp Harmony.

The instructions stated that only one suitcase per individual would be allowed to transport bedding, cooking and eating utensils, as well as clothing and personal hygiene items needed for daily care. In her mind the worrying thought kept circling, *What about the baby? How do I plan for my unborn child? What about clothing for the baby and diapers? How will I be able to take care of my baby?*

Finally, the ordeal was over and the three of them headed back to Capitol Hill and to Mrs. Gibson's house in reflective silence. Hitomi had so many worries, but she didn't want to burden her friends with the many questions swirling in her head. She didn't know how to move the focus away from her situation, but Emily solved that with a question to her cousin.

"Walter, have you gotten your orders yet to enlist?" she asked.

"Henry and I decided to volunteer rather than wait for our draft notices," said Walter. "Henry has already had his physical and taken his exams. He also signed his induction papers. He is to report to a reception center next week where he will be sent to a training camp. With his mechanical engineering background, he will probably end up working on aircraft maintenance. I'm several weeks behind him. I will be getting my physical and taking exams in two weeks."

"Where do you think you'll end up?" asked Emily.

"I don't know and won't know until after my exams and the results of my tests are assessed," responded Walter. "Things are cracking down everywhere and this war effort will be felt by everyone. Life will change dramatically. I wouldn't be surprised if they didn't start rationing food, gas, you name it, by summer time. We already have difficulty getting canned goods and paper supplies for the Market."

"Yes." agreed Emily. "At the hospital we are being asked to conserve certain medical supplies, like bandages. This is just the beginning."

By this time the three of them arrived at Mrs. Gibson's house to find that she had prepared a light lunch and was eager to hear what had happened. Later as they finished eating their tuna sandwiches and cream of tomato soup, they talked about the events of the day.

"How soon do you have to leave, Hitomi, and do you know where you are going?" asked Mrs. Gibson.

"I've been ordered to return to the Civic Control Station the afternoon of May 1, where we will be put on buses and taken down to Puyallup Assembly Center, about twenty-five miles south of Seattle," said Hitomi. "That is all I really know. They did specify only one suitcase for each person in the family. I don't know what to do about packing for the baby."

"You'll need diapers, pins, some sleepers, and blankets," said Mrs. Gibson. "Maybe even a couple of bottles in case your milk doesn't come through after the baby is born."

Hitomi felt shy talking about such personal things in front of Walter, but he didn't seem uncomfortable with the discussion.

"Do you have more than one suitcase?" asked Walter. "I have a couple that I used to cart things back and forth when I was in college that I certainly do not need anymore. I'd be happy to give them to you if that helps you transport your belongings."

"I think you should take some stamped and pre-addressed envelopes when you leave for Puyallup Assembly Center," said Mrs. Gibson. "You can write us and let us know where you are and if you need anything."

"That's a good idea," said Emily. "I wonder how long you will be in Puyallup? It isn't very far for us to drive. Clara and I can drive Mother down there once you are settled. You will write us?"

"Yes, I promise to write just as soon as I'm settled. You are the only friends I have in Seattle."

Mrs. Gibson wrapped her arms around Hitomi and said, "We are your friends, and we care very much about what happens to you and your little family. Our concern is not going to change."

The next day Walter brought two leather bags for Hitomi. They were larger than the suitcase that she currently had. The leather bags were light and flexible so she could stuff them to the brim. She noticed that his initials, WG, were monogramed on the clasp that locked the bags.

"Are you sure you don't need these bags?" questioned Hitomi. "They look like quality leather bags. I hate to take such nice traveling bags from you."

"I want you to have them," insisted Walter. "I don't need them anymore. I'll be living out of an Army duffel bag very soon. It would please me to think that the bags would give you a bit more room to pack things you will need."

"Thank you," said Hitomi. "It looks like I continue to pile on to the debt I owe you, Mrs. Gibson, Emily, and Clara. A debt that I'm not sure I'll ever be able to repay."

"Don't worry about it," Walter said reassuringly. "You've been kind to my Aunt Liz. I know she is going to miss you and your daughter. I wish the U.S. hadn't been dragged into this crazy war."

Hitomi nodded in sad agreement.

The next six days were very difficult for Hitomi. Every day there were reports of increasingly restrictive orders being enforced and Nikkei being arrested. Travel became more limited, some Nikkei had their bank accounts frozen, and some had their business licenses revoked. News of this emerged daily and yet Hitomi tried not to focus on these reports, but instead on the things she would need to do to take care of her children, to survive what was now inevitable, incarceration.

Mrs. Gibson, Emily, and Clara were good to her. Clara brought her two-dozen snowy white diapers and a pack of diaper pins, Emily brought her baby t-shirts and sleepers, and Mrs. Gibson gave her several light swaddling blankets to wrap the newborn in as well as two small baby bottles. She packed these things away with clothes for both Masako and her and toiletries such as soap, shampoo, and dental hygiene items. She saved the second leather suitcase that Walter had given her for a hot plate, small pot, a skillet, two small dinner plates, three bowls, eating utensils, a bag of rice, powdered milk, salt, oil, and a little sugar. She wondered how she would be able to manage Masako, the two bags, and the bedding that Mrs. Gibson had given her. She sighed deeply to herself.

Mrs. Gibson heard her sigh and asked, "What's worrying you, Hitomi?"

"I wonder how I'm going to manage to carry all these items and take care of Masako as well," she said with a sigh. "I wish Akio were here." Tears began rolling down her cheeks. "I'm feeling sorry for myself. It just seems so overwhelming and scary."

"I understand," Mrs. Gibson said with compassion. "I wish you didn't have to do this alone. I'm wondering if we could roll those blankets up in such a way that you could carry them on your back like a little knapsack. Here let me help you."

With some ingenuity they managed to roll and tie the blankets up with some drapery cord that Mrs. Gibson found in her sewing room. Mrs. Gibson even created a small halter for Masako out of some corduroy remnants that she had on hand. The halter slipped over Masako's head and shoulders. She then sewed a short leash on the halter that Hitomi could hold, which kept Masako close to her. It was a small thing, but so helpful and gave Hitomi a greater sense of security and control.

The morning of May 1st arrived, and Hitomi awakened for the last time in the comfort and serenity of Mrs. Gibson's house. She knew she'd miss the feeling of safety and friendship that had developed over the past months. She missed Akio with an ache in her heart that didn't go away. She wondered where he was, if he was safe, and when she'd see him again? The enormity of being on her own weighed heavy upon her slender shoulders.

Hitomi felt the baby move and she knew that whatever happened, caring for and protecting her unborn baby and little Masako would be her responsibility and her responsibility alone. After today there'd be no one else to help her. Hitomi realized the lives of her children depended upon how she handled the hardships and challenges they'd all face. She was no longer the pampered youngest daughter of hard-working immigrant parents. She remembered her father saying when things didn't go her way, "Hitomi, you must have *gaman* to endure what may seem unbearable with patience and dignity." She resolved to take each day as it came and bear it with patience and without complaint. She would have *gaman* to honor her father.

At noon Walter and Emily arrived to help load her things into the car. Then they headed to the Civic Control Station. Mrs. Gibson sat in the back with little Masako and Hitomi, while Walter and Emily sat in the front. The station was busy with families arriving and people milling around waiting for the order to load the waiting buses. Mrs. Gibson's eyes were wet with tears as she kissed Masako goodbye. Hitomi and Mrs. Gibson clung together, neither one wanting to let go of the other. But finally, it was time for them to go as the soldiers came to help Hitomi get her things settled on the bus. She quickly hugged Emily goodbye, shook Walter's hand, and turned to face the future alone.

Chapter Twelve
Puyallup Assembly Center, 1942

The first weeks at Puyallup Assembly Center were miserable. It was cold and rainy that spring and the weather was dismal. Rain dripped through the tarpaper roofs of the hastily constructed barracks, which got bedding and clothing wet with no way to dry them. The camp was only temporary, but week after week passed without any real news where their final destination would be.

The center was made up of four specific sections at the Puyallup Fairgrounds. Area A, B, C, and D all included barracks to house the 7,000 or so internees. Each area had its own mess hall, bathroom, shower facilities, and laundry. Area D also included a hospital with 100 beds to serve the health needs of all the inmates within the camp. There was no privacy for the internees who found themselves sharing close living quarters with perfect strangers. There were no doors on the bathroom or shower stalls and meals were served in large mess halls that seated up to 500 people at a time.

Hitomi and Masako's living quarters were located in Area A. She felt very fortunate that the barrack assigned to her was shared with the Inaba family, which was made up of Mr. and Mrs. Inaba, their three children, and Grandma Inaba. The Inaba's younger daughter, Tome, was close to the same age as Masako and the two little girls enjoyed playing together. The two older children were school aged. It was up to Mrs. Inaba to see that they continued studying, as there was no formal school yet organized.

In order to afford some privacy, Mr. Inaba strung two stout lines with one extending north to south, and the other, east to west creating four temporary rooms. Sheets were hung across these lines in the evening allowing the children to fall asleep without the distraction of the adult occupants. During the day the sheets were pulled back allowing more room for both families. With each passing day, Hitomi felt more and more comfortable with her housemates and a pleasant sense of camaraderie evolved. During the first three weeks they were housed together in Area A, the food consisted of army rations. The two young mothers laughed and joked together about the many ways to make Spam edible. By the end of the first month the food began to improve as fresh vegetables and some fruit became more available.

One morning, after Hitomi had interned at the center for nearly two months, she was surprised to hear her name called over the camp intercom. The message requested that she come to the administration office in Area D. She was now in the eighth month of pregnancy and unable to move quickly. But she gathered Masako up in her arms and headed toward Area D. A soldier escorted her and Masako to the administration building where she was surprised and delighted to find Emily, Clara, and Mrs. Gibson. Masako squealed with joy to see the trio of women. There were plenty of hugs.

"What brings you here?" asked Hitomi. "I'm so happy all of you came, but what brings you today?"

"We wanted to see how you were doing," said Mrs. Gibson. "I was missing the frolicking lamb." She smiled fondly at Masako who snuggled on her lap.

"Two letters came for you," said Emily. "One from Akio and one from Hideo and we wanted to make sure you got them."

Hitomi's heart leapt with excitement! Her hands were shaking as Emily handed her two letters. She recognized the slim Air Mail envelope addressed by Akio's hand and her joy could hardly be contained! She wanted to rip it open and devour every word but restrained herself. She promised herself she would wait to read it in the privacy of her quarters. The other letter was from Hideo and sent in one of the envelopes that she had slipped into his hand at the dock in Seattle.

"Oh, thank you!" She cried. "You cannot imagine how happy I am to receive these letters from my family, and to think you drove all the way down here from Seattle to give them to me."

"We brought you some other little treats as well," smiled Clara. "Here are some fresh strawberries and some apples we got at Pike's Market. We also thought Masako might need a little sundress and overalls for the summer."

Hitomi was overwhelmed with emotion when she saw the strawberries. She wondered if these strawberries had come from Bainbridge Island? Perhaps from her family's farm.

"These are wonderful gifts," cried Hitomi. "I'm very touched by your generosity and so happy to see your faces. It feels good knowing that you think of Masako and me."

The hour passed quickly as the women visited and shared news of their life. Hitomi learned that Walter had left for army training at Ft. Shelby in Mississippi. She learned that Emily was engaged to a doctor at the hospital where she worked as a lab technician. Clara was also engaged, and the sisters excitedly talked about their plans for a double wedding in September.

Hitomi didn't want to burden her friends with the hardships of the assembly center, so she told them funny stories about life in the camp. They all groaned when she told them how she and Mrs. Inaba joked about the many ways to fix spam and rice. Smiles appeared on their faces when she told them about the shrieks in the showers when a little mouse skidded across the wet floor, trying to escape the cascading water. The conversation became more sober when Mrs. Gibson asked about what arrangements were being made for the birth of her baby.

"Are you only a couple of weeks away now from delivering your baby?" asked Mrs. Gibson with concern. "Do they have medical facilities here? Will they let you deliver your baby in a hospital?"

"Yes, there is a makeshift hospital here," said Hitomi. "Over a dozen babies have already been born in the camp. At least that is what I've been told. There are Nikkei doctors and nurses working in the hospital. Mrs. Inaba, my housemate says she will take care of Masako while I'm delivering the new baby. Her youngest child is the same age as Masako and the two girls enjoy playing together. I feel very fortunate to share my barracks with such a nice family. Not everyone is so fortunate."

"Will you be staying here, or will you move again?" asked Mrs. Gibson.

"I don't know for sure, but there is chatter throughout the camp that this is just a temporary place while a more permanent location to house Nikkei is being built," answered Hitomi. "The permanent camp will be situated inland and off the coastline, but I don't have any idea when or where we will be relocated. It leaves a nagging sense of uncertainty, but I guess that is the case for everyone."

"Will you please write and let us know when you do find out?" asked Mrs. Gibson. "Let us know when the baby comes and how you are faring, or if you need any supplies. We'll come again if at all possible."

"I will certainly write and let you know," answered Hitomi. "And I will let you know about the baby. It seems I'm always saying goodbye to you, but I must remember that with the joy of 'hello' there will be sadness with saying 'goodbye'."

Later that evening, after putting Masako to bed, Hitomi pulled out the letters that Mrs. Gibson and her daughters had given her earlier. She began reading Hideo's letter first, as she wanted to save Akio's letter for last. Hideo wrote:

May 9, 1942

Owens Valley Reception Center

Dear Little Sister,

I hope this letter finds you and Masako well. It has taken a very long time to write you for which I apologize. We have been at Owens Valley Center for over a month and are still adjusting to the dramatic change from coastal temperatures with lush flora and fauna to a desert dust bowl where the temperatures rise with each passing day. Our apartment is one of many in an extended building called a barrack. There is no privacy as the bathrooms and showers are communal for men and women with no stalls or partitions. Mother refuses to use the bathroom or showers, preferring to use a washcloth and basin. She cleans herself each morning behind a sheet in the apartment.

There are eight adults living in a single apartment. Our family of four shares the apartment with the Takadas from the Los Angeles area. They are a middle-aged couple who owned a landscaping business in L.A. Their only son and his wife also share the apartment with us. We are still finding ways to accommodate each family's needs and privacy, but they are good housemates. Mr. Takada and I enjoy discussing gardening practices since I am a berry farmer, and he is a landscaper. We are hoping to get permission to start a communal garden, which will certainly help supply the camp with more fresh vegetables.

Enji is seriously talking about enlisting in the armed forces and joining the war effort if the military will allow Nikkei to serve. Kazuko's family is also here at Owens Center, and I think having them here brings her great comfort. Mother misses you and Masako and worries about your upcoming delivery. There is talk around camp that Nikkei from Bainbridge Island and Oregon may eventually be able to relocate with their families.

We are able to receive letters and I've put our return address on the envelope. Please let me know where you are, where to send our letters, and how you and Masako are doing.

Mother sends her love.

Your brother, Hideo

It felt good to hear from her brother and to have an address to send a letter letting the family know where Masako and she were. Hitomi was glad that Mrs. Gibson had encouraged her to bring some pre-addressed and stamped envelopes. She resolved to write Hideo in the morning, but it was Akio's letter that she yearned to read. She opened his letter with trembling hands. Akio's letter read:

May 25, 1942

Somewhere in the Pacific

My darling Hitomi,

By the time you receive this letter I will be on the mainland training at Camp McCoy in Wisconsin. Since I last wrote you, I have been volunteering with a civilian aide group called the Varsity Victory Volunteers, which is made up of former Hawaiian National Guard units and some local ROTC cadets. There are also a few university students, like myself, who joined the VVV, and we have been helping the military construct and establish bases in the Pacific. I'm not at liberty to let you know where I am, but I can tell you that I'm still in the Pacific area waiting for orders to fly to the mainland for military training. We have been told that members of the VVV will now be a part of the 100th Infantry Battalion and we will be activated for training on June 12th.

My uncle and his wife have moved from the big Island to Maui to help my parents with their pineapple harvest. Martial law is still in force on the Islands, and the environment is tense. However, the military has loosened some of the restrictions, which allows farmers to get assistance with harvesting their crops as fresh food is sorely needed for the troops as well as for the markets on the mainland.

I received both your letters that you sent to my parents' address in Maui. In the last letter you said that you were being moved out of Seattle but didn't know exactly where you and Masako would be going. I'm eager to find out where you are now located and especially eager to hear the news of our newborn and of Masako. Wait to answer my letter until I'm stateside. I'll send you my mailing address in the next letter to Mrs. Gibson's home with the hope that she can get my letter to you.

In my naivety, I never thought that the world could change so quickly and vanquish the life that you and I shared. I cling to the memory of our love together and yearn to hold you in my arms. My only comfort is the memory of your beloved face as I fall asleep at night. That memory sustains me every day that we are separated.

My love is forever yours,

Akio

Hitomi felt that she had just lived the most wonderful day since she had arrived at the Puyallup Assembly Center. The visit from Mrs. Gibson, Emily, and Clara bolstered her spirits and hearing from Hideo and Akio made it a diamond day! She wondered if Akio was now in Wisconsin and when she'd see him again. She shared the strawberries with the Inabas as a special treat in the evening. She didn't know who was more thrilled, Grandma Inaba, or the three Inaba children. Their sparkling eyes and red lips from the strawberry juice gave her so much pleasure to see. Never had she tasted sweeter berries and it made her homesick for the berry farm on Bainbridge Island. It brought the memory of her father and mother closer to her heart and she longed for those happy days when they were a family together.

Several weeks later, Hitomi woke up early in the morning with strong contractions. She knew that the baby would arrive that day and she felt both apprehension and excitement. Arrangements had been made for Masako to stay with the Inabas and all of this had been explained to the toddler, but Hitomi did not want to leave for the hospital until the little one was awake, and she could explain where she was going. She lay quietly on her cot as the contractions grew increasingly stronger. Finally, she got up and wakened Mrs. Inaba. She came over to the sleeping child while Hitomi gathered together the few items she had prepared to take with her. Then she quietly wakened Masako and told her that mommy needed to go to the hospital and that Mrs. Inaba would be there to take care of her while mommy was gone. She explained that she would get to play with Tome and that mommy would have a wonderful surprise when she returned. Then she kissed Masako tenderly and told her to go back to sleep. The little one wrapped her arms around her mother's neck, patted Hitomi's tummy and said, "I be fine mommy. I sleepy again."

A contraction gripped Hitomi so hard that she gasped and grabbed the doorframe waiting for it to pass.

"Can you walk to Area D by yourself?" asked Mrs. Inaba in a worried voice. "Let me go with you."

"I think I can make it," said Hitomi. "I've been timing my contractions and they are five to six minutes apart, so I don't think the birth is imminent, but they are getting stronger and some of them nearly take my breath away. I need to concentrate on controlling my breathing. I'll head to the hospital now."

Hitomi walked outside and then headed towards the hospital in Area D. She didn't need to explain to the young soldier why she needed to go. Anyone could see that a woman in her condition would be giving birth soon. The young soldier supported her arm and escorted her to the makeshift hospital. A very kind and efficient woman in a nursing cap and uniform greeted her and took down her personal information:

"Where is your husband or family member to contact?" the nurse asked.

"My husband is in Hawaii and my mother and brothers are at Owen Valley Camp in California," responded Hitomi. "My friend Mrs. Inaba is here and taking care of my daughter Masako back in our living quarters in Area A. Otherwise, I'm alone."

The nurse looked at Hitomi with compassion, but then said in a very professional voice, "Follow me. We'll need to get you in a hospital gown, prepped and ready for the doctor to exam you. Do you know how far apart your contractions are?"

"Yes, I woke up about four o'clock this morning with strong contractions and they've been occurring five to six minutes apart," she gasped as another contraction grabbed her. After the contraction had subsided, she continued, "My waterbag hasn't broken, but with my first pregnancy, once the waterbag broke, the baby came very quickly."

The nurse nodded her head in acknowledgement and led Hitomi down to an area where the beds were separated by curtains. She saw several other women in the area but didn't notice anything that identified it as a maternity ward. She was relieved that at least the hospital was not communal, giving men and women their own wards.

She quickly got undressed and put on the hospital gown and then tried to organize her few things as best she could in the small area that had been assigned to her. A short while later the doctor came to examine her and assess the situation. He was accompanied by a different nurse than the one who had initially taken care of her. Her waterbag broke just as the doctor was beginning to examine her.

She heard him say to the nurse, "It looks like she is going to deliver quickly. We are at ten centimeters and the head is crowning."

The nurse said to Hitomi, "Breathe deeply, but try not to push down hard as the baby is now emerging and we want to minimize tearing as much as possible."

This was easier said than done, but Hitomi concentrated on her breathing and then the baby was there! Hitomi felt as if she were in a fog as she heard the faint crying of her newborn baby.

"Is it a girl or a boy?" she gasped.

"You've just given birth to a strong-looking boy," said the doctor with a big smile. "Let's get him cleaned up so that you can hold him."

A few minutes later the nurse laid the baby in her arms and Hitomi was able to see her son for the first time. He had a shock of black hair, and his eyes were squinty as he cried, but he looked beautiful to Hitomi. Her heart sang with joy, and she longed to share this moment with Akio. He would be excited to have a son. He never talked about his preference for a son and was captivated with Masako, calling her his "little duckling." But Hitomi knew that he'd be very proud to have a son to call his own.

The nurse came to take the baby to the nursery and said, "You need to rest now and get your strength back. We'll take care of the baby and bring him to you when he needs nursing."

"How long will I need to stay in the hospital?" asked Hitomi.

"Oh, five to six days, maybe a week," said the nurse.

"I can't stay here that long," said Hitomi in a worried voice. "I have a daughter I need to get back to. I have no family here to care for her. Mrs. Inaba, my housemate, helps me with my daughter Masako, along with her own three children."

"You'll have to stay in bed for a couple of days," said the nurse. "And then we'll get you up on your feet and see how steady you are before the doctor will even consider releasing you and the baby. So, don't get in a big rush."

Hitomi did not find these words at all reassuring but realized that she would have to listen to what the doctor and nurses told her. She finally got a message to Mrs. Inaba that afternoon to let her know of the baby's arrival and that she would be delayed in getting back to the barracks. Mrs. Inaba came to the hospital that evening with Masako, and Hitomi was able to show the little one her new baby brother.

Masako looked at her little brother with curiosity. She patted his dark hair and said, "Bebee, my bebee." Then she took his little fingers and held them in her hand. The tiny baby looked at her and blinked. In that moment Hitomi knew that something very special had transpired between baby brother and sister. Masako looked at her brother and smiled and kept touching his soft downy tussle of black hair.

"What name will you give the baby?" asked Mrs. Inaba. "Will you give him your husband's name?"

"His name is Hiroki," said Hitomi with a smile. "He is named after my father, Hiroki Tatsuno." She knew her father would be proud to have a namesake and she knew Akio would want this too. She also remembered Walter Gibson's words to her that there was a little bit of her father in each of her children.

"Bebee Hoki," said Masako.

"Yes, that's right," said Hitomi. "This is your little brother, Baby Hiroki."

Hitomi had been out of the hospital for nearly a month and life at Puyallup Assembly Center had taken on a monotonous routine. Although she was very busy with her two children there was very little to look forward to, just nights of restless wondering and worry of what would happen next. Mr. Inaba managed to find two old metal feed buckets that he brought back to the apartment for Hitomi. She used one to rinse Hiroki's diapers and then stored them in the other bucket until laundry day.

Little Hiroki grew and flourished. Masako and the Inabas called him "Hiro" as Hiroki was a big name for such a little guy. Hitomi worried that he would disrupt the Inaba family's sleep when he awakened in the night. But she'd quickly pull him onto her cot to nurse and he'd fall back to sleep. She'd found a wooden apple box that had been discarded in Area A to make a makeshift crib. She lined the box with straw and wrapped the straw with the swaddling blankets that Mrs. Gibson had given her. Grandma Inaba loved holding Hiro when he was awake, giving Hitomi a chance to take care of her daily chores. A routine, of sorts brought order to the boredom and chaos of living in the camp.

Hitomi wrote Hideo and her family, giving them the good news of Hiro's arrival. She hadn't received a return letter but knew her mother would be happy to hear that the delivery had gone well. Hitomi hoped it would please her mother to have Hiro carry her husband's name. She hadn't yet received a letter from Akio, but knew he'd write her as soon as he was settled at Fort Shelby.

One evening in early August, Mr. Inaba came back to the apartment saying that he had heard that the first group of Nikkei at Puyallup Assembly Center would depart on August 12th to another internment camp somewhere in Idaho, with subsequent groups transferred over the next month. Each transfer group would consist of five hundred Nikkei, Mr. Inaba said that the transfers would be by train and would probably take thirty to thirty-six hours of travel time to get there.

The Inaba family as well as Hitomi and her children appeared on the list that was scheduled to leave for Minidoka on August 22nd. That gave them ten days to prepare for the departure, both in packing their bags as well as preparing themselves mentally for the long arduous trip into yet another unknown locality. Hitomi wrote Hideo letting him know of the imminent transfer. She also wrote Mrs. Gibson asking her if a letter from Akio had arrived and to let her know that she and the children were scheduled to leave for Minidoka on August 22nd.

The Saturday before they were scheduled to leave, she heard her name called out on the loudspeaker to come to Area D. She wondered if Mrs. Gibson, Emily, and Clara had come for a visit to see the new baby. Sure enough, there was Emily and Clara seated in the visiting room. She was happy to see them but there was no Mrs. Gibson. The sisters told her that Mrs. Gibson had suffered another stroke in July and was convalescing in a long-term care facility in Seattle.

Masako was excited to see Emily and Clara and to show off her new baby brother. She wore the little sundress that they had given her on their earlier visit. On this visit the sisters brought gifts of clothing for the baby and Masako and greetings from Mrs. Gibson. She sent word of her disappointment of being unable to see her "frolicking little lamb" and the new baby, but not one word of her illness.

Clara brought her Kodak Brownie and took pictures of Hitomi and the children and promised to send copies of the pictures as soon as they were settled in their new location. They also brought a letter from Akio, which thrilled Hitomi. She hoped he was now back in the states and there'd be an address where she could send him a letter. Their conversation was twinged with sadness as they knew this would be their last visit together for a very long time. None of them knew what the future held or what to expect.

"Be sure to tell your mother how much I miss her and her optimistic spirit," said Hitomi sadly. "She always had a good solution to any problem I had."

"Our mother is a spunky Irish woman," said Emily. "Nothing ever gets her down for long. She's already got plans for returning home by September, and knowing her, she'll probably make it."

"I sure hope so," said Hitomi. "One thing that keeps my spirits up is the thought of your mother in her big house on Capitol Hill. It makes me homesick, but also happy to think about her being there. The world is so uncertain right now, but the peaceful memories of living with her and the happy times at the big house keep me going."

That night, back in the quiet of her apartment in the barracks, she read Akio's letter.

August 1, 1942

Fort McCoy, Wisconsin

My darling Hitomi,

We've been training here in Fort McCoy and the training has been brutal. I collapse into bed every night, and morning seems to come before I've even fallen asleep. We run six to ten miles every day, often with boots and full gear on. The workouts are demanding, but I feel myself growing stronger every day. The rigorous physical demands have made this soft university student into a tough soldier.

By this time, you've given birth to our second child. I'm very anxious to hear that you are both well. Let me know if I'm the father of another daughter, or the father of a son. I will be a happy father, regardless of whether we have a girl or a boy. How is my little duckling, Masako? Kiss her and the new baby for me.

My beautiful wife, I love you more than there are shells in the sea, and I miss you more than there are stars in the sky. I long for the time when we can be a family together. My heart aches for you, with a longing so intense that I can hardly bear the pain. I know that you also must endure the pain of our separation and have hardships that I do not know. Your courage makes me stronger.

I am forever yours, Akio

"When will I see you Akio?" whispered Hitomi as silent tears ran down her cheeks. "I miss you. I need you."

She slept fitfully that night, dreaming of Akio running towards her and the children, joy on his face, arms outstretched, but just as he was about to embrace his family, he tripped and began falling into a hole that opened up between them, calling, "Hitomi, Hitomi, my darling Hitomi."

Hitomi woke with alarm and remembered she'd had this dream before. She tried to shake it off, but sleep did not come until the early morning hours when she finally drifted back to sleep.

She woke with a start as she felt Masako's little hand touching her face saying, "Mama, mama, beebe Hiko crying."

Hitomi reached into his box crib and placed him on her breast, worrying all the while that Hiro's crying had disturbed the Inabas. But she could hear the children talking and playing on the other side of the sheet. She heard Mrs. Inaba ask Grandma if she wanted a cup of tea, the normal morning sounds. She would apologize later, but for now she would nurse Hiro, gather her thoughts, and face the day with *gaman*.

Chapter Thirteen
Minidoka Internment Camp, Idaho

The Saturday morning of August 22nd, departure day, arrived with blue skies and sunshine. During the days prior to leaving, Hitomi had fretted herself sick on what she should take to the new internment location. All the internees had been warned that they could only bring what they could carry. This left her in a terrible dilemma as Hiro was just six weeks old, a babe in her arms. Masako was an independent little girl, but still needed her mother's hand to guide her along. She also had Walter's two leather bags that would carry everything that her little family needed to survive at the internment camp.

Hitomi felt an overwhelming sense of helplessness come over her, much like she had experienced at Mrs. Gibson's house when she was preparing to leave Seattle for the Puyallup Assembly Center. She remembered how encouraging Mrs. Gibson had been to help her prepare and pack for Puyallup, and it brought a pang of loneliness.

Hitomi had no idea where they were going or how long the train ride would take. The rumor around camp was that they were being sent to a location somewhere in Southern Idaho, but no official word of their final destination was forthcoming. She wondered how she'd handle the needs of a tiny baby, keeping him diapered, dry, and fresh on the long train ride? What would Mrs. Gibson do? The worry nagged at her as she carefully packed Hiro's diapers, plastic pants, t-shirts, and sleepers. She tried to keep her own clothing to a minimum and decided to wear her winter coat over her clothes, even though it was summertime and plenty warm. She decided that Masako could also wear her winter coat over her clothes. The coat would serve as a pillow or blanket when she slept on the train.

A few days before departure, Hitomi came up with the plan to care for Hiro's diaper and comfort needs. She was going through the few things that she had gotten in the hospital when he had been born. Upon discharge, she had been given a package of pads, designed for postpartum bleeding. It suddenly occurred to her that these pads would work well if placed as a liner in his diaper. She could discard the pads when they were used and minimize the number of diapers needed on the journey. She felt a wave of empowerment and a surge of relief come over her at the thought of this solution. As the youngest child in her family, she had always relied upon her parents and her brothers to take care of things. But this "lightbulb" moment, although small, made her feel as if she could handle anything.

The morning of departure, Hitomi was ready. She used a bed sheet and wrapped tiny Hiro close to her body, leaving her hands free to carry the two leather bags that held their clothing and the necessary essentials for life in the new camp. She placed the small corduroy harness and leash that Mrs. Gibson made around Masako and snapped the leash to her coat. Although awkward, Hitomi got both children and their two bags onto the bus and then to the train station.

At the station Hitomi stayed close to the Inaba family as they boarded the train. She had become close friends with the Inabas during the months they'd shared the makeshift room at Puyallup Assembly Center. Although the Inabas had their hands full getting their three children and Grandma on to the train, Hitomi was able to follow closely and get seats with the Inabas. It was a relief to get settled even though they knew it would be a long and tedious trip. As the train pulled slowly away from the station, a voice came on the speaker saying all the shades on the train cars would be drawn and kept down throughout the trip. Hitomi looked quizzically at her friend, Mrs. Inaba, who shrugged and looked confused. But Hitomi could see anger in Mr. Inaba's face. He did his best to restrain his feelings, but it was obvious the order upset him.

Finally, he said with disdain, "I don't understand why they want us to keep the blinds down, except they don't want the public to see what they are doing. It's so shameful!"

Grandma nodded her head in sad agreement.

Thus began the long train journey. They had traveled for several hours when Hitomi took Masako to the restroom. She left Hiro sleeping on

Grandma Inaba's lap. The train clattered and swayed, which made walking very unsteady. Nevertheless, it felt good to get up and stretch her legs. She and Masako were just returning to their seats when she encountered a young woman standing in the waiting area by the restroom. It was apparent that the young woman was upset as she had tears in her eyes. She was trying to comfort the crying baby she was holding.

"Are you alright?" Hitomi asked. "Is there anything I can do to help you?"

"I didn't bring enough diapers to take care of my baby for this long trip," the woman cried. "I didn't realize it would be like this and now he's soaked without anything dry for him. He just won't be comforted. I'm not a good mother," and she began crying again.

"Don't be so hard on yourself," said Hitomi. "I understand your dilemma. I have a baby, too, and I worried myself sick on how to take care of him while making this long journey. But I've got some extra diapers I can share with you and some pads to line the diapers that you can simply throw away, which will help save your reserve of dry diapers."

"Oh, you are so kind," said the young woman. "I would be so grateful for your help."

"Come with me and I'll get you some dry diapers and pads for him," said Hitomi as she led the young woman back to her seat. She gave the young mother six fresh diapers and eight pads.

"This should help you keep your baby comfortable until we get to our destination," said Hitomi. These pads absorb well, and you can just throw them away. I'm using them for my baby, and it's worked quite well. The pads help conserve diapers, and my son is staying dry and comfortable."

"What a good idea," said the young mother. "My name is Kioki and my son's name is Yuri. I can't thank you enough for your generosity and kindness."

"I'm so pleased to make your acquaintance," said Hitomi. "What train car are you traveling in? Let me know if I can be of further help and please come visit when you get weary of just sitting."

"I'm traveling with my husband and his parents in the train car just behind this one," said Kioki. "I was trying to comfort my baby so he wouldn't disturb other passengers. I would enjoy visiting with you again." She flashed a grateful smile and waved goodbye.

The hours dragged as the train swayed and clacked along. The only diversions were the lunch and dinner meals, which everyone found quite disgusting as they were army C-rations. The meals were pre-cooked, ready to eat, and canned in small tin containers. They were supposed to contain enough calories and nutrition to sustain a soldier, but the food was not appealing or tasty. Hitomi was glad she had gotten some bananas, crackers, and candy bars before she left Puyallup Assembly Center. She happily shared with the Inaba family and was pleased to see the smiles on the children's faces.

Night finally came and Hitomi made a little bed for Masako under her seat. She slept fitfully through the night, waking often to check on Masako and Hiro. The only indication the day was dawning were the tiny pinpoints of light that came through holes in the ancient shades on the train. People began stirring as morning dawned, but the journey was far from over. Finally, the train began slowing down in mid-afternoon and Hitomi knew the long journey had ended.

When Hitomi and the Inaba family stepped from the train at Eden, Idaho they stood in shock at the desolate landscape that met their eyes. There was nothing to see but sagebrush and sand, a landscape so barren that it felt that they had arrived at an alien planet. The bleak atmosphere before them was a stark contrast to the beautiful trees in the Northwest and coastal climate where most of them had spent their lives.

With heavy hearts the exhausted travelers loaded their belongings onto buses, which took them to Minidoka Relocation Center a few miles outside of Eden. Hitomi was bone weary and could see there would be no comfort inside the drab and austere appearance of the unfinished buildings at Minidoka. The day was miserably hot and dusty, but Hitomi kept her coat on and told Masako that she would have to either wear her coat or carry it, which brought the little one to tears. Not a child to fuss much, the discomfort was more than she could handle, and tears began swelling in her eyes.

"I hot, mommy, I hot," wailed Masako. "I want to go home."

Grandma Inaba felt pity for the wailing child and took her heavy winter coat off. She patted Masako on the head and said, "I'll carry your coat for you, little one, just don't cry. We are going to get settled and then we can rest."

Anyone observing the interaction might have wondered if the elderly woman was trying to comfort the child or comfort herself.

Everyone stood in line for what seemed hours waiting to have one of the camp doctors assess their physical condition. Only then could internees register for an apartment in the residential barracks. It took forever, but finally it was Hitomi's turn. The new residents of Minidoka learned that the camp was made up of thirty-six residential blocks that extended over three miles. The Inabas offered to share their apartment with Hitomi and her children. Hitomi accepted their offer with a grateful heart. Permission was granted and arrangements were settled.

The area that Hitomi and the Inabas were assigned was an apartment in block 12, barrack 6, apartment D, known as 12-6-D. The two families found themselves getting settled in a twenty-by-twenty-foot room for the nine of them. The space was slightly larger than the one they had shared at Puyallup Assembly Center but still crowded by any standard. Once again, just as he had done at Puyallup Assembly Center, Mr. Inaba strung cords across the room where sheets could be hung in order to provide privacy for the two families.

The apartment had one small pot belly stove, which was heated with coal during the cold months, and a stack of army cots that were divided among the two families. Hitomi took two cots and situated them in her portion of the apartment. She didn't have a box for Hiroki to use as a crib, but Mr. Inaba found a wooden box by the mess hall that he brought back to Hitomi.

"I know you've been worrying about a secure sleeping container for your baby," said Mr. Inaba. "I was wandering around the camp trying to get acquainted with the layout and I found this large produce box by the mess hall and just took it. I didn't ask permission; I just took it."

Hitomi clasped her hands with joy and said, "Oh, Mr. Inaba, thank you for finding this box for me. I've worried about where Hiro could sleep. He is too little to sleep on a cot, I'm afraid he might roll off and hurt himself. But this box will be ideal for him until he gets bigger. I'll put my winter coat in the box and cover it with blankets and he'll be safe and warm."

The first few weeks at Minidoka passed in a blur as the internees adjusted to the hostile climate of the new surroundings. The high plains heat was insufferable. The first few days, Masako experienced nosebleeds almost daily and Hitomi woke up each morning with a nagging headache. The wind blew continually and there was dust everywhere. The buildings were hastily constructed with green wood and tarpaper roofing. There were cracks and gaps throughout the barracks. The dust filtered into the apartments whenever the wind blew. The women found it a hopeless task trying to sweep it out. The bedding was shaken out daily as the dust constantly seeped through the cracks and gaps in the walls.

But that wasn't the worst of it. Many of the buildings were still under construction and the latrines and water systems were not completed so there was no running water or flushing toilets. The laundry machines weren't hooked up for lack of running water, which made it difficult for mothers with small children and babies to keep an adequate supply of clean diapers and clothes for their little ones. Mrs. Inaba and Hitomi both lamented that no matter how primitive the living arrangements had been at Puyallup Assembly Center, at least they had flushing toilets and hot showers.

Mr. Inaba was a tulip farmer from the Skagit Valley and although he was a farmer by trade, he was also a skilled and gifted carpenter. Little by little he scrounged around the construction areas and gathered pieces of scrap board, nails, and a hammer. With these essential tools he was able to make the apartment more comfortable by sealing most of the gaping holes where dust, rain, and wind came in. He also built little stools for the children to sit on, a table and benches, and shelves along the walls to store necessary items. Slowly the apartment took on a livable atmosphere. It would never be a home, but with the combined efforts of the women and Mr. Inaba, the apartment slowly transformed from an austere military barrack to a sparse living space with a few comforts.

Hitomi had written Mrs. Gibson, Akio, and Hideo shortly after arriving at Minidoka. She received word from Emily several weeks later getting an update of Mrs. Gibson and her improved health. In early October she was overjoyed to receive a letter from Hideo. He wrote:

October 1, 1942

Manzanar Internment Camp

My dear Little Sister,

It was good to receive your letter letting us know that you and the children are well and that you've been transferred to Minidoka Internment Camp near Eden, Idaho. The conditions you describe at the camp when you arrived sound sadly like the situation we found ourselves in when we arrived at Manzanar. Very primitive. I hope by the time you get this letter that your living situation has improved. We are glad to hear that you were able to share an apartment again with the Inabas. They sound very cordial, and it does ease my mind to think that you have friendship and support and are not completely alone.

Our mother is not well, although she doesn't complain. She continues to lose weight and looks very frail. I would be surprised if she weighs 90 pounds. The food has improved modestly since our arrival last March. We are provided with more fruits and vegetables, but it is often not fresh nor appetizing. I will not complain to you about the food as I know your situation is no better than ours. But the simple truth is that Mother has difficulty eating what is offered in the mess hall and at times flatly refuses to eat anything at all. We try to supplement with fresh items that we occasionally obtain from venders who bring produce to sell on the outskirts of camp.

Enji is still hoping to join an infantry battalion if the army will allow him to enlist. There are rumors that an all Japanese American regimental combat unit is being formed and if that happens then he will join. I don't feel that I can leave Mother by herself so I'm not planning to enlist. Kazuko is very kind and helpful with Mother, but she has found her own parents here in the camp and spends time with them. If Enji does enlist, I know that she will find comfort and support with her family.

Many of the Bainbridge Island Nikkei have family at Minidoka Camp and there are efforts underway to allow us to transfer from Manzanar to Minidoka. I'm hoping to move Mother to Minidoka so that she can live with you and the children. She misses her little "duckling" Masako and of course we are all anxious to see Hiro. You have no idea how happy you have made her by naming your son after our father. Her face glows with joy whenever she tells others about her new grandchild who is named after her husband. I'll let you know when the decision for transfer is approved, but I would be surprised if the transfer happens before next spring at the earliest.

Mother sends her love.

Your brother, Hideo

Hitomi felt excitement growing in her heart at the thought of having her family transferred to Minidoka. It would be wonderful to see her family again and the concern for her mother's health laid heavily on her heart. Hitomi knew she must be patient, but the hope of seeing them again was something she savored.

It was early December, just one year since the Japanese had attacked Pearl Harbor, changing lives forever. Life in the camp took on a mundane pattern. The latrines, showers, and laundromat were completed near the end of September and this helped make life more civil, but it was still a hardship. The dust storms that arose suddenly caused misery for everyone living in the camp. The blistering heat during the day had cooled dramatically and the nights were getting colder and colder. Grandma Inaba spent much of her day knitting mittens and scarves for the children. Hitomi knew she was knitting these items for Christmas gifts, but it was hard to keep secrets in such close quarters.

One evening after the children had stories read to them and were tucked in bed for the night, the adults sat near the pot-bellied stove drinking tea. The women knitted and discussed plans to celebrate the Christmas holiday that was just three weeks away. Grandma Inaba's knitting needles clicked busily as she worked to complete the final pair of mittens. The mittens would keep little fingers warm as the first snow of winter had arrived that day. It had been just a skiff of snow, but the drop in temperature was notable.

"How cold do you think it is, Mr. Inaba?" asked Hitomi. "I'm not sure I've ever experienced weather this cold."

"The thermometer this morning said 18 degrees Fahrenheit," said Mr. Inaba. "Some of the local construction workers say that sub-zero temperatures during the winter are not uncommon. I also heard them say that it can exceed 100 degrees Fahrenheit during the hot summer months. Now that is some extreme weather difference!"

"I've never seen it that cold in the Skagit Valley," commented Grandma Inaba. "I've lived in the northern tip of Washington state all my life and have seen some cold winters there, but not sub-zero temperatures."

"It's going to take a great deal of coal to keep these shacks warm if the weather turns that cold," continued Mr. Inaba. "I just hope they don't run out of the stuff, or we could be in serious trouble."

His last statement brought a sober expression to Mrs. Inaba and Hitomi's faces. The children had winter coats, but the nights already felt bitterly cold. If it weren't for Mr. Inaba's faithful stoking of the little pot-belly stove throughout the night, the apartment would be as frosty as the temperature outside.

Mrs. Inaba broke the sober silence with a cheerful announcement that the children's Christmas program would be held on Christmas Eve. The two older Inaba children were attending classes at a school in Block 12 that had been organized by several former elementary education teachers. The children practiced songs, readings, poems, and a skit in their individual classrooms and eagerly looked forward to the event. But the biggest joy for the children were the cookies that their teachers had promised would be served to everyone after the performance.

"It's so nice to have a musical event to look forward to," said Hitomi. 'There is nothing better for the soul than to hear the sweet voices of children singing."

Grandma Inaba had a wistful smile on her wrinkled face. She must be thinking of Christmases past, thought Hitomi to herself.

"Shall we plan a Christmas celebration for the children here in the apartment as well?" asked Mrs. Inaba.

"Oh yes, I would love to plan a special Christmas day for all our children," Hitomi said eagerly. "What ideas do you have?"

The adults had been doing their best to acquire a small gift or two for each of the children. Mrs. Gibson, Emily, and Clara had sent a Christmas package to Hitomi, which had arrived the day before. It was a thrill to receive the package, but even more to get their cheerful holiday greetings. It meant so much in the dreary camp setting.

The cheery note included news of moving Mrs. Gibson back to her house on Capitol Hill and the improvement she was making with her physical therapy. She was now walking with a cane, but there was much optimism that she might one day walk without it.

Emily and Clara had shared a double wedding and there was news about the special day as well as a picture of both the happy couples. Emily had changed hours at the hospital to the swing shift, which allowed her time with her mother during the day while Clara worked. Clara was there in the evenings to help with dinner and assist her mother to bed. The two older sisters each spent one weekend per month with their mother, which gave Clara and Emily some time off.

Clara included several copies of the pictures she had taken with her Kodak Brownie camera in her last visit at the Puyallup Assembly Center. Hitomi was overjoyed at seeing the pictures of Masako, baby Hiro, and herself. She was grateful to Clara for sending multiple copies. She planned to send a picture to Akio in his Christmas letter as well as a picture to her mother at Manzanar. She knew this would be the only picture she would ever have of Hiro as a newborn. He was now nearly six months old and growing rapidly.

There were three gifts in the box wrapped in pretty Christmas paper, one for Hitomi and one for each child. There was also a packet of candy canes, some chocolate bars, a box of chamomile tea bags, two packages of Fig Newtons, and the most prized gift of all, Juicy Fruit gum! Lots of it. Hitomi smiled to herself as she tucked the gifts and treats away in one of Walter Gibson's leather bags and set it on the highest shelf that Mr. Inaba had put up on her side of the apartment. The Juicy Fruit gum would be a treat for everyone to receive on Christmas.

"I thought it might be fun for the children to make some paper chains," said Mrs. Inaba. "I did that when I was a girl, and it was fun to make the chains long enough to drape around the tree. We won't have a tree this year, but we could string it along the walls to make the apartment look more festive."

"What a good idea," said Hitomi. "But I wonder where we could get enough paper to make a long chain?"

"Let me talk to Kame and Mikio's schoolteachers," said Mrs. Inaba. "They may have extra paper they could share with us, or they may know of another source."

"Don't give up on the idea of a Christmas tree," Mr. Inaba said with a twinkle in his eye. "There's lots of tumbleweed around here, and most of it is really big. A little green paint and a big imagination could transform a tumbleweed into a Christmas tree."

They all laughed and immediately felt a warm magical connection in their united effort to make a memorable Christmas for the children.

Hitomi stayed very busy during the weeks before Christmas. She sent Akio a Christmas letter with the picture that Clara had taken during her visit at Puyallup Center. She looked at the picture pensively before tucking it inside the envelope. She wished with all her heart that he could have been in the picture with them. When she closed her eyes at night, exhausted from the cares of the day, Akio's face emerged in her mind. The memory that she treasured most was of the first time he'd smiled at her. She had been a shy university student in Professor Stratton's philosophy class. She was sitting in class, a row behind Akio and a few seats to his left. Professor Stratton said something funny, and the entire class laughed. Akio turned back slightly and smiled at her with a quirky grin which revealed shiny white teeth. Her heart lurched and she knew that she wanted to get to know this handsome guy with the dashing smile.

After class he waited a bit while she packed up her notebook and textbook and then walked out of the classroom with her. At the end of that school year, they got married in a simple wedding ceremony at her family's berry farm on Bainbridge Island. They moved into the small apartment on Capitol Hill and eighteen months later Masako was born.

If her family had been disappointed that she hadn't finished her degree in Home Economics, they had never said anything to her. Her parents and her brothers were proud of Akio when he was accepted into the University of Washington Law School and thrilled when Masako had been born. But life with Akio on Capitol Hill seemed so long ago. The past year had torn their lives and dreams apart in a cruel way. There was so much sadness and loss.

Life with Akio felt like a dream, but she only had to look at the faces of her children to know that it wasn't. Her life with Akio was real and the children were gifts of the love they shared. She often thought of her father's words that life brought situations that must be endured with dignity, hope, and *gaman*. She resolved to honor her father by enduring the indignities that incarceration at Minidoka brought each day.

The Christmas Eve program in Block 12 was a big success. Kame and Mikio said their part of the poem, *The Night Before Christmas*, without a stumble, making Grandma Inaba very proud. The school children's voices sounded beautiful as they sang Christmas carol after Christmas carol. Their angelic voices pulled at the heart strings of everyone in attendance that night. The homemade sugar cookies with the butter cream frosting were delicious. Hitomi wondered where these delectable treats had come from and learned later that the cookies had been donated by a Women's Auxiliary group from one of the churches in Twin Falls, Idaho.

Christmas morning arrived clear and cold. Mr. Inaba came in from the outside rubbing his hands together. He had been up early and gotten more coal to keep the pot-bellied stove in the apartment hot and happy.

"What is the temperature outside?" inquired Grandma Inaba. She was huddled in a blanket by the stove trying to keep herself warm.

"The outside thermometer on the barracks said 5 degrees Fahrenheit," answered Mr. Inaba. "It's a bitter cold Christmas Day."

Mrs. Inaba had a kettle of water on the stove and was making Grandma a cup of tea and offered some to her husband. Hitomi had just finished nursing Hiro and was sitting on the bench chatting with the women. The apartment looked very festive with the holiday decorations. The children had spent the last two weeks making paper chains, paper lanterns, and snowflakes that were hung on the tumbleweed tree and around the apartment walls. Mrs. Inaba had made many colorful origami cranes that were hung with sewing thread on the tumbleweed Christmas tree. The tree looked even more festive with the dozen or so colorfully wrapped gifts that surrounded it. Grandma Inaba had knitted each child a bright red and green Christmas stocking, which they had hung on the nails Mr. Inaba had hammered in the wall. Even though it was brutally cold outside, there was a warm air of Christmas anticipation that was palpable in the small apartment.

The Inaba family and Hitomi shared a breakfast of cereal, milk, and fruit, which they had acquired specifically for the occasion that Christmas morning. After the simple breakfast the two families watched the children open their gifts, play games, and enjoy the holiday festivities. There were squeals of delight from the children and gasps of surprise from the adults as gifts were opened and revealed. The two families spent the next several hours together sharing holiday joy.

Hitomi had knitted scarves for Mr. and Mrs. Inaba and Grandma, her very first knitting projects. The Inaba children enjoyed the candy canes, chocolate bars, and Juicy Fruit gum that she had hidden in their Christmas stockings. Grandma Inaba knitted mittens for all the children and gloves for the adults. The biggest surprise came when Mr. Inaba went outside and brought a crib that he had built from wood scraps for little Hiro who was now six months old.

Hitomi was overcome with emotion when she saw the crib and amazed by Mr. Inaba's craftmanship and ingenuity. Although not fancy by commercial standards, the crib was sturdy, well-constructed, and stood off the floor. Hiro had nearly outgrown the wooden crate that he had been sleeping in for the past four months, but now with this simple crib he would have a safe sleeping environment until he was old enough to sleep on a cot. Hitomi's heart flooded with gratitude as she thanked Mr. Inaba over and over for his generosity in building the remarkable little crib. He smiled in acknowledgement at her appreciation as he patted little Hiro's head. Baby Hiro was a handsome and happy little boy who cooed and babbled to everyone. It was no surprise that he had become the pet of the entire household.

The last gift opened was Masako's gift from Grandma Junko, which had come in the Christmas box from Manzanar. Inside was a beautiful pink dress that Junko had made for Masako. Every stitch was tiny and perfect, as if sewn by a machine, but Hitomi knew that her mother had sewn these perfect stitches by hand. Embroidered on both sides of the delicate white collar were three bright red roses that were connected by a green vine and leaves. The bodice of the dress had small pintucks evenly placed, which gave the dress a delicate look. The dress was exquisite and fit Masako perfectly, with plenty of hem to let out as Masako grew. Hitomi could not wait until the weather grew warmer so that Masako could wear it.

The Christmas of 1942 would be a bright star in Hitomi's memory and would shine clearly through the long years of incarceration. The friendship of the Inabas and the support she felt from this wonderful family gave her strength. The power of their shared experience and sense of caring concern softened the separation from her family and the Gibsons. Christmas came and went as the war raged on in Europe, North Africa, and the Pacific. Hitomi thought of Akio every day, wondering where he was, how he was, and worried about his safety. In the harsh and desolate environment of Minidoka, Hitomi waited out the winter and longed for spring with a yearning that she had never felt before.

Chapter Fourteen
Minidoka, 1943

Early in January, shortly after the new year began, Hitomi received a letter from Akio. She hadn't heard from him since the previous August. Her heart jumped with joy when she saw the slim airmail envelope with his bold handwriting. He wrote:

January 3, 1943
Fort McCoy, Wisconsin
My dearest wife,

I'm still in training at Fort McCoy, but there are rumors that we may be leaving sometime for Fort Shelby, Mississippi where we will continue to receive advanced infantry training. The 100th Infantry Battalion has been recognized for its superior training record and this has influenced President Roosevelt to officially authorize the formation of the 442nd Regimental Combat Team. I have heard reports that Nisei from the internment camps will be given the opportunity to volunteer and join the 442nd RCT. You said in your last letter that your brother Enji wanted to enlist. If he does, there is a good chance our paths may cross.

The Christmas letter you sent with the picture of you and the children was a thrill to receive! Thank you. I was amazed to see how much Masako has grown in the past year. I was especially happy to receive a photo of our son. I'm pleased that you named him, Hiroki. It is the honorable way to recognize and give respect to your father. I carry the picture in the left pocket of my uniform, over my heart. The three of you are the most important people in my life and I miss you with great longing.

There is not much to write about as we train six days out of the seven in a week. The news of the fighting and Allied efforts in Europe and North Africa is not good and all of us are eager to get over there and help. The sooner we can get into the fight, the sooner we can bring it to an end.

I long for the day when we will be a family and I can hold you all in my arms. Until then, I think only of you and our love together.

I am forever yours, Akio

Hitomi was pleased that Akio had expressed his approval of naming their son after her father. It lightened her heart to know that Akio was on the mainland, but she knew that his desire to defend the country and show his loyalty drove him to be among the first to volunteer for the most dangerous missions. This knowledge brought her both pride and fear. She realized there were no certainties, not at this time of her life.

The bitter cold of the harsh winter slowly receded as spring emerged in Minidoka. Hitomi missed the beauty of evergreens and vivid colors of early spring in the Northwest where she had grown up. There were no bright yellow daffodils or red tulips to color a spring day in Minidoka, not like Seattle or Bainbridge Island where these colors would explode around every house in the early spring. That is why she was quite surprised on a morning walk one day to see a large bucket with red tulips blooming outside one of the barracks. The red tulips looked out of place against the ugliness of the buildings. And yet, the vividness of the deep red of the tulips and green of their stems were stunning to behold. She smiled with pleasure when she stopped to gaze at them. Just then a young woman stepped out of the doorway with a small bucket of water and poured it on the blooming tulips.

"Hello," said Hitomi. "Your flowers are stunning!"

The young woman looked up and Hitomi was surprised to see the young woman she had helped on the train ride from Puyallup to Minidoka.

"Why hello!" said the woman with surprise. "I remember you. You helped me with my baby on the train. I still have your diapers and feel bad that I didn't get them back to you. I've looked for you at the assembly centers, but never saw you. What block do you live in?"

"It's good to see you again," said Hitomi. "My name is Hitomi and my children and I live in 12-6-D. Don't worry about the diapers. Diapers are the one thing I brought plenty of with me. How did you manage to find these beautiful tulips and get them to grow?"

"My name is Kioki and I love beautiful flowers," the young woman said. "I managed to dig up six tulip bulbs from my small garden in Centralia and carried them with me to Puyallup and then on to Minidoka. My husband and his family are fruit farmers. But I love flowers and I found this old bucket last fall and planted the tulip bulbs before the weather got too cold. Imagine my surprise when they began emerging about a month ago. I've been excited to watch them mature and now finally bloom."

"It would be fun to grow a few flowers to brighten our barracks, said Hitomi. "I wish I had thought about bringing some seed with me."

"Would you like some nasturtium and zinnia seed?" asked Kioki. "I have quite a few flower seeds wrapped in some wax paper that I tucked away in my suitcase. You were so kind on the train that I would like to return the favor in some small way."

"Oh yes, if you have some to spare, I would love to have a few seeds to plant in front of our barracks," answered Hitomi. "It would brighten the drabness of the buildings."

"Wait right here and I'll bring you some," said Kioki.

A few minutes later she returned with two small waxed paper packets folded like small envelopes, which held zinnia and nasturtium seed. She also carried a plump baby on her hip, her son Yuri. The two women spent a half hour of pleasant chatter sharing flower growing tips, baby teething woes, and tidbits about their former lives. They were the same age and enjoyed growing things as they had both been raised on farms. Kioki had an older brother who was sharing an apartment with their parents in another block in Minidoka. He was married and had two boys of his own. Hitomi talked about her family at Manzanar and the hope that they would be able to transfer to Minidoka sometime soon. As they said their goodbyes, they promised to visit another time. Hitomi left with a warm feeling that she had made a good friend and looked forward to visiting with Kioki again.

Back at the apartment Hitomi showed Mrs. Inaba the packets of flower seed and both women talked excitedly about when, where, and how to plant the seeds to beautify the area in front of their barracks. Just then Mr. Inaba came in from checking the mail at the administration building.

"Here's a letter for you. Hitomi," said Mr. Inaba.

"Thank you," said Hitomi. "It looks like the letter is from my brother, Hideo. I hope he is sending word that the approval has been given to transfer to Minidoka. It's been over a year since I've seen them."

Hiro was taking his morning nap. Grandma Inaba was sitting by his crib knitting an afghan crib blanket for the cold winter months ahead. Masako and Tome, the Inaba's youngest daughter, were coloring in the coloring books they had gotten for Christmas. Mrs. Inaba had taken the family's laundry to wash in the laundromat. The atmosphere in the apartment was peaceful and serene. Once again, Hitomi thanked the heavens above she had met the Inabas and was able to share an apartment with them. They treated her like family and she and Mrs. Inaba had become as close as sisters. Hitomi sat at the bench and opened Hideo's letter. He wrote,

March 10, 1943

Manzanar Internment Camp

My dear Little Sister,

It has been nearly a year since we last saw each other at the pier in Seattle. We have received word that our request for transfer to Minidoka has been approved and that the first group of transfers will take place by the end of this month. I had hoped that we would be among this first group as Mother has been so anxious to see you. But I'm afraid that her health has continued to decline since I wrote you at Christmas. Mother finally agreed to go to the camp hospital and the doctor diagnosed her as severely anemic and suffering from a bleeding ulcer. At this point she has become skin and bones and is extremely fragile. The medication that the doctor prescribed has given her some relief from the acute pain, but she still has no energy and tires quickly. She can hardly walk across the room without feeling faint. At this time, I'm not sure that she could handle the long train ride to Minidoka.

Enji completed the papers of loyalty to the United States and has enlisted in the military. He joined the 442nd Regimental Combat Team and is training with a number of young men from Manzanar who also enlisted. We haven't yet received word from him, but he was hoping that he would transfer to Fort Shelby in Mississippi and make contact with Akio. He had heard that at some point the 100th battalion would also be transferring to train at Fort Shelby.

Both Mother and Kazuko have had low spirits since Enji left. Kazuko spends more and more time with her parents and brother, which gives me peace of mind that she has her family here to support and care for her.

I've been working with a group of farmers in the camp to prepare the soil and develop an irrigation system so that gardens can be planted. Although the ground is very fertile in this area, fresh produce is not easily available, and everyone hungers for fresh vegetables. I'll let you know if Mother's health improves to the point we can travel. However, it may now be late summer or early fall before she will be well enough to make the trip.

It pleased Mother very much to know that the dress she made for Masako fit her and that you thought it was lovely. She spent many hours stitching it and took such care to make it beautiful. She sends her love to all of you, and so do I.

Your brother, Hideo

Hideo's letter brought a cloud of sadness to the sunny spring day. Hitomi couldn't shake the worry that her mother was declining rapidly, and it was distressful to think that she was experiencing severe pain. Hitomi felt herself sinking into an overwhelming sense of helplessness and hopelessness. She missed her mother profoundly and wondered when she might be well enough to travel to Minidoka. Hitomi had been looking forward to the day when she could be reunited with her family and now that hope seemed dashed, certainly it would be delayed.

"Is anything wrong?" asked Grandma Inaba with a concerned look on her face.

Hitomi found herself emptying her heart out to the dear elderly woman that had become a second grandma to her children.

"This news from your brother is a blow to your hopes and plans," said Grandma Inaba with empathy. "But don't let it be a knockout. You have the care of your two beautiful children to inspire your life. Nothing else matters, but your children. I lost my husband in a farming accident when our son was in high school. I didn't know what I was going to do, but with the help of kind friends and my son, I was able to continue. My life has been different from the life I would have had if my husband had not died so young, but it has still been a very fulfilling one."

Grandma Inaba smiled at Hitomi as she shared this sage advice.

"You are right, Grandma Inaba," responded Hitomi. "I needed to hear what you said and give myself a reality check. Life will not always be so uncertain, at least that is my hope and I'm going to focus on that rather than my worries about things I can do nothing about."

A feeling of understanding passed between the two women and a smile of warm companionship shone on their faces.

Over the next few weeks Hitomi and Mrs. Inaba kept busy preparing the soil in front of their barracks. They used sticks to work the soil but found the hoe Mr. Inaba brought them from the communal gardens worked the soil better. Soon they had the areas on both sides of the porch soft and pliable. It was an exciting day when they finally planted the flower seeds. They decided to plant the nasturtium on one side of the doorway and zinnias on the other. Mr. Inaba found some string and with his help they were able to wrap the string to make a fence. This kept stray feet out of the flower beds giving the germinating seeds a chance to take root and thrive.

Every day one of the women would check to see if there was a sign of *green life* as they jokingly called their planting efforts.

"Any sign of green life today?" Mrs. Inaba would ask Hitomi with a mischievous grin.

"Not yet," Hitomi would banter back. "But we should be seeing a pop of green any day now."

And they did, about two weeks later. Mrs. Inaba was the first one to detect the first sign of growth in their garden beds. She excitedly called Hitomi outside to see the emerging plants. Soon the plants began to grow taller and fuller and eventually they exploded in a profusion of blooms. The flowers flourished under the attentive care of Mrs. Inaba and Hitomi. The weather grew more intense as spring gave way to summer. By June the nasturtium plants had bushed out and spread as a hedge filled with glorious colored flowers of yellow, red, white, and orange.

The zinnias were a little slower blooming, but by the end of June they were a stunning show of pink, magenta, yellow, and orange blossoms. During the heat of the early summer the flowers received water twice a day. In the morning, Hitomi would take two buckets and go to the laundry area and bring back water for the plants as there was no running water in the barrack's apartment. Mrs. Inaba would take the afternoon water shift and get buckets of

My Mother Told Me Stories

water while the younger children napped. They took turns "de-heading" the shriveled blooms and the flowers flourished under consistent and watchful care. The brilliant flowers were a remarkable contrast to the drab barrack building. People commented on the beauty and how much they enjoyed seeing the vivid colors.

Kioki came to visit on numerous occasions to admire the beautiful display. She informed them that in the fall the flower blooms would give way to seeds that could be collected, dried, and planted the next year. She told Hitomi and Mrs. Inaba nasturtium and zinnia seeds self-propagated readily and this was why she had chosen to bring them. Hitomi and Mrs. Inaba visited Kioki's flower garden and saw that she had also planted golden marigolds and a flower variety she called vinca, which included a bluish colored bloom that looked outstanding among the pink, orange, and yellow of the zinnias. The three women enjoyed their garden club and shared flower cuttings to cheer up the drabness of the barrack apartments. Kioki showed them how to dry zinnias and marigolds by hanging them upside down on string. The dried flowers made pretty bouquets and wreaths in the fall and winter and added color to a colorless environment.

Sharing the common interest of the beautiful flowers helped alleviate some of the boredom of life at Minidoka, but only some. The high plains summer heat became increasingly oppressive as Hiro's first birthday arrived on July 14th. Hitomi did her best to try and make festive party plans for him, but her heart wasn't in it. The Inabas joined her in the efforts and together they did their best to pull a party together in the dismal surroundings. Mrs. Inaba helped Hitomi plan a few games like Pin the Tail on the Donkey, and a relay game of carrying a spoon with a small pebble that even the adults enjoyed playing. Somehow Mr. Inaba was able to get a dozen Hostess Chocolate cupcakes to celebrate the occasion. Kioki, her husband, and son Yuri also came to the celebration.

Mr. Inaba pulled another surprise out of his pocket when one of the military guards came by with his Kodak camera. He had talked the young soldier into taking some pictures of Hiro's first birthday in trade for a Hostess Cupcake! The young man promised that he would bring the pictures when he got the roll of film printed. It ended up being a very pleasant day, which Hitomi was to remember with fondness.

One morning in early September there was a knock on the apartment door and when Mrs. Inaba opened the door, she was surprised to see one of the military guards from the camp. It was the same young military guard that had become quite friendly with her husband and had taken the pictures of Hiro's first birthday party.

"Good morning, James," she said cheerfully to him. "How are you today?"

"Very fine, Mrs. Inaba," replied James. "I'm sorry to disturb you this morning, but I have a message for Mrs. Murata."

"You mean Hitomi?" she questioned.

"Yes, Hitomi, Mrs. Murata." he responded respectfully.

"Just one moment," said Mrs. Inaba. "I'll get her. I think she is getting the baby changed for the day."

Hitomi came to the door with Hiro on her hip and Masako trailing behind with the curiosity of a three-year-old.

"I have a message for you, Mrs. Murata," said James. "You are to come to the reception room in Administration Building A at 9:00 this morning as there is a telephone call that will be coming for you at that hour from your brother in California."

"Oh, did they say the reason for the telephone call?" enquired Hitomi.

"No, just that a call would be coming in at that time for you," said James.

"Thank you for the message. I will be there," responded Hitomi.

There was quite a bit of speculation in the apartment as Hitomi shared the news with Grandma and Mrs. Inaba regarding the telephone call.

"I wonder what the news is?" queried Hitomi. "I hope nothing has happened to Enji, or Kazuko? Or worse yet, if my mother has taken another turn for the worst?"

"It could also be good news," said Mrs. Inaba. "Perhaps your brother is calling to let you know that he and your mother are transferring to Minidoka. He may even know the exact date. Maybe he just got the news and doesn't have time to write and let you know."

"That's a possibility," said Hitomi. "But I have this sick feeling in my stomach that it's bad news."

"There's been nothing but bad news in the last year and a half, so I can understand your concern," said Grandma Inaba. "I'll watch the children, so you don't need to worry about them. Masako is playing dolls with Tome and that will keep them busy for hours. Hiro will play here on the blanket by my chair so go ahead and walk over to the administration building so you can be there at 9:00. That way you won't be late for your brother's call."

Hitomi checked the children and then left them with Grandma and Mrs. Inaba and headed over to the reception area of Administration Building A. She let the receptionist know who she was and that a telephone call was coming in for her. The woman nodded and told her to take one of the chairs and she would let her know when the call came through. Hitomi sat and waited anxiously for the call.

Precisely at 9:00 a.m. the telephone rang, and Hitomi heard the receptionist say, "Just a moment please and I will connect you."

She then nodded to Hitomi to come with her to a small office behind the receptionist desk where there was another telephone. She instructed her to pick up the receiver when the telephone rang. Hitomi nodded her head that she understood. The receptionist went back to her desk and a moment later the telephone rang.

Hitomi picked up the receiver and said "Hello."

The voice on the other end asked, "Is this Mrs. Hitomi Murata?"

"Yes, this is she speaking," answered Hitomi.

"Please hold one moment," the voice on the other end said. A few seconds later Hideo came on the line.

"Hello, Hitomi. This is Hideo."

"Yes, Hideo, it's wonderful to hear your voice," Hitomi said excitedly. "Is everything fine at Manzanar?"

"No, that is why I'm calling," said Hideo, sounding very weary. "Mother passed away in the evening yesterday. She hadn't been eating much for the past three or four weeks. It seemed that everything she ate caused her extreme pain and discomfort. The doctor said that the internal bleeding increased abruptly, which led to her death. But really, she'd lost her will to live after Enji enlisted and left for Fort Shelby, Mississippi."

Hitomi could not speak. Her throat felt tight and there was a pounding sensation above her eyes. For a minute she felt faint, but she took a deep breath and said with emotion, "I can't believe that Mother is dead. She never got to see Hiro and I'll never see her again." The tears ran down her face unchecked.

"I know your sadness, my little sister," Hideo said quietly. "I miss her, too, and I'm glad that I could be with her during the final hours. If you had seen how much she suffered the past six months, you would know she is now at peace and no longer feels the pain of her body or the sadness in her soul."

Hitomi could hear him crying softly on the other end of the telephone.

"Dear brother, I've only been thinking of my sorrow and not acknowledging that you have been so devoted to our mother and supported her during this terrible time," said Hitomi. "Please forgive me for only thinking of myself. Please come to Minidoka and stay with the children and me. Enji is at war, and we don't know when we'll see him or Akio. But we can support each other through this difficult time."

There was a moment of silence on the other end. Hitomi knew that Hideo was trying to pull himself together to speak to her.

Finally, he said, "I've been approved to transfer to Minidoka, and I leave in two weeks. I hope that I can live near you and see the children daily. I'll bring the urn with Mother's ashes with me. When the war is over, I hope to take her back to Bainbridge Island and bury her ashes with Father on the farm. Will you go with me to do that? I know that is what they both would have wanted."

"Yes, my dear brother," cried Hitomi. "You will live with me, the children and the Inabas. It will be a bit crowded, but all the apartments are crowded. At least half the people in our apartment will be small children, which cannot be said of other family situations. They are noisy and underfoot, but they don't take as much room as we adults. And they clearly bring joy to our lives. Perhaps the children can help heal your heart."

"During the warm months I won't be in the house much during the day," said Hideo. "I hope to join the other farmers at Minidoka and help develop the land, plant seeds, and harvest the crops to help the families in the internment camp as well as help the war effort. I found that very fulfilling here at Manzanar. I'm just a farmer at heart and I feel this is my contribution to supporting the war effort."

"You will be welcome," said Hitomi. "I am comforted at the thought of taking Mother's ashes to the berry farm and laying them near Father's ashes so that they can be together in the place where they shared so many memories. The thought of that eases my sadness."

"It brings comfort to me as well," said Hideo. "I was unable to call Enji, but I will send him a letter to notify him of Mother's passing."

Hitomi and Hideo said their sad farewells and promised to see each other soon and then hung up the telephones.

When Hitomi returned to the apartment she tearfully shared with Mrs. Inaba and Grandma of the news of her mother's death. Both women hugged her, and she slumped into their loving arms as the tears flowed.

Approval was granted and arrangements were made, and another cot was placed in Block 12, Barrack 6, Apartment C. The two weeks sped by, and Hideo arrived by train from Manzanar. He came with his suitcase in one hand and the urn with their mother's ashes under his other arm. Hitomi placed the urn on the highest shelf on her side of the apartment where it could be seen but was not in danger of being disturbed. It was a simple urn but most precious to Hitomi and Hideo and it eased their hearts to see it there. There was also a sense of resolution knowing that when they left Minidoka, they would take Mother's ashes and that she would have a proper burial with Father on Bainbridge Island.

A few days after Hideo arrived at Minidoka, James the friendly guard, stopped by their barrack's apartment and took a picture of Hideo, Hitomi, little Hiro, and Masako in her pretty pink dress Grandma Junko had made. He snapped several pictures and said he would bring them to Hitomi when he got the film developed. Hitomi was pleased that he'd promised to do this as she hoped to send a copy of the picture to Akio, Enji, and Mrs. Gibson in their Christmas cards. James kept his word. A few weeks later he stopped by the apartment and brought the pictures to Hitomi.

Hideo settled in quickly and became friends with Mr. Inaba. They were both farmers and enjoyed discussing everything from the impact of weather conditions on various crops, the quality of the soil, to the kind of fertilizer that worked best for each crop. It was potato harvesting time and both men spent the final days of September and most of October harvesting Russet Burbank potatoes. This variety of potato grew well in the dry loamy soil in Minidoka. The high yield of the potato harvest was a source of pride for those who worked throughout the spring and summer to prepare the ground, keep the crops irrigated, and were now harvesting the fruits of their labor.

The days grew increasingly colder as winter approached. Mr. Inaba and Hideo took turns getting the coal to keep the pot-bellied stove burning night and day. During some of the long wintery evenings around the stove, Hitomi thought back on all that had happened over the past year. It was hard to believe that they had been living in Minidoka for a year and a half. Christmas 1943 was their second holiday season at the camp, and she wondered how many more Christmases they'd spend in Minidoka? She wondered when the war would end, and they would return home?

The sharp pain of missing Akio had lessoned over time although she thought of him daily and worried for his safety. In June she received a letter from Akio saying that the 100th battalion had arrived at Camp Shelby to complete their advanced training. She was happy to hear that he'd seen Enji. The two men were not in the same unit and trained in different areas at Fort Shelby, but they did see each other occasionally and Akio said it felt like being home whenever they were together.

The last letter Hitomi received stateside from Akio was one month later. He wrote to her the night before his battalion left for North Africa saying he didn't know when he'd be able to send her another letter. It could be six months or more, depending upon the success of the campaign they'd be undertaking.

The loss of her mother had wounded a part of Hitomi's heart that she felt could never be healed. Her father's death had been a shock and caused great anguish, but the loss of her mother left her bereft and broken. Only her children gave her life meaning and brought a measure of purpose. That was not to say that she wasn't grateful to have Hideo in her life again. She knew he continued to grieve for their parents as there was a sadness in his face that was permanently set. The hair around his temples had grayed significantly during the past year. But he did his best to hide the sadness and was helpful with the daily care of the children when she had laundry chores or other household responsibilities to complete.

The joy of the Christmas season did not fill the household as it had in the previous year. But the adults did their best to celebrate the holiday and make it a pleasant time for the children. Even the holiday did not take away the realization that they were incarcerated and not allowed to leave the camp on their own free will. Christmas 1943 came and went, and the new year arrived.

Chapter Fifteen
Minidoka, 1944

The war dragged on. Information on how the fighting efforts were going slowly leaked out through the news sources on the radio and newspaper, but the news was always delayed at least a week. Shortly after the attack on Pearl Harbor the War Department stopped accepting Nisei into military service out of fear of further attacks from the Japanese. But as more troops were needed and it became apparent that the Nisei were hard working and loyal, they were allowed to sign papers of loyalty to the United States. They could then enlist and join the newly formed 442nd Regimental Combat Team, made up entirely of young men of Japanese ancestry. This included a number of young men from Minidoka. Everyone in the internment camp was eager to hear about the war efforts, but even more eager to get news of their men training and serving in the 100th battalion or the 442nd RCT.

As the spring and summer of 1944 moved along, the occupants of Minidoka did their best to cope with the anxiety and uncertainty of their situation. Hideo and Mr. Inaba began working with other farmers in the camp to prepare the soil and plant crops, giving the camp access to fresh vegetables, which were difficult to obtain.

The agricultural success of the previous year had encouraged the Minidoka farmers and they redoubled efforts to expand the yields. Their efforts began to emerge in full force as the fields around Minidoka turned green with a variety of vegetables such as beets, potatoes, carrots, turnips, tomatoes, onions and other garden produce. Watermelons did extremely well in the hot dry climate of Southern Idaho and the juicy sweetness was enjoyed by young and old throughout the camp. The dusty and desolate plains environment that the internees had been shocked to see when they first arrived in August of 1942 began to look more hospitable. This was due in large part to the industrious nature of the Nikkei farmers and the access to the North Side Canal for irrigation.

Hitomi and Mrs. Inaba had carefully saved seeds from the flowers grown the previous summer. They found it gratifying to see the fledgling plants emerge. There was a collective effort throughout Minidoka to clean and beautify the camp. Small family garden plots emerged near the barracks and around the grounds. Sapling trees, shrubs, and a variety of flowers were planted, and little by little Minidoka began to take on the appearance of a community rather than a collection of military barracks.

A landscaped park was created in the camp and included a place where families could convene for a picnic. A baseball diamond was built in the camp, giving the youth and young men a chance to develop their skills and compete with teams from some of the local high schools in the area. During the hot summer days, many of the occupants of the camp swam in the North Side Canal to cool off. But the current in the canal was swift and after a tragic drowning accident the occupants of the camp got together and diverted water from the canal to areas where swimming pools could be created. The young people in the camp found the swimming pools a source of fun and distraction from the intense summer heat.

Despite the hardships of the internment camp, little Hiro grew and flourished. He developed like any other normal child. First rolling over onto his tummy, then dragging himself across the dirty wooden floor in a soldier crawl, then pulling himself to a standing position, to finally taking his first independent steps. He was now a sturdy little toddler who followed his sister and the youngest Inaba child, Tome, everywhere. Everyone chuckled when Grandma Inaba would say, "There goes the little caboose."

One morning on a warm July day the two older Inaba children, Kame and Mikio, left the apartment to kick the ball with some of their friends in the compound near their barracks. The younger children, Tome, Masako, and Hiro followed them out to watch. Hideo and Mr. Inaba worked on the agricultural acreage irrigating the crops and the women sat around the table in the apartment fanning themselves and discussing plans for a picnic to celebrate Hiro's second birthday. They had only been chatting for a few minutes when they heard yelling, shrieking, and pounding feet rushing to the apartment.

Hitomi and Mrs. Inaba rushed to the door just as Kame, Mikio, Tome, and Masako arrived.

"Mama, mama, there's a huge snake curled up by a rock where we were playing kick the ball," Mikio said excitedly. "It made a buzzing sound with its tail!"

Mrs. Inaba gasped in horror and Hitomi's heart leaped in fear.

"Where is Hiro?" cried Hitomi. "Didn't he come back with you?"

The children looked around in confusion.

"He was just with us," cried Kame. "But I don't see him now."

Hitomi took off running and Mrs. Inaba grabbed a hoe and quickly followed her. They ran around the corner of one of the barracks to a small field where the children from Block 12 often played. They saw a cluster of children looking at an object that was out of the view of the two women. On the outer edge of the group of children was a small toddler that both women immediately recognized as Hiro.

Hitomi arrived first and snatched Hiro up in her arms. About ten feet away was a large rock with the biggest snake that Hitomi had ever seen. The snake was curled up and shaking the buttons on its tail. It was a western rattlesnake and obviously upset at being disturbed.

"Big nake, see big nake," said Hiro, pointing excitedly at the serpent. "It mad!"

Mrs. Inaba came forward with her hoe and told the children to move back from the snake, which they reluctantly did. Then with one ferocious swing of her hoe she expertly decapitated the snake, striking the serpent behind its neck and slamming the head against the large boulder. It was a scene right out of a horror movie and the children were mesmerized by the writhing body of the dying snake.

"Keep back, children," warned Mrs. Inaba. "Do not touch this snake in any way. I'm going to bury the head because a decapitated snake head still has the potential of biting and inflicting poison."

Near the rock, Mrs. Inaba began fiercely digging a hole. She continued hacking away at the earth until it was about a foot deep. Hitomi gasped when the decapitated snake head bit down on the hoe Mrs. Inaba used to move the head towards the hole she had dug. She couldn't believe what she was seeing! It was true, a snake's head could bite even after being severed from its body. Hitomi was amazed at Mrs. Inaba's calmness as she buried the poisonous snake head. Mrs. Inaba looked for another rock and after locating one she pulled it over and set it on top of the ground where she had buried the snake head.

She looked sternly at the children and said, "Do not disturb this rock, or try to dig up the snake. Do you understand me?"

The children looked at her with big open eyes and in synchrony nodded their heads in understanding. It was apparent that they were all in awe of her bravery and skill in killing and disposing of the snake.

Mrs. Inaba looped the snake's body over the hoe to show Mr. Inaba and Hideo. She walked back with Hitomi and the children to their apartment. Hitomi felt shaky inside, but the children were all chattering and pointing to the snake and gyrating around to enact the death throes of the serpent.

Hideo and Mr. Inaba had returned from the fields for the noon meal and were astounded when they saw the snake hanging over Mrs. Inaba's hoe.

"What in the world!" exclaimed Mr. Inaba. "Where did you get that thing and why is it hanging on the hoe?"

"Mama killed it!" Mikio explained excitedly. "Daddy, you should have seen Mama kill the snake! She cut its head right off with one smash of the hoe!"

"We were playing kick the ball," Kame blurted in, not wanting her brother to get all the glory for narrating the event. "One of the kids kicked the ball against the big rock at the side of the field where we were playing. It bounced off the rock and we saw this snake come slithering out from underneath, coil up like a rope, and begin shaking his tail. The snake made a rattling sound, like Hiro's baby rattle used to sound when he shook it. You know, when he was really little. The snake was so scary, daddy!"

"Why don't you children show me the rock where the snake came out from under?" requested Mr. Inaba. "Uncle Hideo and I will go check and make sure there are no other snakes around."

The two older children took the men over to the field and showed them the rock where the rattlesnake had first emerged. They also showed them the rock and place where their mother had dug the hole and buried the head.

"Daddy, you should have seen the cut off head," said Mikio excitedly. "When Mama started to move the head, it bit the hoe and hung on. She had to shake the head off into the hole and then she covered it with dirt and put a rock on top. She told all of us kids not to dig it up."

Both men looked at each other in amazement and Hideo said, "Your mother is a very brave woman! She is right. Leave that head buried. The fangs still hold venom even though the head has been cut off."

The men conferred together as they walked back to the apartment. "I think we should check that field thoroughly before the children play ball again," Mr. Inaba said. "There could be other rattlesnakes, especially if there is a hole or tunnel they use for their home."

"Yes, I think you are right," said Hideo. "I don't know much about snakes. There are no poisonous snakes on Bainbridge Island where I grew up. There are a few garden snakes, but I've never seen any as big as this rattlesnake."

When they got back to the barracks, they measured the snake from the tip of its rattlers to where its head was severed. It was three feet and ten inches in length.

"If you count the head, this snake was probably four feet long!" said Mr. Inaba as he looked at his wife in amazement and admiration. "I'm going to cut the rattlers off and make a necklace for you as a reminder of your feat!"

"Never mind, I don't want anything more to do with that thing," Mrs. Inaba said with a smile. "If you cut those rattlers off you can make yourself a necklace." Everyone laughed. Later that day Hideo and Mr. Inaba returned to the big rock and arrived just in time to see the last few inches of a second rattlesnake slithering under the rock. They carefully approached and looked closer and saw a small hole situated under the rim of the big rock.

"We've got to do something to close up that den," said a worried Hideo "There are too many children that play around here. We've got to do it before tragedy strikes and one of them is bitten."

Mr. Inaba nodded his head in agreement and said, "We know that at least one rattlesnake is down there. Shall we try to do something about it now? I know where there are some bags of dry cement mix left over from the construction of the camp. I could get a bag and we could mix it right here and dump it down that hole. In this heat it would harden quickly."

"That's a good idea," said Hideo. "Will it take you long to get the stuff?"

"No, probably fifteen minutes, or so," answered Mr. Inaba. "I'll need some water and a bucket. We each brought a hoe so we can use them to mix the stuff."

"Sounds good,' said Hideo. 'I'll stay here and watch to make sure that the snake doesn't come back out. I can push it back with this hoe."

Mr. Inaba hurried away and got the cement mix, some gravel and water and returned in short order. No snake had appeared during his absence and the two men worked quickly to mix the cement and then poured it down the hole. It took a second batch to bring the cement to the top of the hole, which they smoothed over and then stepped back and looked at their handiwork.

"That should do it," said Mr. Inaba. At least that should do it for this den and the snake we saw entering it. We have no idea how many other snakes, if any, were down there."

"No, we don't have any idea,' said Hideo. "But I feel better knowing that we closed that den up. I'm not sure that the kids around here should play in this field until we are sure that there are no more snakes. Let's check the field and surrounding areas during the next few days."

No more snakes were discovered that summer, but Mrs. Inaba's fame as the woman who kills snakes with one slice of the hoe grew to heroic proportions. She became a legend around Minidoka and not only with the younger set who had witnessed her quick action that day, but also among the older occupants of the internment camp. There wasn't a community gathering without someone asking Mrs. Inaba, *Are you the snake woman I've been hearing about? How could you bring yourself to kill a rattlesnake? And thus, the story grew bigger and bigger with questions such as, how many rattlesnakes have you killed this summer? What was the biggest snake you ever killed? Did you kill snakes before coming to Minidoka?*

The Inaba children never grew tired of telling anyone who would listen of their mother's quick action in killing the rattlesnake. But none of this fame turned Mrs. Inaba's head. She remained the calm, steady, matter-of-fact woman she had always been and would just shake her head at what she called, all that silly snake nonsense.

Hiro's second birthday was the highlight of the long, hot, and dreary summer. He was a delightful child and everyone in 12-6-D was captivated by his charming little ways. He was the apple of Grandma Inaba's eye and Masako's shadow, always just a step behind her. The big sister and little brother were close, and she was steadfast in her devotion to him. Both Masako and Tome watched over their little *caboose,* and he benefitted from their united desire to caretake and protect him.

Hiroki's second birthday, July 14, 1944, arrived on a warm sunny day. It was perfect weather for a picnic and birthday celebration. Restrictions had loosened up a little and occupants of the camp could occasionally go to town to get supplies. This was the case for Mr. Inaba and Hideo who were well respected for their agricultural skills and had taken a leadership role in much of the commercial farming efforts at Minidoka. The two men had been instrumental in helping to organize crews to harvest and save the beet crop in the area the previous fall. With so many able-bodied men enlisting and serving in the war effort there hadn't been enough workers to get the beets harvested, but with their organizational efforts the beet crops were saved.

Earlier that spring, seed potatoes, onion starts, as well as other vegetable seeds and fertilizer were bought in Twin Falls, a community about twenty miles from the internment camp. The two men rode to Twin Falls occasionally with the provision truck to get their supplies. Hitomi and Mrs. Inaba made a list of supplies they needed for Hiro's birthday celebration. Twinkies, the delicious crème-filled tube delights, were at the top of the wish list. Luckily, on their last trip to Twin Falls, the two men were able to get a dozen for the festivities. Unbeknownst even to Hitomi and Mrs. Inaba, the men also got one of the first watermelons of the season for the special occasion, which they hid in a bucket under the front porch of the apartment.

Hiro was a sunny-natured little boy, and today was no exception. He seemed to know this was his special day and his laughter and smiles filled the apartment with childish joy. Hitomi's heart felt lighter than it had since the death of her mother almost a year earlier. Sometimes at night when she made the final check on the children before laying herself down to sleep on the cot, she would search each of her children's faces as they slept. Looking at their sun kissed cheeks and golden creaminess of their skin was like looking at beautifully ripened peaches. She saw the strong angle of her father's jaw and broad forehead in Hiro's gentle baby face. But it was in Masako's face that she saw her husband's face. Both father and daughter shared the family trait of a slightly crooked grin and a dimple in their right cheek when they smiled. Hitomi found these traits very endearing, and whenever she saw Masako's dimple it tugged at her heart. She would remember seeing Akio's grin and dimple that memorable day in Professor Stratton's philosophy class when he had first smiled at her.

Hitomi and Mrs. Inaba decided to have hot dogs at the birthday party dinner as all the children loved hot dogs, even though the women got tired of eating them and would laugh together over how many ways to serve rice with hot dogs.

Grandma Inaba refused to eat hot dogs saying, "You don't know what kind of meat or what part of the animal you are eating in a hot dog. It's just mystery meat!"

If there was cheese available at the mess hall, she would slip a slice in her hot dog bun with some of the pickle relish. If there wasn't any cheese, it was just butter and bread for her. They made sure there was cheese for the picnic so Grandma wouldn't be disappointed.

Hitomi invited Kioki, her husband and their young son, Yuri, to the birthday picnic. The three families convened at the picnic area in the early evening. The weather that day was warm, but a slight breeze came up and by the time the juicy red watermelon was brought out the weather had cooled to a pleasant temperature. The evening air was lighter and more bearable. The children had a splendid time playing kick ball and the men joined them in playing some field soccer. For a short time, life seemed almost normal. The conversation did not center around the fighting in Europe or the Pacific. The time spent together was like friends gathering together to celebrate festivities on a lovely summer evening. It was one of the final pleasant days that summer before the weather turned intensely hot and miserable.

August heat came with a vengeance that summer. Hitomi began having headaches during the heat of the day and Masako would wake up in the night with nose bleeds. Once again Hitomi could hear her father's saying, *sometimes one must resolve to have gaman and endure the unbearable with dignity and patience.* His words would come to her as the intense heat and bright sunlight caused her head to throb so sharply she felt dizzy and couldn't see clearly. She would lie down on her cot with a wet cloth on her forehead and wait for the throbbing to lessen.

It was in late August that Hitomi received news from Akio. He had written the letter in May, but it didn't arrive at Minidoka until three months later. He wrote:

May 16, 1944

Somewhere in Italy

My darling Wife,

In March our battalion returned from North Africa where we fought with the Fifth Army as a part of the 133rd Infantry Regiment. We arrived in Italy in late March and have been struggling to open a road to Rome. The fighting is most fierce during the day, but with night it lessens, giving us a chance to sleep. I've been lucky to this point, and I feel certain that my luck holds because of the picture of you and the children that I carry in my left shirt pocket, over my heart. A number of my buddies have been wounded and our unit has sustained many losses. We've been pulled back for a while to rest and recover before we return to fighting. This has given me a chance to pen a letter to you with the hopes that it will reach you at some point.

I have seen and experienced things that no human being should experience. My idealism to fight for my country, to prove my loyalty, to ensure freedom from tyranny, and to save the lives of those who suffer from the aggression of foreign powers still burns strong in my heart. But I have witnessed, first hand, how great the cost is and how deep the suffering can be for the innocent. I feel that the tide is turning as we push the Germans further north, but the fighting is far from over. I fear that the effort will become even more brutal before the fighting ends and a truce is made.

At times I feel sadness even for our enemies, the Germans. They are young men like the rest of us in the 100th battalion, commissioned to fight for something that their leaders have determined is necessary. And for what? If I should survive this war and live the long years after I will not regret how hard I have fought to do my part for America. My only regret is that we were separated for so long and I couldn't be there for you and the children.

Yesterday as I rested outside our makeshift tent, I saw a tiny sparrow sitting on a shrub singing its heart out. In the heat of the battle there are no songbirds, but away from the battlefields the birds do sing. There is still beauty in this ugly war-torn world, and this gives me hope that we'll share that beauty together when all the fighting is done.

My love for you, and my hope to hold you and the children in my arms is what keeps my soul alive.

I am forever yours, Akio

Hitomi's heart was lighter after she read Akio's letter. It had been months since she had last received word from him. She worried and wondered about what he was going through. His safety was always at the front of her worries. His letter reassured her that the man that she had admired, depended upon, and loved was still there.

The idealism that had always guided his thoughts and actions lived on, but his letter helped her realize that this idealism was not blinding him to the reality of the politics of war. Leaders declared hostilities and war, but it was the people who suffered. The most comforting part of his letter was his enduring devotion to her and the children. This thought gave her hope and solace that they'd be able to rebuild their lives together when he came home.

The fall brought an interesting development into the lives of the occupants of 12-6-D. Grandma Inaba was the first to notice the development and shared her thoughts with Hitomi and Mrs. Inaba.

After dinner one evening Grandma asked innocently, "Do either of you know the name of the woman who works in the mess hall serving our block?"

"Mother," said Mrs. Inaba, "there are a number of women working in the mess hall at every meal. What woman are you referring to and why?"

"She is the director or something like that," Grandma went on. "You know, the woman who walks around the room and checks to see if people are enjoying the food. She also tells the servers to get more trays of food when the serving trays get low."

"I think I know who you are referring to," said Hitomi. "The woman with the nice smile and pleasant demeanor."

"You mean the woman who always talks to Hideo?" said Mrs. Inaba in a conspiratorial voice.

"Yes!" said Grandma Inaba. "That woman!"

Hitomi looked at her two friends with surprise in her eyes. She recalled seeing this woman chatting with Hideo on frequent occasions and the more she thought about it, the more unusual it now seemed. Hideo was not shy, but he wasn't the life of the party either. And he certainly didn't go out of his way to visit with women. She couldn't recall him ever having a girlfriend, not even in high school. He had gone to a dance or two, but only when he was asked, he never initiated an invitation. Hitomi knew he was devoted to their parents. As the eldest son he believed it was his duty to support and help them with the family farm. She didn't know what to think about this new development.

"Do you think this woman is interested in Hideo more than just as an acquaintance?" she asked in a wondering way. "It's true that Hideo was a dutiful son and brother. He's always thought of the family first, including me, and now that I think about it, he's sacrificed most of his life and dreams for what he thought was best for the family."

"Well, we can't be sure that this woman is interested in him in any romantic way, nor he in her," said Mrs. Inaba. "But it will be interesting to watch and see what happens." And so, the three women began watching this friendship emerge right before their very eyes.

Hideo was always eager and ready to head for the mess hall before anyone else in apartment 6-D was ready. Hitomi thought at first it was because the children dawdled whenever it was meal time.

Hideo would say to everyone, "Well, I'll head over to the mess hall and save a table for all of us." And off he would go. Often, he would be talking with "the woman" when they arrived. But when the whole group showed up, he would quickly cut off his conversation and she would step away to another table and chat briefly with the occupants there. It was all quite mysterious.

One day, Hitomi asked Hideo if he knew the woman's name that directed the serving of the meals at the mess hall. She was surprised when she saw a redness emerge on his face. *Why, he's actually blushing and is shy about answering this question,* she thought to herself.

"I've heard people call her Mio," he said tentatively. "She's very friendly and asks questions of everyone. I believe she is the director of meal service in our block."

As the weeks passed, Hitomi and the Inabas learned a great deal more about this mystery woman. Her name was Mio Tamaka, she lived in Block 12, but in a different barrack and she was indeed the director of food services. They also discovered that she was single, had been a resident of Tacoma, Washington, and worked in food service at one of the hospitals before being sent to Minidoka Internment Camp. Hideo began spending more and more time in the evenings with Mio and it became apparent that there was indeed a romance blooming right under their noses.

Hitomi could see a change come over her brother, which made her very happy. He had lost that haunting sadness that had characterized his eyes after their mother died. He laughed more and he seemed happy, even in the confinement of the internment camp.

One day Hitomi got her nerve up and asked him, "Hideo, have you fallen in love with Mio?"

He smiled at her and said, "Yes, I think I have. I want nothing more than to be near her. I want to do things for her, to care for her, and to share my life with her. I can't believe that I would find this kind of love in a dismal internment camp!"

"I'm so happy for you," said Hitomi with genuine joy. "Mio is such a lovely woman, and she makes a good companion for you because she is outgoing, and you are content to let her shine. But you give her strength and support. I see that whenever you are together."

"We want to get married," said Hideo. "In fact, we want to get married right away, maybe as soon as this Thanksgiving. People may think we are rushing things, but we've actually become friends over the past year. Most people didn't really recognize our growing interest in each other because they only saw us together in the mess hall where Mio was greeting other people in her work capacity. But we've spent a great deal of time this past year walking and talking after her evening work shift and have come to know each other very well."

"That is such wonderful news," said Hitomi giving her brother a sisterly hug. "I want this for you, Hideo. For many years you've set aside your own dreams in order to help Mother and Father on the berry farm. I know you wanted to go to the university, and you gave that dream up so that Enji could go. I'm so glad that finding someone to love and who loves you back has come to you, my dearest brother."

Hideo's eyes crinkled in joy as he received his sister's blessing.

Hideo and Mio were married on Thanksgiving Day, 1944. It was not a traditional Japanese wedding, but a simple civil service. Hideo wore black slacks, and a white shirt and Mio wore a lovely peach colored kimono that she borrowed from a friend in the camp. Mio's friends and colleagues decorated the mess hall with pumpkins, squash, dried corn stalks, and apples creating a very pretty autumn setting for Mio and Hideo to exchange vows. After the vows were said and rings exchanged a beautiful dinner was served. And what a feast it was! So different from the usual food served in the mess hall. There were a number of talented musicians in the camp who got together early in their incarceration at Minidoka and a small orchestra had been formed. Mio had arranged for them to play at their wedding reception and the music filled the hall with incredible beauty.

Hitomi felt a deep joy for her brother who had found unexpected love and happiness in the unlikeliest of places. She looked fondly upon her children who were all decked out for the wedding. Hiro looked handsome in his white shirt and dark pants that used to belong to Mikio. Grandma Inaba had cut the pants down, then shortened and hemmed them for him. Masako wore the pink dress that Grandma Tatsuno had stitched for her. The pink dress with the embroidered red roses on the delicate white collar. The pink dress twirled beautifully when she danced with her Uncle Hideo and the vision of her pirouetting on the dance floor would live in Hitomi's mind for ages after. The wedding festivities created a lovely memory among all the dull days before and the difficult ones that were to come.

Mio lived in 12-4-F with her older sister, Setsuko, brother-in-law and their three school-aged children. It was crowded, but less so than Hitomi and the Inaba's apartment. Hideo moved into 12-4-F with Mio and her family, and they started their married life together with very little or no privacy. The apartment was certainly not a honeymoon suite, but the two sisters worked out a plan for each couple to have some marital privacy.

Mio's sister and husband spent time alone together when the children were in school. This was also the time when Mio worked at the mess hall and Hideo worked with Mr. Inaba cleaning up the small gardens and larger agricultural areas in preparation for winter. On Saturdays and Sundays her sister and husband would gather the children up and take them to the large assembly hall to play games. This gave Mio and Hideo quiet time alone. Sometimes, they would wrap up in their winter coats and walk outside, hand in hand. But the best afternoons were the ones of lingering kisses and making plans for their future together.

Chapter Sixteen

Tragedy at Minidoka

Snow came a few days before Christmas covering the dirt with a beautiful blanket of white, which gave Minidoka a Christmas card landscape. The lovely landscape didn't last long though as it only took the morning for the excessive foot traffic, snow angels and snowmen to mix the snow and dirt into areas of dirty brown. It snowed again on Christmas eve and the weather took a bitter dip, with the outside temperature dropping to a single digit.

Masako didn't feel well the entire day before Christmas, preferring to lay on her cot and watch her brother and Tome play. She ate poorly that day and complained that nothing tasted good. Not even the brightly decorated sugar cookies served at Kame and Mikio's school's Christmas Eve program tempted her. That evening she crawled onto Grandma Inaba's lap while Hitomi read a bedtime Christmas story to the children.

"Come touch this child's forehead." said Grandma Inaba. "It feels warm and I think she may have a fever."

Hitomi came over to where Masako was snuggling in Grandma Inaba's arms and felt her forehead. It did seem warm, and her little eyes looked dull.

"Do you hurt anywhere, Masako," asked her worried mother. "Tell mama how you are feeling?"

"My tummy hurts," said Masako. "It hurts right here." She took Hitomi's hand and placed it on the right side of her lower abdomen.

"If Masako still has a fever in the morning, I think you should take her to the hospital outpatient clinic tomorrow," said Grandma Inaba. "I know tomorrow is Christmas Day but surely there will be medical personnel available for emergencies and for patients already in the hospital."

"Yes, I will," said Hitomi. "I hope she is feeling better in the morning, but regardless of how she feels, if she still has a fever, I'll take her to the hospital."

Mrs. Inaba got a washcloth and poured cool water over it. She wrung the cold water out and handed the washcloth to Hitomi who placed it on Masako's forehead. The two women did this several times over the next half hour and then it was time for the children to go to bed.

The next morning, Masako seemed to feel better, and the two families had a quiet Christmas morning watching the children excitedly check the stockings hanging by the stove and open their Christmas gifts that were under the tumbleweed tree. Hideo and Mio came over for morning tea, conversation, and to share in the family fun. By mid-afternoon, Masako's fever returned, and it became apparent that the child was suffering again. Hideo carried Masako to the outpatient section of the hospital with a worried Hitomi by his side. They arrived and were surprised to see a young man at the reception desk wearing a white coat.

"Can I be of help to you?" the man said. "Is this your child?"

"Where is Dr. Hamada," Hitomi enquired with a worried voice. "He is the doctor who treats my family."

"I'm Dr. Parsons," he said. "This Christmas Day, Dr. Hamada is spending a well-deserved day off with his family. I'm taking the shift for him today since the outpatient unit is usually very quiet on holidays. Now, let's take a look at the patient."

Dr. Parsons had done his medical training at the University of Oregon Medical School in Portland. He had just completed his medical degree in June of 1942 and had planned to begin his three years of residency at Providence St. Vincent Medical Hospital in Portland, but instead found himself drafted into the army. With his medical background he could have been shipped overseas, but somehow, he found himself stationed at Minidoka working with Dr. Hamada in the outpatient unit of the 600-bed hospital.

He arrived at Minidoka in November of 1942 and was now officially beginning his third year of residency. He wasn't exactly sure how Dr. Canby, his medical school professor, advisor, and mentor had pulled it off, but the University had agreed to let him fulfill his residency in the hospital at Minidoka and the Army had agreed. He felt very fortunate for the support that Dr. Hamada was giving him in fulfilling his residency requirements.

Being a generous fellow at heart, he was happy to give the good doctor a day off to spend Christmas with his family.

Tom Parson had wanted to be a doctor ever since he had been in the fourth grade and had seen his older brother's arm get broken when an overly enthusiastic baseball chum had thrown his bat and whacked his brother's catching arm. Tom remembered the horror of seeing his brother crumple to the ground with his arm dangling oddly from the elbow. Everyone in the family was afraid that his brother Jimmy would never be able to throw or catch a ball again. Although Jimmy missed the rest of that summer's baseball season, he was back playing baseball the next year. Tom marveled at how the doctor had set his brother's arm in plaster and how Jimmy's arm healed as good as new. From that time on, he wanted to help people and make them better.

Tom was a kind man and cared about his patients. But he was still a young doctor and at times made hasty diagnostic decisions without evaluating all sides to the medical situation. Dr. Hamada, a doctor with twenty years of clinical experience, had worked patiently with him to recognize this weakness and Tom had worked hard at slowing down and assessing carefully. But there were still times he tended to rush to judgment, especially when the medical symptoms seemed obvious.

The outpatient clinic was quiet that Christmas day. Masako was only the second patient he had seen all day. The first patient was a seven-year-old boy who had run up the snowy steps to the door of his barrack apartment, slipped, and gashed his forehead over his left eye. The wound required several stitches and the procedure had taken some time. But that was several hours earlier and now he turned his complete attention to little Masako.

He asked, "What is the problem?"

"My daughter had a fever last night and said her tummy hurt," answered Hitomi. "She wasn't her usual active self yesterday and just watched her brother and friend play. This is unusual because she is a busy child, and not normally so quiet. When she woke this morning, she felt better. But after lunch, her fever returned, and she became very lethargic. She complained that her tummy hurt."

"Was she nauseous yesterday?" asked Dr. Parson. "Did she throw up? When was the last time she went to the bathroom?"

"No, nothing like that," said Hitomi. "She wasn't nauseous, just tired with no appetite. She had a fever last night when she went to bed. I don't think she went to the bathroom yesterday, other than to urinate."

"Well, let me examine her," said Dr. Parson. "Let's see what we can discover."

He carefully looked in her mouth and throat, in her ears, took her temperature, pressed her arms and legs, and abdominal area. Masako winced slightly when he pressed her abdomen. He listened to her heart and lungs and then he hung the stethoscope around his neck and turned to Hitomi and Hideo.

"This little one's vital symptoms are normal," said Dr. Parson. "Her throat is clear, there is no infection in her ears or nose. Yes, she does have a slight temperature of 100.7, which is not that high for a child. If there was a serious infection going on I would expect her temperature to run much higher, perhaps 104 or 105 degrees, but that just isn't the case right now. I think your daughter had too many sweets and treats the last few days and her stomach is just upset. I'll send you back to your apartment with some medicine to help her go to the bathroom and I'll also give you some low dosage aspirin to bring down her fever. Make sure she drinks plenty of liquids. In fact, have her take the aspirin with a glass of milk. If she doesn't feel better tomorrow, or if her fever persists, bring her back and we'll do a further examination. Any questions?"

Hitomi looked at Hideo and then slowly nodded her head. She took the medication that Dr. Parson's gave her, and they took Masako back to the barrack apartment. Bedtime came and Masako showed no improvement. If anything, she was more lethargic and except for the flush on her cheeks looked even more pale. Hitomi put the children to bed with a very worried heart.

Early in the morning just as dawn was breaking, Hitomi heard Masako moaning. She got up and felt the child's forehead and realized that she was burning with fever. Masako clutched her stomach and cried, "Mama, my tummy hurts terrible bad." Her child's distress and suffering struck fear in Hitomi's heart and she quickly got dressed. By this time Mr. Inaba was up putting coal in the stove and Grandma had a kettle of water heating for morning tea.

"I need to take Masako back to the hospital right now," cried Hitomi. "She's burning up with fever and is clutching her stomach crying that it hurts badly."

"Let me help you carry her to the hospital," said Mr. Inaba. "I just need to get my boots and then we can go."

Within minutes Hitomi and Mr. Inaba were hurriedly trudging through the snow to the hospital. Mr. Inaba carried Masako gently in his arms as they made their way inside.

"My child is burning up with fever," Hitomi said. "She needs to see the doctor immediately! Is Dr. Hamada here?"

"Just one moment," said the receptionist. "I'll get the attending nurse."

The receptionist got up quickly from her desk and disappeared through the double doors that led into the outpatient and emergency examination rooms. She returned quickly with the attending nurse who guided them into one of the examining rooms and had Mr. Inaba put the suffering child on the bed.

Hitomi held Masako's little hand and brushed her bangs off her feverish forehead. Dr. Hamada came and began talking in a soothing tone to Masako, trying to calm the little one's fears and to get a quick assessment of what was going on.

"My tummy hurts, my tummy hurts right here," she cried as her hand touched her lower right abdomen."

"Alright, sweetheart," Dr. Hamada said in a kindly voice. "This is what we are going to do. The nice nurse here is going to take your temperature and then you will be given some medicine to go to sleep while I take care of your tummy. When you wake up, I hope it won't hurt as much as it does now." He gently caressed her arm and motioned to the nurse to take Masako's temperature.

He asked Hitomi if she could step out of the room while the nurse took Masako's temperature and other vital signs. Mr. Inaba followed them out into the hallway.

"Your daughter," Dr. Hamada began, "is exhibiting all the symptoms of an infected appendix. In fact, I think your daughter has appendicitis, which is when the appendix becomes inflamed and fills with bacteria laden pus. I'm concerned that her appendix may have ruptured, and if that is the case, peritonitis may occur. Peritonitis is very serious and sometimes life threatening, especially if the infection from the rupture results in sepsis. I will need to take her to surgery and remove the appendix and if it has ruptured, there is an increased risk of sepsis. Do you understand what I'm saying?"

"But Dr. Parsons said she just had stomach discomfort because she had eaten too many sweets and treats during the holiday season," cried Hitomi.

"In the early onset the symptoms can be very similar to gastrointestinal distress," Dr. Hamada quietly continued. "But let's not worry about that now. Let's get her comfortable and ready for surgery."

Hitomi looked at Dr. Hamada with terror in her eyes. *How could this be happening to her beautiful child? Was there something that she could have done to prevent this?* She felt as if the walls of the hospital corridor were closing in and would crush her. For a minute she felt faint, but Mr. Inaba supported her arm and steadied her. She had no voice; she couldn't speak and just nodded her head in understanding.

The nurse opened the door and beckoned Dr. Hamada back into the room, which he did quickly, leaving Hitomi and Mr. Inaba standing in the hallway. Hitomi moved to go back in the room, but Mr. Inaba said, "Let's give them a moment." Just then another nurse appeared from down the hallway and entered the room. Dr. Hamada and the nurse came out as she went in.

"I'm going to go now to prep for emergency surgery," the doctor said. "The nurse will have you fill out forms of consent and information about Masako. Try not to worry. We'll do our very best to take care of her." He looked at Hitomi with compassionate eyes and then walked quickly down the hallway to the surgery unit.

"Hitomi," said Mr. Inaba. "Stay with Masako and get the hospital forms completed. I'm going to go get Hideo. I'll come back with him."

Hitomi nodded, but her only concern was Masako. She walked back into the room and saw her daughter propped up in bed with the nurse hovering over her.

When Masako saw her mother, she cried out, "Mama, mama, hold me," and stretched her hands out to her mother. Hitomi quickly sat on the edge of the bed and put her arm around her daughter and drew her comfortingly to her breast.

"Mama's here," comforted Hitomi. "The nurse will put you to sleep, and the doctor will fix your tummy ache. I'll be here when you wake up my little duckling."

Hitomi completed and signed the required forms and then held her daughter's hand as the nurse wheeled Masako to the operating room. The kindly nurse gave Hitomi a moment to kiss her daughter and caress her before Masako was taken through the double doors and the surgical wing. Hitomi was distraught as she stood outside the door with her hands clutched to her chest watching her precious daughter disappear behind the double doors. She felt a hand on her shoulder and turned to find her brother and Mio standing by her side. They both put their arms around her shoulders and supported her back to the waiting room outside of the surgical unit. And the waiting began.

An hour into the surgery Mr. and Mrs. Inaba came to join them. Mrs. Inaba told Hitomi that Grandma Inaba was watching Hiro and the other children. Hiro had asked for her and Masako. He didn't fret after he was told that his sister was at the hospital with mommy. Hitomi thanked them for telling her and for watching Hiro, but she said no more. She wondered how she could go on breathing when her precious girl was in such peril. She begged all the powers of the universe to bring her daughter back, whole and healthy again. The panic she felt earlier had evolved into naked fear. And the waiting went on.

Finally, the door to the surgery unit opened and Dr. Hamada came out, still in his surgical protective clothes, and walked towards the waiting group.

"There were no complications with Masako's surgical procedure. However, when we opened up her abdominal cavity to remove her appendix, we discovered that her appendix had already ruptured and infected the peritoneum, which is the membrane that lines the abdominal cavity. She has a serious infection and we have started her on some medication in hopes that we can reduce any serious destruction to her major organs and eliminate the danger of sepsis."

"What is sepsis?" asked Mr. Inaba. "What kind of damage does that do?"

"Sepsis is how the body responds to an extreme presence of infection that the body is already fighting," answered Dr. Hamada. "If not treated in time, sepsis can quickly cause organ failure and worse. Masako is being closely monitored and still recovering from anesthesia. In a couple of hours, the nurses will take her to the post-surgery unit here in the hospital. I would suggest all of you go and get some nourishment and then return back in a couple of hours when she wakes up from the surgery. The next twelve hours are extremely crucial. There is a new medical treatment now being used in these kinds of cases. It's medicine derived from the sulfonamide family and very effective for severe bacterial infections, but we don't have any sulfonamides here at the hospital. If the medicine we have available to treat Masako can reduce the infection with no sign of sepsis, then I have hope for a full recovery."

Dr. Hamada did not continue with what might happen if the medication didn't work quickly enough, but his unspoken words thundered in the silence.

They returned to their barrack apartments in quiet thought. Each in their own way tried to bolster Hitomi's spirits, but this was not the time for empty words, and they knew it. Masako's onset of appendicitis had been so sudden that none of them had adjusted to the shock of the last twenty-four hours. Especially Hitomi. She hadn't wanted to leave the hospital until she had seen Masako, but the nurse said that she would have to wait until Masako was taken to the post-surgery unit as she was still in the recovery room.

Hitomi picked up Hiro and hugged him tightly when she got back to the apartment. "Where is Sako," he asked in his baby voice. "Where is my Sako?"

"Mama had to leave Masako at the hospital," Hitomi said as she tried to reassure Hiro. "She's sleeping right now. Mama will need to go back and be with her when she wakes up. Can you be a brave boy and stay here with Grandma Inaba while Mama is gone?"

Hiro soberly nodded his head yes and then trundled over to Grandma Inaba and raised his arms for her to lift him on her lap.

Hitomi had no hunger and couldn't bring herself to eat, but she did sip some tea that Mrs. Inaba prepared for her. It was warm and soothing and helped calm her anxious heart. She finished her tea and put on her coat and boots, kissed Hiro, and went back to the hospital.

Masako hadn't awakened from the anesthesia, but the nurses took pity on Hitomi and let her come and sit with her daughter in the post-surgery room. Hours passed and still Masako didn't waken from the anesthesia. The nurses transferred her to a hospital room in the surgery recovery unit where Hitomi quietly sat, holding her daughter's small hand. She stroked Masako's arm and hummed little nursery rhymes as she lay quietly in the hospital bed. Masako looked like a small doll lying in the big bed. Tubes ran out from under the white sheet, which covered her body. Dr. Hamada came to her room in the late afternoon to check his small patient. Although he had a calm and professional demeanor, Hitomi could see concern in his eyes.

"Why doesn't she wake up, Dr. Hamada?" asked Hitomi in a worried voice. "When will she wake up?"

"It isn't unusual for people fighting this kind of infection to make a slower recovery out of anesthesia," explained Dr. Hamada. "She's lying there quietly but her body is working hard to fight the infection. As I said earlier, the next twelve hours are crucial. She's resting and is not in pain. I think that is a good thing for now."

Hitomi sat quietly by Masako as the early winter night arrived and darkness fell. She sat through the midnight hour, dutiful, hopeful, diligent, looking for signs of Masako's awakening. But the little duckling slept on and in the early hours of the following morning, Hitomi's darling girl slipped away without ever opening her eyes. She was gone. Hitomi had been listening to her small breaths for hours. Breath in, breath out, and suddenly there were two short breaths, then nothing, just utter stillness.

Hitomi ran out of the room crying, "Nurse! Come quick. Masako has quit breathing!"

The nurse came in quickly and inspected the child, then rushed out and soon there were several nurses working on Masako, checking this, checking that, but to no avail. One nurse tried to lead Hitomi out of the room, but she begged to stay.

"She's gone, I know she's gone, but please let me stay with her." The nurse nodded her understanding and left the room to call Dr. Hamada.

Dr. Hamada arrived and examined Masako and confirmed the worst. He turned to the grieving mother saying, "I'm sorry Hitomi, but your little daughter is gone. If only we had operated on her a day earlier, before the appendix ruptured, she probably would have made it. I'm sorry I wasn't here to make that decision."

Hitomi went over to the bed and laid down beside Masako, cradling the child in her arms, sobbing with the broken heart of a mother who had lost her beautiful child.

"My darling girl!" she cried. "How can I live without you?"

She could not, would not leave her child. Only when Hideo came and said that Hiro was calling for her and that he would see that things for Masako were taken care of did she finally lift herself from the bed and with shattered eyes stumble out of the room.

In the hallway she saw Dr. Hamada talking to Dr. Parson. Dr. Hamada had his back to Hitomi, but Dr. Parson was facing her direction. He looked up and for a long moment their eyes met and then he looked quickly down at the floor. Hitomi turned and walked out of the hospital.

For a week she laid on the cot unable to talk, to move, to eat. She didn't get off her cot except when Hiro needed her attention. Then she laid back down, closed her eyes and lay motionless. It was only when Hideo brought a small urn with Masako's ashes and placed it next to their mother's urn on the top shelf that Hitomi began to come back to the world of the living. But Hitomi was changed. She was shattered inside. No one could see her brokenness. She tried to function normally, for Hiro's sake. Those who loved Hitomi were heartened to see her heroic efforts. They encouraged and supported her in loving ways, and she was grateful for their love. The loss of her father and mother had been painful, but those wounds had slowly healed as she cared for and lived for her children. But Masako's loss had broken everything inside, her heart, her hopes, and her dreams. She thought to herself, *"I breath, I walk, I appear to live, but I'm dead inside."*

The Christmas season passed, and the year ended. The new year arrived and for many in the camp the new year brought hope that the war would soon end. But Hitomi's heart had stopped hoping and the little urn on the top shelf was a daily reminder that the dream to have her little family back together was gone, gone forever.

Chapter Seventeen
Going Home

The War Department began allowing a few internees at Minidoka to start preparing to leave in late January of 1945. Hitomi and the Inabas were not among the very first group to leave the camp. However, they would leave in Spring, perhaps as early as April or May.

Hitomi, Hideo, and Mio began talking about their future and where they would go after their release. Hideo wanted to return to Bainbridge and the berry farm. He told Hitomi that Mio and he wanted her and Hiro to come live with them, but they'd leave that decision to her. All of them had been incarcerated for three years, their lives disrupted and in limbo. So much had happened during that time. Hitomi had not heard from Akio since the previous fall when he wrote saying he was in Italy. She had received the sad news from Emily that Mrs. Gibson had suffered a third stroke and had passed away, just before Thanksgiving of 1944. There would be no motherly Mrs. Gibson to welcome her home.

The Inabas planned to return to the Skagit Valley, near Mt. Vernon and asked Hitomi to come live with them. Hiro had become extremely attached to Grandma Inaba and Tome after the loss of Masako. Hitomi wrestled with the decision. She knew that taking Hiro to Bainbridge Island would be a hard adjustment for him as the Inaba children had been his surrogate siblings for the past three years. He had spent his infancy, toddlerhood, and early preschool years trundling after the three of them. Tome, who had been the same age as Masako, had become his sister and protector since her passing.

One morning Hideo came to the apartment and asked Hitomi to come walk with him as he had news from Bob and Barbara Sabers on Bainbridge

Island. Hiro was playing school with Tome; she played the teacher and he the student. She was teaching him the alphabet, and together they sang the ABC ditty. Grandma Inaba drank her morning tea and kept a watchful eye on the two youngsters.

Hitomi slipped on the red sweater that Akio had given her the Christmas of 1941. She'd worn the same sweater at the Port of Seattle to say goodbye to her family the day they were sent to Manzanar. That seemed a lifetime ago, so much had happened since that day. At five-feet four-inches, Hitomi stood taller than many of her friends and had always had a slender and sapling figure. She'd lost considerable weight since Masako's death. The red sweater hung on her bony shoulders, but she didn't care what she looked like. When she put the sweater on it felt as if Akio was putting his arms around her. It gave her comfort to wrap herself in the familiar garment.

"I received a letter from Bob and Barbara Sabers yesterday," began Hideo. "I want to share the news with you. Bob wrote saying that the farm was in good condition and the last two years the yield from the harvest has been especially heavy. He said when we come home, we can buy the farm back for the same amount that he bought it. Bob also said he put twenty percent of the revenue from the past three seasons in a bank account for us."

Hitomi looked at Hideo with amazement. Tears glistened in her eyes. Hideo grabbed her shoulders and gave her a quick hug. His eyes misted as the two looked at each other. The experiences of the past three years had aged them both in very visible ways. They had endured much, so this sudden gesture of generosity and kindness shook their souls deeply.

"Hideo, I can't believe the kindness of the Sabers!" she cried. "I'd stopped believing such goodness still existed in the world!"

"That's how I feel too, my dear sister," said Hideo. "Bob said there is over $4,000 in the bank account waiting for us. He said it's there to help us get started again. I hope you will consider coming to live on the berry farm with Mio and me. I'll work for Bob in getting the strawberry harvest taken care of this year, but I'm hoping that Enji will be home from the war before next year's harvest."

"I've been in such turmoil as to where Hiro and I should go after we leave Minidoka," said Hitomi. "But I think going home to Bainbridge Island is the right thing for us to do. You are a good brother to give us some security until

Akio comes home." Hitomi looked at her brother and gave him a sad, but grateful smile. It was the first smile that he had seen on her face since the loss of Masako, and it lightened his heart. Perhaps Hitomi had begun to heal.

"Then it's settled," said Hideo, relief resonating in his voice. "I'll write Bob and Barbara back and let them know that we're coming home to Bainbridge Island. Perhaps we'll be home by May, before this year's berry harvest really takes off."

Hitomi smiled again at her brother and was surprised at the feeling of relief she felt. She'd be going home, back to the berry farm, back to the comfort of familiar surroundings. Mother and little Masako would be laid close together, next to Father. The thought of the ones she loved so dearly resting together eased her broken heart.

The pace at Minidoka quickened as plans to leave the camp emerged. Hitomi and the Inabas were approved to leave their barracks and apartment on the first of May as were Hideo and Mio. They would travel together on the train to Seattle and then go their separate ways. The Inabas would return to Skagit Valley to begin rebuilding their lives on the farm they left behind. Hitomi and Hiro, Hideo and Mio would finish their journey to Bainbridge Island. The departure date was nearly six weeks away, more time than they'd had to prepare to leave their homes three years earlier. They'd forged friendships in their shared struggle. It would be a wrenching sadness to say goodbye to the Inabas and Hitomi dreaded that moment. But sharing those final days together held a quiet support and friendship they all needed.

"We won't be hauling buckets of water to keep our flowers blooming this summer," commented Mrs. Inaba one beautiful March morning. "I still have some nasturtium, marigold, and zinnia seeds I'm taking home with me."

"I have some seeds as well," responded Hitomi. "If it's not too late in the spring I'll plant flower seeds too. Whenever I see nasturtiums, zinnias, or marigolds, I'll think of you."

Mrs. Inaba smiled and said, "I'll think of you too, my dear friend, and how eagerly we looked for those flowers to bloom."

"Do you think the seeds would last another year if I kept them in a dry place?" asked Hitomi. "Just in case I'm unable to get them in the soil this year."

"I think they'd keep," chimed in Grandma Inaba. "But we can ask my son, he's the flower farmer."

"Yes, I think they'd keep well," said Mrs. Inaba. "But if we leave the first of May, the seeds could be planted as late as mid-June and they would still bloom this year."

The women chatted about their plans in companionable conversation. Every moment of the day held a special quality, as they treasured and savored these final days together. They promised to visit once they got settled. Grandma Inaba knitted some potholders for both women. All conversation and planning centered on what they would do when they got back home, never on the past.

In the evenings Hideo and Mio came over, and the adults would sit around the pot-bellied stove drinking cups of tea, while the children played games on the floor. There was an atmosphere of anticipation coupled with a feeling of anxiety for what the future held. The conversations around the stove helped lessen the anxiety.

One early morning in late March, Hitomi woke up with a start, her heart pounding and Akio's voice calling her, "Hitomi, my darling, I'm coming home, I'm coming home." She sat up on her cot and pulled the quilt around her shivering shoulders, willing her heart to stop pounding. She had dreamt this dream before. Once in Seattle and once at the Puyallup Assembly Center.

In the dream, Akio ran across a field towards her and the children. The wind blew through his straight black hair. He stretched out his arms to embrace his waiting family. She could see his handsome face clearly in her dream, looking at her, smiling at her with that crooked grin and his glistening white teeth. His eyes crinkled with joy and the dimple she loved so deeply indented in his right cheek. He was almost there, ready to wrap his arms around her, Masako, and Hiro, when suddenly the earth opened up and he began falling, falling, falling. She could not stop his falling. She could only hear his voice calling, "My darling, I'm coming home, I'm coming home to you."

Hitomi clutched the covers to her heart. She shivered as she sat bolt upright in bed. Hitomi knew Akio was dead. He was gone, just like Father and Mother, and her sweet Masako. He would never come home to her. Their time together had been so short, so full of promise, so full of tender love, and now he was gone forever. An incredible sadness came over Hitomi. She didn't feel the crippling pain she felt when Masako died. Akio had been gone for three years and his loving letters were so few and far apart, she'd almost grown used to his absence. Or perhaps her already broken heart was simply too numb with grief over losing Masako to feel anything more.

Later that morning, Grandma Inaba asked, "Hitomi, you seem so quiet this morning. Are you feeling ill?"

"Akio is dead," Hitomi said with a heavy heart. She told Grandma Inaba about the dream. "This morning I heard his voice clearly calling my name and saying that he was coming home. But I know in my heart that he is dead. He is gone." Tears welled up in Hitomi's eyes.

Grandma Inaba pulled Hitomi into her arms. Then she said quietly, "The heart loves what the heart loves. And the heart knows what cannot always be seen."

Ten days later Hitomi received a letter from the military informing her of Akio's death. He had died after his battalion successfully crossed the Arno River in the Northern Apennines. His unit had run into strong German resistance near Pisa where Akio had perished, throwing himself on a grenade and sacrificing his life to save seven of his fellow comrades. He was awarded a purple heart, a bronze star, and the Medal of Honor for his personal bravery and sacrifice. These recognitions and honors would come later, but they would not bring Akio back. Ten days after receiving news of Akio's death, Hideo received a letter from the Department of Defense saying that Enji had been killed in heavy fighting in the Vosges Mountains. Like so many Nikkei soldiers in the 100th and 442nd Enji was also recognized for his bravery, receiving a Purple Heart and Silver Star. Akio and Enji would never come home, and all that Hitomi and Hideo would have to remember them were the dog tags they had worn around their necks.

Fighting in Europe intensified. The Germans were pushed back from many of the areas they had controlled. The tide slowly turned as the Allies got the upper hand in Europe and in the Pacific. As the end of the war neared, the number of internees leaving Minidoka increased. In mid-April of 1945, the Inabas, Hideo and Mio, and Hitomi and Hiro received permission to leave Minidoka. They had been planning and preparing for their departure for weeks. They carried their few possessions to the loading area and none of them turned around to see the camp before they boarded the bus that took them into Eden. At Eden, they transferred from the bus to the train to Seattle. Their future was uncertain and there was no joy in the return because of all they had lost. But they felt relieved that the years of incarceration were finally over. And there was hope, ever so small, that they'd be able to rebuild their lives.

At the end of their long train journey to Seattle, the two families parted ways. The Inabas taking another bus north to their tulip farm. Hideo, Mio, Hitomi, and little Hiro headed down to the pier to take the ferry back to Bainbridge Island.

Before parting Hideo said to Mr. Inaba, "I'll miss working in the fields with you. If things don't work out at Mt. Vernon, I invite you to consider moving to Bainbridge Island to work with me on the berry farm. With my father and brother gone, it will be challenging to get things up and going again."

"Thank you for the offer," said Mr. Inaba. "I need to see what's left of our farm. We only had a few days to get our things together before we left, so I didn't have time to sell the farm, or make arrangements with any of my neighbors. I don't know what I'll find when we get back. It may take some time to clean things up and sell if that's what we need to do. I enjoyed our work together at Minidoka. The one positive thing that happened there was meeting you. Thank you for your generous offer. I'll think it over and let you know."

The two men shook hands and said their goodbyes.

Then it was time to say goodbye to the Inaba women. Hitomi wished with all her heart it would not be a permanent separation, but she knew better than to make an empty promise of coming to see them. Who knew what the future held? If the last three years were any indication of the chaos and disruption that could turn lives upside down, then there was no guarantee what the future would hold.

"Goodbye, my little caboose," said Grandma Inaba to Hiro. "I'm going to miss that mischievous smile of yours and reading you a bedtime story each night."

"Bye, bye Gamma," said Hiro. "I take good care of Mama for you." He smiled and wrapped his little boy arms around Grandma Inaba's neck and hugged her hard.

"Goodbye Hitomi, my little sister," said Mrs. Inaba. "I'm going to miss you terribly, but I'll write you and let you know what we find when we get back to Mt. Vernon. I've got your address on Bainbridge Island. Let me know how you get on and perhaps when things get better, we'll be able to come see you and Hiro. I know Mother is going to miss the little guy very much."

"Goodbye my sister and my mother," Hitomi replied to the two women. "Your goodness and kindness sustained me through the long hard years, more than I know how to express. I'll miss your love, your friendship, your support, and hope we can see each other occasionally as times get better."

They held each other without speaking until there nothing left to do but let go and walk away.

The ferry ride to Bainbridge seemed to take only a moment and then they were at the dock unloading their meager possessions. Bob Sabers was there to welcome them home. He brought his Ford Woody station wagon to take them back to the berry farm. Barb waited at the farm for their arrival. Hideo proudly introduced his wife, Mio.

"It's good to meet you," said Bob. "I never thought Hideo would find a woman that would put up with him, but I can see that he did very well for himself."

Mio smiled demurely at Hideo as Bob patted her on the shoulder.

Bob turned to Hitomi and took one of her hands in his work-worn and weathered hands and said, "Welcome home, Hitomi. It's good to have you back again. I know these past few years have been difficult ones. I can't imagine how difficult, but I hope that the serenity of the Island will bring you peace."

Hitomi was touched by his genuine concern and grasped his hands back.

"Thank you, Bob, for being such a good neighbor and friend. Your generosity and support mean everything to Hideo and me." Her throat tightened, but she continued. "My parents are gone, and you really didn't owe us this level of care, but my brother, my son and I are deeply in your debt."

"Who is this little guy?" asked Bob as he nodded towards Hiro standing shyly beside his mother. "I don't think I've seen a more handsome young fella."

Hitomi smiled as she introduced her son to Bob. "This is Hiro, my son. He'll be three years old in July."

Bob laughed when Hiro put his little hand out to shake Bob's big hand, just like Uncle Hideo had done. "Well, you are a mighty fine young man," smiled Bob, "with good manners, just like your grandfather."

Hideo and Bob put their luggage and bags into the station wagon and headed for the berry farm. Hitomi could see her brother's mix of excitement and anxiety about seeing the farm. She sat in the back with Mio and Hiro and drank in the familiar sights of the Island. She didn't share Hideo's excitement, but there was a sense of coming home to the familiar that soothed her heart.

Soon Bob's old station wagon turned the corner and veered left down the lane to her family's farm. She was amazed at how well-maintained the farm looked and she knew that Bob and Barbara had worked hard to keep it this way. Her heart flooded with gratefulness as she knew that other Nikkei were not having this same kind of coming home experience.

Barb met them at the door with a huge smile and hugs for everyone. Hiro was engulfed in her arms, and although she was a stranger, he seemed to sense that this woman was a special angel to their family.

After unloading the station wagon, the two men began a slow walk about the property to assess the farm and discuss turning it back over to Hideo and Hitomi. Bob updated Hideo on the plans for the year's berry harvest, what he thought the yields might be, and where Hideo might get a crew to help harvest the strawberry crop. Hitomi and Mio put their suitcases and bags in various rooms and then came out to help Barb set the table for an early evening meal. Barb baked a large salmon and stuffed it with a delicious rice, mushroom, and onion dressing. She'd put together a large salad, baked fresh bread, and topped the entire dinner with a strawberry shortcake. The strawberries were frozen from last year's crop, but Hitomi thought she had never eaten a better meal in her life.

That night, Hitomi lay in her bed and felt a quiet peace as the soft island breeze slipped into her bedroom. She was home now, back in the room where she'd spent her happy girlhood. Hiro slept in the room next to her, the bedroom that Enji and Hideo had shared as boys. Hideo and Mio settled downstairs in Mother and Father's old bedroom. She thought about Akio and felt a sadness, not just for herself, or even for Hiro growing up without his father, but a deep sadness for Akio. He would forever be twenty-eight years old, and he wouldn't get to see his son grow up. They wouldn't grow old together, he would miss so many things. Hitomi longed for Akio, she longed for her mother and father, but it was the loss of Masako that crushed and broke her. Each time she thought of her sweet child, pain engulfed her like the surf of the sea.

But here on Bainbridge Island with all the familiar surroundings and memories of earlier, happier days, she felt she could go on. She was finally home. Hitomi closed her eyes and slept more deeply than she had in years.

Chapter Eighteen
Fate Calls

For the next couple of years, life on the Tatsuno Berry Farm was intensely busy and filled with back-breaking work and long demanding hours. Bob and Barbara Sabers, good friends and neighbors that they were, sold the berry farm back to Hideo for the $5.00 they had paid in 1942 when the Tatsuno family were forced to relocate. Their generosity also extended to the nest egg that Bob put in the bank for Hideo. It was a sizable sum, $4,100, which was twenty percent of the profits that had been taken in during the three years that the Tatsuno family had been incarcerated. The first year was difficult. It seemed to Hideo, Mio, and Hitomi that they were always a step behind. They managed to just keep their heads above water.

Their father had built good relationships with vendors in Seattle, Tacoma, and other market sources over the years and they reconnected with many of them. It wasn't as if they didn't experience prejudice and mean-spirited bias at times. It always felt like a body blow when someone called them out for being *Japs* and *slant-eyed traitors* who bombed Pearl Harbor. But after the first couple of years that type of hostility began to subside. They never experienced that prejudicial hate in the community on Bainbridge, but it did occur occasionally at Pike's Market in Seattle, and with a few venders in Tacoma and Puyallup. Some of the markets that Enji had developed in the larger communities around Washington state refused to work with them. But slowly things began to turn around. Hideo had the same quality of calm resilience and perseverance that helped his father to succeed, and this quiet persistence began to pay off as people recognized that Tatsuno Berry Farm's business dealings were dependable and fair.

Mio and Hitomi reopened the berry stand Kazuko and Junko started before the war. After the first couple of seasons, they developed a loyal customer base that returned again and again throughout the berry season. Kazuko returned home to Stockton, California with her parents after they left Manzanar. At first, Hitomi exchanged letters with Kazuko every month. After the first year, they only exchanged Christmas cards and holiday greetings. It was too hard to keep that feeling of closeness after Enji's death. What do you say when there's nothing to say? Kazuko was rebuilding her broken life as best she could. So was Hitomi.

Hitomi grew to enjoy living and working with Mio. She was different from many of the women that Hitomi was naturally drawn towards. Mio was bold and always sure of herself. She made a great partner for Hideo, both personally and on the farm. She was outgoing, friendly, and a successful salesperson, having the ability to talk almost anyone into buying produce grown on the farm. She treated Hiro with kindness, but she didn't dote on him the way Mrs. Inaba and Grandma Inaba had. The two women never talked about their incarceration at Minidoka and since Mio had never known Akio or Enji, there were no common memories to share.

Minidoka and Puyallup Assembly Center receded further and further into distant memory, but each time Hitomi saw the memorial garden that Hideo built on the east side of the house, she remembered. Hideo put in a little fountain, planted some bamboo, flowering azalea, and a miniature maple. He added a small concrete bench and put up a shrine, which held the ashes of their parents and Masako. It was a peaceful place and Hiro liked to play there with his little toy trucks while Hitomi sat on the bench, thinking and remembering.

The strawberry harvest of 1948 was a bountiful one. It was only mid-June and the harvesting had been going strong for two weeks. Hitomi loved this time of year. The hours were long and the work grueling, but she found joy in the work and knew that if her father was still alive, he would be pleased to see how the farm prospered. This Saturday morning, she and Mio planned to take the strawberries to Pike's Market where they leased a small vending table. Hideo typically oversaw the vending table at Pike's Market on the weekend, but he had acquired a new contract in Tacoma with a company that serviced a number of restaurants. He needed to make a large delivery of strawberries.

It was early morning when the two women loaded the old farm truck with the strawberries for Pike's Market and Hideo loaded the new truck, they had recently acquired to accommodate their expanding business. Young Hiro was excited for the ferry ride over to the Port of Seattle. Hitomi could hardly believe her son would turn six in a month and that he would start school in the fall. He was a busy little fellow with a big imagination and he loved to stand at the window of the big ferry and pretend he was the captain of the ship.

"This beautiful weather will bring the people out to the market today," commented Mio.

"Do you think we packed enough flats?" asked Hitomi. "I wondered if we should have packed another dozen flats, but Hideo didn't think it was necessary."

"Well, you never know," responded Mio. "Sometimes on sunny days people go to other events and even though you think you'll be busy things can be quite slow. Hard to tell for sure."

"If we sell out early," suggested Hitomi, "I guess we could do some shopping ourselves." She looked at Mio with a smile. The two women grinned at each other.

The ferry ride seemed very quick this Saturday as the water in Puget Sound was smooth and calm. They carted the berries from the truck to the vending table on the appliance dolly Hideo recently bought for the farm. Little Hiro helped Hitomi and Mio move the strawberry flats to the vending table. Even at his young age they expected him to help, and he did so without fussing. By 8:30 in the morning, Hitomi and Mio had moved all their flats from the truck into the vending area, ready for the surge of customers seeking sweet summer berries. People began arriving well before 9:00 a.m. when Pike's Market opened for business.

Hitomi had just helped one customer and was wrapping the cartons of strawberries in newspaper when she heard her name being called out. She looked up and recognized two faces she hadn't seen for six years. Emily Gibson and her cousin, Walter Gibson walked towards her.

"Hello Hitomi," Emily said with a warm smile. "I was hoping to see you here. Let me introduce you to my husband, Frank Ballard."

Hitomi didn't recognize the man standing next to Emily, but she knew they belonged together when he stepped forward and took Emily's hand. Frank smiled and held out his other hand to Hitomi, saying, "I'm pleased to meet you. I've heard so many good things about you from Emily."

"I'm so pleased to meet you, Frank," said Hitomi. "I knew Emily got married, but it's very nice to meet you in person." Then she looked up at Walter who had been quietly standing beside his cousin Emily. He seemed thinner than when she last saw him in 1942, but he still had those beautiful blue eyes.

"Walter, I'm surprised and pleased to see you," said Hitomi. "I've wondered how you were. Are you were still living in Seattle?"

"I'm actually visiting Frank and Emily this weekend," said Walter. "I live in Walla Walla. My father passed away while Henry and I were overseas. I've been living with my mother and helping her now that my father is gone. It's been good to live near family since the war ended." Hitomi understood exactly what Walter meant and she nodded her head slowly.

"We're celebrating Frank's birthday," said Emily. "I was hoping to get some Tatsuno Farm's famous berries for strawberry shortcake. Is this little guy the baby I saw in Puyallup so many years ago?" She turned to look at Hiro and smiled at him as she spoke.

Hiro put out his hand and said, "My name is Hiroki and I'm named after my grandfather." He shook Frank and Walter's hand as well. The adults smiled at his gentlemanly manners. Hitomi was proud of her son and put her hand on his shoulders to draw him close.

Hitomi looked at Mio and said, "This is my sister-in-law, Mio. She and my brother Hideo married a few years ago." Mio looked their way, nodded, and smiled, but she continued helping another customer. Hitomi looked apologetically at Emily and said, "I should get busy helping Mio. We have many customers this morning."

"We won't keep you," said Emily in understanding. "But before we leave, I'd like to buy half a flat of berries for our dinner tonight. Could you stay in Seattle after the market closes and have dinner with us?"

"I would love to," said Hitomi regretfully," but we need to get back to the farm to prepare for tomorrow's market. It's a busy time for berries. Nothing stops them from ripening."

"Of course," said Emily. "But let's get together when things aren't so busy. I know Clara would like to see you, too"

Hitomi wrapped the boxes of berries for Emily and wished Frank a happy birthday. She remembered that Emily had been engaged to a young doctor. In fact, she recalled that both Emily and Clara had told her of their plans to have a double wedding when they visited her at Puyallup. She realized that Frank must have been Emily's fiancée.

Mio and Hitomi ran out of berries by mid-afternoon and closed their vending table. They purchased some fresh produce from other venders and then drove back to the pier to catch the 4:45 afternoon ferry to Bainbridge Island. It had been a very busy and successful day at the market. Both women were tired but happy with the day's results.

"I'm sorry I didn't get a chance to chat with your friends today," said Mio. "They came right when the big morning surge began. Who was the tall, good-looking man with your friend? He has nice eyes."

"Some friends before the war," said Hitomi thoughtfully. "I took care of Emily's Mother, Mrs. Gibson, for a year while Akio studied law. Mrs. Gibson was a sweet, wonderful woman who helped me before the internment. Our apartment was located on Capitol Hill and so was her house. It was an easy walk from our apartment to Mrs. Gibson's house on 15th Street. She suffered a stroke, and I helped her with shopping, housekeeping, and her physical therapy exercises. She was very good to me, and I grew to love her."

"What happened to her?" questioned Mio. "It sounds like she's passed away."

"Yes, she passed when we were at Minidoka," said Hitomi sadly. "She came to see me after Hiro was born at Puyallup with two of her daughters, Emily and Clara. She had four daughters, but I didn't get to know her older daughters as well as Emily and Clara. The older sisters had families of their own. I remember the day Mrs. Gibson, Emily, and Clara visited me as one of the happiest days I spent at Puyallup Assembly Center. I heard my name over the intercom system asking me to come to the administrative building. I had no idea what was going on. When I got there, I couldn't believe it when I saw the three of them. They brought baby gifts for Hiro, a sundress for Masako, and letters from Hideo and Akio. I was happy that day." Hitomi sat reflecting upon the happy memory. They had reached the terminal and were waiting in line to drive onto the ferry.

"Mrs. Gibson sounds really nice, and I wish I could have met her," consoled Mio. "But you still haven't answered my question about the good-looking man with the dark hair and blue eyes." She smiled at Hitomi as she continued to probe.

"Oh, that's Walter Gibson, Mrs. Gibson's nephew and Emily's cousin. He grew up in Eastern Washington, a place called Walla Walla," explained Hitomi. "I've never been there, but I think it's located right on the border of Washington and Oregon."

"Well, that still doesn't explain why he was watching you with such puppy dog eyes," laughed Mio. "I saw the way he looked at you."

Hitomi blushed. "I'm not sure that was the case," she said. "I only knew him for a brief period of time, and that was long ago. It was before the war and before all the turmoil of the internment camps. He was Mrs. Gibson's nephew and worked at a grocery market on Capitol Hill. He was very kind to me during the chaos. It seems a lifetime ago."

The two women didn't speak again of the encounter at Pike's Market. The berry season took all their attention and energy as the summer's harvest intensified. They took a day off mid-July to celebrate Hiro's sixth birthday, and then they went back to the summer grind as raspberries and boysenberries ripened.

Chapter Nineteen
The Visitor

One day in late September, Hitomi was home alone. Hideo and Mio had gone to Tacoma with the final shipment of fall boysenberries for local restaurants in that area. This was Hiro's first year in primary school, and he would get off the old school bus about 3:30 in the afternoon. Hitomi had spent the morning cleaning and organizing the shed. She had come in for a quick bite of lunch when the doorbell rang.

"*Who can that be?*" wondered Hitomi.

She dried her hands on a dishtowel and went to answer the front door. When she opened it, she was shocked to see Walter Gibson standing there smiling at her.

"Walter, my goodness, what are you doing here?" she exclaimed. "Please come in and sit down."

"Am I catching you at a bad time?" questioned Walter in an awkward voice. He seemed suddenly shy and not sure of himself.

"Please, come in and visit," insisted Hitomi. "I'm the only one at home. I wish you could meet Hideo, my brother, but he and his wife are in Tacoma today."

Walter seemed even taller than she remembered him and yes, he was thinner. Walter took the big stuffed chair that Hitomi pointed to and sat down.

"Can I offer you a glass of water?" she asked. "Or would you like a cup of tea?"

"I don't want to put you out," said Walter, "but a cup of tea sounds nice after my ferry ride across the sound. It was breezy and cooler than I planned for this time of year."

Hitomi slipped into the kitchen and put on a pot of water. Then she arranged a tea service, English style, with sugar and a small pitcher of milk. Hitomi brought the tray in the living room and poured Walter a cup of tea.

"How did you get to the farmhouse? If you'd let me know, I could have picked you up at the ferry terminal."

"I got a taxi," said Walter. "It was a spur of the moment decision to come to Bainbridge Island. I had a few days off and came to visit Emily and Frank. I thought about you quite a bit this summer, especially after I saw you at Pike's Market. I should have called ahead, but I wasn't sure if you'd be home, so I just took a chance and caught a taxi."

"I'm so glad you did. How are Emily and Frank?" asked Hitomi. "I've thought about contacting her to arrange a visit, but I was waiting until after the end of the berry season."

"They are doing very well," answered Walter. "Frank's an emergency care doctor at Virginia Mason Hospital in Seattle, the same hospital where Emily works. I think that is where they met. Emily's expecting their first child in January. As you can imagine, they are both excited about the new arrival"

"What wonderful news," said Hitomi with a smile. "It will be a thrill for them to have a little one in the house."

An awkward quietness fell between them as Hitomi's head swirled with surprise and questions about why Walter had suddenly appeared on her doorstep. She felt a stirring in her heart, a feeling that she hadn't felt for many years, and it confused her. She didn't quite know what to say.

Walter broke the silence. "Hitomi, I learned from Emily that you lost your little daughter Masako at the camp in Idaho. I remember her sweetness and how much my Aunt Liz doted on her. She called her the frolicking lamb and I know that Masako brought my aunt a great deal of happiness in her final years. I hesitate to bring up such terrible memories to you, but I wanted you to know that I was aware of the losses and pain you experienced during the war. I wished that you hadn't had to go through such terrible sadness."

Hitomi's eyes misted over, and she swallowed a large lump before she spoke. "Walter, you were always kind and gave me support and friendship after Pearl Harbor. I'm getting by, but there isn't a day that I don't miss my daughter and imagine what a lovely child she would be now. I've tried to forgive the doctor who misdiagnosed her ailment, but my heart is too broken for that. She didn't need to die and if we hadn't been in those dreadful surroundings, she would still be with me today."

A single tear ran down Hitomi's cheek as she attempted to compose her emotions. She reached for a tissue and carefully wiped her face.

"The war years were difficult times for everyone," continued Hitomi. "I know you lost your father."

"Yes, my father passed away shortly after both my brother Henry and I enlisted," said Walter. "I visited him and my mother before I went to basic training. That was the last time I saw him alive. Emily told me that you also lost your husband and brother during the war."

"They're all gone," Hitomi said quietly. "My father, my mother, everyone is gone, except my brother Hideo and my son Hiro. Do you remember meeting my son and Hideo's wife, Mio, at Pike's Market last June?"

"Yes, I do remember," said Walter. "Emily said that Hiro was the child you were expecting when you lived with Aunt Liz on Capitol Hill in '42."

"Yes, that's right," responded Hitomi. "What I remember of that time was how you and Emily helped me pack and move everything from my apartment to your Aunt Liz's house in one day! And then you came back and helped me clean the apartment before I turned in the key. I couldn't believe how well you vacuumed and mopped the floors." They both laughed at the memory. "You said your mother expected you and your brother to clean house and do chores," continued Hitomi. "She did a fine job of that!"

"Would you like to meet my mother sometime?" Walter suddenly asked. "I'd really like you to meet her."

Hitomi was taken back by Walter's question and didn't know what to say. Instead of answering, she asked a question of her own. "How has your mother fared since losing your father?"

"It's been very hard for her," Walter said sadly. "My parents were married thirty-five years, and no one could ever take my father's place in my mother's heart. She worried incessantly about my brother and me, our safety, and whether we'd come back from the fighting. But I think that was every family's worry." He looked at Hitomi soberly realizing that he'd touched a sensitive nerve. "Here I am, bringing up sad memories for you, Hitomi. I don't mean to keep doing that," he said with a worried look in his eyes.

"The war changed everyone's life," said Hitomi. "Losing Akio and my brother was terrible. But their deaths didn't shatter me in the way that losing my daughter did. My heart beats only for my son. He is the one reason I keep breathing, moving, and living."

Hitomi could see that Walter wanted to say something, but she wasn't sure she wanted to hear it. Before he could say anything, she said, "Speaking of my son, there he is! That's his school bus. Can you stay for dinner, Walter? I would like to repay you for the kindness and support you gave me during that difficult time in Seattle. A dinner isn't much, but it would be a small gift." She looked at him with asking eyes.

"I'll only stay if you let me help you fix dinner," said Walter with a smile. "My mother also thought men should know how to cook. She taught my brother and I how to get around in the kitchen."

Just then Hiro flew through the front door hollering, "Mama, mama, I'm home." He stopped short when he saw the tall stranger in the living room but smiled in recognition when Walter put his hand out and said, "Hello, Hiro. Nice to see you again. Do you remember meeting me at Pike's Market last summer?"

"I remember you," said Hiro. "Want to play catch with me? Uncle Hideo says I can try out for Little League next spring if I can catch the ball." Walter looked at Hitomi and she nodded saying, "Go ahead. I'm going to go freshen up. I can't believe we've been sitting here talking and I'm still in my work clothes. I'll call you when I start dinner. How are you at cutting vegetables, Walter?"

Walter smiled and said, "I'm a whiz." Hitomi laughed and said, "Well, you'll get your chance to prove that tonight."

Hideo and Mio drove in from making deliveries in Tacoma about 5 o'clock that evening, just in time to wash up for dinner. Walter and Hitomi had been preparing dinner for an hour and the kitchen smelled savory and welcoming. Hideo and Mio were surprised to see Walter, but they welcomed him warmly and the conversation around the dinner table was comfortable and congenial. After dinner, despite protests from Hitomi, Walter helped her clean and put away the dishes. Hitomi and Walter smiled at each other when he said, "And yes, my mother taught my brother and me how to wash and dry the dishes along with other housekeeping skills she insisted we learn."

Hiro asked if Mr. Gibson could please read a book to him before he went to sleep, which Walter did. It was a pleasant evening, but when 9 o'clock rolled around Walter said that he needed to call a taxi so he could catch the 10:15 ferry back to Seattle. Hideo insisted one of them drive him to the ferry terminal. He looked at Hitomi who nodded and said, "There's no need for you to call a taxi, Walter. I'll be happy to drive you."

Hitomi waited in the terminal while Walter bought his return ticket. It was a thirty-minute wait for the return trip to Seattle. Walter and Hitomi walked back outside to the farm truck and stood quietly leaning against the hood, looking up at the soft stars and sliver of a moon in the evening sky.

"I've really enjoyed seeing you today," began Walter, "and I want to see you again. Would you be agreeable to that?" Hitomi's heart beat a little faster and she caught her breath before answering.

"Yes, I would like to see you again," she said. "But you live so far away. I'm sure it must be a drudge to drive all the way from Walla Walla to Seattle."

"It's not a drudge if I'm coming to see you," Walter said in a teasing voice.

Then his voice became serious as he turned toward her and lifted her chin toward him. "You have no idea how much I've thought about you over the past years, wondering where you were, wondering how you were doing, and longing to see you." His voice broke as he uttered these last words, but he continued. "There have been a couple of other women who I've briefly been interested in, but only because I knew you were married. The moment I saw you in the market on Capitol Hill, I was drawn to your gentle and lovely ways. The graceful way you moved, the shine of your hair, the beauty of your eyes, and the shape of your mouth. My heart yearned for you Hitomi, from the moment I first saw you."

"Oh Walter, I have always felt there was something very special about you," Hitomi said softly. "You have empathy and understanding like no one I've ever known. I feel so safe with you. But I'm not sure that I'm the same woman you met so many years ago. I'm different now. I'm broken inside. There has been so much sadness and pain that I don't know if I have anything to give you, at least not what you deserve."

Walter drew Hitomi into his arms and held her gently, stroking her hair. Finally, he said, "Hitomi, I don't know what I deserve or what I don't deserve. But I know that I want you and have wanted you for many years. I can't get you out of my mind. You're always there, in my thoughts, in my heart. Back in Seattle when I met you at Aunt Liz's house, I knew you belonged to someone else, so I tried not to think about you. But when I saw you at Pike's Market last summer, the feelings flooded back. Emily and Frank encouraged me to get in touch with you, and I didn't know if I should intrude into your life, but here I am." Walter looked at Hitomi with his heart laid bare.

"Should we take some time and see where this goes?" questioned Hitomi. "I'm still surprised to see you. This is all so overwhelming. I don't want to make you feel bad, Walter, but I didn't think about you, at least not in the way you say you thought about me. I knew you were a special kind of guy, you were Emily's cousin, and Mrs. Gibson's nephew, but I didn't have stirrings in my heart. At the time I met you I only thought of my daughter and Akio. And there is the difference between us in family background. I'm Japanese and my parents were traditional Buddhists. Your family is of English and German ancestry, and you grew up in the Methodist Church. These are strong differences to adjust to. What about your family? Will they accept an Asian woman with a son into their family? I'm not the naïve girl I once was. I've lived with the ugly reality of discrimination and racism and have learned how mean ordinary people can be. I've learned where my place is in this country."

Walter was quiet for a long time and then spoke. "I know there are differences between us and there will be people who judge us as an odd couple, but I don't think it will be my family. Having the same skin color, or religion, may make it easier for others to accept a person. But love is a mysterious thing, and those things don't make a difference when the heart feels at home with the other. I want to take care of you Hitomi and be a father to Hiro. We can be a family and the hell with the rest of the world!" Walter said these last words with such passion that his intensity surprised Hitomi. But it also opened her heart to him, and she knew she could not let him go.

"Oh, Walter, I want to believe you," she cried. "I do believe you! I'm just scared of upsetting the serenity of the life I've found here on Bainbridge Island since the war ended."

"I know, I know," said Walter. "I feel urgency because I've longed for you since the first time I met you. I will be thirty-five in a few months, Hitomi. I'm not the young idealist I once was. I know what I want, but I'm willing to wait until you feel ready. I'll wait for you; I'll wait for you as long it takes."

"Thank you, Walter," Hitomi said softly. "I need some time to adjust and to prepare my family, especially Hiro. Since the war, I've felt numb inside. I feel broken and I'm not sure I could be whole again. But you give me hope and courage that life can be good, even with all the bad things that happen."

"The ferry is coming in to dock so I'm going to have to leave you now," said Walter. "I hate to leave, but I'll write and let you know when I can come. We'll make plans to see each other again, my darling Hitomi."

Walter gently kissed Hitomi goodbye and held her close. Hitomi felt faint with joy. The sensation of being in this wonderful man's arms was surreal, so dreamlike. This man with the warm beautiful blue eyes who made her feel safe and wanted. Walter let her go and gave her another quick kiss goodbye and then walked to the ferry terminal. He turned at the entrance and waved to her. She touched her heart and waved back.

Chapter Twenty
Walter Gibson

Walter was a man in love. He was happy as he drove the curvy road over the pass towards Walla Walla. The fall leaves were changing color and he had never seen them so brilliant, so beautiful. He wished Hitomi was sitting by his side so he could share the beauty of the world with her. What a difference a day could make. Yesterday morning as he rode the ferry to Bainbridge Island, he felt doubt and uncertainty. He wasn't sure what Hitomi might say when he suddenly appeared on her porch. But today the future looked bright, hopeful, and exciting.

Walter had never been a risk-taker. As an accountant he was comfortable in the world of accuracy, detail, and neat number columns. It wasn't as if he was socially awkward or inept, but he wasn't accustomed to the tumbling emotions that he was experiencing. The uncertainty he felt didn't align with his need for surety and security. He hoped his family would accept Hitomi so they could make a life together. He wanted that more than anything he had ever wanted in his life.

He arrived home that evening and found his mother in the kitchen canning the last of the beets from the garden he had helped her plant earlier in the spring.

"How was your trip to Seattle, Walter?" she asked. "How were Emily and Frank?"

"They're doing well," answered Walter. "Emily hasn't had any complications with her pregnancy. The baby is due in January and her doctor advised that she stay off her feet as much as possible until the baby is born. She's no longer working in the lab at the hospital, but Frank's still doctoring in the emergency room. They're very excited about the baby"

"I wished your Aunt Liz could be here to see Emily's baby," said Mabel, her voice tinged with sadness.

"Yes, me too," responded Walter. "I know she'd be thrilled with the new baby, but she got to see both Emily and Clara get married." His mother looked at him and smiled as she remembered happier times

The following evening, Walter and his mother went to Henry and Mary's apartment for dinner. Mary had prepared a tasty meal of meat loaf, scalloped potatoes, and green beans. She topped the meal off with double fudge cake and coffee. As they sat around the table enjoying the last bites of dessert and coffee, Henry said, "I have some news to share with all of you."

"You're not planning to move away?" asked his mother in a worried tone.

"No, Mary and I are happy here, but I am changing jobs." said Henry. "The U.S. Army Corp of Engineers is opening an office on November 1, in Walla Walla. I've been hired to oversee flood control and maintenance of waterways in the Snake River Basin in the new district office."

Smiles emerged around the table as Walter and his mother gave their congratulations. Walter saw relief in his mother's face. He knew she was concerned about Henry's future and this new development soothed her worries. He wondered if he should share his own exciting news. He was in love, but didn't want to risk sharing the news prematurely, at least for a while. But his resolve was challenged when Mary innocently asked, "How was your trip to Seattle, Walter? Did you do anything interesting?"

"I took a ferry ride out to Bainbridge Island," answered Walter.

"What possessed you to do a thing like that?" asked Henry. "What's to see in Bainbridge Island?"

"I went to see an old friend, someone I knew before the war," answered Walter. "She was a friend of Emily and Clara and helped Aunt Liz for a time after her stroke."

"You visited a woman?" questioned Mary. "You never mentioned knowing any woman from Bainbridge Island."

"Like I said, I knew her briefly before the war and lost touch with her," answered Walter. "Emily, Frank, and I ran into her last summer at Pike's Market. She lives on a berry farm with her brother and sister-in-law on Bainbridge Island."

"Hmmm," said Mary with a twinkle in her eye. "What's this woman's name and when do we get to meet her?"

The three of them looked at Walter with expectant eyes.

"When the time is right," Walter said thoughtfully. "She lost both her husband and daughter during the war, and she has a six-year-old boy. She's been through a great deal of sadness. I don't want to rush her, but I do want all of you to meet her."

"Don't worry son," said his mother. "We'll look forward to meeting a woman you find interesting. You do care about her, Walter? Right?"

"Yes, I care deeply for her, Mother." answered Walter. "When I say she'd been through great sadness, you need to know that Hitomi is Japanese-American. She was born in this country, but she and her family spent the war years in an internment camp, unable to leave. She lost most of her family during that time and returned home with only her son and a brother." Walter looked around the table at the thoughtful faces. His family sat in quiet consideration. Mary was the first to speak.

"I don't care if she is Japanese-American," she said with passion. "If you care for her, she'll be my sister."

"I feel the same way," said Henry. "I'll stand by you." The three of them looked at Mabel, waiting to hear what she said.

"Walter, your brother and you are good sons. I'm proud of you both. If you care for Hitomi and want her, then we'll do everything to make her feel welcome and comfortable."

Walter let out a deep breath. The tension he felt was gone. Things might not always go smoothly but knowing that his family supported him gave him confidence. Later that night, in the solitude of his room he wrote Hitomi. Walter had never written a love letter in his life, and he felt unsure of himself as he began.

September 26, 1948

Dear Hitomi,

I hope this letter finds you well. I've thought about you every minute since our time together last Saturday. I must confess I was nervous to come visit you unannounced, but with with Emily and Frank's nudging I got the courage and I'm glad I did. My feelings for you have been bottled up for a long time. There were times when I denied the feelings even to myself or tried to put them out of my mind. But when I saw you Saturday, they resurfaced in a way I could not ignore. I thought fate only gave one opportunity for happiness, but I was wrong. Sometimes, fate smiles more than once, such as meeting you at Pike's Market last summer. Emily had asked me to come to Seattle and celebrate Frank's birthday. Little did I know that during my visit our paths would cross. Emily may have had a hand in playing Cupid. However, when I asked her whether she knew you'd be at Pike's Market that day, she just shrugged and mischievously smiled.

Last evening, Mother and I had dinner with my brother Henry and his wife Mary. Henry had good news that he now has a permanent job working at the U.S. Army Corp of Engineers' new district office in Walla Walla. He'll oversee flood control and maintenance of waterways in the Snake River Basin area. He's very excited to begin his work and Mother is happy to have him finally settled in a position that keeps him in Walla Walla. Last night I told my family about you and Hiro. I told them about your loss and sadness during the war and how you and other Japanese Americans were treated. They knew about the internment camps, but it's more shocking when you personally know someone who lived through this experience. They were saddened by what you and your family had to endure. I told them I cared deeply for you and hoped we would spend our lives together. They were accepting and supportive of my love for you. I knew they would, but it's reassuring to hear. They are eager to meet you and Hiro.

As for me, Hitomi, I can't wait to see you again. I wake in the morning and long for the day when I'll look over and see you sleeping next to me. I sit at the breakfast table, drinking my coffee and imagine you sitting across from me. When I walk outside, I feel you everywhere. I hope your feelings will continue to grow for me, Hitomi. I will wait with great longing to receive your reply.

Love,

Walter

The next day Walter stopped by the Post Office and mailed his letter to Hitomi. He knew it might be two or three weeks before he heard back from her, but there was a lightness in his step as he walked into his office in the Drumheller's Building.

"Good morning, Walter," said Jack Reed, one of the salesmen at the Drumheller's Company. "How was your weekend?

"Good morning, Jack," answered Walter. "I had a good weekend. How about you? Did you do anything interesting?"

"Yeah, Zach and I scouted for deer in the Blue Mountains. White tail deer season opens next weekend. My boy is fourteen and this will be his first deer season, so we were trying to scope out a herd."

"Tell your son good luck for me," smiled Walter as he sat down at his desk to begin the day's work.

It was nearing the end of the month and there were accounts payable and receivable to review. Walter also had a pile of receipts that he had to look over and sign, so it would be a busy day at the office.

The days passed quickly and two weeks later, almost to the day that Walter had mailed his letter, Hitomi's letter arrived. It was lying on the small side table near the front entryway closet where he hung his overcoat and hat. His heart quickened as he picked up the letter addressed to him in small, neat handwriting. The legible and dainty handwriting pleased his sense of order. He walked into the kitchen and said hello to Mabel who was bustling around preparing the evening meal.

"Did you see the letter from Hitomi on the hallway table?" inquired his mother.

"Yes, I have it here," answered Walter, as he patted his shirt pocket. "I'd like to read it before dinner."

"Of course," responded Mabel. "The pot roast still needs another ten minutes, and the potatoes and carrots also need more baking time, so there's no hurry."

"That's what smells so good," smiled Walter. "Mother, you make the best pot roast. I'll pop up to my room, read the letter, and wash up for dinner. Leave the table to me and I'll set out the plates and cutlery."

In his room he picked up the letter opener his father had given him as a gift when he graduated from the university. He slit the envelope open, pulled the slim sheets of paper out, and sat on his bed to read Hitomi's letter.

October 3, 1948

Dear Walter,

Thank you for your letter. I read your words with joy and happiness. It's hard to believe I could ever feel this happy again, but I do. It felt like a dream when I opened the door and saw you standing on the front porch that Saturday afternoon. I was surprised, but more than that, I couldn't believe how my heart jumped with gladness when I saw your face. Your letter thrilled my heart when you said you wanted me as your sweetheart.

Life has slowed down on the farm now that the berry season is over. Mio and I closed the produce stand for the season and Hideo is building new berry crates and repairing the old ones. Hiro is enjoying his first year in school and had a good progress report. Now that the season is done, Mio and I are taking time to do a thorough fall house cleaning.

I'm anxious to see you again, hopefully before the winter weather makes travel difficult and treacherous. I want to meet your family, but I worry that they may think I'm not the right one for you. You are a wonderful man, kind and good to others, so this gives me reassurance that you didn't become that way on your own. Your family must also be good to raise a son like you.

Walter, my heart is at home when we are together. Could it be that this is our chance for happiness? I had given up hope that I would ever feel like this again. You said in your letter that fate smiled when our paths crossed last summer. I feel that way too. I am lucky to have a second chance to love such a wonderful man.

Goodbye for now. I hope to hear from you soon, Walter.
My heart is yours,
Hitomi

Walter sat on the edge of the bed and read the letter three times before he stood up and put it in the top drawer of his bureau. He smiled as he came down the stairs. Mabel looked up and saw his smiling face and said, "You're here just in time. I'm pulling the pot roast out of the oven now."

"Dinner smells wonderful, Mother," Walter said as he put the plates and eating utensils on the table. "I can't wait to eat your good cooking."

"You're certainly in a good mood tonight," his mother said. "Does it have anything to do with the letter you got today from Bainbridge?"

"Yes, it does," smiled Walter. "I really want you to meet Hitomi and her son, Hiro. What do you think of inviting her here for the Thanksgiving holiday? I'd like to travel to Seattle and bring her and Hiro back here. I can take a day or two off from work and make the trip."

"I think this is a good idea, son," said Mabel. "It will be nice to have guests for Thanksgiving. Hitomi will meet Henry and Mary and also get a chance to see Walla Walla. I don't have to tell you that it's a community quite different from Seattle or Bainbridge Island. I wish your father could be here to meet her."

"Father would like Hitomi, I know he would love her quiet and gentle ways," responded Walter. "Father was a farmer at heart, and he'd have enjoyed talking with Hitomi about her family's berry farm."

"That he would." agreed Mabel. "Your dad was a smart college man, but I don't think he ever quit pining for the wheat farm in the Palouse where he grew up."

"I'll write tonight," Walter said thoughtfully. "If she agrees, then we can make plans."

That evening he wrote to Hitomi.

October 15, 1948
My dear Hitomi,

Everywhere I look I see you. Everywhere I go I wish you were with me. I think of you every minute of the day. When I got home from work this evening, your letter was waiting for me, and I read it three times. I'll read it again, at least three more times before I go to bed tonight. Waiting to hear from you was like a thirsty man eager for a glass of water to quench his thirst. My heart leaped with elation when I saw your letter today.

I want to see you again and hold you in my arms. Would you consider coming to Walla Walla and spending the Thanksgiving Holiday with me? I could take off work early on the Tuesday afternoon before Thanksgiving and drive to Seattle. I'd stay with Emily and Frank that night. If you and Hiro take the first ferry out of Bainbridge Wednesday morning, I'd meet you at the ferry terminal and we'd drive back to Walla Walla that day. It's a seven-to-eight-hour drive, which will be hard on Hiro, but we can pack a little lunch and picnic along the way. My mother is anxious to meet you and Hiro. I have so many things to show you and I want you to meet Henry and Mary. I can't wait to spend a few days with you. I wish it could be forever, but I know I must be patient. Please say yes!

I love you, Hitomi. Keep me in your heart.
Walter

I. M. Ramsey

The next morning Walter mailed the letter at the Post Office on the way to work. He could hardly focus on work that day as his mind kept wandering to thoughts of Hitomi and their future together. Yes, Walter Gibson was in love. This was a new feeling for him, and he found it both thrilling and unsettling. He was a quiet guy who was a spectator, but not an active player on the stage of life. People who knew him best would describe him as unassuming and preferring routine to an adventure. Walter never had a serious love interest. He found girls interesting, but Walter was an observer, never acting on his interests. And there was plenty of interest amongst young ladies he was acquainted with over the years. They made it known that they found his tall, dark, handsomeness appealing. And especially those stunning blue eyes. But it never turned his head until he met Hitomi. Maybe her appeal was enduring because she was unavailable to him. He found it all so confusing.

At noon, Walter walked to Falkenberg's Jewelers on main street. He asked to look at rings and chose a simple gold band with five tiny diamonds set in a floral pattern. It was simple, but elegant and he hoped that Hitomi would like it. The clerk placed the ring in a small square box and handed it to Walter. He tried to still his heart wondering if he was rushing things, but he had every intention of proposing to Hitomi at Thanksgiving.

That evening over dinner he asked his mother how she had met his father. Mabel laughed recalling the event. "I met your father when I was eighteen, right here in Walla Walla. I grew up in Portland, but we had relatives that lived up this way. The summer after I graduated from high school, there was a big family reunion. My entire family came to Walla Walla. It was an exciting adventure and I met cousins I never knew existed. A distant cousin invited his college roommate, your father, to attend the potluck reunion, which took place at Pioneer Park. There were many people, perhaps a hundred or more. I remember it being a very festive day, with a dozen large picnic tables loaded with all sorts of picnic treats.

My mother's cousin, Allie, grilled hamburgers and gave one to me on a bun. I put my plate on a table and walked over to get some ketchup when a large dog suddenly appeared, grabbed the hamburger on my plate and took off running. Your father and I ran after the black Labrador yelling at the poor thing. The thief was your father's dog, but by the time he intercepted him, the hamburger and bun were gone. That was how we met. Your father would laugh and say, *my dog got the hamburger, but I got the girl!"*

Walter smiled as she continued. "Your father was the only man I ever loved. We had a wonderful life together. He was good to me and a good father to you boys."

Walter nodded in acknowledgment and then glanced at his mother saying, "Today I bought a ring at Falkenberg's Jewelers. I plan to ask Hitomi to marry me at Thanksgiving. Do you think I'm rushing this?"

His mother looked at Walter thoughtfully and finally said, "When you are young it seems you have your entire life ahead of you. But with each passing year, the time seems to move more quickly, and the realization begins to dawn that life is short. You're still young, Walter, but the war brought chaos and disruption to normal life. I can understand how you may be feeling. The more important thing is how Hitomi feels toward you and once that feeling is evident, I wouldn't waste a minute."

Walter smiled at his mother and took the ring out of his pocket to show her. "The ring is beautiful, son," said Mabel as she admired it. "Like I said, I wouldn't waste a minute."

Hitomi read Walter's letter with interest. Her heart fluttered as she read his invitation to spend Thanksgiving Holiday in Walla Walla. Should she? It was a big step to take.

Later that day she mentioned the invitation to Hideo and Mio as they worked on inventory and organizing the berry shed.

"Walter invited Hiro and me to spend Thanksgiving with his family in Walla Walla," Hitomi said cautiously. "He would drive to Seattle and stay with his cousin Emily and then meet us at the ferry terminal. What do you think I should tell him?"

"Do you want to see him?" asked Hideo. "Do you want to spend the holiday with his family?"

"Yes, I want to see him very much," answered Hitomi. "But truthfully, I'm worried about meeting his family and wondering if they will accept me."

"Love is curious," said Hideo. "You never know when it will come, but when it does, you have to take whatever risks needed to have it. When I met Mio in the camp something in my heart began to grow. I tried to ignore it. I mean, love in an internment camp?" He smiled and exchanged glances with Mio.

"When I was younger, I didn't see how I could leave Mother and Father with the burden of the farm squarely on their shoulders. Not after all the sacrifices they'd made for me, for us. But the war changed all that. I'd given up the idea of ever falling in love. When I realized that Mio had feelings for me, I was amazed that love could come to me. But it did, Hitomi. Love is like a leaf in the wind. If you don't grab it when you have the chance, it will flutter away."

Hitomi thought about Hideo's words as she moved through the day. When Hiro got off the school bus that afternoon and was sitting at the kitchen table with Hitomi and Mio eating a snack, Hitomi decided to ask him about the invitation.

"How was your day at school, Hiro?"

"It was good," he replied as he munched on a graham cracker and took a sip of milk. "I hit a ball at recess, mama. I hit it hard and made it to second base."

"I'm proud of you, son. It's fun when you make it to first base and even better if you make it to second." Hitomi smiled at him. "Do you remember Walter Gibson? We met him and his cousin Emily at Pike's Market last summer. He came to visit us here a month or so ago and he played catch with you in the back yard. Do you remember him?"

"Yeah, I remember him," said Hiro. "He was nice and read me a story before I went to sleep. You know, the wolf story."

"That's right. Walter, his cousin Emily, and I were good friends when I lived in Seattle, before you were born. He invited us to spend Thanksgiving with his family. Would you like to do that? It's a long drive to Walla Walla from Seattle, but I'll pack us a basket of goodies to lunch on along the way."

"Can I bring my baseball mitt and ball?" asked Hiro. "Maybe Walter could play catch with me at his house."

"Of course," replied Hitomi. "If you ask him, I'm sure Walter would play catch with you every day we are there."

"Sure, I like Walter. It'd be fun to see where he lives. Do you think Uncle Hideo and Aunt Mio will miss us?" he said, looking at Aunt Mio.

"I talked with both of them, and they think we should accept the invitation, but I wanted to make sure you would like to go as well."

"Hooray!" yelled Hiro as he ran out the back door. "Uncle Hideo, can you play catch with me? Mama and I are going to Walter's house, and I've got to practice catching the ball so I can be really good at flyballs when I play catch with Walter."

Hitomi and Mio smiled at each other as they cleared the table and tidied the kitchen.

After supper that evening, she wrote Walter.

October 22, 1948
Dear Walter,
I've spoken to Hideo and Mio and also Hiro and they all agree that I should accept the invitation to spend Thanksgiving with your family. I write to say, "yes, we will come." Hideo will take us to board the first ferry on the Wednesday morning before Thanksgiving and we'll meet you at the dock in Seattle at 7:45. Don't worry about lunch. I'll pack a few sandwiches and slip in some fruit and other nibbles.

It worries me a little to meet your family, but I trust you, Walter. Hiro is very excited to come, and he is bringing his baseball and mitt. He is hoping you will play catch with him.

I miss you, Walter, but it makes me so happy to know that in a few weeks I'll see you again. I can't wait to see your face and look into those handsome blue eyes.

My heart waits for you.
Love,
Hitomi

A week later Walter received Hitomi's letter. He shared the news with Mabel and plans for the holiday began in earnest. Mabel loved to cook, especially for guests, and she was determined to prepare a sumptuous feast for this special occasion.

Although the days dragged by for Walter, the weeks passed quickly. Finally, Thanksgiving week arrived. He left early on the day of departure, delayed just long enough for Mabel to pack a box of goodies for Emily and Frank. She also tucked in a receiving blanket she had knitted for the baby's arrival in January.

Late in the afternoon, Walter arrived at Aunt Liz's house where Emily and Frank lived. They had moved in after they had married in order to help Aunt Liz, but with her passing they had made the residence their permanent abode.

Emily answered the doorbell with a big smile and welcoming hug for Walter. It was obvious that she was heavy with child as she swayed back into the kitchen calling, "Put your suitcase in the upstairs guest room, Walter, and then pop down and set the table for me. Frank went to the market for some ice cream. We'll eat as soon as he gets back."

Walter hadn't seen Emily and Frank since early fall and there was much to catch up on, especially news of Hitomi.

"What time are you meeting the Bainbridge ferry in the morning?" inquired Frank.

"I'm meeting Hitomi and her son Hiro at the dock early, for the 7:45 ferry," answered Walter. "It will be an early morning getaway for us. The drive back to Walla Walla is a long one and I'm eager to get home before dark."

"That's a good plan," acknowledged Frank. "Driving in the winter is always unpredictable and the days are short. We don't have much daylight now."

"Yes, that's my concern," agreed Walter. "Hitomi is bringing a lunch, so we won't make any long stops."

"My mother would be thrilled to know that you and Hitomi are an item," smiled Emily with a mischievous grin. "She's probably smiling in heaven right now."

Walter laughed at the thought and then said soberly, "I miss Aunt Liz. Do you think she'd be happy for Hitomi and me?"

"Oh yes," insisted Emily. "She thought the world of Hitomi, just like another daughter. You were like a son to her, the son she never had. She would have loved the idea of you two being together."

"I think she would have," agreed Walter. "My family is yet to meet Hitomi, but I know I have their support, which means everything to me."

Walter woke early the next morning. Frank had already left for the hospital, but he had left some coffee warming in the pot. Walter ate some cereal, toast, and drank his coffee in quick fashion. He wrote a note to Emily who was still slumbering in bed and took his suitcase to the car. He knew he was early, but he wanted to get a parking spot near the ferry terminal. It was a wait, but eventually he saw the Bainbridge ferry coming across the sound.

The ferry anchored at the dock and his heart quickened as cars started exiting and passengers began walking off. Then he saw her – his beloved. Hitomi had a suitcase in one hand and held Hiro's hand in her other. Hiro had a little rucksack on his back and carried a small basket, which Walter assumed was the picnic that Hitomi had prepared for their journey. He couldn't stop smiling as he walked briskly towards them, arms outstretched, ready to embrace them both.

"Hi Walter!" Hiro said excitedly. "I brought my mitt and ball to play catch in your backyard. Is your yard big enough to play catch in?"

"It sure is, buddy boy," responded Walter. "I dug my baseball mitt out of storage with the plan to play catch with you. How about a little batting practice, too? If you are going to be a standout baseball player you've got to hit the ball as well as catch it." Walter smiled at Hitomi as he took the suitcase and opened the door. Hitomi smiled back at him and gave an apologetic look to indicate she knew that they had a chatterbox in the back seat. But Walter didn't care. He had spent most of his adult life alone and the fact that he had this beautiful woman sitting next to him and a fascinating boy in the backseat filled his heart with more happiness than he had ever experienced.

Soon they were out of the city and making their way along the winding road through the mountain pass. Hiro found every tree, rock, and bird interesting and asked a hundred questions. The highlight of the journey was when they came around a corner and saw several elk standing among the trees near the road. Walter slowed the car as they passed the three majestic creatures.

"Those are the biggest horses I've ever seen!" Hiro said with excitement. "Wait 'til I tell Uncle Hideo."

"They look like horses," explained Walter. "But they are called elk. They are rather shy and not often seen by travelers along the highway. We were lucky to catch a glimpse of them."

Several hours into the trip Walter pulled over at a roadside rest area to let Hiro run and stretch his legs. Hitomi pulled out the basket, which she had filled with sandwiches and tasty treats. She poured a cup of hot coffee from a thermos for Walter and a glass of milk for Hiro from a small jug. They didn't tarry long as the air was so cold, they could see their breath. Walter worried they might encounter snow before they made it to Walla Walla.

After their lunch break, Hiro curled up in the back seat and took a nap. Hitomi covered him with a blanket that Walter carried in his car. They chatted quietly, sharing little stories of their lives. Walter took Hitomi's hand in his and she sat close to him, feeling safe in his love as they traveled the long miles.

It was late afternoon and daylight had almost vanished when they arrived and drove into the Gibson driveway on Catherine Street. Mabel turned on the front porch light. She had patiently waited through the day for their arrival and was relieved when Walter's car finally pulled into the driveway. Mabel had a warm supper of soup and fresh bread ready for the weary travelers. It was the perfect meal after a long journey.

Mabel was not a woman who wore her affections on her sleeve. She was known for her blunt and pragmatic look at life. But she sensed Hitomi's anxiety and as she took her to the guest room to put away her suitcase, she said, "Hitomi, I'm glad that you and your son are able to spend Thanksgiving with us. Walter has told me how much he cares for you, and I want you to feel right at home."

Hitomi was deeply touched by Mabel's simple words. She gave Mabel a quick hug and thanked her for her kindness.

The next morning, Mabel was up early and had the turkey baking in the oven by 8 o'clock. The two women kept busy in the kitchen preparing the Thanksgiving feast. Hitomi enjoyed working alongside Mabel in the kitchen. And Mabel appreciated the way Hitomi peeled the potatoes while she rolled out the dough for her apple and pumpkin pies. Hitomi had always liked working with other women and had grown accustomed to sharing the household tasks through her experiences with Aunt Liz, Emily, the Inabas, and Mio. It felt very comfortable to help Mabel in the kitchen and let her take the lead. Mabel enjoyed Hitomi's quiet companionship and assistance with the work in the kitchen.

Henry and Mary arrived in the early afternoon and while Walter and Henry played catch with Hiro in the backyard, the women set the table and pulled the food out of the warming oven. Soon the table was groaning with the holiday feast. And what a feast it was! Turkey baked to a golden brown, mashed potatoes with giblet gravy, dressing with cranberry sauce, corn casserole, green beans, fresh buttery rolls topped with the strawberry preserves that Hitomi had brought as gifts for Mabel and Mary. Everyone ate until they couldn't hold another bite, that is until Mabel brought out her pumpkin and apple pie for dessert.

After dinner Walter and Henry set a game table in the living room and played Parcheesi with Hiro. Hitomi's heart warmed to hear Hiro's happy voice chattering. Mary and Hitomi both insisted that Mabel should put her legs up in the reclining chair while they cleaned the dishes and tidied the kitchen. It was a pleasant atmosphere in the Gibson house that Thanksgiving afternoon – a memory that would long live in Walter and Hitomi's hearts in the years to come.

That evening after Henry and Mary left for home, Walter read a bedtime story to Hiro. Both he and Hitomi tucked Hiro into bed, in the room that Walter had shared with Henry when they were boys. As Walter pulled the covers around Hiro's shoulders, Hitomi bent down and kissed the sleepy boy goodnight. She asked, "Did you have a good day, Hiro?"

"Yes, Mama," yawned Hiro. "Today was the happiest day ever!" With that he rolled over, closed his eyes, and was out like a light.

Walter smiled at Hitomi, took her hand and pulled her to him in a loving embrace. They kissed tenderly and then smiled at the sleeping child. Walter led Hitomi down to the living room. Mabel had said goodnight and gone to bed as they tucked Hiro in for the night. It was just the two of them sitting close together on the sofa watching the embers of the fire slowly burn out. They hadn't had time alone since Walter had met Hitomi and Hiro at the ferry terminal. It seemed like an eternity since that moment, only yesterday, but their closeness had grown with intensity as they spent Thanksgiving Day together surrounded by loving family.

Hitomi looked up at Walter and asked, "Did you have a happy day, Walter?"

Walter looked at her with those beautiful azure blue eyes and said, "Yes! I feel just like Hiro. Today was the happiest day ever! How about you, Hitomi? Are you happy?"

"Oh yes, my heart is overflowing," Hitomi said with joy in her voice. "I loved helping your mother today. I learned many cooking tips from her. And Mary was sweet and friendly. Your family is good, just like you, Walter. It was so nice of you and your brother to pay attention to Hiro and give him a fun day. It seems I will always be indebted to you."

"That's good," laughed Walter. "You can be indebted to me." Hitomi joined him in laughing.

Walter's voice sobered as he looked at her and said, "Hitomi, would your indebtedness include marrying me? I mean, I want you to marry me for love, but if indebtedness could help convince you to say yes, I'd be the happiest man in the world."

Hitomi smiled at Walter, he looked so serious. "Walter, I want you and that has nothing to do with my feeling of indebtedness to your kindness. I want to build my life with you. I say, yes, I will marry you."

Walter pulled Hitomi into his arms and kissed her with the hunger of a man who had waited a lifetime for this moment. He pulled out the little box from his pocket and placed the delicate diamond ring on her finger. "I love you, Hitomi, I will love you my whole life."

Twelve months later, exactly a year from the time their paths crossed at Pike's Market, Hitomi and Walter were married at Tatsuno Berry Farm on Bainbridge Island. It was a small wedding celebration of family members, a few neighbors, and a few friends. The Inabas, Mabel Gibson, Henry and Mary, Emily and Frank with their new baby, Clara and Tom, and Bob and Barbara Sabers were all there to share in the festivities of Walter and Hitomi's wedding day.

Barbara catered the wedding dinner and made all the strawberry cheese cakes for the wedding celebration. Hideo walked Hitomi along the Zen Garden path in their back yard, which led to a latticed archway that Mr. Inaba had built from grape vines for this special occasion. The garden path was lined on both sides with a stunning growth of yellow, orange, red, and white nasturtiums. Hitomi wore a simple lavender-colored dress with a matching bolero jacket. Mrs. Inaba styled her hair and Hitomi was a vision of loveliness with white baby's breath and dark blue lobelia weaved in her luxurious black hair. Hiro looked handsome in his white shirt and black suit that matched Walter's suit.

It was a glorious day for Walter and Hitomi to share with the people they loved. When they spoke their vows and Walter drew Hitomi into his arms to kiss her, they both knew that this would be a day treasured and cherished in all the years that were to come.

Hitomi hated to leave Hideo and Mio with all the farm responsibilities, but she felt better knowing that the Inabas had sold their tulip farm in Mt. Vernon and had moved to Bainbridge Island to work with Hideo in expanding the berry farm. The Inaba children were now teenagers and Tome was in elementary school. They had waited until the children completed the school year and had arrived at Bainbridge just as the strawberry season opened. Hitomi was happy that Hideo and Mio had help and support for the busy summer months ahead.

The Gibsons settled into married life on Catherine Street. They moved Hitomi's few possessions into the house. Among those items were the two old leather suitcases that Walter had given her so many years ago. Inside the leather suitcases were the important belongings that she had kept from her years in Minidoka. Walter knew that Hitomi would need time to sort through the bags and decide what was important to keep and what needed to go.

Mabel had eagerly awaited the arrival of Hitomi and Hiro. She was content now that Walter had a family of his own and was grateful to have the big house full of boyish chatter again. She knew it would take some time for Hitomi to adjust to her life in Walla Walla, but Mabel was determined to make Hitomi and Hiro feel at home. She was a no-nonsense type of woman, very practical, blunt, and straight forward. She hadn't a sentimental bone in her body. But she was generous, kind, and loving in her own way. Having raised two boys of her own, Mabel understood Hiro and enjoyed having his lively presence around the house. It wasn't long before Mabel became Grandma Gibson to Hiro. On summer evenings the family walked to the ball park and watched Hiro play little league baseball. Although he was still working on hitting the ball, there wasn't a fly ball that could get by Hiro in center field.

As the days and months moved along, Hitomi became acquainted with the people in the community. She attended Pioneer Methodist Church with Walter and his mother for Sunday services, which extended her circle of acquaintances. She also became friends with several of the neighbors that lived on Catherine Street: The Barnetts, Bakers, and Bill and Bitsy Sheldon. Hitomi woke one spring day and realized that she had never been so happy. The love that she shared with Walter was not the love of the young: intense, passionate, and tumultuous. Their love was not a stream that tumbled and fell over boulders on the mountain side but was calm and deep like a serene alpine lake. Hitomi was happy sharing her life with Walter and she knew by the light in his blue eyes that he was happy, too. Life seemed sweet in spite of all the losses she had endured.

Mabel enjoyed Hitomi's company and was happy to have a companion to share the toils of the day while Walter worked as the accountant for the hardware store in the Drumheller's Building. A warm and pleasant friendship grew between Walter's mother and Hitomi, and then bloomed into a close loving relationship.

Hitomi never expected to become pregnant again. It was a surprise to everyone when three years later, she conceived at the age of thirty-three. Walter worried and fretted about Hitomi's health, but Mabel told her son, "Stop fussing about Hitomi and the baby! She may look fragile, but she is as strong as any woman I know. She will be fine, and so will the baby!"

Megan Elizabeth Gibson was born at St. Mary's Hospital on June 7, 1952. She weighed seven pounds, one and a half ounces and was nineteen inches long. When Hitomi saw her beautiful baby girl she cried with joy. "Walter, God is giving me another chance with our baby daughter. We won't let anything happen to her. Will you promise me that? Please promise me that, Walter."

"Hitomi," said Walter. "I will be here with you, and we'll raise our baby daughter together. Just as we've raised Hiro together these last few years. Don't cry my darling, we'll do this together."

Tears flowed down Hitomi's face. The tears were of joy, of worry, but mostly they were tears of gratefulness, to have another chance at loving and raising a daughter.

Part III
Walla Walla, Washington

May 1964

Chapter Twenty-One

Forgiveness

I lay on the exam table in the emergency room at St. Mary's Hospital waiting for the emergency doctor to come in and check my arm and forehead. I was still in shock from the bicycle accident at Pioneer Park and I could see that my mother was very upset about my injuries. She looked at me and said reassuringly, "Megan, the doctor will be here soon. He'll make you feel better." She held my hand and patted my uninjured arm as she tried to comfort me. But everything hurt; my broken arm, my head, my entire body felt like it had been run over by a big truck.

The door opened just then and in walked the nurse and Dr. Parsons. I recognized Dr. Parsons as he had gotten Christine from school several times when the weather had been snowy and icy. But it was my mother who caught my attention. When the nurse and Dr. Parsons walked in the door, she began squeezing my right arm so hard that it hurt worse than my injured arm. I heard her gasp and saw the oddest expression of fear, shock, and sadness come over her face. She was staring at Dr. Parsons.

Dr. Parsons looked up from the file he'd been reading. When he saw my mother the expression on his face changed to one of surprise. He obviously recognized her, and I wondered how he'd met her, because she hadn't been to the hospital recently. Father stepped up to Dr. Parsons and introduced himself, giving a brief description of what happened to me.

Then my sweet, dear Mother shocked everyone in the room by saying, "Walter, we can't have this doctor treat our daughter. I want another doctor to see Megan."

Father looked at Mother in great shock. She was not a forward speaking woman and her statement seemed so out of character with her gentle way of being. But the distress on her face was obvious and my father said, "Hitomi, let's talk in the hallway."

"I'm not leaving Dr. Parsons in here with Megan. I insist on having another doctor treat Megan."

"It's alright," said Dr. Parsons. "I'll step out and talk with both of you. Nurse, please take Megan's vital signs while I speak with Mr. and Mrs. Gibson."

The nurse looked puzzled but did as the doctor had requested. I didn't know what was going on, but I'd never in my life seen or heard my mother speak to anyone that way. A short time later Dr. Parsons and my parents returned to the room. I could see from my mother's face she was still upset by Dr. Parsons, but evidently, he had said something to change her mind because he began assessing my injuries in a very kind and careful way. He asked me about school, and I told him how his daughter Christine stayed with me after my accident and kept other people from trying to move me. He smiled at me and nodded. He explained to me that I would have pictures taken of my injuries with something called an X-ray machine. He also explained that my arm was broken. It would be necessary to reset the bone and put it in a cast to hold in place while it healed.

"Now Megan," Dr. Parsons said. "The X-ray machine will not hurt you. It's just a big machine that takes pictures of injuries inside your body. I need to look at those pictures before we set the broken bone in your arm. The nurse will give you some medicine when I put the cast on, so it won't hurt when I reset your arm. We'll also need to take an X-ray picture of that nasty bump on your head. Do you understand what we need to do to help you feel better?"

I nodded and then asked Dr. Parsons, "Will my friends at school be able to sign their name on my cast and draw funny pictures?"

"Indeed, they will," smiled Dr. Parsons. "I hope you'll let me sign your cast, too."

This time I smiled and nodded. Dr. Parsons turned to the nurse and gave her instructions to take me to the X-ray department with my parents.

He turned and said to my parents, "I recognize your concerns, Mrs. Gibson. "Thank you for letting me treat Megan. When we have Megan comfortable and all taken care of, I hope we can talk. I've been waiting nineteen years to ask for your forgiveness."

The nurse looked shocked but didn't say anything. She retrieved a wheelchair from behind the door and helped me get into it. Mother's face looked distraught, and she gripped my father's arm to steady herself.

Father looked very sober, but he spoke for both of them and said, "Thank you Dr. Parsons. We'll hear you out."

Dr. Parsons nodded his head and then opened and held the door as the nurse pushed the wheelchair out to the hallway and towards the X-ray department. My arm ached. I just wanted to get this over with. After my X-rays the nurse wheeled me back to the emergency room where Dr. Parsons re-set my arm.

I didn't like the shot the nurse gave me for pain, but Dr. Parsons explained it was necessary so he could manipulate the bone and align the broken ends. He explained how bone cells would begin forming between the two broken ends until my arm was as good as new. Dr. Parsons also explained that I had a slight concussion. But he assured my parents that there was no evidence of a fracture as he showed them the X-ray.

"I think it's best to keep Megan overnight," explained Dr. Parsons, "to make sure that nothing more serious emerges. If she's here in the hospital, we can take care of any concern that might arise. Do you have any questions?"

"I want to stay here with my daughter, all night," Mother said. "I don't want to leave her alone."

"I understand," said Dr. Parsons. "That won't be a problem. We can bring you a cot to sleep on."

"No, I don't need a cot," my mother said. "I doubt I could fall asleep. I'll sit in this chair and watch my girl through the night."

There was one large stuffed and cushioned chair in the room. Dr. Parsons stepped out for a moment and returned with two folding chairs. One chair he handed to my father and one he unfolded for himself. He motioned for my mother to take the large cushioned chair, and then he and my father sat down on the folding chairs. I was hungry because the accident had occurred just before lunchtime and now it was mid-afternoon. The nurse had brought me some graham crackers and some strawberry Jell-O, which tasted refreshing at the time, but that seemed hours ago. I wanted to ask for more food, but I didn't dare interrupt Dr. Parsons and my parents.

He began quietly. "I'm not sure just how to start this although I've rehearsed what I wanted to say many times over the years. I've often wondered what it would be like to finally meet you and make my peace with you, Mrs. Gibson. I've prayed about this many times and I know God has forgiven me, but there has been a wound in my heart that only you could heal."

His voice cracked and the tension in the room grew heavy. I had no idea what had happened to make Mother so upset with Dr. Parsons, or why he looked so sad. He was silent for a moment and then he continued.

"No matter how hard I tried I could not forget how grief stricken you were when your daughter died," said Dr. Parsons. "The look on your face haunted me for years along with the sweet voice of your child saying, 'Mama, Mama, my tummy hurts.' She shouldn't have died, and I know she died because I was overly confident and jumped too quickly to a diagnosis before taking time to evaluate and assess all the symptoms. Dr. Hamada told me on more than one occasion there were no simple diagnoses. I wish I'd heeded his words that day."

My mind raced with this revelation. *Who were they talking about? Was it the little girl in the picture? Was she, my sister?*

I looked at my parents sitting side-by-side. Father held my mother's hand and stroked her arm. Tears glowed from Mother's eyes, and she took deep breaths to avoid weeping uncontrollably. So many questions swirled in my mind, but I was also beginning to get some answers. Dr. Parsons spoke again.

"I long to change the events of that Christmas Day in Minidoka. But I know I can't ever repair the terrible outcome. What I've tried to change is myself and how I approach my practice of medicine. At that time, I believed that I was the doctor with all the answers. But the events of that day made me realize nothing could be further from the truth. From the moment I learned what happened to your daughter, I've tried to treat my patients with more empathy, to assess and evaluate all the symptoms, and not to rush to judgment before I set up a treatment plan. As tragic as it is, your daughter's death led me to become a better doctor, a better man, and a better human being. Mrs. Gibson, I am deeply sorry about your little one's death, and I ask you to forgive me for my arrogance, and for all the pain I have caused you."

Dr. Parsons let out a big breath and then sat silently looking at my mother with pleading eyes.

My father had given my mother the large white handkerchief he always carried in his back pocket. She dabbed her red eyes. It took her a moment to get her emotions under control. She slid forward in the chair and reached for Dr. Parsons hands and spoke in the gentle, lilting voice that always soothed my troubled spirit.

"Dr. Parsons, the death of my daughter left me shattered and so broken that I thought I could never be whole again. In my mind you were an unfeeling monster, and I blamed you for Masako's death. But I can see that you have also suffered deeply. I'm not sure that you caused her death, but you were an easy target to blame and someone I could vilify in my mind. I see that you are truly regretful and deeply wounded by Masako's death. I forgive you, Dr. Parsons and I ask you to forgive me for the hateful feelings I've carried toward you all these years. A load has been lifted from my heart, and I hope that this is true for you as well."

There was a moment of silence as all the tension seemed to leave the room.

"Thank you," said Dr. Parsons. "Thank you for opening up your heart to hear my apology and for granting me forgiveness. Your forgiveness has finally let me forgive myself." He got up to leave the room, but at the door he turned and said, "I'll be back to check on Megan when I make my evening rounds."

Then he closed the door behind him leaving my parents sitting there looking at each other.

I was too young to really understand what I had just witnessed, but I knew it was powerful. The questions I had pondered after discovering the little dress and the pictures in the old leather suitcases were partly answered, but there was still so much to understand.

I saw my father embrace my mother in a tender hug and then he said, "Hitomi, I'm going to go home and get Mother and bring her back so she can see Megan. I called her after Dr. Parsons set Megan's broken arm, but I'm sure she is still fretting and worrying. I know she will want to see her."

"Can you please bring Karl into my hospital room?" I asked. "He won't be able to go to sleep tonight if he isn't in bed with me. Can't you please sneak him by the nurses?"

Father laughed and said, "Megan, I can't bring a cat into the hospital! They would kick us all out if I brought Karl to you. I'm wondering if it's you that can't go to sleep without Karl, not the other way around?"

"I think he needs me," I pleaded. "He always cuddles up by my side in bed. Karl will miss me if I'm not there."

"Don't worry," said my mother. "I'll be with you through the long night." And she was.

The next morning, I felt much better. The bump on my forehead had begun to recede, and although I still felt bruised and battered from my bike crash, I was ready to go home. The nurses and Dr. Parsons signed my cast. He asked me what my favorite animal was, and I told him, it was my black and white cat named Karl. He drew a cat face that looked remarkably like Karl!

"You've been a very good patient," Dr. Parsons told me as he signed some papers releasing me to go home. "No strenuous activity for a week and don't be surprised if that area around your eye turns black and blue as that knot on your forehead begins to drain."

He reached into his pocket and pulled out an envelope with my name written on it. I recognized Christine's handwriting and when I opened the envelope, I discovered a pretty picture she had drawn for me with a note saying, *I'm sorry about your bike wreck and I hope you will feel better soon. I can't wait to sign your cast!* Christine had also slipped a couple of tootsie rolls in the envelope for me to enjoy. I smiled when I saw the treats.

Father shook Dr. Parsons' hand and thanked him for taking care of me. Mother and Dr. Parsons talked quietly for a moment or two by the door, but I wasn't able to hear their conversation.

Dr. Parsons turned and waved goodbye to me saying, "Remember now, Megan, no crazy activities for a week or so. I'll leave it up to your mother to decide, but it might be best to stay home from school for the first few days of next week. I'll see you in a week to check your arm and your concussion."

Then he was gone. I wasn't too happy with the news that I would be stranded at home Monday and possibly Tuesday as I wanted my friends at school to sign my cast. Especially Christine and Sarah.

Grandma Gibson was waiting at the front door when Father drove us into the driveway. She gave me a hug, being careful not to squeeze too hard. I smiled and held up my casted arm.

Grandma Gibson tapped on the hardened plaster and said, "My goodness! You scared the pudding out of all of us, but remember you are a Gibson and the Gibsons are tough. You'll mend just fine and be as good as new in no time flat."

I found Karl waiting for me in my room, snoozing on the bed. He greeted me with a meow and a stretch, then he closed his eyes again.

My brother, Hiro called to check on me. I laughed when he said, "Megan, next time you'll know better than to get in a tangle with the sidewalk. I'm an engineer and concrete will always win!"

He told me he was studying very hard at the university, but he would be home for my birthday. He reminded me to save him a place to sign on my cast. I promised him I would.

Uncle Henry and Aunt Mary also came over to see me. Aunt Mary knew just how to fuss over someone to make them feel better. It was great being home with Mother, Father, Grandma Gibson, and Karl. I knew that this was where I belonged because this was where I was loved.

That night Mother sat by my bed and told me stories about my sister Masako. She told me stories of how Grandma Junko and Mrs. Gibson called Masako the frolicking lamb and the special Christmas when Masako received the beautiful pink dress that Grandma Tatsuno made for her. She told me about the little mouse that came out of the wall in the women's shower room at a place called Puyallup Assembly Center and how Masako laughed and laughed to see the poor creature skidding in the water trying to get back to the little crack in the wall. I giggled, thinking about the tiny mouse sliding on the floor as the shower water came pouring down like a summer thunderstorm. But my favorite story that night was the story of Mrs. Inaba killing the rattlesnake with one powerful swing of the garden hoe. I was horrified and thrilled to think of her courage and quick action in protecting the children from the rattlesnake.

My mother told me stories, stories of my sister, of Puyallup Assembly Center, and Minidoka. Places I had never heard of. Even now, after all these years, if I am in a quiet place and close my eyes, I can hear her voice rise and fall in a lilting singsong rhythm. Back then I knew my mother was beautiful and wise.

The End

Printed in the USA
CPSIA information can be obtained
at www.ICGtesting.com
LVHW080755011123
761763LV00007B/300/J